Praise for *When the Forest Dreams . . .*

"A layered, character-driven novel about finding one's inner strength and purpose in the midst of falling in love."

—**Emily Wakefield Cyr**, owner of Folklore & Fable Booksellers

"*When the Forest Dreams* is magical, a delightful tale with a setting that feels real and characters that live in your heart long after you turn the last page of the story."

—***Readers' Favorite***, 5-star review

"The fun lies in how fresh the retelling feels. . . . If you love birds, if you have ever stared out a city window and longed for a different path, or if you simply want a romance that blends warmth, humor and a touch of fairytale shimmer without losing sight of real-world stakes, Emma Jablonski's story is well worth your time."

—***Book Trib***

". . . I kept turning the pages, captivated by Emma's choices and evolution. I needed to believe that happiness, much like the rare and elusive ivory-billed woodpecker, was within her grasp."

—**Lucille Guarino**, author of *Elizabeth's Mountain*

Also by Andrea Ezerins

Again and Again Back To You

When the Forest Dreams

When the Forest Dreams

A Modern Retelling of
The Blue Castle

A NOVEL

ANDREA EZERINS

SHE WRITES PRESS

Published in 2026 by
She Writes Press, an imprint of The Stable Book Group

32 Court Street, Suite 2109
Brooklyn, NY 11201
https://shewritespress.com
Library of Congress Control Number: 2026900610
ISBN: 979-8-89636-310-1
eISBN: 979-8-89636-311-8

Interior Designer: Tabitha Lahr
Interior graphics © Shutterstock.com

Printed in the United States

To my mother, Erica, who instilled in me
a love of birds and reading

Chapter 1:

The Morning

Stepping from our apartment, the hallway light momentarily blinds me. Our apartment's lamps are fading while everything else shines brightly. A tentative "Hello" breaks the silence. I freeze, as this can mean only one thing. *Jake*. There is one other apartment in our hallway, and while I have rarely ever seen the parents, I have certainly seen their son over the years.

Sure enough, Jake is standing next to the elevator. I tense but can't control the stab of exhilaration that lances through my stomach. First my dream and now Jake, this is a special day.

I drop my head and watch through hooded eyes, making sure my father can't see my interest. Jake is holding on to someone and appears to be dragging her while pulling a large suitcase behind him, one of those roller bags. He's having trouble maneuvering her down the hallway.

"Hello," he calls out more firmly, "can you help me here? I just need to get her into my apartment. It will take only a minute."

I glance at my father; his eyes have turned steely, angry at the request. Knowing I should ignore the request, I look toward Jake, and I can't bring myself to do that. I hesitantly walk, reaching for the girl's arm, looping it over my shoulders. She's much taller than my five-foot-two frame, so she drapes over me. Jake has her other side, and she takes a few unsteady steps. Her head is lolling down on her chest and her eyes are closed. Jake drops the handle of the suitcase, and I'm relieved when my father picks it up, walking behind us.

We slowly make our way to his apartment door; the hallway feels alive, and I take a deep breath of air that invigorates instead of stifles. Jake fumbles for his key and opens it. I've never been this close to Jake, and I peek at him, studying his hair. I've always loved his hair. A piece falls across his forehead and I immediately remember reading all the Harlequin Romance books I devoured a few years ago until I lost interest in such nonsense. The man's hair was constantly falling over his eye, and the woman was always pushing it back or thinking about pushing it back. A blush creeps up my neck and settles in my cheeks. Jake's is cut close around his ears but still has waves on top that make him look even taller than he is. The deep auburn color is so lovely, reflecting the bright lights of the hallway. *Oh, to reach out and touch it.*

Once inside, I force my eyes away from his hair to glance around the apartment. We stumble down the hallway like a giant spider with legs and arms sticking out here and there. Jake turns on an overhead light and I'm mesmerized. The splendor of the hallway is shocking and overwhelming. It has pillars with plants on them, and I see an ivory statue peeking out from a recessed corner. There are pictures with lights set on top of each one, so the beautiful landscapes appear to glow from within. My feet sink into a rug that is rich and plush. We continue down the hallway, and I marvel at how opposite this apartment is to ours, despite having the exact mirrored layout. It is as different as a scarlet tanager is to a drab house sparrow. The difference between having money and not. I scan the living area quickly for any sign of his parents. *Nothing.*

We continue past the first bedroom on the right and turn into the room that is my bedroom in our apartment. The room smells citrusy and woodsy but has none of the fanciness of the hallway. It is solid and peaceful. The walls are a serene blue-gray, like the color of the early night sky. The overhead light has a delicate glass covering with an intricate design on it. It shines down onto a gigantic bed with a dark blue quilt and sumptuous pillows. The light creates spots on the quilt that look like bright stars against the night sky. The bed is made up nicely, and I wonder if a maid did that or if Jake made his bed before he went out for the night.

Despite being fairly strong, I struggle to get the necessary leverage to hoist the girl onto the bed because of our height difference. Jake reacts quickly: he swings her into his arms and deposits her on the bed.

He turns to us and says sheepishly, "Thank you, both, I wasn't sure how I was going to manage."

We stare at the woman sprawled across the bed on her back. Now I can see her face.

Papa crosses himself and mutters, "Saint Michael, defend us."

I've never seen such a delicate and beautiful thing. She has a pert nose and an oval-shaped face. Her lips are a perfect bow, and her hair is cut in a very fashionable bob, even though it is fanned out in a tangle framing her pale face. I touch my plain blonde hair self-consciously. Mine is pulled back in a simple ponytail and doesn't have half the style hers does. My eyes drift slowly down her body; she is rake thin and must be almost six feet tall. I exhale and ask softly, "Is she a model? Is she okay?"

Jake steps in front of me, blocking my view, ruefully shaking his head.

"She'll be okay," he replies before quickly ushering us out of the room and then out of the apartment. I'm disoriented for a moment as I stand in the hallway. I lean against the wall, still back in the blue gray bedroom with the angel. Papa tugs at my arm, and I slowly focus on his frowning face and stand upright, trying to remember where we were going.

We don't speak until we are out on Fifth Avenue. I know what is coming.

He sputters, "Emma, how could you? Who knows what that no-good boy is up to? And now we are part of it. What if something happens to that girl?"

I respond meekly, "Papa, he needed our help—"

He slices his hand through the air to silence me, "How many times have I told you? American boys will be the ruin of this great country. And now this could be the ruin of us. This . . . Jake doesn't know how lucky he is to be born in America. No! Everything is handed to him. He hasn't worked a day in his life. You know that." He looks sharply at me, and I'm unsure if he wants a response. "He knows nothing of hard work or the freedom he takes for granted." His voice drops. "We don't know what kind of trouble we could get into. I don't like this, I don't like any of it."

My father's fear is talking. He's not angry with me—well at least not very angry—he's fearful of what could happen. My parents worry about getting caught in some misdeed or illegal activity they didn't understand, and because of a minor mistake or misunderstanding, they lose their tenuous hold on the American dream. They know they can try their hardest and do all the right things but still get caught up in something that results in it all going up in smoke, which would be the ultimate affront to my grandfather's perilous journey from Poland and the death to every other Jablonski that remained.

I can't imagine how helping the pretty girl into Jake's apartment will get us into trouble, but I know better than to share my opinion. No matter what I say, the weight will not lessen or change; it is always there, and I can't do anything to lift it and dispel my father's concerns. He has enough worries that weigh down his broad, stooped shoulders. So, I simply nod my head in agreement as he continues to fret and mutter to himself until we reach the bakery and enter through the back door.

Once inside the shop, my father's attention quickly shifts to the making of bread, mixing the flour and sugar, and starting the yeast to rise for the pumpernickel, the one the patrons stand in line for. He no longer looks quite so stooped as he relaxes against the large stand mixer that whirls and twirls the dough. His hair sticks up in gray and white tufts. His broad face would be unremarkable except for his dark eyebrows, which slash so forcefully across his brow that they look like they are trying to smooth the deeply furrowed lines that crease his forehead in the opposite direction.

I set about mixing the fillings for the pastries. As I stir and stir, my mind flashes back to the morning, remembering the suit Jake was wearing. It was steel gray and looked soft to the touch. Next, his hair flashes through my mind. It was short as it has been for the last few years. Up close, it was lovelier than I imagined. *What if I had dared to touch it?*

The first time Papa and I bumped into Jake was ten years ago; I was fifteen and figured Jake was around nineteen. It was 4:00 a.m., and Jake was walking in from what I imagined was a night on the town. His hair was long and tousled, he was wearing tight-fitting jeans and singing some popular song of the day. As we passed him in the hallway, he reached out for my father's hand and tried to spin him in a twirl. Papa shrank back against the wall to evade him, and Jake then reached his corded arm out for me.

I smelled the alcohol on his breath and froze—unable to move, never mind spin.

Without missing a beat, he did a jaunty bow to us and, with a cheeky grin, said, "Top of the morning to you both."

I stood rooted to the floor, staring at Jake with his wavy chestnut hair, his aquiline nose, and smooth cheeks, as he made his way past us, toward his apartment door. His face was open and carefree. His eyes had a humorous glint, as if he and only he knew a secret joke. As I watched, a wave of longing hit me that I had no explanation for. He was something so exotic, so different from the large, blonde, flat-faced Polish boys who work at the bakery. He was narrow at the hips, almost slight, but sinewy with shoulders that looked strong. My gut tightened with hunger despite the bagel I had eaten.

At fifteen, I knew in my heart of hearts he was wildly dangerous, and my father confirmed that to me in no uncertain terms during our walk to the bakery. That was the first of many lectures about rich American boys and how they will be the downfall of this great country. Papa loves America but holds Americans, particularly American boys, in very low regard.

"You must never forget the sacrifices made to give you the life you have," he admonished me. Then he quickly launched into his oft-repeated lecture of how his father Ernest came to America when he was eighteen, leaving his family behind to perish in the great war. Repeating his well-worn phrase—"My father came here with nothing but the shirt on his back"—with force.

Back then, my rebellious self had to bite my tongue, fighting the urge to respond with a flippant, "while technically true, the shirt did have jewels and gold sewn into the lining, so maybe not quite *nothing*."

I smile now, remembering that moment and my disobedient thoughts. I don't know where this devilish side of me comes from. Sometimes Papa seems to sense my insolence even when I haven't said a word, as he will launch into some lesson grounded in our family legacy. I think it is my eyes that give away my uncharitable thoughts.

Since that first embarrassing run-in with Jake, we've bumped into him sporadically over the years. Each encounter was both mortifying and fascinating and I remember each one vividly. When I ran into him in the hall at seventeen, Jake had even longer hair that fell almost to his shoulders in a wavy, coppery mane. That time, when he walked past me, I stared with my mouth agape and had to clench my fist at my side to keep my hand from reaching out to touch his hair in all its wildness. He said nothing, but I saw a quick quirk of his lip as he passed us, as if he knew exactly what I wanted to do.

I saw him a few more times with his hair long and continued to be mesmerized by it. My father stepped up his condemnation of Jake and all American boys as he seemed to understand that my reaction to Jake was not waning but was getting stronger.

After that, Jake's hair got progressively shorter, but never *short.* I fancied he knew his hair only added to his allure, and to tame it would be a shame.

When I turned nineteen, I reined in my infatuation. Maybe I finally grew up . . . or maybe his shorter hair gave me enough strength to control myself. Dreams are for the young and the foolish, the real world doesn't allow such dreams to breathe and take flight. That is when I began to take my father's lectures to heart, realizing the silliness of my interest in the rich, handsome boy next door. Jake was not of my world, and it was stupid to pay him any more attention than I do to the wealthy patrons of the bakery who drop a dollar in the tip jar as they smile at me condescendingly. I still had my special dream of flying free in the forest, and that would have to be enough.

I pull myself out of my reverie when I smell a sweet acrid smell of burnt sugar. *Oh, no! I've let the filling burn.* I rush to dump it in the garbage, covering it with an empty bag. Staring at the waste, I give myself a stern admonishment: *Be the dutiful daughter my parents want and deserve!*

Chapter 2:

The Birds

The bread is baking in the oven when I open the front doors at 7:30 a.m. A swarm of customers rushes in, breaking the quiet melancholy of the morning. Some regulars greet me with a "Hi, Emma." Others smile pleasantly as they place their orders. Watching the people step off the street, I imagine their busy, exciting lives and wonder how I missed having a little life of my own. Smiles, nods, and greetings come my way, but nothing more. I'm stuck in a bubble I built to protect myself and now I'm not sure I know how to get out or if I want to. I'm alone, removed from this life that for everyone else, the connection seems as natural as breathing.

The picture of the blonde angel sprawled on Jake's bed pops into my head as I knead the dough for another batch of bread. *I hope she is okay.* I weave a wonderful life for the angel. One that is full of friends, excitement, and gaiety. Her life is magnificent. Smiling, I fill a box of Paczki. Sprinkling the sweet, fried dough with powdered sugar. Inhaling the homey aroma, I think, *Why can't this be enough?*

On my way home midafternoon, I walk through Central Park and do the only thing that brings color to my world: I watch the birds. As always, I have John Foster's guidebook *Birds of Central Park* tucked into my pocketbook. I've spotted some species he meticulously describes in his book.

I look for new birds on each of my walks as well as the regulars, through the ever-changing seasons, year after year. Some birds remain in the park, others pass through on their way to far-off wintering or breeding grounds. These solitary walks are the high point of my day. In the park, I'm connected as if I belong here, among the birds and the trees. For the hundredth time, I wish I had binoculars as I could add a lot more birds to my life list if I had even a cheap pair. My fingers idly rub the spine of the guidebook; it has given me my connection to this special world.

It was shortly after 9/11, my family moved to New York City to help care for my ailing grandmother after the old Ernest died, fortunately, the young Ernest remained to help me deal with a world that had turned upside down the instant the planes hit those towers. My world had imploded as I grappled with a move from Connecticut to the city. Both the world inside my grandmother's rent-controlled apartment on the Upper East Side and the world outside were in shambles. It was during this time that the bubble fully encased me, protecting me from the chaos and the sharp jabs the kids in public school directed at me. All of them assumed I was a rich girl kicked out of her snobby boarding school, who now was slumming it with them. The humiliations were too many to count. Sitting alone in the cafeteria, the little pushes when walking down the hallway, always the last one to be partnered up with when the teacher assigned a group project. While my bubble protected me, the library nourished me—showing me worlds I couldn't begin to imagine, and I devoured them wanting to be far away from this crazy foreign world we were stuck living in.

When I was seventeen, I stumbled upon *Birds of Central Park* in the NYC Library and that changed everything. Finally, our location across from the most famous urban park in the world helped me. The book gave me a purpose and a distraction that went well beyond me getting lost in the pages of a book. John Foster's guide showed me how to walk and commune with nature. While my parents and the customers at the bakery might see me every day, they never see the real me, the person who has dreams and hopes and too many funny comments. Only John Foster and the birds and the trees see me and feel me. I write down in his book not only bird observations, but my thoughts and feelings that go well beyond the birds. He invites me to share, and share I do. He is a good listener. Now I had John Foster and young Ernest for company, what more could I need?

As I wander through the park, I scan the tree limbs, trying to peek through the leaves and peer into the low shrubs to spot one of my feathered friends. It's mid-September, and there are still migratory birds flying south, stopping to rest up and put on necessary fat to see them through to their faraway wintering grounds. *Oh, to be wild and free.*

John Foster explains that you must first listen for the bird and then get your eyes and ears to triangulate to where the bird should be sitting. Once you spot the bird, you use your binoculars, if you have a pair, to bring the bird into focus. His descriptions of the nesting habits of these *feathered friends,* as he calls them, as well as what each bird eats and where it winters and summers, is a secret world unto itself. A world I have the magic key to enter. Describing the purple finch, he writes *its proclivity to build nests on any outside, manmade structure, which the park has several of leads you to look up into the nooks and crannies of the carousel or Wollman's rink to locate them.* He encourages readers to find *the secret world of finches on these buildings that are part of our world, but they have purloined a piece for themselves to use in their world.*

When I first took the book out from the library, I kept my dictionary nearby to help me understand many of the words he used, but in time, John Foster expanded my mind to include his fancy words as well as birds.

People walk through Central Park every day, but it's only those of us who know about this secret world of lovely, chittering, feathered beings that get to peek at it. If I ever meet him, which could happen because the book jacket says he lives in NYC, I will thank him and may even dare to hug him. His book has been a lifeline for me during my long and lonely teenage years, which now are stretching right into my twenties.

He explains in the book, "We come from nature, and we all would be much better off if we walked more in nature instead of viewing nature as a separate thing apart from humans."

I would not have survived living in the city without my connection to the world of flora, fauna, and the birds of Central Park. I discovered a peace within the park that I never found anywhere else, except at Seaside Park's ocean beach back in Bridgeport, where I could feel the power of my favorite myth, the story of Halcyon and Ceyx. John Foster helped me put words around the peace I found in nature and made my connection seem normal. He opened my eyes to the passing of the seasons, and the migration of birds north to south and back again. Giving me an understanding of how living by the rhythm and cycles of nature is better for the human condition than the artifice of clocks and our obsession with small increments of time—minutes instead of seasons and millennia. He woke me up, giving me a thin rope that tethered me a bit to this world.

Thanks to him and Central Park, I am alive.

Stopping at my favorite bench in the Ramble section of the park, I sit and immediately spot a bird poking its head out from under the witch hazel bush with its yellow spidery flowers, I note a yellow circle around a bright eye and a gray head: a white-eyed vireo. It looks right at me with an inquisitive cock of his head and gives its distinctive three-part song. My bird bible tells me he is only looking for insects to forage for on the ground and isn't making eye contact with the likes of me. But that doesn't stop the surge of happiness from filling my chest, and this one time I dismiss John's teachings and instead believe that the little, gray-headed bird with its yellow sides and two white wing bars is looking right at me and acknowledging my presence.

The bird takes a few more hops, then disappears back under the shrub. I am seen, even if it is only by a bird.

My eyes travel from the bush to a couple strolling by. They lean in towards each other, murmuring and holding hands, they're in their own magical world.

Oh, to have someone to tell your thoughts and feelings to and have them care about what you say, and more importantly, what you feel. When I was young, my parents had little interest in me, only making sure I was eating, sleeping, growing, and doing all the *right things*. They never wondered what I was feeling or thinking. They are of the generation or maybe of the culture that believes parents must feed and clothe their children, teach them the importance of hard work, and anything more is unnecessary and may actually spoil them. Spoiling a child is the worst thing a parent can do and is why my father rails against all the "spoiled American children" like Jake, who take their freedom and good fortune for granted.

My parents decidedly *do not* spoil me, quite the opposite, but I don't blame them. They are trying to cope; they don't have the time or energy to focus even a tiny bit of attention on me unless I force their hand like I did this morning. My mother is trying to survive her MS, a degenerative and debilitating disease, with as little attention or complaint as possible. Despite her stoicism, many things fall to my father. And the stress of my grandmother's constant threats saps his energy even further. *How many times has she threatened to throw us out over these intervening years? Too many to count. They don't need me dreaming and wishing for something more.*

Glancing up at the sky, I realize the sun is getting low and I need to head home to help with dinner. Mama has been having some good days lately, but I should be home helping and not staring up at the sky and the trees, dreaming and hoping. My father's voice rings in my head: "There is no time for hope, only hard work." I don't know why I can't do better and just accept my life, but a vice tightens around my chest when I think of these endless days with no color or hope sprinkled in.

I sputter, *Dammit, that can't be all there is to live for?*

Pressing my hand against my mouth to hide my smile, I look around for any passersby who may have heard me. Instead, I spot the vireo peeking out at me and I chuckle. Feeling downright defiant, I don't even cross myself.

I sit for five more minutes and am rewarded with first the raspy call of the belted kingfisher, and then I triangulate his call, and I spot him. Perching on a branch with his blue-gray little body, his ragged crest makes his head look too large for his body. He is an odd-looking little bird, but he is my favorite.

A bubble of happiness expands in my chest. *Maybe God has a sense of humor and doesn't mind my blasphemous inner voice. Wouldn't that be something?*

The kingfisher was the first bird I documented in my guidebook, which contains a whole Life List section full of blank pages, to help one start building their list of bird sightings.

I don't get paid for working in the bakery, as that is a family obligation, so it took me until I was eighteen to save up enough pin money to buy my own copy of the book. That was my one luxury since I have few other needs—no iPhone, no makeup, no jewelry. Six months later, I finally dared make my first entry on the blank, crisp white pages in the *Life List* section. It took spotting my first kingfisher to get me to mark down the sighting on those lovely virgin pages. It was the sign I needed.

My connection to the kingfisher goes back to seventh-grade English class when I first read the myth of Halcyon and Ceyx. Princess Halcyon was married to the mortal king Ceyx and their love for each other was known throughout the realms. Because of their pridefulness and blasphemy, one day when Ceyx was sailing to Delphi, a great storm capsized his boat and as he was drowning, he begged Poseidon to bring his body to his wife's arms. Halcyon, meanwhile, had the God of Dreams tell her about the awful fate of her husband, and she rushed to the coast where she found Ceyx's body and immediately threw herself into the blackness of the sea. Amazed by her love and devotion, the gods decided to save her. They transformed her and Ceyx into kingfisher birds so they could be together forever.

But Zeus ordered that Halcyon must lay her eggs in winter, nesting always near the spot where she found Ceyx's body. This was impossible for the two birds, as the waves kept sweeping away the eggs. The kingfishers were heartbroken and desperate. Zeus finally took pity on the lovers and ordered the gods to give them fourteen days of pleasant weather around the winter solstice, so they could keep their eggs safe.

This story of love and commitment sustained me. It spoke to me of the need to keep trying and never give up. It convinced me that we all have our Ceyx or our Halcyon out there somewhere, and we will find them when the gods decide it is time. This was when my dream made its first appearance and that comforted me as well. It has sustained me while I wait on the gods.

After seeing the kingfisher that very first time, I realized I needed to do what John Foster preached in the book: "One needs to track and make note when and where they see their first bird of a particular species, so you can hold on to the memory." So, I wrote down belted kingfisher and described the park that day. The weather, the sun shining down, the exact location of the bird.

Now I'm up to sixty lifers. That is what John Foster calls this list of specific identified birds. There are over two hundred species of birds that visit the park, so I have a long way to go on my list, but that gives me a reason to get up in the morning when there isn't any other compelling reason to rise. A surge of pride makes me straighten my shoulders, but almost as soon as that happens, I deflate. How I wish I had someone to share it with. While I love him dearly and he is a good listener, John Foster isn't the best conversationalist and Ernest is even less so.

I tuck my guidebook into my industrial-sized bag that holds my umbrella, wallet, and the other items one needs to walk the city streets and hurry home. I take a deep breath, and the air feels alive and energizing. As I walk the path getting closer to home, my feet drag and my lungs constrict.

Well, I think as I step off the elevator, *at least my father's story of the morning's situation will remind my parents I'm still alive and breathing.*

I pause outside our door and steal a glance at Jake's door. A picture of the plush hallway with the rich carpet and the muted lights flashes through my mind, followed by his bedroom. I wish I had touched his quilt. It looks like it would feel like a cloud.

"Hmm." A dreamy smile tugs at my lips as I turn the knob. "Mama, I'm home."

Chapter 3:

The Limp

Days later, walking home through the Ramble, I stop and look down at my legs encased in my smudged, checked bakery pants. A thought slowly dawns and unfurls in my mind like a snake. *I'm limping*. I haven't been feeling well, but I thought it was from the change of the seasons. Fall, with its shorter days and brisk temperatures, signals the slow opening of the door to winter and that always brings with it a sense of melancholy. It means the end of the fall bird migration when the outside world becomes brown and drab—too much like my inside world. Each fall I go through a period of sadness when winter takes over, muting out the vibrant greens and splashes of color of the trees, birds and flowers.

I glance around; the leaves are still green, but they look ready to shrivel and dry as the tinge of fall grips the air in mid-September. Winter is coming even if it hasn't yet started painting the trees, the magic colors of fall.

I frown at my thoughts. What I'm feeling is something altogether different from my normal seasonal grief. Recently, my knees and hips have been aching all day instead of just in the morning. Today they feel almost swollen. My stomach knots into a state of panic as my mind immediately jumps to MS. "Noooo!" screams in my head.

Taking a deep breath, I stare up at the clear, blue sky. The picture that comes into focus is my mother, sitting at the Formica kitchen table with a bunch of pamphlets spread out in front of her. She just came from one of her first doctor's appointments after her diagnosis. I was eighteen. My grandmother is sitting in her recliner, facing the table. I'm stirring soup on the stove. Mama is reading out loud, translating the pamphlet into Polish. Mama and Grandma glance sharply at me and silence hangs heavy in the air. They rarely pay me much attention so, at first, I think I've done something wrong with the soup. But, when I meet their gaze, I don't see the disapproval that I expect for my cooking — instead, I see pity reflected in their eyes. Now sensing that I should have been paying more attention, I review my mother's words, translating them to English and connecting the dots to make the most regrettable picture: "MS can be a genetic disease." Fear and anguish flood my being and my mother looks contrite. She shakes her head as if trying to nullify the words.

Leaving my soup pot unattended, I sit down at the table, taking the pamphlet from her hand. I skim it, silently calculating how many more years I have before I, too, will need to start taking the heavy dosages of medication my mother has started on. She is struggling with the new regimen of pills that make her sleepy and not herself, but the doctors assure her they are all necessary to help manage her disease. It was sitting at the table that I worked out the timeline for me, and that timeline became etched into my psyche.

My mother's symptoms began when she was thirty, right after I was born. For the first couple of years, she believed the symptoms were related to caring for a new baby. She struggled to get her doctor to listen to her complaints because of language barriers and her own reticence to complain. So, for eighteen years, she dealt with the cruel fickleness of MS without knowing what was happening. Bouts of unsteadiness, muscle weakness, and vertigo, coupled with periods of feeling normal and fine. She struggled along, living the physically demanding life of a baker's wife, never knowing when her symptoms would strike or what they meant. Finally, her diagnosis gave a name to her many ailments. The timeline I had counted on gave me until I was thirty before I had to start worrying and looking for symptoms, but here I am at twenty-six. *Of course, my timeline was wrong.* I stumble along until I find my favorite bench and sit. My symptoms are real, and now that I'm conscious of them, I realize they've been getting worse for the past couple of weeks. *Could it happen this fast?*

Of course it could. MS is a tricky disease, sometimes disappearing completely only to come roaring back for no apparent reason.

A dark wave engulfs me. *What is the point? Why am I even here? Is it truly just to suffer? I haven't begun to live—and now it is too late.* I had 2017 in my head, not 2013.

Getting up slowly, I trudge back to the apartment. I serve the sauerkraut and pork chops and then clear the dirty dishes. I'm disconnected from my body, lost in my head, removed completely from this apartment and this life. Robotically, turning on Babcia's TV when it's time for *Wheel of Fortune*. My parents settle in for the evening and no one glances at me.

Do they see me at all? Don't they sense my anguish?

Instead of sleeping, I assess my life in fits and starts throughout the long, miserable night. My life in review is so painfully dull. I haven't done one thing that is significant in my twenty-six years. Unless you count the many embarrassing events and humiliations. Certainly, nothing I experience resembles the life that the individual in Jake's bed likely enjoys simply existing.

Life is so unfair.

I quickly cross myself with a pang of guilt. Jealousy of others and thinking God owes you is counter to everything I've been taught while sitting on the hard pews of St. Augustine Church. And these teachings apply doubly to a Jablonski whose family made the ultimate sacrifice. I do ten Hail Marys in quick succession and promise to do more at church on Sunday.

With my penance over, my painful past continues to roll behind my closed eyes like a sad movie—the sleepover my parents had to collect me from when I cried and screamed when we watched *ET*. It was absolutely terrorizing when the monster screamed and stretched his neck up. For years after that, I threw away every Reese's Pieces pack I got trick or treating, petrified he'd come find them in our apartment above our bakery. Or the time I brought pierogis to school for Cultures within Our Class, and the kids snickered, "Emma, didn't bring anything," pretending they couldn't see the pale pierogis against the white plate. The girls from my class who always went out of their way to make my school days lonely and miserable, excluding me from recess games.

In the inky darkness just before dawn, the last painful memory drifts into focus: I'm fourteen and we're attending my mother's cousin's wedding, a small, family affair. I am wearing my best Sunday dress and feeling quite grown-up.

It is a light-blue dress, and when I look at my reflection in the bathroom mirror in the banquet hall, my light-blue eyes look downright sparkly. As the afternoon progresses, people start to dance, and the music gets loud. My mother and father are all smiles, looking so relaxed, I barely recognize them. Mama has been having a good month, with barely any weakness, so they look like every other couple at the wedding: drinking, talking in Polish, and laughing.

A boy approaches our table.

"Hello, I'm Jimmy," he introduces himself. "Would you like to dance?"

My father says loudly, "Yes, Emma, go dance with the nice boy." He gestures wildly toward the dance floor.

My mother sees the shock in my eyes and she more sedately motions me toward the dance floor. I wonder where my parents have disappeared to.

I get up obediently and follow the boy to the dance floor. We dance.

After another dance, Jimmy asks, "Want to go outside? It's getting kinda hot in here."

I quickly glance at my parent's table, and it is empty. I spot them near the bar with Uncle Leo and a group of others. Feeling emboldened, I shrug a yes, and we walk out onto the patio.

Others are milling around outside, enjoying the fresh air. Jimmy pulls me in close and tucks us into a corner. He feels even warmer than the air in the reception room, but I don't pull away. I think he is going to kiss me, and my stomach jumps with nerves. All the girls at high school talk about kissing boys, and I very much want to see what it is like. But suddenly, I hear Father Kowalski's voice in my ear—"Harlot!"—and I jump and pull away, running back to our table, my cheeks flaming red with embarrassment.

If I had only known—how could I have known?—that this was going to be my only chance for a kiss, I would not have fled. I wish a warning bell could sound, signaling, "Last chance, take it or leave it." I would have been so much braver and not run away from a secret kiss in the corner of the patio at Clark's Restaurant and Banquet Hall. Right after this, we moved to New York City, and I sealed myself off completely. My bubble kept me safe from all the hurts and taunts leveled at me for reasons I could not fathom. A few things could get through. Some unwelcome, like my father's voice that echoed within about the sacrifices one must make or Father Kowalski's booming voice, also ricocheted off the walls each Sunday. But some good things made it through too. My mother's soft squeezes when she sensed I had a particularly bad day. The birds, trees and velvet moss of the Park eased through my walls. And Jake. Jake could break through until I finally sealed the hole when I was nineteen. Crazy dreams were just that . . . crazy.

I stare up at the ceiling through the long night of my painful review. As dawn is breaking gray and bleak, I clasp my hands together, not sure if I am praying or wishing, and whisper in a hush, "Please, anyone. I don't want to be cured. I know that is impossible. But please let me live a little before I start to die." I spot the tenacious little spider web in the corner of my room and make out the delicate threads and the intricate design. That lifts my spirits a bit.

Getting out of bed, I'm not sure if the aches are from lack of sleep or the MS continuing to assault my nerves and muscles. I feel a hundred years old as I bend down to kneel beside my bed. I bow my head, resting it on the thin mattress. I can't think of a single prayer to say this morning. *Does it really matter when I'm in hell already?* I shake my head, shocked at my audacity. I really need to get a grip.

During a slow time at the bakery, while my father is taking care of a flour delivery, I call my mother's MS specialist and make an appointment. They have an opening next week because of a cancellation, and the receptionist shares how lucky I am to get this appointment.

I refrain from saying, "Lucky? Let me tell you, anyone calling your office for an appointment is the exact opposite of lucky." I suppress a grin then sober up. It's a morning appointment, so I'm going to have to figure that out.

I go through the week on autopilot, but the world does not notice. Although my father seems to tire of having to remind me to focus on my tasks at the bakery.

Chapter 4:

The Appointment

When my father raps on my door at 4:00 a.m., I call out weakly, "Papa, I don't feel well today. I'm sick."

My father pauses for a moment and then I hear him continue to the kitchen. A short while after, I hear the door open and close, and silence blankets our apartment. *Well, now I can add lying to my list of recent sins.*

I dress quickly, then go back and lie back down on my bed pulling my quilt up to my ears. My mother gets up and shuffles into the kitchen with her walker to get the breakfast plate with the bagels and cream cheese my father left carefully draped with a tea towel. The smell of the strong coffee reaches my room as my mother pours out two cups from the percolator. There is a soft clink as my mother sets the tray onto her walker's shelf, designed so she can sit down on it if she needs to, and she wheels down the hallway to bring the tray to Babcia. Stuffing down the pang of guilt I force myself to stay in my room and not help despite knowing she is struggling again with numbness in her feet and hands. Once I hear her open the door to Babcia's room, I silently ease out of bed and am out the apartment door in an instant.

An unexpected bubble of happiness flares in my chest as I realize I have an hour to kill before my nine-thirty appointment in Midtown. This means I can birdwatch this morning and John Foster says mornings are the best time to birdwatch. I'm thankful for this small gift on this day of potential ruin.

Walking through the park, I spot a northern flicker with his long, pointed bill making its way around a dead tree, and a cedar waxwing with his crested top, happy to hear its high-pitched call. Ambling along the path, I spot more ordinary birds—a noisy blue jay and a tufted titmouse—filling my lungs with the fresh and wild air I can breathe.

Making my way past the Pond, which I rarely get to walk by, as it is far off my trek to and from the bakery, I spot one of my most sought-after birds. A wood duck! They are quite common in Central Park, but I've never seen one before. Staring with my mouth open, a bit of warmth unfurls in my chest. It is so lovely, its coloring is unbelievable, it looks fake. John Foster describes the duck as looking like a little Chinese man wearing the most wonderfully crafted kimono, and now I see his description is spot on. The duck has white stripes in the most unexpected places, his red beak adds even more color behind the iridescent-emerald coloring of his hood with its special little backward point, that makes it look like he has put a baseball cap on backward like one of those wild American boys. *How can Mother Nature create such a striking creature?* I don't ask for much, really. All I need is a duck occasionally. A smile quirks at my lips.

The minutes tick by, and slowly a wave of queasiness replaces my excitement as it dawns on me that the only explanation for finally spotting this special bird is that God or fate or whoever is trying to balance out the pending bad news. Rooted to the ground, I screw my eyes shut, trying to block out the awful thought. I feel a steadying arm wrap around my shoulder and know it is young Ernest once again mysteriously appearing just when I need him most. I turn away from the duck and the bad news it portends. We walk together towards the future I now know unequivocally awaits me. I stare miserably towards Hallett Sanctuary, no longer in the mood to explore.

Sitting in the nicely appointed waiting room, Rebecca, the doctor's assistant, calls my name and greets me with a friendly, "Hi."

She doesn't seem surprised to see me without my mother, which makes me wonder if they too had a mental timeline of when I would show up for an appointment of my own. I can't muster a smile in return.

Rebecca takes my pulse and temperature, weighs me, and I take a seat on the bed. The noise of the paper rustling beneath me sounds like a scream to my ears. I try to sit perfectly still as I wait for Dr. Liam.

She arrives a few minutes later with a big smile, and I wonder why everyone is acting like this is a perfectly normal visit.

Haltingly, I tell Dr. Liam my suspicions and my symptoms. Her smile slowly disappears as I describe my swollen and painful joints, my clumsiness, and my weakness in my legs and arms. She talks about genetics and the advancements in the medications used to treat MS.

She doesn't add that all they can do is treat the symptoms because they can't cure the disease. After all, she knows she doesn't have to.

She completes her exam, checking my reflexes and eye movements. It feels like a *Freaky Friday* situation where, somehow, I've switched bodies with my mother. My mind wanders to the movie and how funny it was having young Lindsay Lohan stuck in a grown-up mom's body. Now it doesn't seem funny at all. I'm just a kid, but I'm going to be stuck in my mother's failing body. Dr. Liam is speaking, and I try to listen, but I keep seeing Jamie Lee Curtis getting her hair cut short and spiky. Dr. Liam is listing other things my symptoms might be, and then she writes out a prescription and hands it to me.

I quickly hand it back and state emphatically, "I don't want to start any MS medicine for a while. I just need a bit more time before I do that."

Dr. Liam pushes the slip of paper back into my hand and explains, "Emma, this isn't for MS, take these for twenty-one days and then come back to be re-evaluated. Then we can discuss MS medicine. But take these."

"This isn't MS medication?"

She shakes her head no. There is no actual test for MS, which I already knew, but Rebecca takes blood work, and I take the script but don't stop at reception to make the follow-up appointment.

A plan starts to form in my head as I walk back toward Central Park, and it is based on the wish I made last week after my sleepless night. Since I don't have six years anymore, it only seems fair to squeeze out six months to live before I face my diagnosis. I want to live a life, any life, for just a bit before I disappear into the beige walls of our quiet, lonely apartment and step into my mother's shoes. Raising my eyes to the sky, I state solemnly, "After six months, I promise I will accept my fate and be the dutiful daughter who will never complain again."

A thought develops in my consciousness. *My parents may be happy about my diagnosis, as it will finally ensure my grandmother won't throw us out.* How could she? She can't throw us out on the street, leaving her son with two struggling women and no roof over their heads. That would be too cruel to even threaten.

I shake my head to clear such an awful thought as I walk along the main path of the park. My parents would never be happy about my MS. They may determine if it must be, then the one good thing is we are a little more secure in our precarious living situation, but they wouldn't ever want this for me.

I glance at the pond; the wood duck has disappeared.

I stare at the empty pond, I think, *Maybe it is not true, maybe my symptoms are from some other ailment.*

Just then, the stunning little beauty paddles out from behind the reeds, and my little bubble of hope bursts. God is giving me this duck to make up for my fate. I want to shake a fist at the sky and scream, "This is not a fair trade, God!" but I don't. I turn away. The wood duck is all the things my world is not and now never will be.

Sitting on my bench, I don't birdwatch; instead, I sit and wallow in the universe's unfairness. After a few minutes, I get up, step behind the bench, and ease into the dark woods behind it. Needing more solace than my bench offers, I walk the short distance to the immense oak tree directly behind my special bench. I press both of my palms against the bark and my stress eases. The weight of my ancestral ghosts lifts off my shoulders, the noise of the fear-inducing sermons of the church fades, and the painful memories of my past ease. I inhale and my chest fills with a peace I struggle to capture anywhere else. The diagnosis has altered how I see the world. I can be part of things, there is a way.

Touching the old tree, I ask, "Please Lord, just six months. Please, I want to try to live."

I continue pressing into the tree and try to conjure up a picture of what *living* could be. *What am I asking for?* Something fun and daring, but what is that?

After sneaking back into the apartment, I don't even have to feign illness. I'm sick and tired of everything. Sitting at dinner that evening, I watch my parents.

"How did you two meet?"

I want to know their love story, as maybe it will show me the path. Wouldn't it be lovely to have someone for these next six months to see what it is like—holding hands in the park, kissing and cuddling on the bench, sharing dreams?

"What?" my mother asks in surprise.

I blush when a steamy picture pops into my head. My eyes widen as it dawns on me that I don't want to be a virgin after these six months.

"Are you still feeling sick, Emma?" she asks pointedly.

I shake my head and stubbornly repeat my question, "How did you two meet?"

This time my father responds, "At church, of course. Why?"

Then my grandmother barks from her room, "Emma, I need my tray cleared and turn on the TV, *Wheel of Fortune* is starting."

"Freakin' church." I mutter. I've been going to church with my parents every Sunday at noon since *forever,* but I've never seen, never mind met, a male under the age of fifty. I'm certain church isn't the answer to find love anymore, but what is?

That evening, my prayer is one that I repeat over and over like a mantra as I kneel: *I want a life.*

Chapter 5:

The Favor

Walking to the closet next to our front door to retrieve the large soup pot we store there, I nearly jump out of my skin when I hear a rap on the door. I clutch my chest; I can't remember the last time an unexpected visitor knocked on our door. My aunt and uncle are our only visitors, and they never knock but just barge in, but we are always expecting them.

I tentatively open the door. Peeking through the crack, my eyes meet bright brown ones. *Jake.* I drop my gaze, letting my hair fall over my face.

Smiling hesitantly, he says, "Hey, I've got a big favor to ask. Can you come over at four today and stay with Veronica? Uh, she's the girl you met kinda the other day? It will be for a couple of hours. I teach a class over at Columbia and don't want her to be alone and was hoping . . ." His voice trails off.

I raise my eyes; he looks so sincere and a little unsure. If this were two days ago, my answer would have been an immediate no, but today, even before I think, I respond, "Yes, I can do that." I like the way his cheeks angle up to his sharp cheekbones. He's all angles and sharp points.

Jake quickly lets out the breath he must have been holding and smiles brightly, "I will pay you, of course. It should be until six or so. Does that work?"

Trying to match his easy smile, but my face doesn't seem to know how to do it. "Yes, that works." I quickly incline my head and close the door. Leaning against the wall, I take a deep, cleansing breath. Suddenly I'm a bundle of nerves coupled with a rush of adrenaline, feeling more alive than I was just a minute ago. *Could this be what living feels like?*

Getting ready in my room later, I picture the angel. Her name is Veronica. Pinching my cheeks to give them a bit of color, I pause and furrow my brow. Why do I need to *watch* her? That seems strange, but I push the question out of my mind, straighten my shoulders, and whisper under my breath, "Be brave."

At 3:45 p.m., with my stomach in knots, I announce to my mother, "I have to babysit a neighbor, and I won't be home until after dinner."

Mama stares at me in disbelief. I've never babysat a neighbor as I don't know any of our neighbors, other than the poster child of jaded American youth down the hall, and my mother would never suspect I'm heading into that den of iniquity. I'm hoping she assumes I made an acquaintance of some mother in our building. Taking advantage of her shocked surprise, I make my escape. For this moment, I'm brave and I jauntily throw open our door. My steps falter just a touch, as I know

I won't be able to avoid my parents' consternation when I return. I bravely think, "I won't worry about that until I must."

Knocking softly on Jake's door, I glance nervously down the hall. My father shouldn't be home for another forty-five minutes, but I can't help but shrink against the doorjamb. Jake opens the door, and I almost fall into his arms. He smiles and seems pleased I'm early. I'm relieved, as some Americans don't like my family's tendency to be early for all appointments and gatherings. We believe on time means at least fifteen minutes early. It has proved to be embarrassing on the few occasions we were invited somewhere outside our small circle of family. It's an Eastern European thing, and I gave up trying to convince my parents to abide by America's more relaxed, almost lax approach to time.

Jake ushers me down the same sumptuous hallway, and we turn right, stepping into the living area. Veronica is curled up in a graceful ball on the sofa. Her face is free of the makeup from the other night, and she looks sixteen. She turns toward me and smiles, but her smile doesn't reach her eyes. She looks lonely and young.

I immediately sit down next to her and say, "Hi."

Veronica responds with a tired, "Hi."

We sit quietly, watching Jake gather up a few papers on the coffee table and put them into a beat-up brown satchel. He looks tired too.

"So, I'll be back around six. You guys order anything you want when you get hungry." He drops a bunch of bills on the table and turns to Veronica, "Vee, please eat." He heads for the door.

I feel like I'm involved in something, though I'm not quite sure what it is. We sit quietly together. It is not an uncomfortable silence. I watch Vee. She is curled inward and not fully engaged with the outside world, as if she's encased in her own little bubble.

Since Jake seemed so concerned with eating, I think maybe I'm here to cook for her. I say brightly, "Do you want me to make you something to eat?"

"Like what?"

I pause and run through a couple of recipes I can make in my sleep. Most call for some special ingredient, such as the mountain cake that requires custard powder. I can't imagine Jake, or his parents, have that, although from what I can see of the kitchen, they may have every ethnic spice I can dream of. I don't dare run to my parent's place to grab something as Papa could be home by now and I'm not sure what I would ever say to him to convince him to let me go back over here. Babysitting, cooking . . . it all sounds crazy.

I respond, "Let's make crepes."

Veronica shrugs, but she unwinds her arms and legs from the ball and stands up. I impulsively take her hand, and we walk to the kitchen.

She drapes her long torso over one of the stools lined up at the island as I spin around the immaculate kitchen, opening drawers and cabinets as I go. The kitchen is lovely, all soft grays with splashes of warm cream. I locate the bowls and a whisk and place everything on the island so Veronica can be part of the preparation. The stove is part of the island, and I'm glad, as we'll be able to mix and cook everything facing each other.

I open the massive steel door of the refrigerator, extracting milk, eggs, butter, and sparkling water—our bakery's secret ingredient. I find the door to a walk-in pantry and look around until I find an assortment of jams and jellies.

"Are you a strawberry girl or a marmalade girl?"

I hear a smile in her voice as she responds, "Freakin' strawberry."

I carry the jar of jam over to her. "We are going to make Polish crepes. They're called nalesniki."

Veronica replies, "Nah-lesh-nee-kee."

I nod in approval. "Close."

I whisk the flour, eggs, milk, sparkling water, and butter together, then cover the bowl. "Now it must rest. What shall we do while we wait?"

Veronica scrunches up her forehead and, with a slight quirk of her lip, asks, "How do ya know how to make nah-lish-ka? You didn't even measure anything."

I laugh. "Nah-lesh-nee-kee. I've worked in my parent's bakery for as long as I can remember. Nalesniki is one of the first things my mother taught me how to make. I've made it thousands of times."

"Hm, a bakery." She frowns and sighs wistfully, "That sounds cool. I'd love to make stuff like that."

Cool? I have never thought of working at the bakery as cool.

I reply pertly, "It's not so cool when it's a hundred degrees in the middle of summer, but it does always smell sweet, no matter what."

Veronica straightens up, looking more alive, and continues, "So, you live across the way from here. That's pretty cool too."

Tilting my head, I state simply, "It wasn't so cool when I first moved here. I was just starting high school, and I didn't know anything about New York City and certainly didn't know our address meant I must be super-rich. Because we weren't super-rich, far from it. You see, my grandparents have had this apartment for years and years. I guess she doesn't pay much 'cause it's rent-controlled." I stop and fall silent.

"That doesn't seem so terrible."

"Well, when kids found out where I lived, they all teased me and assumed I was a spoiled, rich girl who flunked out of some fancy boarding school and now was slumming it with the public-school kids. I tried to explain, but no one listened, and I wasn't even sure what I was trying to explain. I guess what I was trying to say was that I was one of them and they shouldn't hate me. But they never gave me a chance and I certainly never fit in. It was a miserable four years." I blush. "I can't believe I told you that. I never told anyone that before. Not even my parents."

"Everyone has it tough, one way or another," Veronica replies, sounding tired and wise beyond her years.

"Hah! I can't believe that. Your life must be filled with fun and excitement at every turn."

A cloud passes over Veronica's eyes, and she smiles thinly. "Even me. I'm getting hungry. How much longer?"

Realizing she's deflecting, I announce dramatically, "It is time."

We pour the dough into the pan, and it sputters and sizzles. I flip the little round crepes confidently and set them out on plates. I show Veronica how to roll them up with the strawberry jam in the middle. The sweet aroma of strawberries floats in the air.

Veronica gets up and pushes a few buttons on a ginormous, fancy coffee machine. "Looks like these go perfectly with a cup of latte."

I remember seeing some tea bags in the pantry and go find them and a teapot and make myself a cup of Earl Grey. We munch on the sweet crepes, sipping our hot beverages. I've made crepes at the bakery and for my family, but this feels totally different. Special and totally ordinary all at the same time. I realize I'm comfortable here despite the fanciness of the furnishings. Maybe I'll be able to learn how to live after all.

Veronica eats with gusto and, with her mouth full, mumbles, "Aah, this is fucking fantastic."

I squeak out, "It's only crepes."

She leans in and whispers, "Only crepes! I'm twenty-one and had to look up how to boil an egg the other day."

I burst out laughing but stop when I realize she wasn't joking.

She pouts and punches me lightly on my arm. "Well, not how to cook them, but for how long. My mom never really liked to cook. My dad cooked a few things but never tried to show me or teach me. He worked a lot, so if we ever wanted a hot meal, we would scrape up enough money to order a pizza." She lets out a sigh. "Kind of sad, I know."

Rubbing my arm absentmindedly, it dawns on me; it has been a long time since someone touched me like this. My mother clutches me for balance periodically, I bump shoulders with my father in the bakery, but a punch in arm, I can't remember the last time. I grin and mirror her, leaning toward her and whisper, "It depends. We've never ordered a pizza, and I've always wondered what it was like to have food delivered right to your door, especially pizza."

Veronica gapes at me. "Shit." Oh no, she's realizing I'm a complete freak.

I quickly add, "I've had pizza before. I buy a slice occasionally, on my way home from the bakery just never had one delivered."

Veronica nods, looking relieved.

I can't believe the stuff I'm sharing with her, but it seems so easy. I'm not sure what has changed, but I feel lighter and happier instead of hiding myself away.

We continue talking quietly, and I'm cleaning up the kitchen when I hear the apartment door open. I look at my watch, Veronica looks at her phone, and we both look at each other with the same where-did-the-time-go expression, and chuckle.

Jake steps into the kitchen, breathes deeply, and says, "Wow! Something smells delicious."

"It was delicious." Veronica jumps off her stool, gives Jake a quick hug, and heads down the hallway.

Jake gives me a surprised smile and says softly, "I haven't seen her this relaxed in—" he pauses and frowns, "—like forever. What did you do?"

I look at him in alarm and blurt out, "We made nalesniki, that's all."

Jake cocks his head, clearly perplexed.

"Oh, Polish crepes, I mean," I say in a rush. "There is extra, if you're hungry."

Jake straddles the stool Veronica just vacated and leans over the island to grab the plate, giving it a deep sniff. He proceeds to eat the two remaining nalesniki in record time. I try unsuccessfully not to stare while he eats.

He finishes and licks his fingers, then he looks up and notices me. I'm fidgeting with the towel, trying to finish tidying up the kitchen.

Standing, he states, "Those are amazing. How many did Veronica eat?"

"Two."

Jake exclaims, "Incredible!" and continues, "I should have had you over days ago. I've been trying to get Veronica to eat something, anything, for days. She eats like a goddamn bird."

I laugh and he raises his eyebrows.

"Birds eat constantly and have to consume half their body weight, so that expression really makes no sense," I inform him.

Jake gives a low chuckle. "Oh really! Well, I'm just glad she ate something." He reaches into his pants pocket and takes out a slim wallet, handing me two twenty-dollar bills.

I put up my hand in protest, "That's too much, we just hung out."

"Please take it, you got her to eat, you cooked it yourself, which saved me twenty bucks right there; I've been ordering anything and everything and then throwing most of it away."

I hesitate and he reaches out and takes my hand and folds the bills into my palm, closing my fingers around them. I freeze at his warm touch.

"Really, thank you. Can you come again on Friday? I have classes Monday, Wednesday, and Friday, and I don't want Vee to be alone."

I nod my head and think, *The money may be the only thing that stops my parents from forbidding me to do this again.*

Walking quickly down the hallway, I look back as my hand reaches for the doorknob. He's poured himself a big glass of milk and is settling back down on the stool with some notebooks and papers spread out around him. He's completely forgotten me in these few minutes, while I will never forget this day for the rest of my life.

John Foster suggests taking mental pictures when you spot a bird if you don't have a good camera to take an actual picture. *You must remember the feel, the smell, and the look of where you spotted the bird,* he writes. *If you engage all five of your senses, the memory will be much clearer.*

Snapping a mental picture of Jake sitting in his kitchen, he is totally absorbed in the papers in front of him. I will never smell nalesniki again without picturing him and remembering his hand on mine.

I attempt to swing open the door to my apartment with authority, but even to my ears, it sounds tentative, scared. I throw up a quick prayer, "Please God, let this work."

Quickly surveying the kitchen, I see Mama and Papa are sitting at the kitchen table with their plates cleared, so I slide into my regular seat. I don't put my head down, as I normally would when I'm waiting for a lecture. I look each of them in the eye and slide the forty dollars across the table figuring a preemptive strike may be my best course of action.

"Look: for two hours' work, I got forty dollars, so I couldn't say no."

No need to tell them I said yes without having any clue what Jake would pay me. I continue hesitantly, "I'm just helping out a friend of Jake's who wants to, er . . . learn to cook . . . I thought it was babysitting, but it turns out it's cooking and stuff."

And then it just starts flowing.

"You remember that nice girl?" I ask my father. "She's going to get married soon and doesn't know the first thing about cooking, so wants to learn. I guess Jake figured because of the bakery, I could help her."

I cringe. I've never lied to my parents before. It's definitely breaking one of the commandments and an important one. I've always honored my parents. But I feel I have my wish on my side and that gives me courage. Clasping my hands tightly under the table, I hold my breath. It is now in God's hands.

My father glances at my mother, and then they both glance at the forty dollars.

My mother slides a twenty back towards me and asks, "Well, what did you teach her?"

And just like that, my prayer is answered, without even a lecture.

Chapter 6:

Cooking

For the next couple of days, no words pass between me and my father as we walk to the bakery each morning. He glances at me but swallows back the words he wants to say, shaking his head. I'm sure he wants to launch into his normal lecture about *American youth,* but knows he can't when he continues to take a portion of the money from said American youth. This eliminates even the few words we normally speak to each other. When I'm at home, too, the silence is expanding, taking up more space than it used to. The only words Mama directs at me are instructions to get Babcia's tray or to clear the plates. Nothing more, certainly nothing about my new job. I know my endeavor has added another ripple of worry to the already heavy air in the apartment. My parents don't know what to make of me, heading out into the world as I am.

The guilt lodges in my chest, causing me to struggle to draw a breath. Babcia is mercifully ignorant of the little drama playing out in the quiet apartment. And by some tacit agreement, we keep it that way. She wouldn't be able to bite her tongue and now that she is bedridden, her mind is forever grasping for something to latch onto from which she will never let go. At least we agree on one thing.

Friday afternoon finally comes, and when I leave the apartment, I'm clutching a bag full of ingredients and spices, and I hold my head high as I throw open our door. When Jake answers my knock, he grins widely when he spots my bag.

He exclaims, "Oh super! What do I have to look forward to tonight?"

I redden and demur, "I figured I'd see what Veronica feels like making."

"Excellent! I'm looking forward to anything those lovely hands make."

I'm sure he is talking about Veronica's hands, as everything about her is lovely, but he playfully grabs my hand and swings it in an arc reminding me of that first time I met him in the hallway when he tried to dance with Papa and me. A flush rises from my chest to my cheeks. I pull my hand back in surprise, turn quickly, and head down the now familiar hall. Veronica is sitting on the stool and smiles weakly at me when I circle into the kitchen.

Jake calls out, "I'm leaving. Be back at six."

We both say, "Goodbye," in unison.

I turn to Veronica and inquire, "How are you doing?"

Veronica shrugs. The weight of the world appears to be resting on her slim shoulders. She's wrapped in a lovely white and green kimono. Wanting nothing more than to distract her from her heavy thoughts, I start chattering—about birds, of all things.

"I was walking in Central Park and saw a wood duck the other day," I tell her. "Have you ever seen one? Honestly, it looks just like your kimono." I leave out the unfortunate circumstances surrounding the sighting.

She forces a smile but appears to perk up slightly. I gauge she still isn't in the right mood to select a recipe, so I make an executive decision. "Are you hungry? I'm going to make some pierogis."

She nods her head and settles her elbows on the counter, leaning her head on her hands so they encircle her lovely face.

I quickly mix up the dough and give Veronica the ingredients for the filling: ricotta cheese with eggs, sugar, salt, and pepper. As she stirs them together, I tell her, "Now we have to let the dough rest for twenty minutes."

"Rest, why would dough ever need to rest?"

"Er, you know I don't really know. I just know it's very important. We all need our rest, right?" I giggle.

A little wisp of warmth unfurls in my chest when I see Veronica smile back at me. The first proper smile I've seen.

Leaning my elbows on the counter and resting my head in my hands, matching her pose, I whisper conspiratorially, "I told my parents I'm giving you cooking lessons because you're getting married and wanted to learn to cook. So, if you ever bump into them when you're going in or out, can you go along with the story?"

Veronica eyes me and then shrugs. "Sure, but I'm not going in or out these days. I'm lying low."

"If I looked like you, I would be out every night," I blurt—and then, realizing I may have overstepped, I add, "Or at least that is what I imagine I'd do."

Veronica nods sagely. "It's not as fun as it looks, and shit can really mess you up." Waving her hand gracefully in a circle around her beautiful face. "It's really all an illusion."

Suddenly she jumps up and exclaims, "That's a great idea! We must do it."

I frown. "Do what?"

"A makeover, of course. What fun."

My frown deepens, and I cross my arms across my chest, withdrawing a bit. Ignoring my shaking head, Veronica pulls a chair away from the large oak kitchen table and pushes it over toward the window, then heads down the hallway. Instead of turning to the right, into the room I helped Jake carry her to the other day, she moves past it, entering the room that is my parents' bedroom in our apartment.

In no time, she returns with a little suitcase and lays it on the table. It opens like a clamshell. Inside are hundreds of nooks and crannies filled with little bottles of this and tubes of that.

"What is all this?" I exclaim.

Veronica laughs. It is deep and unexpected. She ends it with a little snort, which immediately makes me smile. I'd do anything to make this sad waif of a creature smile and laugh, even if it means putting on makeup.

Setting out several bottles and brushes on the table, Veronica keeps glancing at my face. She tells me to sit and dramatically twirls around my chair. I catch my breath at the fun of a spinning chair. All our kitchen chairs are ancient and certainly do not spin. What could be the purpose of a spinning kitchen chair? Veronica, though, has no doubt about its usefulness, as she rotates me back and forth while holding her finger up to her mouth and staring at me with frank intensity.

"I've never really worn makeup before," I rush. "I bought foundation once from Duane Reed, but it made me look kind of orange, and my mother banned me from ever putting any-thing on my face again. She used the word *harlot*, although *pumpkin* would have been more fitting."

Veronica smiles indulgently. "You have the complexion of a porcelain doll. You just bought the wrong shade. The secret is to put on makeup so it doesn't look like you're wearing anything at all."

"But then, what's the point?"

Veronica states dramatically, "Ah, just wait and see," and then she sets to work.

She hums to herself and periodically tells me to close my eyes or press my lips together. I can feel the feathery touches of the various brushes stroke my face, and I relax under her ministrations. My mind drifts and I wonder what the little wood duck is doing now. This is the first time I've thought of him without immediately remembering the associated curse, and I'm glad of that. I don't want to blame the colorful little bird for my issues or think it is a curse of any sort. Maybe he simply appeared to me when I needed him most, and he was saying, "I'm here for you." I let out a sigh, feeling better.

I'm jolted from my reverie when Veronica waves her arms with a flourish, spins me around in a complete circle, and announces triumphantly, "Tah dah!"

"Come, come," she orders and leads me into Jake's room.

She turns on the fancy overhead light I remember from that morning, and I see the little stars dancing on the quilt. She pulls me over to a large mirror on top of a low bureau.

I approach it hesitantly. And then I stare. It is me, but it isn't me. I'm enhanced. My eyes look wide and more pronounced. They've always been large and the color of blue cornflowers, but today they are luminous. My lashes are long but very blonde, so you normally can't see them. Now, suddenly, they stand out and seem to have a life of their own. They sweep up and down as I blink; my eyelids glide up and down in slow motion and seem to be speaking a mystical language, saying, *look at me*. My skin looks dewy and has a rose tint that, no matter how much pinching I've done to my cheeks, I've never achieved. It is a faint blush of perfection. My lips are a perfect little bow, and the color isn't a daring red or anything close, but they look larger and almost sumptuous.

I turn and clap my hands to my face and exclaim, "Oh my gosh, you are magic!"

Veronica hoots, "Em, you have a solid base, I just played it up."

She called me Em.

Staring at the mirror some more, I bat my eyes and tilt my head to one side. I really look so different, yet the same, and I certainly don't look like a harlot. I look almost younger than my twenty-six years.

I breathe, "You'll have to teach me." I almost say Vee but at the last minute stop myself.

"Perfect!" Veronica says. "You will teach me to cook, and I will teach you makeup."

"Oh, the pierogis!" I exclaim. "The dough must be ready."

We start to walk out of Jake's room, and I catch a flash of movement at his window and walk over. There is a plastic birdfeeder attached to the window, and a few white-breasted nuthatches and chipping sparrows are picking at some seeds. What a marvelous idea—having the birds come to you instead of always having to go to them. Why haven't I thought about doing something like that?

Veronica takes my arm and pulls me away from the feeder. I hand her a spoon and the cheese filling, and I find a jar lid to cut out circles from the dough. Then I show her how to put a dollop of cheese filling in the middle of each dough circle and then pinch the edges to seal them. She eventually gets the hang of it but a few of her dumplings will struggle to keep their seal during the next steps.

I plop the little rolls of dough with filling into the pot of boiling water and remove them after a few minutes, layering them onto the sizzling frying pan to brown and crisp.

Veronica is watching me flip the pierogis in the pan when suddenly a loud voice says, "Yum! Something smells delicious."

We both jump. "Christ, Jake. You scared the bejesus out of us." Vee shrieks smiling. "Em is just finishing teaching me how to make pierogis. Isn't that cool?" Veronica announces proudly.

Em again. I never had a nickname before. Do I dare call her Vee like Jake does?

I grab another plate and divide up the first batch between the three plates, and we dig in. We don't have any sour cream to dip them in, but you don't really need anything when the pierogis are right out of the pan.

Jake is munching quietly when he tilts his head to one side and stares at me. He looks slightly confused. "What did you do?"

Now it's my turn to look confused.

"I gave Em a makeover," Veronica inserts. "What do you think?"

Jake examines my face slowly and expertly. I turn a bright red, ruining all of Veronica's subtle blush application.

Jake finally tips his head and declares, "Perfection—you do good work, Vee."

I realize he isn't talking so much about me as Veronica's makeup job, and my embarrassment reduces some. I smile tentatively, and Jake looks momentarily caught off guard but recovers and grins back at me. A warmth creeps back to my cheeks, so I look for something to move the subject away from my face, but I keep thinking of the word *perfection* and can't quite convince myself Jake was talking about the makeup.

I blurt out, "You have a birdfeeder. You are so lucky."

Jake looks a little taken aback for a beat, but then he nods. "Huh . . . it's my mom's really." He says dismissively.

I shrug unsure as he doesn't seem eager to continue this topic, so I dole out the last batch of pierogis from the pan, and we cut into them more slowly this time.

Jake gets up. "What do you guys want to drink?"

"We have water," I say.

He pulls out two beers from the fridge and a fancy can of sparkling water, handing that to Veronica. They exchange a look, but it passes so quickly I can't begin to figure out what it means. Jake hands me one of the beers. It is cold and slick in my hand.

Beer, makeup and a nickname all in one night.

I took my first sip hesitantly. I've never had a beer before. I let the taste pool in my mouth. It's frosty cold and bitter but it pairs perfectly with the pierogi and I almost groan. This is perfection. *Oh, that word again.*

Jake drains his beer quickly and returns to the fridge for another. "Do you want another one too?" he asks.

Looking up, I state in a rush, "Oh my, no. I may get drunk."

Jake laughs and glances at Veronica.

She raises an eyebrow. "You won't get drunk from one beer, will you?"

I respond nervously, "Oh, I don't know. I've never had a beer. Are they strong?"

Veronica chuckles. "Beer is what I drink when I don't want to get drunk. Vodka is my poison of choice. Aww, the burn as it goes down your throat and the warmth when it hits your belly and then straight to your head . . . I reckon that is as close to Heaven as I'll get. But *that* will get you drunk, sometimes quicker than you want. Ain't that right, Jake?" This is the first time I've heard Vee's southern drawl.

"Cut it out, Veronica, this isn't doing anyone any good." Jake scowls.

Veronica trails off down the hall, looking wistful as she drags her fingertips across the table, touching the statue in the hallway as she glides past. She eases into what I assume is her room, and the door quietly closes.

I look at Jake; he tilts his head toward Veronica's room, and shrugs. He offers nothing more, so we both start to clean up.

"Sorry about the mess. The pierogis took a while. I can clean up now if you have work to do." I start washing and rinsing the pans and plates in the sink.

"No problem. It's great that this fancy kitchen is getting used by someone. Cereal and coffee don't really count, so glad to have a homemade meal. It's been . . . well since forever."

He looks young and sad, "I love coming home to such lovely and savory smells."

"Pierogis are meant to be comfort food," I tell him. "Every culture has a dumpling of some sort, made slightly differently with different fillings, but they are all designed to comfort and sustain the people. Italians have their ravioli; China has potstickers, right?" I pause, as I'm not sure where all this came from.

"I love Thai gyozas," Jake says. "That must be Thailand's comfort food."

I nod, relieved that my outburst didn't result in laughter, or worse, scorn. I can still feel the sting of my classmates' disdain when I brought pierogis to my class in fourth grade as if it was yesterday.

I'm brought back to the present when Jake clears his throat and inquires cheerily, "Penny for your thoughts. You look like you're a million miles away."

Smiling sheepishly, I shake my head apologetically. I don't want to ruin anything by sharing my pathetic story.

"Well, this is an exciting Friday night, huh?" he says.

I nod my head earnestly before realizing he was being sarcastic. I cringe. Then feeling brave decide to be truthful. "Well, it is for me. I don't think I've ever cooked food for someone, gotten a makeover, and had a beer—certainly not all in the same night. This definitely is one of *my* most exciting Fridays." I glance around making sure the kitchen is spotless.

He smiles. "Good, I'm glad you had a nice time. Are you available next week?"

Sensing no condescension, I smile broadly, nod affirmatively and head to the door, Jake walking behind me.

At the door I turn, "What exactly am I doing when I come here?" I hesitate a beat, "for Vee?"

Jake looks toward Veronica's room and steps out into the hallway with me. Frowning, he says quietly, "Vee has some drug and alcohol issues she's working on. I'm giving her a little break from the rat race, hoping it will help—modeling is brutal. It eats up girls like her and spits them out. I'm not sure I can really save her, but I'm trying."

I nod, trying to look like I can relate. "Thank you for letting me know. I'll see you Monday."

I walk to my door. Though it's only a fifteen-foot journey, it is worlds away. I've watched some TV shows about addiction issues, but it always seems like the stuff they show is from a place far from my world. I never imagined someone like Vee being the subject of those TV programs. The last show we watched was about the opioid problem. I remember some-thing about a celebrity who just got out of rehab. I can't recall much else as it seemed so far away.

As I open the apartment door, I hunch my shoulders feeling smaller than my five foot two inches; my parents barely acknowledge me. My mother is watching TV, and my father is sitting in his matching recliner, dozing.

For a moment, I watch them and wonder for the first time why I don't have a comfortable chair to watch TV. There is plenty of room. Jake's living room has six spots for people. Six doesn't seem necessary but three certainly does. Why have I never asked for a chair in all this time? My grandmother doesn't like things to be changed, and back when we first moved in, she would wheel in to watch in her wheelchair. But now we have a TV for her bedroom and she rarely gets out of bed, we could add a chair. Instead I just pull the unforgiving kitchen chair over when I am desperate for some sort of conversation, even if it is only banter between Pat and Vanna.

Suddenly my old life feels even bleaker and smaller than before Jake knocked on my door and introduced me to beers on Friday night.

I watch Vanna flip a letter and shake my head. My parents love this show, though they have never solved a single puzzle, not in all their years of watching.

In my bedroom I pull out the new book I picked up from the library: a bestseller I've had on the waiting list for two months. The reviews say it's wonderful, but what piqued my interest is the description that it has a lot of nature and flowers in it.

I flip open *The Language of Flowers* and start reading about the sad, lonely life of Victoria Jones. I read late into the night. My eyes are burning, and my body is aching with tiredness, but I can't put it down. I feel a kinship to her, and it only grows when she ends up all alone tending her flowers in the park.

I know her loneliness.

Chapter 7:

Kapusniak

Snapping *The Language of Flowers* closed on Monday afternoon, I sit quietly and think about Victoria and all the sorrows in her life. How they make mine pale in comparison. She built a fortress around her heart but had to since the day she was born and abandoned. She didn't even know her actual birthday. Beyond tragic and yet she overcame it all. In a trance I throw on a fresh shirt, as I can't remember when I last changed it. I haven't been able to do anything but read or think about reading since I first cracked open the book. I lay a hand over the hard cover and feel the connection to Victoria's world of flowers and their meaning. Love vibrates up through my palm. Books are the thing that slip easily into my bubble and they fill the empty spaces.

I step out of my room and my mother is sitting in her usual chair at the kitchen table. Her eyes follow me, but she doesn't say anything. Perhaps because I was immersed in my book, I only now realize she hasn't spoken to me all weekend.

Keeping the hurt out of my voice, I say pleasantly, "Hi, Mama."

She inclines her head in my direction.

Sighing, I take a bag out of the closet and start putting the ingredients into the bag for kapusniak. I hope Vee is in good spirits today, as I need her to pull me out of my doldrums. Aching for Victoria and her difficult life and feeling the sting of my mother's disapproval of me stretching my wings, I hope a nice soup will make me feel better. Although merely thinking about a visit to Vee improves my mood. I honestly think we are becoming friends.

Vee is in an upbeat mood, and we have fun making and then eating the sauerkraut and sausage soup.

When Jake comes back from class, he inhales appreciatively. "Well, it isn't crepes or perogies. What is it?"

I hand him a bowl. "Kapusniak."

Jake repeats gamely, "Ka-pus-niak."

"Sauerkraut and sausage soup, if that's easier," I say.

"Oh, I'll get it. Kapusniak!"

I beam, marveling at our simple exchange. Only a short time ago, I had barely spoken a word to this person—or if my father is to be believed, *the devil incarnate*. Now we are playfully pronouncing Polish words and breaking bread. The world is a wondrous and mysterious place.

Jake keeps practicing his pronunciation of the soup until he sounds like someone right from the old country. He shares a funny story about one of his students that keeps us all in stitches. The soup has worked its magic on all of us.

When he is done with the soup, Jake hefts his briefcase onto the kitchen table and takes out a few papers.

"What do you teach?" I ask.

Jake responds dismissively, "Bio to a bunch of snot-nosed premed students. God, they are awful."

"Weren't you a snot-nosed premed student just a few years ago?" Vee chides.

"I never was as obnoxious or as pretentious as these kids. If they're our next generation of doctors, we're all in trouble."

Vee gives a loud snort and adds, "Jake is going for his doctorate, so we will all have to call him Dr. Henderson one day. As my mama likes to say, 'He's getting a little too big for his britches.'"

I scrunch my forehead and breathe out a soft, "Wow." *Jake is going to be a doctor. That is so impressive.*

Hating having to leave the warmth of the kitchen, I hang around for as long as I can without being obvious. It's feeling like a cozy blanket I get to wrap myself in each time I visit. This is what I imagine friendship feels like.

Somehow, after one short week, I've broken out of my protective shell without even realizing it. Calling Vee, *Vee* doesn't feel strange anymore and I respond without a thought to my nickname Em.

Saying my goodbyes, I drag myself away and head back to my dull existence, back to living in the shadows. Somehow it feels even bleaker, now that I have seen the bright colors that shine just next door. *I'll be back in two days*, I remind myself. *It is so wonderful to have something to look forward to.*

I continue to "babysit" Vee for the next few weeks, and I like her more and more. Some days she is down and other days she's just fine. Whatever her mood is, she is beautiful inside and out. Sometimes when she talks about modeling, she sounds tough as nails, talking about the girls who throw up to stay so thin. Other times, she sounds lost and lonely.

I share details about my life with her, and Vee listens and seems to understand.

"How does one get into modeling?" I ask today.

She is curled up in one of her graceful balls, and for the first time, she doesn't immediately change the subject. Instead, she gets a wistful look on her face. I wonder if she is nostalgic for the remembrance or rueful, wishing it never happened.

In a small voice, she shares, "I was discovered at a mall in Mississippi when I was just seventeen. One minute I was hanging out with my friends, and the next minute my mother and I were in New York City trying to figure out what the hell this all meant. It was overwhelming. My mom was a tiger, but not really in a good way. She wanted success at any cost. And it turns out the cost was me. But back then, at the beginning, she was beyond thrilled, and I went along with everything because it made her happy. She came to every job with me.

"It was hard at first. You think fourth graders are mean? Models are the worst. They made so much fun of me and Mama's accents and expressions. On my second shoot, I said 'I was fuller than a tick' because Mama and I had breakfast right before the shoot. That was the last time I ever said that, or ate breakfast in fact, for years. They called me tick girl for a long time. It was mortifying."

"Oh, that is awful. What does it mean to be fuller than a tick?"

"Oh God, no. I refuse to answer that question. I have wiped that part of me clean away." Vee smiles, but then, looking pensive, says, "I worked hard to get rid of my southern drawl. I even took voice lessons, to get that cold, nasal twang just right. Half nose, half mouth instead of all mouth. Now my accent only comes out when I talk to Mama or Papa or . . ." she pauses, "when I drink."

She closes her eyes and inhales and exhales softly. Her eyes flutter open.

She continues, "How did we get on this topic?"

"You were telling me about modeling and your Mama."

"Oh right, things were good for a while, I was working nonstop. But the modeling agency and my mother didn't see eye to eye on some things, and as soon as I turned eighteen, my agency started pushing me to ditch her." Vee shifts uncomfortably in her seat and bites a nail. "Honestly, I was getting tired of her, too. She controlled everything: what I ate, how I dressed. It was getting annoying, and I figured I knew everything there was to know. I'd been doing it for a year now and I was eighteen and wanted to have a little fun instead of working all the time.

"So, I told her I was all set and she could go home. When you're eighteen, you have no idea of the dangers out there. Right? You think you're unstoppable. I'll never forget the look on my mother's face. It was a lot of hurt with a dash of hate thrown in. She never forgave me for pushing her away. She loved modeling more than I did, and I took that away from her. I now know I was young and stupid, but I can't undo what I did. And after my mom left, it became so easy to make the wrong decisions. I started hanging out with a pretty wild crowd, and there were always drugs available. It was all too easy."

I try to picture a younger Vee all alone, feeling sad and surrounded by a bunch of people who didn't really care about her.

"That must have been scary. I never thought about not having my parents around. Mine are *always* around." I try to sound like the girls in high school when they talked about their parents, with exaggerated exasperation, but it doesn't ring true to my ear.

Vee sighs. "I've only realized recently how much I needed my mom. I knew I was getting out of control, and I wanted to fix things between us. So, a couple of months ago, I called her and asked her to come back up to help me."

"Did she come?" I ask softly.

"Nope," Vee responds, sounding lost and forlorn. "She didn't even want to hear why I was asking. I'm not sure she would've been able to help me or if I even wanted her to come running, but when she refused to come, it hurt and made everything twice as bad."

I look at Veronica, needing her mother, and instead all she has is Jake—and me, three times a week. For the hundredth time, I wonder about their relationship. I have yet to figure it out. There is something between the two of them. The sun angles in the window, and Vee looks like an angel with her blonde hair framing the most beautiful face I've ever seen. I picture Jake and Vee all dressed up, heading somewhere fancy. They would make the most perfect couple.

I push these thoughts out of my head. It doesn't really matter. Jake is completely out of my league. A freakin' doctor and rich.

Our unlikely threesome is working despite our differences. Jake and Veronica educate me on all I'm missing by not having a phone or being connected to the internet. I'm skeptical of the whole thing, but listen as Veronica states emphatically, "I would absolutely *DIE* without my phone."

Jake admits, "I don't think I would die without my phone, but I might not be able to live without it."

I look at them and then at their phones and shake my head. I state simply, "I don't find anything compelling about those contraptions. If I need to be connected to the internet, I go down to the library and use their computers. I can't imagine needing one in my bedroom or my pocket."

Jake stands up and flips open his laptop and responds with a challenge in his voice, "I may be able to change your mind. Look at this."

He shows me the website for the NYC Audubon Society, scrolling through all the information on recent bird sightings, tours, and other information that makes John Foster's guidebook come alive. The pictures are spectacular and much larger on Jake's laptop than in my paperback book.

Captivated, I look into Jake's smiling eyes and state sheepishly, "Well, maybe it would be nice to have a computer . . ." I take my book out of my purse. "But this is still the best. That website doesn't quite have the heart John Foster shares in his prose." I gush on, "He says that a true birder will always stop and glance up to see an ordinary bird they may have seen a thousand times because even a chipping sparrow is lovely and special."

Jake visibly shudders. "What garbage!" he mutters.

The sharpness of his words hits me in my gut, and I take a step back. John Foster is special; I have a kinship with him and his musings. I would not have survived without his voice in my head.

Jake sees the hurt in my eyes.

"Don't listen to me," he says quickly. "What do I know? If you like it, that's all that matters. A book that speaks to even one person is not to be taken lightly."

Immediately, I feel better—but I guess I'll stop quoting John Foster in front of Jake. He doesn't seem to like it.

Chapter 8:

Pasta Bolognese

Getting out of bed, I head over to my small calendar pinned up on my bedroom wall. The one the library gave me for free. As I started doing four weeks ago, I place a big slash through today's date, October 15. Five months left before I must fit myself back into my bubble.

Through my bedroom window, I catch sight of the leaves in all their glory. Yellows, reds and oranges are shimmering against the blue sky as if they are alive. They are going to drop soon and fade into nothingness for the winter. My connection to their journey is so strong I feel a sense of contentment despite what it means for me; I press my palm against my window.

Later that day, I'm with Vee and she is bent over her laptop. We've moved on from Polish staples and now are finding fun recipes on the internet to make together. I pull up a chair at the kitchen table, our heads are almost touching as I check out the recipes she is scrolling through.

Suddenly, Vee leans back, takes a deep breath and announces, "I think I'm ready to go back to my apartment."

I don't say anything and wait expectantly, no longer interested in the recipe for Bolognese pasta she had pulled up.

"I need to get back to work, to the real world. This has been great, and Jake really did save me, but I can tell my agency is getting frustrated. I can't hold them off much longer; it's been over a month now. Honestly, I'm afraid they'll forget me if I don't start working again." She pauses. "I know I will disappoint Jake, but here's my plan. I want you to come live with me for a while. That's the only way Jake will let me go."

I gape at her. "Wow, I would love that." I hesitate, unsure whether to finally ask the question that has been on my mind since day one. Taking a deep breath, I blurt out, "Can I ask you something?" I press my lips together.

"Sure."

"Umm, why does Jake care so much?"

Vee grins. "We never told you. Jake is my cousin. Er, or his mom and my mom are cousins, so maybe that makes us second cousins. I'm not sure, but we're family. When we moved here four years ago, we stayed in Carol's apartment for a while when they were in the Hamptons. I'm not sure where Jake was—I think a safari or something. My mom and his mom don't really like each other, but you know, blood is thicker than water, so they let us stay here for almost three months. My mom and Carol used to be like best friends. After I sent my mom packing three years ago, Jake's parents took me under their wing. And clearly, Jake takes his big-brother role very seriously. Sometimes a little too seriously for my liking."

Relief floods my chest. I've been—watching and waiting to pick up on any undercurrent of emotion or feelings. My relief at Vee's words makes me color. Grinning like an idiot,

I struggle to tamp down the happiness that threatens to split my face in two. Why am I so happy to hear they are practically brother and sister? I'm under no illusions that I have any hope with Jake. We're from two different worlds; the idea that the two of us could ever be together is completely preposterous. A picture of a smiling Jake flashes through my mind, and I shake my head to clear it.

"So, what do you say? Want to move in with me?"

Chewing my bottom lip, I take stock of *things* in my head. With five months left out of the six I allotted myself before facing my reality, it's the perfect time to do something a bit more drastic, and Vee has dropped *drastic* into my lap. Maybe I do have a guardian angel watching over me. Wouldn't that be nice? A warmth flows through my body.

Vee is observing me, and while I'm sure she can't imagine what is running through my head, she knows enough about my parents and the world I come from to understand this is a big step. My parents won't approve of this, but I push that worry out of my mind and think, *One step at a time*. If I truly do have a guardian angel, maybe they will drop some fairy dust or other magic to get my parents to agree to such a crazy plan.

Nodding affirmatively, I say confidently, "I would love that. What do we need to do to convince Jake?"

Veronica shrugs. "He really can't stop me or us, right?"

I think he can stop me, but I shrug too, trying to look as self-assured as Vee does. "Where do you live?"

"In Chelsea." Vee responds.

"Oh great, that's closer to the bakery than the Upper East Side, so that will work. I'll miss my walks through Central Park, but I'll survive."

We finish the Bolognese sauce and mix in the pasta and start eating our bowlfuls with the most delightful sprinkling of real parmesan cheese on top. Veronica can't believe I've never had freshly shaved parmesan cheese before.

She explains in her most snobbish voice, "All the best Italian restaurants grate it fresh, right onto your plate."

I smile. Sometimes I get tired of explaining I haven't eaten in *any* restaurant, never mind an Italian restaurant that has staff standing at the ready to shave parmesan cheese on top of your pasta.

Vee nudges me. "I didn't mean to make you feel bad. It's no big deal; just a little cheese."

I shrug and reply nonchalantly, "I know."

Vee laughs with her classic snorting sound. "Oh, dear Emma, your face shows every one of your emotions. Don't try to mask that. It's so refreshing. No guile, no deceit. I really am sorry."

Before we are halfway through our bowls, Jake swings the door open and stops, inhaling deeply. "Is this Emilio's?" he asks enthusiastically. "My God, it smells delicious. You know Italian is my favorite."

I look at Vee; she planned this all along. All her *Oh, let's do something different, maybe Italian,* was all a plot to get Jake in the best mood possible. Maybe she is a little worried that Jake *can* stop her.

Jake grabs a bowl and fills it overflowing, and Veronica shaves the cheese on the top with a flourish.

She gives me a wink and says brightly, "Guess what?"

Jake looks up with a mouthful of pasta and shakes his head, clearly indicating he has no idea, nor does he care too much.

"I'm going to move back to my place and finally get out of your hair, and Em is coming with me," she says in a rush.

Jake sets his fork down with a grimace. He gives me a steely look, and I reflexively cast my eyes down at my bowl. He turns his gaze to Vee.

She meets his stare confidently, but her voice gives her away. It sounds strained and unsure. "I've thought about it a lot, Jake. I need to get back to work. I'm fine. I'll just do the modeling and no partying. Em will be there and everything will . . ."

Jake shakes his head, cutting her off. "Vee, if it was just the modeling, that would be fine, but it's not. You know you will have to go to the parties and then the after-parties. *That* is the problem."

Veronica looks at me and quickly retorts, "How about if I promise that if I must go to some stupid party, I'll take Em with me. She'll watch out for me. And I promise I won't drink—not a thing—or take anything else."

Jake pushes the bowl away, clearly having lost his appetite. He narrows his eyes. "I don't like it. You should try something else. Modeling holds too many temptations."

Vee shrugs. "It's what I know, and it's what I'm good at. If I don't have modeling, I don't have anything."

Jake walks over to her and wraps an arm around her shoulders, "Vee, you can do anything you set your mind to. You are more than your face. You know that."

Vee lays her head down in her arms.

Jake looks resigned and sad. "You can do anything, but if you want to stay modeling, I can't stop you. Anyway, my parents called last night. They're coming back to the city next week, and it's going to get crowded in here with all of us, so maybe it is the right time."

With a shriek, Vee jumps up and gives Jake a quick hug. "Don't you worry, everything will work out. Em and I will stick together."

Jake whips his head around and gives me a hard look. "What about working at the bakery?"

I look up in surprise. "What about the bakery?"

Jake shakes his head. "You won't be able to work in the bakery. Modeling jobs are at all different times of the day and night, and I can't imagine you will do that and still get up at four in the morning to get to the bakery."

I feel foolish; I clearly didn't understand what I was agreeing to before I jumped in. *What will my father do without me?*

"I have to go to modeling jobs?" I ask timidly. "Can I even do that?"

"The deal is, Emma needs to be there with you for everything—or no deal," Jake says to Vee.

Pacing around the small area, Vee finally looks worried too. "I know!" she exclaims triumphantly. "Emma can be my new PA. Rachel was awful, so this will work out great. I'll fire Rachel if she hasn't left me already, and I'll tell every-one Emma is my new PA. The agency may have an issue, but I'll tell them Emma is my cousin, and I'll just demand it. What can they do?"

I hesitantly ask, "What is a PA?"

Jake smiles and looks more relaxed. "A personal assistant. Just someone who looks after Veronica and does whatever she needs you to do as long as it doesn't involve parties, drinks, or drugs, right?" He looks Vee right in the eye.

Vee nods decisively—and the deal is done.

We've just finished cleaning up from turning the kitchen into Little Italy. I'm sitting quietly at the table nervously chewing my lip. Vee is scrolling through her phone, and Jake is engrossed in some papers.

Vee glances over at me, "Em, what is it? You're back to looking scared. I told you; you will be a great PA."

Shaking my head, I state, "I'm still nervous about that, but now I'm worried my parents won't let me do it. They need me at the bakery and won't understand any of this."

Jake responds smoothly, "Emma, I'm sure your parents can replace you at the bakery. I'm sure you're good, but no one is irreplaceable."

"But that means they'll have to pay someone, and family is, well, family. They trust me."

Jake's brow furrows in confusion, "But they have to pay you too."

I shake my head. Jake is at a loss for words.

"Your parents don't pay you to work?" Vee pipes up. "Don't you get up at four every morning and work until noon or something?"

I nod.

"Emma, that isn't right." Jake glowers. "You should be getting paid." He continues, "You're being treated like an indentured servant, which may have been okay when you were fifteen, but it is not okay when you're . . . ahh—how old are you?"

"Twenty-six. But you don't understand. You're American. It would be disrespectful for me to demand money from my family. We're just trying to survive and need to make sure we don't squander our family's opportunity. When there's extra money, I get some, so I can take a few community college classes or buy things my parents know are important to me."

Turning away, I slump down in my chair, crossing my arms. *They don't understand what it means to be a Jablonski. How could they?*

Jake walks over to me and gently turns me back toward the table. "Come on, we aren't being mean. I know you've said you come from a different world, and I can tell you don't believe what we are trying to tell you, but really it's wrong. You need a life of your own. That's what every parent wants for their child."

I almost blurt out, *That is exactly what I'm trying to get.* But I don't want them to ask more questions. So, I hold my tongue.

"Emma, if money is the issue, I will try to get the agency to pay more than the fifty-thousand salary," Vee says. "I can push them on that."

Staring, flabbergasted. "Fifty-thousand dollars? Are you kidding me?"

Doing the math in my head, I estimate I'll be paid almost twenty thousand in the next five months. There is no way my parents will argue against that kind of money. I turn and gaze at Veronica in wonder.

"Plus, it will be free room and board, right? Cause you'll be staying at my place. Oh, never mind, you get that at your parents already."

I respond quickly, "Wow! That is amazing. All that money, plus room and board?"

I glance toward the ceiling expecting to see a guardian angel smiling down at me, sprinkling magic dust from above.

With the number 20,000 dancing in my head, I march into my apartment. My parents have stopped speaking to me almost completely, except to give me some chore or errand to do. Which isn't a huge change from the number of words we normally exchange, but it is the chill that is different. I'm sure they aren't doing it to be mean; they're just worried and aren't sure how to deal with this new Emma, so shutting me out is their answer. With only commands coming my way, it does make me feel like a scullery maid, but Jake and Vee don't need to know that. And now, with Vee's crazy offer, I can do something about it.

The TV is on, and my parents are watching *Wheel of*

Fortune. When I stand in front of the TV, they meet my eyes for the first time in weeks.

Taking a deep breath, I try to expand as big as I can; I don't want to be a shadow tonight.

"I've been offered a job for five months, and I'll need to move out because that is part of the job," I say firmly. "I'm going to be a live-in cook for a famous model."

While it is a lie, it is something they may be able to understand, as I am still not sure what a personal assistant is and I know my parents won't either. A whisper of a smile crosses my mother's face, my father grunts and looks down. I try to read his expression. Maybe resigned.

"I'm really sorry but I won't be able to work at the bakery while I'm doing this," I continue in a rush. "I guess I need to be on call at all hours, which is why I need to live there."

My father says softly, "Well, Emma. That is sudden. Are you sure it's not some scam or something?

"No Papa, it's not a scam. Vee is very nice and honest. It is real. I'm very excited to try something different."

My father nods his head. "Well, I will miss you at the bakery. Good luck, Emma. Work hard. That is all you can do."

"You will come to church though?" my mother asks. "The bakery is one thing, Church is another."

I nod yes.

My mother angles her face in my direction with a furrowed brow. "Be a good girl, Emma."

Stepping away from the TV, I breathe a sigh of relief. I'm glad I didn't need to convince them by telling them about the salary. I wanted to keep that information to myself. Some of Jake's comments earlier did land, and I'm no longer clear what it means to *honor thy mother and father*. Does it mean I need to share everything with them? They've continued to take half of what I make from Jake, and each week when I hand over the money, a brief flare of resentment flickers in my gut. I need to carve a little spot out for me and my future—all five months of it.

I'll always help my family if they ever need it. But I've decided the seventh Commandment doesn't say I need to hand over half of my money and I'll be back in five months, anyway.

Lying in bed the night before I move into Vee's, my gut is in knots. The idea of leaving and starting this new job seemed like the perfect answer, but now it seems like the most foolish endeavor ever. I don't even know what a model really does, never mind a model's personal assistant. The only thing keeping me from backing out of this whole scary idea is the belief that being scared actually may be what living feels like. Something scary and unknown is exactly what has been missing from my life, and I can't back out now as I still have five months to go. So, I figure this is all part of the wish I made when I leaned into Mother Tree and asked for guidance. She didn't show me then, but I must trust she's showing me now.

Mother Tree, my guardian angel? Maybe.

I cross myself, knowing my thoughts must be blasphemy, but stop in mid motion when a picture of a bill with $20,000 on it pops into my head. My mind tries to wrap around what that much money could mean. Once I'm back with my parents, maybe I'll be able to do a few things, and MS won't rob me of everything. Maybe I'll get my associate's degree. I've taken quite a few community college classes over the past five years and done well in all of them. I finished the prescription Dr. Liam gave me, and I'm feeling better than I was. Is it because I'm finally living a life? Or is it the natural ebb and flow of the disease that, for no discernable reason, can retreat and then flare up? I've seen this happen to my mother for my whole life.

I grab my bird book to take my mind off things and flip to the back. *Binocular Recommendations*. I reread that section. Swift, Leica, Swarovski, Zeiss. My lips curl into a tiny smile. The very first thing I'm going to buy with my very first paycheck is a shiny, new pair of binoculars. I've seen groups of birders walking through the Ramble with their binoculars trained on a bird. Sometimes I can see the bird they are looking at with my naked eye, but most of the time I can't. A good pair of "bins," as John Foster calls them, costs two hundred dollars, and these recommendations will be perfect to help me decide.

Light and warmth unknots my gut and expands to my chest. My wish is coming true, even if it is only for these next five months. Getting a real chance at a life that isn't the bleak and colorless world I've been stuck in is all that matters. I have a little color in my world and a kernel of hope for some sort of life.

I set my book aside, wrap my arms around my body, give myself a tight squeeze, resting my head on my pillow contentedly.

That new bubble of hope churns up into my chest. I've tried not to acknowledge it, but tonight I didn't succeed. It wasn't the hope for a life I wished for with Mother Tree; it is the hope of love. A love as deep and never ending as Halcyon and Ceyx.

As I drift off to sleep, the image of Jake eating a forkful of pasta with his eyes closed flashes through my mind. Jake morphs into a small blue kingfisher, sitting on a branch—and I am right next to him.

Chapter 9:

Moving Day

Although Papa didn't knock, my eyes fly open with my clock blinking 3:45 a.m. I listen as Papa eats and leaves the apartment at our usual time. I snuggle back under my worn quilt and struggle to keep the wave of guilt from engulfing me. It's moving day. It's been just over four weeks since I began my *life*.

At 7:00 a.m., I step out of my room and into the kitchen. Mama sits slumped at the table. Hesitating in the doorway, the kitchen sink drips in a slow cadence, combining with the hollow ticking of the clock. I break the sad rhythm, saying, "Well, I am off. I won't be far, and I'll stop by to visit whenever I can. I won't call unless it's an emergency."

They hate phone calls. My mother bobs her head and mutters, "Emma, it is worlds away from here," drawing the words from deep within. "You must take care."

I nod and grab a bagel off the tray, taking a quick bite.

Sounding more like herself, she scolds, "Emma, sit and eat. Do not take the bagel and eat like those uncouth Americans, stuffing food into their mouths as they walk down the street."

Sitting obediently, I take a few small bites but refuse to pour myself my usual half cup of coffee. From this day forward, I will have tea with my breakfast, and I fight the urge to pound my fist on the table for effect, knowing my mother will think me mad. I smile inwardly, noting ruefully that I don't quite have the nerve to make myself a cup of tea, but tomorrow at Vee's, just watch me.

Rising, I give my mother a brisk hug. As I release her, her hand clutches at my sleeve.

I hesitate, "Mama, will you be all right?"

Collecting herself, she says briskly, "Oh, of course we will. Papa has already hired someone. We will be fine."

I quickly head down our hallway with my small valise in hand.

As I open the door, I call over my shoulder, "Bye, Mama. I will visit when I can." Then I step out and shut the door behind me.

The excitement swells as I put a little distance between me and the apartment, and it's as if the weight of being a Jablonski lightens and shifts. Knocking on Jake's door, I feel taller, like I'm taking up a little more space in this world.

Vee is in her room, working to zip up one of the three large suitcases she has lying on the bed filled to overflowing. Lovely outfits are in a pile, looking soft, expensive and beautiful. They are all the colors of the rainbow. I spot her wheelie bag of makeup near her door, zipped up and ready to go. She hasn't opened it since she gave me my makeover.

In the one open corner of the bed, I flop down, "For someone whom I've only seen wearing leggings and sweatshirts, you certainly have a lot of clothes."

She grins and responds lightly, "Ya never know when you'll be invited to some party or outing, and at a moment's notice, must don your armor. I'm super glad I never had to dig out a single thing these past weeks. Of course, with your cooking, I'm not sure I still fit into any of them."

I look her up and down and shake my head. "You haven't gained a single pound. You could eat a dozen pierogis, and you wouldn't get a bump or a bulge."

Vee darts across the room and gives me a hug. "You're such a doll. All the girls who have said those sorts of things to me in the past always sound like they're conjuring up a hex. But you sound like you mean it—all milk and honey with not a bit of vinegar. You're sooo sweet. Don't let this mean old world change you."

I shrug embarrassed. Jake and Veronica have said things like that to me before, and I never quite know how to respond.

Jake pokes his head in Vee's doorway and Vee shouts, "I am ready, my prince."

Her enthusiasm is contagious. Jake does a jaunty bow and grabs for two of the bags. Taking my one medium-sized bag and Vee's makeup suitcase, I leave her to wrestle with the ginormous one.

And we're off.

It is a lovely day in October, and despite Vee's protests, Jake and I win the argument, and we walk through the park for a bit before we head to Chelsea. As we stroll along the sidewalks with trees and shrubs on either side, a feeling of peace seeps into my soul or into some part of my being, who knows for sure? I pause and close my eyes for a brief minute. The morning sun is shining down on my face, and I feel such a sense of relief. I'm leaving my dreary room in that dreary apartment. I didn't under-stand until now how it all weighed me down: the stress of my grandmother, the bakery, the silence, my mother's unpredictable illness, the Jablonski legacy. The park always made these stresses bearable, spending time with the birds and the trees, but today the sensation of lightness keeps increasing the farther I walk away from 933 Fifth Avenue. I may float away, like the leaves that are cascading down all around us. Gripping the two bags I'm carrying tightly, as if they are keeping me anchored; I blink my eyes open and realize Jake has stopped and is watching me. The wind tousles his copper hair; the fall leaves make a perfect backdrop, surrounding him with a warm palette of color. A blush rises in my cheeks; I must look like a crazy person. Vee continues walking on up ahead.

Jake points to the ground a bit off the path and whispers, "Look at that bird."

I turn and catch my breath. "Is it a palm warbler?"

Dropping Vee's bag, I dig through my purse and pull out my guidebook, searching for the right page. I look from the book to the bird on the ground with his little tail flitting up and down. I struggle to suppress a shriek, "It is! It is!" and I impulsively turn and hug Jake, giddy with excitement. "Thank you, thank you," I gush. "I would have missed it. That's a bird I've been trying to spot for years."

We both quietly watch the yellow-bellied and brown-speckled warbler with its lovely brown cap. The bird takes a few more hops, then disappears into the thick shrubbery, still pumping his tail.

"He needs to be heading south soon," Jake says.

Grabbing my pen, I start to mark down the details in my bird log.

Jake shakes his head. "Really, you can't wait until we get to Veronica's to document the sighting?" he says sternly, but I see he is grinning.

Smiling, I say mock-primly, "I guess I'll wait, since you asked so nicely and because you were the one who spotted a lifer for me."

We turn and rush to catch up to Vee, who stopped a hundred feet ahead. I practically skip the entire way there.

As we near her, she asks in an exasperated tone, "What did you spot, Jake?"

"A palm warbler, can you believe it?" I rush. "Well, Jake actually spotted it, I would have missed it completely if not for him. Isn't that so lucky?"

Jake frowns a little. Vee looks back and forth between us a few times, then shrugs and says flippantly, "A lot of excitement for a silly bird, eh?" and we continue our trek.

We enter Vee's third-floor walk-up, dragging the bags behind us. The hallway is bright yellow, and the large main room is a muted mossy green. Everything feels bright and alive. There are black and white pictures of cityscapes on the walls: Paris, London, and a place called Dubai. Each has the location and date printed in bold, black print below the frames. The large room has comfortable couches around the edges and is open to an island kitchen like Jake's, except this kitchen has warm wood stools and a lot of wood tones throughout. I take a deep breath and my chest loosens.

"That's your room." Vee points me toward a door down the hallway.

Bag in hand, I open the door slowly. It is a lovely room painted light blue and trimmed in white with large windows that allow the sun to shine into the simple but elegant space. As I start to unpack, a weird feeling fills my chest again. I pause in my folding; I think the weird feeling is the feeling of *being alive*.

The bathroom through a side door has everything I could ever dream of, and it is all mine. Mirrors, chrome, bright lights, some sort of fancy shower spout that is a large rectangle hanging down from the ceiling instead of the small spout we have in our apartment. I take out my one bar of Dove soap but don't see a soap dish, so I slip it back in the box to figure out later. I lay my toothbrush and toothpaste on the edge of a glistening white sink that looks like no one has ever used it. No water marks on the sink or rust stains around the handles. I finish hanging my sparse wardrobe in the walk-in closet and do a little twirl and flop onto the bed.

Hearing voices, I pop up and head out of my room; Veronica and Jake are sitting at the kitchen island. When I move back home, I'll see if I can get Babcia and my parents to renovate and add an island to our kitchen. I will tell them; *they are all the rage*. They'll think I've completely lost my mind, because of my MS or from being out in the world for five months. I can just hear them saying, *an island belongs in the ocean, not a kitchen*. I break into a wide grin.

Jake looks up and sees me smiling, and his lip quirks. The sun is hitting his hair just so and I realize his hair is the same color as the cap of the palm warbler we just saw. They both have rust-colored streaks for a multi-toned color.

Following the sunbeams, I look up higher and see skylights and exclaim, "Skylights, I've always wanted skylights. Being able to watch the sun and the moon, how perfectly lovely."

Veronica looks up and cocks her head as if she is seeing the skylights for the first time. She laughs and muses, "I forgot I paid extra to rent the top floor of this building, solely because of those skylights. It's been years since I've even noticed them." She pauses and continues wistfully, "Isn't that sad and such a waste? I wanted them so badly and paid through the nose for them, and I stopped appreciating them as soon as I moved in. Life is funny."

Sighing sadly, she drifts out of the room, touching many items as she goes, as if reacquainting herself with her apartment after her month-long absence.

Jake and I sit together, not saying anything for a while. It's not an uncomfortable silence, but Jake breaks it when he leans over and asks, "You'll keep an eye on her, right? She seems fine now, but people are always trying to get her to make bad choices, and she is often too willing to oblige them."

I chew on my lip. "But what would I do? I'm not sure I even know what a bad choice is, never mind how to stop Vee from making one."

Jake says confidently, "You know what is right and what is wrong, I can clearly see that. It's just who you are."

I knit my brows and shake my head. "But I've never even been to a party before."

"Don't worry," he insists, "you'll do the right thing."

Just then Vee comes out of her room with an armful of colorful shirts and sweaters and other items. She throws them on the couch and says, "Here are a few things that should fit you. None of my pants will fit you, so we'll need to pop down to Barneys for some bottoms and a few pairs of shoes."

A flood of panic rises in my chest. "Oh. I have pants, and I brought shoes too."

She shakes her head. "We need you to look the part, sweetie. You know—to keep the hounds at bay."

Having no idea what she is talking about, I do know I don't have money to *pop* down to Barneys. I'm just glad I know what Barneys is, so I know for sure that I can't afford a pair of socks from there, never mind some pants and shoes. A sense of panic rises in my chest at the thought of standing at the cash register and pulling out my wallet with all my cash, which adds up to a paltry $155.00. Paltry by Barney standards, but this is a huge amount for me. I straighten my shoulders. I have no plans to spend it on clothes. Binoculars maybe, but not clothes.

Just as I'm getting ready to say no, Jake smoothly interjects, "Vee, you'll be giving Emma an advance on her paycheck to cover these essentials, right?"

Vee pauses and looks quizzically at Jake, then at me.

"Oh, we can expense this. You don't need to spend your hard-earned money on pants and shoes. The agency will never know if they are for you or for me. I have plenty of clothing stipends to cover this—unless you plan on buying out the store." She puts her hands on her narrow hips and looks at me sternly. "You aren't going to buy out the store, are you?"

We all laugh. How nice and considerate they both are, even though clearly the concept of not having enough money to buy a few pairs of pants and shoes is completely foreign to them.

Over the next few days, we poke around Vee's neighborhood, buying a few *essentials* at Barneys, as well as buying some makeup of my own from a store that only sells makeup. I had no idea such a thing existed.

With Vee at my side, New York looks and feels differently. It's as if Chelsea is a fresh start, and everything and everyone is seeing a new Emma. People treat me differently. But I'm not sure if that is because some of Vee's shine is reflecting on me or because I'm not so weighed down by the Jablonski legacy now that I'm out of my family's apartment.

Chapter 10:

The Photoshoot

I wake up, turn over, and avoid looking at the small calendar hanging across from my bed. Ugh! There is no way to avoid it. Today is the day I start my new job. This past week has been all fun and games, but that ends today. I want to crawl back under the covers. *A personal assistant. Who am I kidding?*

I steel myself and try to remember all of Vee's coaching. *Fake it, till you make it* is the only one I recall as I pull on my outfit for my first day. I make a slash through October 22. I'm counting down the days until March 15; to make sure I don't squander a minute of living, as these next five months will need to sustain me for the next thirty or, God forbid, forty years. This is all part of living.

Vee and I head out and I enjoy our walk to the Twenty-third Street station, as the sun shines down upon us. Vee looks completely in her element. I stumble along behind her as we jump on the E train and head down to the Village with a bunch of other commuters.

I've ridden the subway before, but just like wandering around Chelsea, this feels different. Sitting next to Vee who, even though she is fresh-faced with her hair pulled back in a ponytail, gets glances from men and women alike, I feel their eyes upon me too. Normally I could be sitting naked as a jaybird on the subway and people wouldn't notice me, but today they are noticing me. Amazing what a little makeup and clothes can do.

I've been getting better at putting on my makeup, although my eyes are still a bit of a problem. It's awfully hard to put makeup on one's eyes when said eye needs to be closed to do it properly. Vee assures me I will get the hang of the one eye squint in no time.

Vee did my makeup today and when I looked in the mirror, I realized she does have the magic touch. My blonde hair is pulled back in a low pony and Vee has pulled a few strands out of the elastic band so they artfully frame my face. Of course, when I tried to do that, the hair hung down like strands of dry hay, but when Vee wielded her magic hot wand, she made these loose strands twirl around my face like graceful dancers.

I meet people's eyes and smile, and they smile back. Energy is racing through my veins, and I struggle to sit still. What a wonderful feeling to not be a shadow as I walk around the world. These are people I've always seen but who had never seen me until now.

I lean over and ask Vee the same question I've asked her for two days straight: "What do I do when we get there?"

She shushes me and gives my fingers a quick squeeze. My stomach does a little flip, which is better than what it did at five this morning when I thought I was going to throw up.

We exit the subway at Spring Street, walk a few blocks, arriving in front of a large building that looks like an industrial warehouse. It's gray and forbidding. Vee walks up to a door that blends into the wall, making it almost invisible, and pushes a ringer. The door opens, and a large man shouts, "Vee!" and crushes her to his chest, lifting her off her feet. Vee suddenly looks like a small rag doll.

He sets her down and exclaims, "Well, nice to see you. Where ya' been?"

Vee gives him a big smile and shrugs, "Nowhere," before hurrying past him.

The man puts his beefy arm across my pathway and asks gruffly, "And who might you be?"

I see a twinkle in his eye as he says it, but I'm so nervous I can't squeak out a response.

Vee does an about face and laughingly scolds, "Carl, she's with me. Leave her alone."

Carl says in a low voice, dripping with innuendo, "Ahh! Fresh meat."

Vee hustles me past him and whispers, "Don't worry about Carl. He's harmless. He loves to do characters; his pimp character gets pretty raunchy if you let him go too far with it."

Vee steers me around a group of people with clipboards that look harried and eases me through another set of doors—and we step into sheer madness.

Bright lights fill the room reflecting off a long row of mirrors that appear to go on into infinity. The glare is blinding. People are running around with hairspray in one hand and brushes in the other. Others are dabbing and blotting the skin of the most beautiful women I've ever seen. This place makes Vee's suitcase of makeup look like child's play.

Vee plops down in an open seat and two people rush over and start working on her. She motions for me to take a seat in a folding chair set up a little off to the left and out of the path of sprays and spritzes that are being liberally applied.

I watch, fascinated. There is a buzz in the room that comes from many animated conversations, the constant hiss of spray bottles, and the swishing of brushes. Clutching my notepad to my chest, I take a deep breath; this is what life smells like. Not flour and sugar, but powders and perfumes. Where beautiful things become too beautiful to be believed.

Once Vee is transformed, we head to the photographer's area. Vee keeps a bright smile on her face the whole time. She parries questions about her absence with playful responses, and she poses for what seems like hundreds of pictures. She changes into three different outfits and has her hair and makeup redone each time. Her smile is bright and unwavering. She catches my eye and signals for water. I hand her a cold bottle and she takes sips without a word.

After seven hours, we leave the shoot, stepping out of the same steel door and Vee wilts in front of my eyes. The bright smile is gone, her eyes look dull and tired, her shoulders slump, and while she is still beautiful, the camera has sucked out her energy. She looks hollowed out, as if each click took a bit of her soul.

She hails a taxi, and we quietly ride back to Chelsea. While I'm giddy with the splendor of it all, I understand what I saw today isn't real. What shows up on the magazine covers are just surface beauty; it doesn't show the robbing and stripping away of someone's spirit that occurs while the glossy photos are being created. I watch Vee in the dark of the cab and hope she can replace what was taken today.

When we get home, Jake is there with a pizza, and we sit quietly munching. Vee picks at the slice on her plate.

Finally, she announces, "I'm going to bed. I'm plumb tuckered out."

Jake shakes his head, "But you're going to do it again tomorrow, aren't you?"

Vee smiles and gives me a hug as she walks by.

"I'm glad you were there today. It made it so much better," she says tiredly.

I hug her back and say, "Thank you. That is so nice."

Looking at Jake, I explain, "I didn't do anything except sit all day. Oh, I did get her water a couple times."

Jake nods his head, "Hydration is important."

We all laugh, hollowly, and Vee drifts out of the room.

The next morning, I'm relieved to see Vee doing her thirty sun salutations on a mat in the sunny little alcove she calls her meditation room. Back when I was *babysitting* her, I learned from Jake this means she's going to have a good day. If Vee can't muster up the energy for her morning yoga routine, he told me, life was going to be too much for her to bear. On those days, he would go into protector mode and try to keep life from running over Vee so she could make it to the next day and hopefully her *namaste* would return. He explained it kind of joking, but I've since determined it is very true.

I watch Vee with the sun shining down on her wispy blonde hair and when she is almost done, I join her, struggling through the last ten sun salutations. After those ten, Vee stops and takes a big drink of water from her bottle. "Okay, keep going Em. You're looking good."

"Ugh." I groan. Then I slide back on the mat and push myself up into a downward dog.

"Okay, breath in, plank, chaturangas, breath out, upward dog, to downward dog. Let your breath lead the way."

My breath is loud and fills the tiny space. My arms are aching by the time I've done five more salutations under her watchful eye. *Chaturangas* are killers. While I'm strong from the years of working at the bakery, it turns out your triceps are not often used when rolling dough or serving pastries, and triceps seem to be the most important muscle in yoga, other than your lungs. Vee keeps trying to teach me about the importance of breathing to get through the routines, but it doesn't make any sense to me. I've never had to think about breathing before, so it's hard to see how concentrating on something that happens no matter what, helps you do one more *flow*.

After another impromptu lesson, Vee skips off to the shower and I try a few more moves. I giggle when I see myself reflected in the large mirror on the wall. My hair is a mess and Vee's too-long sweatpants have come unrolled, making me look like a child playing dress-up and Twister at the same time. I need to buy some sweatpants that fit me, as Vee's castoffs fit around my waist but are so long that they will surely trip me up one day, and that will be the end of me. Vee keeps threatening to go back to her favorite hot yoga studio and drag me along with her. If that happens, I can't show up wearing rolled-up sweats. I will need to try to appear as if I belong, while at the same time I try to disappear.

Today's shoot is back at the same warehouse building. This time Carl gives me a salute and states grandly, "Welcome back, little one."

I smile and stop. "Hello, Carl."

Vee gives my arm a yank and I stumble behind her toward the makeup room.

Today the shoot is for a fitness company, and Vee is in the cutest pair of shorts and a tank top. At one point, she is supposed to be catching a basketball. The photographer looks around and spots me at the edge of the far wall. He gestures, waving me toward him.

Approaching tentatively. He points to Vee and barks, "Hurry, hurry. Here, take the ball and toss it to her."

Vee is in a jaunty pose in her shorts. I'm frozen. Balls and tossing are not things I have much experience with. Picking up the ball tentatively, I bounce it in my hands, trying to figure out how to do this. I mean, I know how to throw something; it's just the ball is big, and the space is small with a lot of lighting and expensive equipment all around.

The photographer is looking at his camera display. He raises a finger and counts, "One, two, three."

I reach the ball down between my legs and heave it up in the air. The ball sails up and up and then starts coming down. I hold my breath. Vee sees it and does a graceful pirouette, jumping up with an athletic grab, a triumphant smile on her face. The photographer's camera clicks away.

"Again," he demands.

I trot over to Vee, retrieve the ball and she gives me a grin that says she's glad I'm now even more a part of the shoot.

We repeat the sequence several times. I'm no longer nervous but almost enjoy tossing the ball. At the end, the photographer turns the camera in my direction, and I hear the shutter snap. He gives me the slightest nod; his eyes coldly scanning me up and down.

Vee changes quickly, and we head out to the street and jump into a waiting cab. It is getting colder and I'm wearing one of Vee's coats that hits her at her waist but hangs down almost to my knees.

"That was so much fun having you be part of the shoot. What did ya think?" Vee gushes.

"I didn't like how the photographer looked at me at the end," I say, making a face. "It felt like he was appraising me—analyzing my features. Maybe even my worth?"

"Oh, he definitely was," Vee says. "They can't help themselves, it's what they do. That's pretty much what it feels like to be a model. Everyone looking at your hair, your face, your body—thinking, does it work? Does it not? Uhh, too athletic, too edgy, too pretty." Vee sighs. "I was told once I was too pretty for the shoot. It made me feel so bad about myself. Even my mother was disappointed that I was too pretty. This is a crazy industry. Sometimes when I'm posing, I think I could start gushing blood or something, and the photographer would say 'Hold that look, the blood is just perfect. Stop it right there,' and then I picture myself collapsing in a heap as they continue to *click*, *click*, *click*." Vee laughs quietly.

I frown, imagining what it would be like to have the photographer's cold, appraising look constantly focused on me. He took one picture and looked at me for just a minute or two and my soul was chilled, and I felt unworthy of breath. Vee just went through hours of being treated to that feeling. *Do you ever get numb to that?* Glancing at Vee slumped against the seat. *It doesn't seem so.*

Chapter 11:

Yoga

We spend the following day relaxing with coffee and tea, enjoying our day off. Each morning since moving in with Vee has been a joy. I enjoy the comforting warmth of my teacup as I noisily sip my favorite Earl Grey tea, happy at the freedom I have to pick it each morning. While Vee is absorbed in her phone, I begin making pancakes.

She looks up beaming and announces, "Perfect. There are two openings for the 10:00 a.m. yoga class at my favorite studio, and I just signed us up."

"Nooooo! I'm not ready," I wail. I've been getting stronger and have had no aches, pains or swollen joints for weeks, but yoga with people watching? I'm sure it will be mortifying. Vee gives me a fake pout and says, "Please. I promise, you will love it." The thing I don't share is that MS doesn't do well in heat. After my mother was diagnosed, her doctors required that she stop working in the hot kitchen of the bakery. I sit quietly and turn over the pros and cons in my head. Vee watches me clearly seeing the conflict play out on my face. Ultimately, I land on taking the chance. I gave myself these six months and I'm not going to limit myself from one potential experience even if it is something as scary as freakin' hot yoga.

Vee immediately claps her hands together. Able to read my face like a book.

Two hours later, we are out on the street making our way to the Hot Asana Yoga lounge. Underneath my sweats, I'm wearing a pair of Vee's yoga shorts if you can call them that, feeling like I'm buck naked. They fit, but I'm very uncomfortable wearing something so revealing. They are skintight and come down to mid-thigh. Of course, Vee is wearing a matching pair and hers are even shorter, but she can pull it off.

"Hush up you look adorable," she scolds.

I yank the loose-fitting sweatshirt down lower. The sweatshirt covers the half bra, half tank top thingy she gave me for my top. I'm glad she knew not to push me on baring my midriff.

She sees my discomfort and states serenely, "You do your own practice in class. Stop worrying. It will be fine."

"What happens if you don't have a *practice*? What do you do then?"

She laughs. "Don't worry, the heat makes you more flexible. Wait and see how much better you do at ninety degrees than in my sunroom."

I shake my head in despair. "Nothing is better at ninety degrees. I've worked in a bakery my whole life, and in the middle of summer, it's always ninety degrees, and no one ever said, 'Why don't we start a yoga class in the kitchen?'"

Vee gives me one of her classic snort laughs and swings open a door. "We're here."

Before I enter, I try to peek through the frosted window and my palms feel clammy. Vee glides in with her yoga bag slung carelessly over her shoulder and I follow closely behind, feeling like a complete imposter, clutching my borrowed mat and slouching in with my borrowed clothes.

I step into an open and airy lobby; chimes sound softly in the background. I imagine a Buddhist temple and feel a slow release of the muscles in my shoulders. The soft lights glow and flicker like candles leading you from the lobby area into the high-ceilinged classroom.

Settling into a spot in the back of the room, I look around. No one is looking back. Everyone seems to be in their own little world. Some are lying prone while others are curled up in child's pose. The heat isn't as hot as it is in the bakery kitchen in the middle of summer, so I'm pretty sure I won't pass out from it. I may survive this yet. When I gather my courage to look at myself in the mirror, I don't look different from the others in class. There are people of all shapes and sizes.

I take a deep breath and sit up straighter saying to myself, *I can do this*. Vee's been telling me about the importance of positive self-talk, and this seems to be a good time to practice.

Closing my eyes, I inhale lavender and some other citrusy smell. We make a roll at the bakery that includes a bit of lavender and orange zest, and my anxiety eases as I picture the familiar bakery.

The instructor walks in with white tights that fit smoothly over the most womanly but athletic body I've ever seen. She's barefoot and looks free of any makeup or other artifice. I stare; she could be Mother Earth incarnate with her grace and her strength.

She comes over on cat's feet and gives Vee a big hug, then turns to me and does a little bow. "Welcome, I'm so happy you are here. I'm Jasmine."

Good vibes fill the whole place. The combination of the chimes and the aromatherapy wafting through the space gives me permission to quiet my mind.

Jasmine tells us to start in child's pose. We slowly work on stretching every part of our body and then move to sun salutations. My cheeks turn pink and the sweat drips down between my breasts. I look around embarrassed, but see everyone has sweat dripping down some part of their body and some have pools around their mat. Everyone is wiping themselves with the little towels they handed out when we checked in. I take mine and drag it across my face and neck.

I can do most of the basic postures and stick with the easier version of the trickier ones. The instructor's voice is encouraging and soothing and she is like breath itself—filling you up and letting you release with her words. She instructs without judgment, telling folks to stay with the version of the pose their body needs today. Vee and a few others are doing the more advanced side crows while I stay in side angle, but no one is even looking around except me.

Vee was right. Everyone is doing their own practice.

I hit a wall thirty minutes in and worry that I may have made the wrong decision, but as if sensing my rising panic, the class shifts to balance poses and a ton of core work which is more in my wheelhouse. I swell with pride when I hold tree longer than Vee, then feel bad at my petty comparison, as it doesn't belong in this space.

Vee's eyes are closed throughout the class, and she looks at peace. Free despite the sweat and the shaking of muscles as we hold a chair pose forever. I breathe deeply and think I might just be enjoying this yoga class.

Vee and I get into a groove. On workdays we go to her scheduled photoshoots, and on off days we squeeze in yoga and cooking in between meetings at her agency to work out future jobs and scheduling. Sometimes at shoots, I'm sent to get a different pair of shoes or a handbag from wardrobe; once I even had to run out to a trendy shop in the Village to buy a replacement for a belt the director found wanting. It was a thrill to see my selection being modeled by Vee. I can see how Vee's mother could get swept up in being part of this action. It's captivating.

I make sure Vee eats and drinks and gets a break when she starts to fade. I take notes in the meetings and point out conflicts or issues with the proposed schedule. I'm being useful, and it turns out that is what a PA does. Vee calls me indispensable, and while that is an exaggeration, I think I'm doing a good job.

We spend a lot of time together slowly revealing our secrets. Sometimes Vee seems on the verge of spilling more but then retreats, after which she gets sad for a while.

The other night she told me about a male model she dated a year ago and how he was more insecure about his weight than most of the female models.

I laughed and shared, "I've never had a boyfriend. The closest I ever got was an almost kiss at a wedding when I was fourteen."

Thankfully, she didn't make a big deal about it, but I notice she now occasionally looks at me kind of speculatively, like she's trying to solve a puzzle and is looking for clues. I immediately get uncomfortable when she looks at me like that, but she never responds when I ask her pointedly, "What?"

I'm continuing to do my own yoga practice. The studio is a special place, truly a no judgment zone like Vee had promised. I've stopped watching the others and comparing myself to them, instead I spend the hour trying to listen to my body and pushing it sometimes and sometimes stepping back. What a wonderful, novel idea. I've always watched the world and therefore watched others. Now I'm thinking about me and what my body needs and where my head is at. I've learned that breath can ground you and focus you to help reduce anxiety and keep your mind from racing too far ahead. Even some sayings and readings the instructors share each class start to make some sense.

Walking home after class today, Vee asks, "You know the message Jasmine shared today during class about masks? I can get behind something like that. It makes perfect sense. Don't ya think?"

"Hmm, what was it?" I ask. "We're all the same when we are born . . ."

"And only as we go through life, we start to put on our masks that cover our sameness," Vee finishes. "I love that. I believe that, more than I believe any of the dumb sermons I listened to when I was growing up. We are all alike, some just have put on masks that make them appear different and it hides the real person." She grows more animated by the second. "If you got to pick one of the yoga beliefs Jasmine teaches, which one would you pick? You know, what one should they teach in church instead of all the crap they try to shove down our throats?

"You can't do that," I blurt. "Yoga isn't a religion."

She chuckles, taking my hand, "I'm just asking, if you were to believe in something other than church—or if your God wanted to know which yoga belief you really liked, what would you tell him . . . or her?" Vee's eyes are mischievous.

I can't help it; a smile tugs at my lips. Vee looks so happy and earnest.

"Okay," I concede, "if my God were to ask me such a thing, which *he* would never because he doesn't need my ideas. But I'd pick the yoga teaching from a couple of weeks ago. It was about if blue skies fill you with joy, if grass growing in the field has the power to move you, if nature has a message you understand, be happy, for it means your soul is alive." I laugh self-consciously. "Well, it was something like that. I liked it because I'm most comfortable when I'm in nature, with the trees and, of course, the birds."

"Oh, I remember that one." Vee nods. "I liked it too, but it didn't do anything for me. We each must find the beliefs that speak to us and that serve us, and everyone can pick something different."

Vee sounds like Jasmine. "You aren't saying yoga beliefs can replace church beliefs." I frown. "That isn't true."

"Why can't it replace church teachings?" she demands. "If they don't serve you, find something else. Who can say one is right, and one is wrong?"

Stopping, I stare at her. "That's crazy. Replace church with yoga?" I glance up nervously. "I'm surprised we aren't being struck dead on the spot."

She nudges me forward. "Who wants a God who might strike you dead when you are saying nature makes you happy? That isn't any God I want to hang with. God is in everything and everywhere, and he doesn't care if we find him in yoga class or in church or Central Park or your silly birds. Those things were all created by him or her, so he or she doesn't mind."

Stopping again as I'm unable to digest these concepts and walk at the same time.

I reply tentatively, "Find God where you find him? I've always thought he was in church, but honestly, I never felt him there. Maybe I kinda feel *him* in the park, but not at yoga. That can't be right."

Vee replies primly, "Well, I find him—*or her*—at yoga."

Clutching at her arm, I respond, "Dear Lord, please forgive me and my friend for this blasphemy."

"Don't include me in your old-school, guilt-induced requests for forgiveness," Vee states chuckling and yanking her arm free. "My yoga God or your Central Park God is all forgiving and wants you to know you are your own higher power." She raises her arms beseechingly to the sky.

I glance around and see people staring at us. I yank her arms down. "People will think you're crazy. Come on. We're finally home."

The next day at the agency meeting, Janet, Vee's agent, shares excitedly, "There's a *Vogue* party coming up on November fifth to celebrate the tenth anniversary of owning *Vogue Paris*. You are on the invite list and absolutely must attend."

Vee gracefully replies, "Oh, I can't. No one will notice if I'm not there."

"Top models need to attend, and you are a top model," Janet states crisply. "It will be the usual scene, just bigger and better."

She moves on to other topics. Clearly, she considers the matter settled.

Out on the street after the meeting, I ask, "Should we talk to Jake about the party?"

Vee doesn't respond for a bit. "No," she finally states firmly. "Let's go to the party and have fun. Have you ever been to a fancy, over-the-top party?"

"Of course not," I say, nudging her. "I've barely ever been to a birthday party, at least not since I got scared watching *ET* at Julia's party when I was eight. I cried, and they never invited me to another one. And of course, I became the leper of third grade."

Vee snorts. "Oh, right, I remember that story. Well, we will have to make up for that bomb. Tomorrow we'll go shopping for dresses. We'll have to find two within the $3,000 budget they gave me for the event. I'm sure we can do that, don't you?"

"Y-yes, I can stay within that budget," I stammer.

I've never spent anything more than fifty dollars on a dress before, and she knows it.

The next day, we head off arm in arm to a chic boutique on Fifth Avenue, and I insist we walk through the Ramble on our way. Vee puts up with my bird obsession to a point, but today she doesn't let me sit on my favorite bench. Walking, I spot a bright-red male northern cardinal, who shyly disappears into a nearby bush. As soon as the crimson flash disappears, I see a chipping sparrow giving a soft trill. I'm happy with that.

The shop, which smells of luxury, would be intimidating if not for Vee. She's totally relaxed and at home here.

A salesclerk with a severe bob who looks pretty enough to be a model herself picks out dresses for us. All the dresses are divine. They're made of the softest, silkiest material that feels lush and beautiful against my skin. Vee makes sure the ones she picks for me are modest by her standards. So, most are long sleeves and come to mid-thigh or lower. But each one either has a slit or a plunging neckline or back. I keep tugging at the dresses, trying to cover whatever the designer is trying to draw attention to.

Vee gives a thumbs up when I try on a deep-maroon,

velvet dress with a plunging neckline, but this one has a translucent netting that holds the two front panels together. This allows for a more significant plunge, but I don't feel naked in it with air brushing my stomach. As long as I don't glance down, I feel I'm covered.

Naked or not, I feel like a princess in every dress I try on. The maroon one fits me perfectly, though—as if made for me.

Vee picks out a pair of size-seven, silver strappy sandals that aren't as high as the shoes she normally wears but certainly higher than my normal flats. I slip them on, and feel like Cinderella, they are a perfect fit too.

"Absolutely stunning. You look amazing." Vee gushes. Blushing, I peek at myself in the mirror again. I want to stare but know that would be unseemly.

"I don't know Vee. It must be very expensive." I drop my voice. "There aren't even price tags on anything."

"We're good. Don't worry. You look stunning, doesn't she?" Vee turns to the salesclerk. Cindy nods her head approvingly and that seals the deal.

Vee continues to try on a few more strapless dresses and ultimately picks out a bright-red dress with a flared skirt that ruffles around her thighs in the most enticing manner. She skips the shoes commanding, "We must economize, Emma."

I giggle, as she is clearly in a good mood. We leave the dresses at the shop, Vee wants hers shortened a touch more, to which I state primly, "There won't be anything left of the dress if they shorten it more." Vee does her classic snort laugh and even the sales lady cracks a smile.

"Don't you just love her?" Vee exclaims.

We stroll out of the store arm in arm just the way we came in. As we step onto the sidewalk, I glance up Fifth Avenue toward my parents' apartment; it's only been a month since I left, but it feels like forever.

Chapter 12:

The Dinner Party

The echo of the knock still lingered as Jake threw open the door, launching into a story about being forced by his parents to attend his father's charity awards ceremony. In sweatpants and running shoes, he's sweating profusely, despite the forty-degrees and the biting wind making it feel like December, not late October. He mumbles a hello in my direction before collapsing into a chair, clearly venting to Vee, who knows his parents. She makes small sounds of outrage in solidarity throughout his tirade.

"Besides the stupid charity event, they're hosting a dinner party this weekend. I need you, Vee," he concludes with a plea. "You must come to dinner. If it's just me and my parents and Jessica, I will go batshit crazy. Please."

Vee quirks an eyebrow in my direction. "If I have to go, Emma has to go. That will make it much better."

Jake tilts his head in my direction as if realizing for the first time I'm sitting in the room and responds, "Hell yeah!

That's an excellent idea. Christ, that could almost make it fun."

"A dinner?" I ask nervously.

He announces grandly, "Emma, I'd like to invite you to dinner at my parents' this Saturday. It will be a lovely affair, just a few of us, and we will have some good food, good drinks, and kind of okay company."

Hearing the sarcasm in his voice, I'm unsure of what I'm missing, I nod. "Sure."

I've been curious about Jake's parents for ages. I rarely saw them when I was living across the hall. They didn't seem to be home much of the time.

Jake stands and gives my shoulder a squeeze. "Six o'clock sharp and dressed to the nines." His mood has lifted.

I look at Vee who gives me a confident nod.

I muster another less than confident, "Sure."

"Phew! I was so annoyed with my parents that I needed to get out of there," Jake says, "So, I ran around Central Park before heading here for a visit. Thank you, ladies, you have probably saved my life." Jake pauses and frowns. "Oh, let's not tell my parents you live next door. Let's just say Vee met you at the bakery and hired you as her PA. We don't need to get into any other details."

He turns and gives us both a wave, heading out the door. Glancing at Vee, she is chewing on her bottom lip. A niggle of worry worms its way into my head despite the flare of excitement at the thought of spending Saturday night with Jake. I've missed our conversations in the evening when he returned from class every Monday, Wednesday and Friday. I have loads to tell him.

"Saved his life! That seems serious." I say

"Oh, don't pay him any attention. He's being dramatic as usual."

On Saturday, Vee frowns at me as I stand in front of her in my black work slacks and gray sweater. She rummages around in her drawer and pulls out a gray and cream silk scarf and artfully drapes it around my shoulders, it falls in soft folds around my neckline. I glance at myself in the mirror, touching the luxurious material. I'm wearing my only pair of hoop earrings, and my shiny, patent leather flats. Vee is wearing a gray-checkered sweater dress that hangs straight down from her shoulders, and she belts it with a large, black belt that matches her knee-high, black boots. She looks smashing.

Vee sits down at her make-up table. I still can't believe there are special tables and chairs just for putting on makeup. She starts applying her makeup. When she finishes, she points me to the seat and spends more time than normal on mine. When she is done, I stare at my reflection, she hasn't done her normal "less is more" approach. Instead, she has emphasized everything. My lips are a deep red hue, and my eyes stand out with shimmers of browns and creams, enhancing my blue eyes. My eyes are always large, but now they look like saucers. She has put on extra coats of mascara, making my blonde lashes look like brown spikes surrounding a deep pool of blue.

I stare. I look so different. My skin and cheeks are still pale, almost translucent, but my skin has a shimmer to it.

"Wow, you can make anyone look beautiful."

Vee smiles. "Emma, you *are* beautiful. Makeup just enhances what you already have. That's all it does." I wonder for a moment, why all of this is necessary, but forget it as I step out the door. I feel I can conquer the world. Boy, maybe clothes and makeup are worth the price if they give you this kind of confidence.

We hurry by my parents' door, and I glance surreptitiously at it. Vee knocks on Jake's door with a little three knock, two knock rhythm; like she hasn't a care in the world.

It's 6:15 p.m. and I'm nervous as Jake said 6:00 sharp. I hate being late and we are late because of the extra time Vee took on my makeup. The door swings open wide, and Jake smiles brightly at each of us.

"Ah, my two angels of mercy have arrived. I was getting worried."

We hand him our coats and walk down the familiar hallway toward the sound of voices. Jake grabs both of our hands in his as he seems concerned we may fly away leaving him all alone. My stomach jumps a little when we veer into the formal dining room off to the left of the kitchen. We never spent any time in this room when Vee was staying here, as it's stuffy and uncomfortable.

Jake announces grandly, "Veronica is here, and she brought her friend Emma. Emma, these are my parents, Carol and Oliver."

Frowning a little at Jake's use of the word *her friend* instead of *our friend*, I hesitate at the threshold but quickly put a smile on my face as Jake's mother and father stand up.

They give Vee a hug, then take turns reaching out their hand to me. Jake's mother is wearing a rose-colored dress with matching pumps. She has pulled her hair back in a tight bun. She has pearls dripping from her neck, ears, and wrists. The term *well put together* pops into my head. Jake's father has a bit of a paunch and while he has a smile on his face, it easily could be a grimace. His suit is impeccable. They both level cold eyes at me and don't hide their looks of surprise. I assume they were expecting another model like Vee instead of plain, old little me.

Jake ushers me over to the one other person in the room, who has remained sitting.

"Jessica," he says pleasantly, "this is Emma."

I smile wider, glad he didn't add *Veronica's friend* this time. I reach out my hand to Jessica. Jessica turns ever so slightly in my direction, placing her hand into mine, and then pulls it back quickly.

She remarks in a nasal voice, "Oh, so pleased. Now, Jake come back and sit. Before being interrupted, you were telling me such a marvelous story." Jessica shifts back in her seat, smiling encouragingly at Jake. *Simpering* pops into my head. She is pretty, but in a cold, haughty sort of way. Her brown hair is pulled back tightly in a ponytail and her lips are a little thin.

Standing awkwardly, I jump when someone claps me on my back.

"Well, what can I get you to drink, Emily?" Oliver asks loudly.

I murmur, "Emma."

Barely acknowledging my correction, he says, "Right-o, so what would you like?"

"Water is fine."

Jake's father barks out a laugh, "Water, water! Let's get you some white wine, hey?"

A maid I hadn't noticed darts forward with a long-stemmed wineglass. I take hold of it with both hands, immediately worried I'm going to drop it. I spot Vee with a large, sturdy glass of water with a refreshing slice of lime in it and wonder how come she got to have water. Ah, maybe this is a dinner where you get the opposite of what you want, as I'm pretty sure Vee isn't thrilled with her option either. I hear my name and realize I've drifted off in my musings.

"Emma, what do you do?"

Glad Carol got my name right. I respond, "I'm Vee's personal assistant." Dismay replaces my happiness as Carol turns away from me.

Fortunately, Jessica steps in. "That sounds interesting. How did you get into that?"

"They knew each other because Emma ran the local bakery," Jake interjects quickly, "and when Vee needed someone, she figured Emma's experience could be perfect. It turned out she was right. Plus, Emma makes a mean pierogi."

There's polite laughter.

"Everyone says the best way to a man's heart is through his stomach," Carol says, "but I think it's through his mind." With a slight pause, she continues, "Jessica is a lawyer, graduated top of her class from NYU."

I turn to Jessica to give her a warm smile, but she has a hard look in her eyes and is looking at me challengingly. My smile wavers and I turn around to see if Vee can save me from whatever is going on, but she is chatting with Oliver. Thankfully, I catch her eye and she waves me over.

"Oliver is just telling me about his upcoming charity event. It sounds just marvelous."

She perfectly rolls her eyes, conveying utter boredom, and smoothly changes the subject by asking about Oliver's recent Hamptons stay. They chat about a few people they both know from the Hamptons, and then Carol ushers us to our seats at the table. I'm glad to be part of any conversation even if it is one sided.

Oliver sits at one end; Carol at the other. Carol pointedly motions for Jake to sit next to Jessica, and Vee and I take the seats across from them. Dinner starts with a pale soup. I can't determine what it consists of. It's not unpleasant, just not wildly flavorful, and rather watery.

As if reading my mind, Jake exclaims, "Well, this is no ka-pus-niak, is it?"

I look at him and he winks; I smile gratefully. He seems to want to see me smile. It never takes much attention from

Jake to get the pink to start inching up from my chest to my cheeks. I hope it doesn't ruin the effect of Vee's makeup magic.

"What the heck is kapsnup?" Jessica asks pointedly,

I reply happily, "Oh, it's a sausage and cabbage soup, we made it the other—"

"Cabbage and sausage!" she cuts me off. "Why would anyone eat that? Did they want to get fat *and* bloated?"

Looking down at my soup, I take a spoonful. *Fat and bloated is better than eating something that looks like dish-water and has only a bit more flavor.*

Jessica proceeds to monopolize Jake in conversation, and Vee is politely listening to another Oliver story. Carol looks like she would rather start a conversation with the maid than with me, so I sit quietly, feeling dampness under my armpits. The ability to form words and speak seems to have completely escaped me.

Finally, remembering Carol's bird feeder in Jake's room, I turn to Carol and ask, "Uhm, have you seen any interesting birds lately at your feeder?"

Carol turns her icy stare on me, and I shrink in my seat unsure of what I've done.

"Oh, Emma," Jake suddenly says, "I saw the same palm warbler we spotted heading to Vee's. At least I assume it was the same one as it's strange that one is still hanging around this time of year."

I throw Jake a grateful nod, glad he saved me from Carol's confusing reaction. I feel the warmth from the glow of his warm brown eyes. "It *is* late for a palm warbler. When we saw that other one, I checked my book—normally they are gone by now."

Jake nods in agreement. "So, what birds have you seen lately on your walks?"

"Oh, just on the walk over here, I saw a blue jay and a

northern cardinal." I reply enthusiastically, "Nothing out of the ordinary but still lovely."

Jessica lets out a little huff and my heart warms that Jake is trying to save me by talking about the one topic he knows I love. I'm still confused as to why Carol isn't joining in as I remember Jake mentioning the bird feeder in his room was hers so she must like birds. But Jake's interest is enough to stop the flop sweats and get my brain reconnected to my lips.

Jake leans across the table toward me and whispers dramatically, "I hear there's a snowy owl in the park, down from Canada for the winter. You should be on the lookout for it."

I clasp my hands at my chest and my eyes widen. "Really! Oh, I've never seen any owls, never mind a snowy one."

Carol clears her throat and gives the maid a terse nod of her head. The maid jumps forward and clears the soup bowls, and then she starts delivering the food from the kitchen. It is some sort of fish in a cream sauce with sweet potato and a green vegetable on the side.

"What kind of vegetable is this?" I ask politely.

Jessica responds with distain dripping from her voice, "Broccoli rabe."

I don't think she said *idiot*, but she certainly implied it. I'm glad I recognize the sweet potato side dish, although it has some sort of little round red seeds or kernels mixed up in it. I certainly will not be asking what those are.

As we begin to eat, conversation stops, and the room gets quiet. The trickle of sweat restarts under my arms and grows as no one so much as scrapes a fork or lets a knife touch their plate. I can't wait for this dinner to be over. I can't believe I was looking forward to it. No wonder Jake wanted us to *save him*. I think back to the last time I stopped at my parents' for a quick visit, where I sat in my regular chair, and we enjoyed a pork dinner. I didn't think anything of it then, but right now I would give my right arm to be over there instead of here, trying to keep out of the dangerous quicksand that seems to surround this table.

I'm halfway through my meal, and it tastes pretty good compared to the soup, when Carol asks sweetly, "Jake, do you have anyone to take to your father's charity event? It's next week you know."

Jake grimaces and Jessica smiles widely. It dawns on me that Jessica must be the girl Jake's parents want him to marry, and everything suddenly becomes clear. It's not that they don't like *me*, they just didn't want anyone who may be competition for Jessica. I'm relieved as I know I'm not competition. How could I be? She's smart, polished, well educated, maybe a little unfriendly, but certainly a good match for Doctor Jake. I'm sure they know the same people, because according to Carol, they both grew up summering at the Hamptons and traveling in the same circles. My stomach sours when I glance over at Jessica.

While I'm mulling all of this over, I stretch my legs to get the muscles to relax a bit when I hit something solid with my foot—which is bare, as I've slipped my shoes off under the table. Jake's twinkling eyes meet mine and I blush again. I pull my legs back, slipping my feet quickly back into my shoes.

Carol pushes her plate forward a few inches, even though it's still half full, and drops her napkin onto the food. Standing, Jake takes his plate, which is completely clean, reaches for his mother's plate, and plops it on top of his. While I normally would never leave food on my plate at my house, I decide if this will get me out of this place sooner, I'll gladly waste some food just this once. Picking up my plate, I reach for Vee's as I stand. Jake takes Jessica's plate, looking a little worried about the two dishes already stacked in his left hand. I expertly stack Vee's on top of mine and place Oliver's on top of that. I move the silverware to my other hand, so I can carry the bowl of purple dotted sweet potatoes, and I head to the kitchen right behind Jake.

Walking past Carol, I catch her eye, and she gives me a cold stare.

Oh Lord, what did I do now? Maybe I shouldn't be helping clear, but I've done it a thousand times at my house, so it's an automatic response. *Ugh, maybe she thinks I'm trying to get Jake alone.* I bite my lip as I enter the kitchen.

Jake glances at the neat tower in my one hand and large casserole dish in the other and remarks, "Show off."

Grinning, I immediately feel better, glad there is a little distance between me and the icy stares. The maid is toiling over a large mixer and a lovely smell fills the kitchen. I sniff appreciatively, it is some concoction of vanilla, cream, and sugar. Looking up from the noisy machine, she jumps when she spots us. Panic rises in her eyes. She leaps toward us grabbing the plates. Jake fends her off, stating firmly, "Maria, we're fine. We'll just put them in the sink. You keep doing what you're doing, it smells divine."

The fancy coffee maker is bubbling and hissing. Jake sets his plates down and grabs a cup from the nearby shelf and starts rummaging around. Finally, he asks, "So, where *do* we keep the tea bags?"

Beaming, I gush, "Oh, that is so nice, right over here."

I reach up and take down a box of chamomile tea, and Jake fills up a cup with hot water from the coffee contraption. He gestures for me to lead the way back to the dining room.

I forget all about the cold stares waiting for me until I sit back down at the table. Jake slides my teacup into the middle of my placemat and then goes over to the other side to sit down. Carol looks ready to explode. I realize it looks strange that Jake served me tea while everyone else is waiting for the maid to bring coffee. I stare at my tea, wondering if I will be able to drink a sip under these tense circumstances. Thankfully, the maid bustles in with a tray with the cups filled with coffee and creamers and sugars.

Carol turns to me and bites off, "Cream or sugar for your tea?"

Shaking my head, I try to take a sip. Carol's eyes narrow and I wonder if I should have said yes for some reason. As the maid returns with fluffy confections in fancy wine glasses, I state, "The meal was just delicious. I loved everything."

Carol pins me with a stare for a quick second and pointedly turns to Jake, "So, what is going on with school?"

She says the word school like it's offensive, indicating that she prefers discussing something offensive over responding to me. I take a small scoop of the dessert, and it melts in my mouth. I take a bigger spoonful. I could eat the whole thing and then some, but Jessica is staring at me and just playing with her dessert, taking small spoonfuls. I set my spoon down, disappointed.

Jake quirks his eyebrow in my direction and cajoles, "Come on, eat the rest. It's heavenly, isn't it? Like eating a cloud."

Smiling, I pick up my spoon again and take a big scoop, feeling defiant. Rich people are so wasteful and kind of miserable. They can't even enjoy the most marvelous dessert ever. Maybe my beige apartment down the hall isn't as pathetic as I've always thought it was. Jake nods encouragingly, so I take another scoop and a sip of my tea. My back muscles relax a little.

Suddenly, Vee places her napkin on the table and says loudly, "Carol, Oliver, this was absolutely marvelous. Can't thank you enough. But Emma and I have an early shoot tomorrow, so we need to get our beauty sleep."

I look at Vee in confusion; tomorrow is a day off. She faces me and winks, then smoothly pulls me up by my hand. She seems to have had enough of Oliver's stories.

Glad I caught on, I stand obediently and bob my head in agreement as Vee continues to say what a lovely time we had.

We're collecting our coats in the guest room when Jake emerges from his room with his coat on.

"We're all heading out together," he says brightly. "Safety in numbers."

I'm not sure what happened after Vee and I left the room, but something did. Jessica is now standing with her coat on, and we all walk out the door and pile out onto Fifth Avenue. Jake takes command and we head down a few blocks and take a right.

He declares with a forced smile, "Ah, here's Jessica's place. Hey, have a nice night."

I offer a sincere, "Nice to meet you," and before Jessica can say more than a quick goodbye, we turn in sync and head back the way we came. I didn't realize I was holding my breath until I let it out in a whoosh.

Jake lets out a hoot and exclaims, "Amen sister. My God that sucked. I really owe you guys one."

Vee snorts. "It wasn't that bad. Seeing them trying to figure out the Emma thing was kinda fun. Boy, the tea delivery really was a nice touch. They're probably throwing away every damn tea bag in the house right now so it can never happen again."

Vee gives out a gleeful *woohoo* and Jake smirks.

Stopping in the middle of the sidewalk, I demand, "What is going on? I mean I figured out halfway through dinner that Jessica is who your parents want you to marry, but why am I involved? I didn't mean to cause trouble."

Jake looks sheepish, "You didn't do a thing to cause trouble. They just keep pushing Jessica on me, and can you imagine? Ugh, Jessica in bed would be like the fish we just suffered through—lukewarm and a little mushy."

Vee snorts a loud laugh. "Exactly."

I'm still mystified but I can't help but smile at the fish comparison. Vee tucks her arm in mine and her other in Jake's and marches down the sidewalk. We walk through Central Park, but unfortunately, no nightbirds are calling.

"Remember to keep your eyes peeled for snowy owls," Jake says. "They can sometimes be seen perched atop a post or telephone pole or broken-off tree."

This distracts me from my thoughts of Jessica; how thrilling it would be to see a snowy owl. As the darkness surrounds us, I feel a connection that is more than just our linked arms. These two are my friends. I scan the shadows looking for the elusive owl and the contentment in my chest simmers softly inside me. A picture of Jake's dancing eyes when he was encouraging me to eat the fluffy dessert flashes through my mind.

When I'm back alone in my room, I can't stop myself from running the whole dreadful evening over in my mind. I clearly see how unsophisticated I am compared to everyone else who was at the table. The cold stares, awkward conversations and my many missteps make my heart feel heavy in my chest. *How am I going to survive the Vogue party?* I fall asleep feeling depressed, but the reappearance of my special dream assuages those feelings:

Flying over the most wonderful forest, the trees are first below me, until I swoop in between the branches finding small pockets of space to cruise. Everything smells of earth and life.

Now I'm down on the ground, transformed into a human, picking my way along a faint trail, and there is the fluttering of wings and flashes of movement up in the dark canopy of the forest. Owls on their silent wings keep me company as I search for something.

I look up ahead. I know my true love is there, just out of view, ready to protect me.

Awakening, I lie still, letting my dream wrap itself around me like a pair of strong arms. My dream morphed a little and somehow connected our walk back to Vee's last night into the story. The feeling of belonging and comfort that I've always found in my dream, I realize I was feeling on our walk last night.

I get up and flip the page of my calendar. Time is so fickle. Until now, my life plodded along, but these last two weeks have flown. I'm going to need to try to slow down time. *Is that even possible?*

Chapter 13:

Snowy Owl

Striding through the park, I feel strong and confident. I'm visiting my parents because Vee and I don't have any shoots or meetings today. As I approach the apartment, I slow my pace, then knock tentatively, unlocking the door with my key. It's 4:30 p.m., so everyone should be home.

"Hi, Mama, hi Papa," I call out. "I'm here."

My mother is stirring a pot at the stove, and my father is dozing in his chair. Mama gives me a wan smile. My father opens his eyes, and he tilts his head in my direction. I didn't know what I was expecting, but I can't help feeling a little deflated. But then I remember the dinner on Saturday night and how tense and miserable it was making *this* seem so much better.

Walking over to my mother, I take the ladle from her hand, "Sit, I will stir the soup and can serve it tonight. You go put your feet up."

She pats my shoulder as she passes the spoon to me and sits down heavily at the kitchen table. I stir, and the warmth of the soup works to dispel my little bit of hurt and discontent. Yes, the silence here feels different from the silence I often share at Vee's. A little cold and unfeeling but not intentionally mean or bad. As Vee has been telling me, a lot of my worry and anxiety is in my head and I'm in control of it. I'm still not sure that is true, but it helps me shake off the voice in my head that wants to stamp my foot and yell, *pay attention to me, please.*

I remember coming home from school one day when I was in fourth or fifth grade, when the girls had been particularly mean. I told my mother how Dolores had taken the leaf I had found for an art project. I was crying and hiccupping as I recounted the story of ending up with a broken leaf that I had use for the project. Mama listened as she stirred a pot on the stove and finally said, "All this over a leaf, Emma. There are people dying in this world. One can cry over that, perhaps, but not over a leaf."

Reaching over with the spoon, she stated, "Keeping busy is the best thing to take your mind off your troubles. You know what they say about idle hands."

I certainly did, and I grabbed the spoon and poured all my anger into my task turning the soup into a fine puree which my father did not enjoy one bit.

Now I turn toward my parents as I stir and say quietly, "The job is going well. I get to do some interesting things. I schedule meetings for Veronica—so more than just cooking."

My mother replies encouragingly, "How nice. One should always keep busy."

I can't help but smile. I keep expecting something more from them, and I need to stop being disappointed. A special leaf or a little life, they don't understand what I want or what I need. I must find it for myself, or if Vee and yoga is to be believed, I need to find it within me.

After serving everyone their bowls of soup, I clean up and leave quietly, walking back to Vee's with a spring in my step. I stop on the path through the park and stare down at my legs, remembering the limp months ago. I shoot up a prayer of thanks for my current strong legs and arms. Vee has told me to be thankful for the little things. Although, as the picture of my mother sitting wearily in her chair flashes through my mind, I know that working legs and arms is not a little thing.

Vee and I are curled up on her couch. It's close to 8:00 p.m. I'm reading a new book I picked up at the library after leaving my parents' apartment. Vee is flipping through one of her many magazines.

Vee's phone buzzes: she picks it up. "Hi, Jake." After a pause, she leans toward me, holding out the phone. "He wants to talk to you. If only you would get a cell phone, I wouldn't need to play secretary."

She is joking, but she *is* getting aggravated about the situation, so I think I'm going to have to cave soon. I hate spending money on such a contraption and I'm afraid I won't know how to answer it, but Vee assures me I just need to google stuff like that, and I will be able to find the answers to all my questions. She lets me use her computer in her apartment, but I tend to google bird sightings in Central Park and not how to use an iPhone.

Focusing on the phone in Vee's hand, I take it and tentatively say, "Hello."

"Hello, Emma, I was wondering if you want to come see the snowy owl. It's been spotted on top of a barn by the large, open grassy area, and I have it on good authority it is there right now."

"Oh my gosh." My eyes widen. "Yes! Yes! Yes!"

"Okay, okay, I'll be over in twenty minutes."

I quickly change out of my old sweats, pull on a pair of hand-me-down leggings from Vee, and put on a big sweater I recently bought on clearance from Barneys. I already have my coat on when Jake rings the buzzer, and I bound out the door and down the stairs.

Vee calls out, "Well *bye* to you too."

My bursting from the apartment building startles Jake, who clearly expected to have to come up to the top floor to get me.

"I'm ready," I announce enthusiastically.

Grinning, Jake does an about face and we head out into the dark towards the park.

This is only the second time I've been in the park at night, and again just like the night with Jessica, I notice how at night everything feels so different, as if the moon above has replaced the bright sun's cheerful mood with a deep, somber magic. I practically skip along beside Jake, babbling, "I don't have any owl sightings on my life list and John Foster writes that owls are a different species from most birds as one must experience them on their terms: in the dark, when the world doesn't belong to humans as much as the daylight world does."

I realize too late I'm talking about John Foster, but Jake doesn't seem to mind it and even smiles slightly, as if he agrees with the sentiment.

When we arrive at the edge of a field, we see the barn in clear view before us. There are a few other people with binoculars standing around in loose groups. They must be here for the owl as well. I suddenly feel a part of the birders around me as if we are part of our own special *gang*.

Jake pulls out a pair of binoculars from a backpack he has slung over his shoulder and puts it up to his eyes. He aims where the couple closest to us are pointing their binoculars, and he plays around with a few nobs and moves his head in a tight circle.

"Ah, got him. Here you go. Just aim at the barn, he's perched on the very peak of the roof."

I take the glasses and follow his instructions. My path to the bird is rather herky-jerky, but after the second try, I spot him. He is gorgeous and so large, his disk-like face is staring directly at me. His yellow cat eyes look molten and they burn a path straight into my heart. It is almost too much, and I take the glasses down, spotting him with my naked eye where he can't see into my soul so easily. He is sitting thirty feet off the ground, unperturbed by us humans down below.

I turn to Jake and gush, "Oh my gosh, he is so big. Just beautiful."

The owl's white feathers are radiant with fine black barring on the front and sides.

Suddenly the low murmur of voices rises, and Jake whispers, "He's taking off. Look."

I turn back to the spot; the owl has swooped off the barn and is heading towards us. On silent wings that absorb all sound, he crosses directly overhead, and I grab Jake's arm. *Magnificent.* I watch the owl fly until night swallows his shimmering white body.

I whisper, "I've never seen anything like that. Thank you so much. It was magical."

Jake grins. "Good thing you made us bolt out of Vee's, or else we would've missed it."

Still clutching his forearm, I feel the color rise in my cheeks, and I pull my hand back, thankful for the dark. Jake swings his arm around my shoulders in what I imagine a brother might do to a sister and gives me a quick squeeze. My embarrassment evaporates, but I can't stop thinking about how his corded arm felt under my fingers, smooth and strong.

Jake pulls away, but I still feel the length of him imprinted along my side. I shiver as I feel cold without him close. I need to stop this or else I might do something stupid like imagine *What would it be like to kiss him?*

We wander back towards Vee's place. Jake asks a few questions about how Vee is doing, and I ask how his teaching and thesis are going. Both are big stressors for him. Jake responds lightly to my inquiries, and we walk on with silences interspersed between our conversation.

"I can't believe I've lived here for all these years and never knew something so majestic and beautiful lived right next door." I muse.

"Oh no, this is a special year for snowy owls—an irruptive year," he says. "Normally they don't come down this far south."

Intrigued, I ask, "An irruptive year?"

"It means for some reason birds of a certain species or group move far from their normal range. Lack of food or some other unknown factor might cause these winter irruptions, but we are unsure. Most of the snowys that come down are juveniles like the one we saw tonight. Did you see the fine black bars on it?"

I nod; he gives me a smile of approval.

"Either way, it's a pretty rare and special event. Snowys haven't been here for years."

"Oh! That's why John Foster doesn't talk about snowys in my book. I couldn't figure that out, but now this explains it. He talks about other owls, like the northern saw-whet and barred, but not snowys."

I smile to myself at my mimicry of Jake's use of the term *snowys*, but he frowns and looks uncomfortable.

"Maybe we better try to find John Foster to tell him the news so he can update the bird bible."

I can hear the disdain in Jake's voice, but I'm able to ignore it as I'm still marveling at what I just experienced. Again, I picture the glowing owl flying directly over our heads.

When we're on the front steps of Vee's apartment building, I ask Jake if he wants to come up. He demurs politely. I suddenly feel he is farther away than just the three feet of space separating us.

He's already started walking away when he spins back around and calls out, "Oh hey, I almost forgot. These are for you." He strides back over to me, the pair of fancy binoculars in his hand.

I clap my hands against my cheeks in astonishment. "Really?"

"Yes."

"Why?"

"So, you can see more birds."

I laugh, "Yes, I know that—but why?"

Jake looks at me sternly and replies with pauses between each word, "So—you—can—see—more—birds."

I reach for them and look into his eyes. "Thank you. I was going to buy a pair, as I can finally afford them, but this is so unexpected and nice."

When our hands touch, Jake leans toward me and I think he may be going to kiss me, and I falter. Jake catches himself, folding my hand around the binoculars and says brusquely, "Enjoy."

He turns and marches away. I stand for a minute, watching him walk, confused, then glance at my very own Nikon binoculars.

Chapter 14:

Vogue

The following Wednesday, our dresses arrive, and we try them on. I twirl around the room, feeling like Cinderella. "Thank you, thank you, thank you."

Vee frowns, "I didn't buy it, the agency did. You can thank the agency if you want, but please stop thanking me."

"Okay," I acquiesce, though I know she's the one I owe my gratitude to. Changing the subject, I ask, "Does Jake know we're going to the party on Saturday?"

Vee, looking guilty, says, "He doesn't. He has enough to worry about. He's roped into going to his father's charity event with that dreadful Jessica, so he isn't a happy camper. We'll tell him all about it afterwards."

My heart drops and I have a hollowness in the pit of my stomach. Suddenly, I'm not as excited about our party as I was a minute ago.

She pauses and states more assuredly, "And then we can hear how wretched his party was, too. He really doesn't want to go with her. He's trying to keep the peace. His parents are really pushing him to get engaged, and he's okay with losing a battle here and there, as long as he doesn't lose the war. His words, of course, not mine. He doesn't want anything to do with that dead fish."

I smile, remembering the walk home after the dinner party. Feeling a little better, I drop my eyes to my dress, brushing my hands across the soft fabric. "Why Jessica?"

"Oh, no reason. She's just the most convenient and willing prospect. His parents would be happy with anyone, if it resulted in Jake settling down and stop focusing on his *hobbies* as they call his PhD work."

"Gosh, his PhD work doesn't seem like a hobby." I shake my head in disbelief. "They must be so proud he's going to be a doctor."

"Doctor, Shmoctor is what they think. All they want is for him to start working at his stepdad's investment firm. That's the actual goal, and they know someone like Jessica or really anyone will add more pressure to make that happen. The real money is in hedge fund management, and Jessica and most of *the women* want real money. It sucks for sure."

I ask, "*Stepdad*? Oliver is Jake's stepdad? I didn't know that."

"Yeah, his real dad died when he was young. Overdose—which is why Jake hates my . . . tendencies." She grimaces.

I take a moment to process all the revelations Vee just dumped on me. But my mind keeps getting stuck on "his parents would be happy with anyone." I plop down on the couch with a sigh. "Well, it can't be *anyone*. It can't be me. Can you imagine what they would say about that? Boy, they hated me."

Sitting down next to me, Vee looks me dead in the eye and says, "You hush up. They don't know what's good for them or Jake. It most certainly could be you. You are the nicest, most down-to-earth, sweetest person I know. If they didn't have their head up their bums, they would most definitely love you."

My face flushes crimson. I sounded like I was angling for praise, or even worse, that I revealed my secret crush. *Ugh! How stupid.*

With my cheeks burning, I fumble, "I meant they would never let Jake marry the little Polish girl from next door. They might let him marry another Jessica, but they won't let him marry just anyone."

For a long moment, we sit quietly. When I look back over at Vee, she is studying me in her puzzled, thoughtful way again, but this time her eyes are sparkling.

I respond with my usual, "What?"

"I think I have a crazy, wonderful idea." She pauses. "You *should* be the one to marry Jake. I mean, why not?"

"Are you crazy? I mean, Jake would never—" I search for words, "—I couldn't, he wouldn't."

Vee pats my knee absentmindedly. "You're probably right. I was just thinking it would be nice."

Saturday dawns bright and clear, with just the beginning chilly hint of the winter that is coming. Staring at the eighth that is circled on my calendar, I shiver slightly, even though the room is warm and cozy. I want to tell Vee I'm sick and can't go, but I know I can't.

The day crawls by until finally Vee announces dramatically, "Ready to transform? Remember, we are Cinderella, and we must get ready for the ball."

I force a giggle—until I notice how pale and drawn Vee is. My eyebrows knit together in concern. "Are you okay?"

"The show must go on," she responds brightly.

I watch her closely as we shimmy into our dresses. Then Vee drapes the makeup cape over my shoulders and I'm relieved when color dots her high cheekbones and her eyes flash when she twirls me toward the mirror. I resolve to keep a sharp eye on her all night.

As we approach the *Vogue* party, I'm busy doing my yoga ujjayi breathing, feeling both excitement and a bit of nauseous churn through my stomach. *God, just like high school all over again.* I give myself a shake and square my shoulders. *It is not like high school.* Glancing upward before we cross the threshold of the massive front doors of the building, I catch sight of the stars twinkling up in the sky. Smiling, I give a quick prayer of thanks, as I am truly *living*.

We find ourselves in the most impressive room I could ever imagine. The tall walls are splashed with large projections of red paint. The lights appear as bright stars high in the ceiling, but at our level, the muted light is more like twilight. Crystal glasses of champagne are floating around on silver platters, carried by servers who are wearing tuxedoes.

Vee spots Janet and starts weaving her way over to her, dragging me behind. On her way, she says *hi* and drops my hand to hug a bunch of lovely people who look as if they stepped right out of the glossy pages of the magazines Vee has lying around her place.

Glancing left and right, I notice that half the people look like ethereal beings who have dropped down from heaven and the other half look bored with an air of wealth dripping off them. My breathing is failing me completely and a wave of panic rolls through my stomach.

We finally reach Janet, who gives Vee a big hug and reaches for me, giving me a squeeze too.

Janet says offhandedly, "You look just lovely, Emma."

I nod and my panic subsides a bit solely because she remembered my name. She quirks an eyebrow and inclines her head to the left. Vee looks over in that direction and takes my arm, leading us along a slow and meandering path over to the left side of the ballroom. There are a bunch of models standing around chatting, and there are men who keep glancing at their phones as they flirt with the girls.

Vee exclaims enthusiastically, "Danny, it's great to see you. Where have you been hiding yourself?"

A smartly dressed, fiftyish man turns and beams. "Well, now the party can begin. Vee has arrived." He engulfs Vee into a hug.

Vee extracts herself and says brightly, "Danny, this is Emma."

He reaches out with both hands, enfolding my hands in his, and smiles. While his eyes don't look me up and down, I feel I'm being assessed. My smile wavers, but then I remember Vee's coaching for the party and for life. *Don't wear your emotions on your sleeve. Fake it and put a smile on even if you feel like crying inside and especially if you feel like slapping someone for their insolence.* The last one, she said in her fake English accent and left me in a fit of giggles. Confidence is key, she has told me over and over. So, I raise my eyes and stare directly into his shining brown eyes.

He expertly pulls me in for a hug and exclaims loudly, "Any friend of Vee's is a friend of mine." His hand brushes my lower back, and I stiffen.

I think I've passed some sort of test. Maybe Vee is right. I wonder if I had only been braver, maybe I would have had a friend or two in school.

Danny turns to the group and announces loudly, "Drinks for everyone. My two favorite party girls are here."

I turn to Vee and give her a questioning look. Is he talking about me and Vee? She smiles wanly and gives me a quick nod. A server appears from nowhere with a silver tray of champagne flutes.

Vee and I talked about this, and we have a plan. We hold the bubbly-filled glasses. We clink and cheer and pretend to sip from them. Our plan is to drop the full glasses surreptitiously on any empty tray or table we find. I worriedly told Vee people would notice such blatant waste, but Vee assured me no one would. Now, seeing the mayhem, I realize she was right. People are leaving half-finished glasses everywhere. Danny suddenly pulls a server aside, "Tequila, the best stuff, glasses for eight with the full set up." Just as the Tequila bottle is being delivered with a bunch of tiny glasses and bowls of limes and salt, Vee melts into the background, pulling me with her, and we move back toward the center of the party.

Vee whispers in my ear, "Well done. Now, we are working the room."

I sneak a few tiny sips of champagne each time we stop to say hi to a different group, as I can't stand the idea of wasting it. I love the feeling of liquid air sliding down my throat with the bubbles tickling my nose. Keeping an eye on Vee, I make sure she is sticking to our plan of no liquid allowed to pass through her lips.

Maybe because of the sips of magic bubbles or the repetition, but gradually, my shoulders relax, and I ease into the mindless chitchat, and then our choreographed disappearing act. Vee is in charge. As the evening wears on, I notice the strain around her eyes, like when the cameras have stolen a little too much out of her at one of her shoots.

A DJ starts playing music that just seems to have a pulse or a heartbeat and nothing else, and people are dancing in ways I never imagined. Some look as if they are taking part in some horrific exorcism right on the dance floor, while others look like they are having sex out there. I watch from the edge of the dance floor, mesmerized. Vee chats with yet another group, but I can't tear my eyes away from the dance floor.

Suddenly someone grabs me from behind and propels me forward, into the chaos. I try to turn around, but they are gripping my hips firmly in their hands and are steering me through the crowd, turning me in one direction and then the other, until we are right in the middle of the dance floor. I'm spun around and I stumble, tripped up by the sudden change in direction and my fancy shoes. Falling hard into someone's chest for a minute, I think it's Jake. Pulling back, I look up with a smile on my face, and I'm appalled at my error. Danny is leering at me and gyrating suggestively.

"Let's dance," he shouts over the din.

The music is even louder on the floor. I shake my head no, but he grabs one of my arms and pulls me toward him and then releases me. I stumble forward and back like a puppet on a string.

Remembering Vee's guidance, and really having no other choice, I stop fighting and lean into the motion. I can handle one dance; maybe this is all part of living. I try to copy the people dancing around us—not the ones doing the sex act, but the ones trying to expel the devil from their bodies. I feel ridiculous. Danny doesn't notice my discomfort. The music keeps pounding and I realize this is one of those times when time has slowed to a crawl, or this is the longest song ever. I sense a slight change in the beat, but it's hard to tell for sure. Maybe this is another song, and I won't ever get a chance to stop. The picture of Vee's disappearing act pops in my head. *God, I hope this works*. Doing some serious dance moves, I back up little by little as I flail my arms around. It's getting more crowded on the dance floor and when a large man in a suit gets between me and Danny, I backpedal as fast as I can, breaking through the border of the dance floor. I wipe a piece of hair clinging to my sweaty forehead, relieved that I am now back to the normal insanity.

Vee would be proud, I think—but looking around, I don't see her. I check my watch; it's midnight, which is the time we planned to leave. Damn, we didn't plan on being separated.

Heading toward the entryway, I dodge the crowd that is eating, drinking, gesturing, and talking way too loudly. Everyone looks crazed. I try to keep the panic that is building in me under control, but I can feel my face flushing red. I'm torn as I need to locate Vee, but I also have to pee really bad.

Making my way along the hallway off to the right of the entrance, I ask a server where the bathrooms are. He points in the direction I'm going. I spot a door with a large gold W on it. Pushing it open, I enter a marble castle and the fanciest bathroom I've ever seen. Attendants are handing out towels after handwashing and girls stand ready with makeup brushes to freshen up faces.

Not bothering to take any mental pictures of this marble oasis, instead I dart into a stall with a deep, dark-paneled door and quickly pee. Checking my watch again, it shows 12:30, and panic rises in my chest.

I quickly wash my hands and glancing in the mirror note that I look more like the other crazed attendees than I would like; feverish and agitated. I try to calm my features into a serene smile, but I'm not fooling anyone. Vee is right, I wear my feelings on my sleeve; I didn't believe her until now.

As I'm walking out of the bathroom, one of the other models I recognize from a photoshoot enters. I reach out my hand to stop her. “Brittany, have you seen Vee by any chance?”

She pauses, her eyes are unfocused, but she squints at me and says, “Vee . . . Ah, yes. She said she was leaving a while ago. I think she was looking for you. She told us if we see you to tell you she has left. You’re Emma, right?”

I nod my head in a quick jerk and my breath comes out in a whoosh.

“Thank you so much. I was so worried.”

Brittany smiles and wobbles past me.

Stepping out into the hallway, my limbs loosen with relief. I head to the coat check, remembering the fifty dollars Vee insisted I put in my coat pocket tonight. I think, *Thank god, I guess she knew things can happen at these parties.*

I’m thrilled I’ll be saying goodbye to this party soon. As I pass the men’s room, Danny bursts out of the door and takes one look at me and grabs me in a bear hug. This time, it doesn’t feel like Jake at all. He is squeezing me too tightly, and he smells sour.

He twirls around, still holding me pressed to his chest, and says with a touch of irritation, “Ah, there you are. I’ve been looking and looking for you. We’re now up on the second level, having our own private party.”

Releasing me from the bear hug, he keeps a firm grip on my wrist, pulling me towards a staircase that is the opposite direction from the exit. I try to protest, but he pays no attention. Glancing around frantically, I intuitively know I don’t want to go to any private party with Danny or anyone else, but he pulls me up the stairs.

As we approach the landing, I see the open doors leading to a dimly lit room. There are two security guards standing outside the open doors. Maybe Jake is right. Maybe I do know right from wrong. Because I know in my bones, it will be very wrong if I go through those doors. Reaching out with my free hand, I tug at Danny's arm to get him to stop.

"Danny, wait a minute. Let's spend a minute getting to know each other before we go in to the party." My voice quavers, but Danny doesn't notice.

He turns, his eyes glitter like shards of glass, "Yes, let's do that, little one."

He veers to the left and pulls me around a corner. I have absolutely no plan, but anything is better than going into a room with security guards at the door. I stumble a bit and fall into Danny's chest as he turns to face me. He seems to mistake it for a move, and suddenly I'm engulfed in a wet, sloppy kiss. His tongue slides into my mouth and I fight the urge to gag. Although I've never been kissed before, I'm sure no one would enjoy this kind of kiss. As his tongue continues to press and explore my mouth, I react without thinking, making a vicious twisting motion with my body and yanking myself away. Danny has his hands loosely around my shoulders and his back is leaning against the wall, so he isn't in a good position to make a grab for me and I take off running.

Danny explodes, "Bitch," as if I've done something to him. Running blindly back the way we came, I have no idea if he's coming after me. This is unbelievable. *Could someone maul or even rape me in the middle of a huge party like this?* My heart is pounding and I'm down the stairs in a flash. Should I stop at the coat check or just keep going? I look behind me, figuring if Danny is giving chase, I will leave the coat and the money—and I smash into a brick wall.

How did Danny get in front of me? I think frantically. *He must be some sort of devil.*

But then I hear a familiar voice and smell the citrusy, fresh scent I know so well.

It's Jake.

I collapse against him and cry out, "Thank God."

Jake looks down at me with alarm, concern showing in his deep-brown eyes.

"Please get me out of here." I gasp and a tear streaks down my cheek. I know more are going to follow.

He immediately hustles me toward the door, but I pull on his hand and ask, "Can we get my coat? I think I'm safe now."

Jake bursts out, "You *think* you're safe, Jesus Christ! What happened in there?"

He rushes over to the coat check with me still clutching his arm. Then we head outside, into the bracing air; it feels clean on my face, but I wipe my hand against my mouth to wipe away the feeling of Danny's vulgar kiss. I know Jake sees me do it; I'm grateful he doesn't say anything.

When we're in the taxi, though, he turns to me, tilting my face up to the light of the streetlights and demands, "What happened?"

Mortified, I plead, "Not now. I don't want to talk about it now. I just want to go home. I'll tell you tomorrow?"

Jake shakes his head, "No. It can't wait. I need to know if I need to kill someone or not."

Laughing a bit hysterically, "No, nothing like that. Well, except—I don't know, really. It was just awful. This guy Danny made me dance with him and when I left him, he found me later and wanted me to go to a private party room or something on the second floor. I had to escape him because I just knew I didn't want to go into that room. They had security guards, and I think the guards were there to keep people in, not out. Could that be true?"

"Yes, these parties get Vee in so much trouble." Jake shakes his head, "They are over the top in every way. You may not have made it out alive." He sees the horror in my eyes and quickly declares, "That's just an expression, but let's just say I'm glad you got away. Why the lip wiping?"

I shrug. "I don't want to talk about it."

Thankfully, he doesn't press.

"How did you know I was in trouble?"

"Vee called me on this really convenient thing called a cell phone."

This gets a feeble smile out of me.

"When she couldn't find you at midnight, she said she had had enough, so she asked if I would come and make sure you got home. I was at the Roosevelt down the block, at Oliver's charity event, and once I got over the shock of you both being at some party, I agreed to make sure you got home safe. I was there just to escort you home; I had no idea you were in danger. Vee never would have left if she thought you'd have any trouble."

I lean my head against the back of the taxi seat. I whisper a soft, "Thanks."

"Oh, I was glad to do it. The charity event was rubbish, and my so-called date was even worse. Ugh!"

I smile sinking into the darkness of the cab. The stress of the past hour eases ever so slightly. With my coat wrapped tightly around me, I feel warm and protected.

Chapter 15:

Vee

We exit the cab at Vee's building and climb the three flights of stairs. I can hardly wait to get my shoes off because my aching feet can't take it anymore.

"She must be in bed already." I say, noting Vee's closed door. "Give me a minute, I need to wash up and take these, um, damn shoes off." I head to my room, wanting to brush my teeth, too. My clock shows 1:45 a.m.

"Emma—hey, Emma." Jake calls with an edge to his voice.

I dart out of the bathroom with my toothbrush still in my hand. He's in the kitchen holding a partially empty bottle of vodka.

"Did you have some vodka before you went to the party?" he asks.

I shake my head, completely at a loss. "No! Absolutely not. That wasn't there when we left."

Jake strides down the hallway and calls Vee's name outside her closed door. The dots connect for me, and I rush behind him as he slowly opens the door. The lights are on in Vee's room, and she is lying face-down on her bed, still in her beautiful red mini-dress. There is a bottle of pills on her bedside table I've never seen before.

Jake gently turns her over, and her eyes flutter a little as if a bumblebee hummingbird is rapping against her lids, but they don't open. He gives her a rough shake, and she mumbles something—it's unintelligible, but at least it's a sound.

Jake reaches for his cell phone and punches in 911.

"933 Fifth Avenue apartment 3C," he says into the receiver, his face stricken. "Suspected overdose."

Time freezes.

Oh my God! I left Vee alone—I caused this.

We follow the ambulance to New York Presbyterian in a taxi, not exchanging a word. In the waiting room, we learn Vee is already inside somewhere and doctors are working on her. Finding the quietest corner of the waiting room, we settle in. My mind keeps repeating the same refrain, *This is all my fault. I killed Vee.* My heart is beating to the rhythm of those words.

As if Jake can read my mind, he states simply, "Vee will be all right. She's strong."

I notice idly that he is wearing the loveliest navy suit I've ever seen. It fits him like a glove. And the tie he's wearing is maroon and light-blue. I look down at my maroon dress; we look like we are a couple dressed to match perfectly in a very understated way. How much fun it would have been to go to the award ceremony with Jake instead of the awful *Vogue* party.

I ask quietly, "So, how was your party? I hope you didn't get lured into any secret party room."

Jake smiles tiredly. The gold usually sparking in his eyes is now dulled. "It was rubbish. It may have been as miserable as yours. I think I'm slowly but surely getting lured into the devil's den, and I don't see any way out."

I shake my head, mystified.

"I don't talk about this much, but Oliver is my stepdad. He adopted me when I was five and saved my mom, my sister, and me from ruin after my dad died. We were destitute—or at least as destitute as you can be with a luxury co-op and a house in the Hamptons." He lets out a grim chuckle. "I was young and I didn't really understand the whole situation, but when my dad died, he left my mom in tough financial shape. When she married Oliver, that saved us all. Oliver doesn't have any other kids, and he expects me to take over the family business—or at least start working there, so eventually I will take over. It's Henderson's Investment Fund, so trading of stocks and bonds. Shit, I hate. Shit, that fucking killed my father. But I may have to get over myself. My mom did what she had to do twenty-five years ago, and now it's my turn to pay the piper, so to speak." Jake inhales a deep breath and stares down at the floor. "They have a prenup: if Oliver ever divorces my mom, she won't get a thing. We have that always hanging over our heads."

Putting an arm tentatively around his shoulders, I probe, "That's an awful lot of pressure. But is it really up to you to give up your life for your family? You've been telling me how unfair it is of my parents to ask me to do that. Isn't this the same thing?"

Jake looks at me and with a little spark in his eye states, "Touché. I guess it's easier to give out such nice-sounding advice than it is to take it. My mom sacrificed a lot for me and Sandy. You've met Oliver. He's no picnic, and I know she doesn't love him, but she did what she had to do for us kids. Freakin' Sandy is a doctor, so she's out of the running."

"But you're going to be a doctor, too. So doesn't that protect you, too?"

"Ahh!" Jake snorts. "Sadly no. Wrong kind of doctor."

"How can it be the wrong kind of doctor? There is no such thing."

Jake shakes his head. "It doesn't matter. I can't be the person who gets my mother kicked out on the street. She can't survive without a staff, summers in the Hamptons, and her bridge club."

Silently, I consider this dilemma. Having money doesn't solve your problems like I thought it did. Miserable situations can trap you just as easily in a plush, beautiful apartment as in a dumpy, drab one. It seems the prenup and family obligations weigh Jake down just like the Jablonski legacy does me.

Sitting up a little straighter, Jake continues, "I just want to finish my doctorate and then I'll see what Henderson Investment has to offer. Maybe it won't be as bad as I think."

A doctor comes into the waiting room and asks, "Family of Veronica Mason?"

We stand and Jake replies, "Yes."

I'm silent, but the doctor doesn't seem to need another affirmative response.

"We've pumped her stomach. She has an IV in and is lightly sedated. You won't be able to see her until morning, but she'll be okay. So, go home, get some rest and come back tomorrow."

We are too relieved to thank him and instead do as instructed, numbly walking out of the hospital into the dark of the night.

It's 4:00 a.m. and I must be hallucinating from exhaustion, my focus is narrowed; while I'm bone-tired, I'm also so keyed up my body feels like it needs to go for a run or something.

"Do you want to walk back?" Jake asks. "It's only a couple blocks."

I nod; I'd agree to walk to Florida with him, if he asked. Together, we head down the sidewalk.

I stumble along like a sleepwalker, trying to keep a tight lid on my thoughts and not think about Vee and how I almost killed her. I will fall completely apart if I think about that.

Before I know it, we're at the apartment. Taking my key out of my bag, I open Vee's door. Every light is ablaze, making the apartment look like a police interrogation room. I hang up my coat and quickly make a circuit, turning off most of the lights. Jake is sitting on the couch with his head tilted all the way back against the couch, his eyes shut.

I walk over quietly, looking at the dark circles under his eyes and the curve of his cheek. He has a slight outline of a five o'clock shadow. I'm staring down at him when his eyes flicker open, and his hand reaches out to me, and I collapse onto him.

All it took was him raising his hand, and I lost all resistance. I wonder idly, *Have I been waiting for any sort of signal all this time? Or is it the sheer exhaustion that's letting my instincts take over?*

Our lips meet and there is both an urgency and a desperation in his kiss as Jake presses his mouth to mine. His arms pull me closer. The connection fills the emptiness of the apartment and the hollowness in my chest and keeps me from thinking about Vee in a hospital bed, all alone, hooked up to machines. Jake deftly flips me to one side and pushes my dress up around my waist. Cool air tickles my thighs and then his hand follows, caressing them, leaving a burning sensation as he slides his hand toward my waist. He tugs at my underwear, and I inhale sharply. Jake's eyes are unfocused, but with my inhalation, they sharpen, and he pulls back, working to pull my dress back down. He shifts a little to the right, opening a fraction of space between us. I feel emptiness from the sudden loss of connection between our bodies. A need or an ache I don't understand pushes me to lean towards him, reaching my hands around his neck, threading my fingers through his hair. The dull ache in my chest eases. I've wanted to touch his hair forever, and the feeling is excruciating. I lean in and kiss him, and a throbbing low in my gut starts to thrum against my insides.

Jake breathes against my mouth, "Can we go into your room?"

I can't speak, so just nod my head. He stands and reaches out to me again and I'm like a moth to a flame. Not understanding why, but knowing this is what I must do to survive not only this night but maybe my life.

Jake sits on my bed, drawing me between his legs. He turns me around and unzips my dress, slipping it off my shoulders. With a faint rustle, it drops to the floor. Stepping out of it, I stare down at the most expensive dress I've ever owned pooled on the floor. When I don't reach to straighten it and hang it up, I know unequivocally I've lost my grasp on reality. Looking up toward the heavens, I send a silent prayer asking for forgiveness and for it not to hurt too much. My lips quirk at the juxtaposition of my requests and I shiver—waiting to see if God demonstrates his lack of humor, right then and there.

When lightning doesn't strike, I meet Jake's eyes. He's been sitting perfectly still, waiting and watching me as if he knows I'm waiting for something. *He can't know*. His eyes are burning with something I've never seen before.

I smile timorously, and he tugs me down onto the bed next to him. Collapsing, the feelings coursing through my body roll over me like a strong wave. I've never felt so alive; every nerve ending is on fire. I've expanded into a real living, breathing person, someone that is no longer looking out through her shell, trying to find the secret portal that everyone else found easily years ago. I've finally found my way out.

Jake traces his fingers up my arm and a tingle follows the path he charts. He reaches around the nape of my neck and pulls me closer. When his lips touch mine, I'm lost. Something within me is leaning in, demanding more connection and it's hungry and demanding. I tangle my fingers into Jake's hair and fight the urge to pull hard. My mind disconnects, swept away into the feeling and longing surging through my body. I am liquid and the feelings flow like water within me. Contained but wild and powerful.

Jake lays me back and quickly unbuttons his dress shirt. Then he slips off his shoes and slides out of his pants, and I stare, mesmerized. Jake turns to me, and I feel my ragged breath rise and fall in my chest. He reaches behind me, unclasping my bra.

Jake's mouth explores my body, raining kisses down on spots I had no idea could be so sensitive. My body responds, no longer under my control. He stops his gentle assault, and I come back into my body for a moment and gaze into his eyes, suddenly worried as to why he stopped. His eyes fill with fervency as he looks at my body; it's how I imagine a starving man stares at a banquet. Running his hand lightly over my cheek, down my shoulder, then around my full breasts. Finally, tracing a trail down my stomach and below. Something I don't understand erupts within my body. It's as if a piano string is being plucked in my gut that is pulling and pulling.

"Ah, yes," I squeeze out, unbidden.

Jake rubs and teases and I feel the pressure mounting. Inhaling sharply, I'm arching and arching, opening myself as I've never imagined I would. Points of darkness appear when I close my eyes and then flash into a white light, the release is swift and wonderful. I lie back and my muscles melt into the bed. I watch as my hand rises, and I caress his smooth chest, I'm unsure who is guiding my hand. Tonight is the start of everything. He leans into me, angle his body over mine and I feel him pushing me apart.

My mind is slow to comprehend, and my body remains limp and pliant. I bite my lip suddenly worried as I connect what is happening, I think, *It's going to hurt, but I can't cry out. That wouldn't be right.* But my body is still not under my control, staying relaxed and willing. I'm stretched and stretched, I clamp my lips closed. *It's Jake. He won't hurt me unless he has to.* Jake moans, and I gaze into his face, his eyes are closed. He suddenly moves against me and pushes, and the pressure builds and then a flash of pain, and Jake slides out and then back. *My God, I'm going to be split in two.* He moves faster, and I thrash, unable to take anymore. He grabs my hip with one hand, and he drives into me over and over and then he freezes, and I feel his muscles convulse, and the pain is gone then he sinks down slowly and comes to rest by my side. I lie still, stunned.

I just made love for the first time, and it was amazing and strange and completely unexpected, but now I can't remember what I ever expected. Staring at Jake, he opens one eye, giving me a half smile and drapes a languid arm over my bare shoulder. He closes his eyes and falls asleep. I could never sleep; the next minute I'm opening my eyes to the harsh morning sunlight streaming through the window, and Jake is sleeping soundly next to me.

Chapter 16:

The Morning After

In the morning light, Jake appears peaceful. A wave of happiness bubbles up inside me. I have the urge to touch his cheek, but I don't dare. Last night I could, but this morning in the sun, I hesitate. Suddenly I remember—Vee. Clutching my stomach; it feels as if someone kicked me, and the walls are closing in. *How did I forget about Vee and the fact that I wasn't there when she needed me?* I again picture her all alone in a hospital, hooked up to every kind of machine.

How can my body hold two such distinct feelings simultaneously? An art lesson on the primary colors from long ago flashes through my head. I was yellow when I woke next to Jake but thinking about Vee, the color blue washes away the yellow or maybe mixes with it and that morphs into something completely new, a strange green, containing both happiness and horror but dulled and transformed into feelings that are nothing like the originals. Frowning, I drag myself stiffly out of bed.

My dress is laying on the floor like a dark stain, and I pick it up, draping it over a chair. *Phew!* My sanity is returning. I see the discarded wrapper on the ground, and I breathe another sigh of relief. *My God, I wasn't even thinking about that last night. Thank God Jake was.*

Grabbing my robe, I head to the bathroom. Things feel swollen and a little uncomfortable down there, but not too bad, considering. I close my eyes and lean against the sink for a moment, remembering Jake inside me, and a tingle runs from my toes to the top of my head. A little more of a hue of yellow takes over, shading the strange green that seems to be painting my bones a bright lime color. Quickly brushing my teeth and then dragging a comb through my hair, I take extra time to clean off last night's makeup. Staring at my bare face, I check to see if I look any different, now that I'm no longer a virgin. I tilt my chin this way and that, thinking I look more worldly and maybe like I'm part of this world a little more than I've been. My heart flips when I think about Jake sleeping in my bed right this minute.

Heading out of the bathroom, I float down the hall to the kitchen, starting Vee's fancy coffee machine and the hot pot for my tea water. When they are both ready, I load up a tray and head back to the bedroom. Jake is awake and is standing next to the bed in his underwear. He is staring at me with a look of horror, or is it revulsion? I'm not sure which. *Oh God, he remembers what I let happen to Vee. It is my fault.* My smile falters and the tray almost slips from my shaking hands. I quickly set it down on the bureau.

He spits out, "You were a virgin!" He snaps the top sheet, and I see the red streak on the bedding.

My hands fly up to my cheeks and I feel the rush of heat. The green within me that I thought was bad, disappears into black, an empty, hollow black. When you mix too many colors you kill all of them to become a dead black. I'm unable to formulate a response.

"Why didn't you tell me?"

I stare at him numbly.

He whips the sheet back into place and comes toward me, "Why didn't you tell me?"

I put up a hand, not sure if it is to ward off his anger or to touch the glass wall that is reemerging and encasing me. Shaking my head, I expected Jake to be angry with me over Vee, but this is a shock. Was I supposed to tell him *that?* Last night just happened so fast. I try to think when I could have squeezed it in. We never talked about sex before. Vee knew I was a virgin, but I couldn't imagine telling Jake something like that, at least not until now. But these thoughts that are a torrent in my head get stuck in my throat. I continue to stare at him mutely.

"You should have said something," he mutters,

When? When was the right time to bring it up? I'm getting angry as I consider the ridiculousness of his statement.

Just as I feel my voice returning and I'm ready to start asking questions of my own, Jake's cell rings. He reaches down for his pants and finds his phone in the pocket.

"Hello, yes, this is Jake. Oh great, can we come visit her this morning? Okay, yep, we will. Thanks for calling."

I look at him expectantly.

"We can go visit Vee at ten today," He pauses. "Umm, if you want."

I state hollowly, "Of course I want to. Your coffee is over there. I need to shower."

Jake stiffens. Realizing it sounds harsh, like I need to wash away last night, I stammer, "That isn't what I meant at all—"

"Yep, and I need to go home and get clothes and stuff," he cuts in tonelessly. "Let's meet at the hospital at ten, okay?"

I nod.

"Do you need directions?"

I shake my head, once again the words are stuck in my tight throat.

He pulls on his dress pants and shirt from last night and drapes his suit jacket and tie over his arm. I watch him, fidgeting with the tie to my ratty robe, standing awkwardly. The gulf between us widens, and I shrink back into the sliver of the world I normally occupy. He turns to me and looks like he is going to say something, but turns on his heel and walks out of the room.

I hear the apartment door click shortly after, and I collapse onto the bed.

My jumbled thoughts flow like a mad river current. *Why was he mad I was a virgin? Perhaps I did it all wrong last night, and that's why he's angry. Dammit. I really liked it.* The fact that Jake hated it is a punch to my gut. I can't imagine it could get any better than what he did with hands and his mouth. *But what do I know—I'm just a virgin.*

Quickly, I correct myself: *I* was *just a virgin.* My fingers trace a circle on the bedspread, and I relax into the softness. I remember watching a monarch butterfly emerge from a cocoon at the Museum of Natural History one summer, and I thought *that* was a miracle. Even Jake and his anger can't take away the magic of last night.

After I shower, with my leggings and sweater back on, I feel a little more even-keeled. The maroon dress draped limply over the chair doesn't look magical but I hesitate to touch it. A picture of Danny flashes through my mind and I taste the sourness of his kiss. This dress cast some sort of crazy spell on people last night. First, Danny, then Jake, after all this time, finally showing interest—only for it to be ruined when he saw me in the morning out of the bewitching dress. Staring at the offending dress, I wonder if I should ever wear it again.

I quickly head out the door, and as I retrace our steps from last night, I replay the night in my head. The ups and downs leave me dizzy. *Is this really what I wished for?* In the magic of the dark, I thought my guardian angel was looking out for me and answering my prayers, but now, in the bright morning sun, it was just a cruel joke. No angel was answer-ing my prayers, quite the opposite. Fate is teaching me a lesson—to be careful what you wish for. I wished for a life and a life doesn't mean you get just the good things. Life holds equal parts joy and sadness. No one gets the good without the bad. Turns out having no life at all may be better than what happened. Touching my finger to my lips, I wonder if that is true.

As I approach the hospital, I see Jake in the emergency room entrance. The wool jacket stretches tight across his broad shoulders. Staring, I remember raking my fingers across his back. When I see his face, he looks pensive and a bit sad. Remembering the anguish of this place last night, I approach cautiously.

"She's been moved to the fifth floor," he says blandly, "so we need to go around to the main entrance."

We walk side by side but with a good bit of space between us. I feel a vibration thrum between us, and I have a new consciousness of his body despite the space. I shake my head, trying to dispel my fanciful imaginings.

Approaching the main visitor desk, Jake states in a hushed tone, "We're here to visit Veronica Mason."

The attendant consults a computer screen and responds crisply, "Only one visitor allowed at a time on the fifth floor."

I look at Jake questioningly, and he tilts his head toward the sign on the wall. I scan it, 5th floor—Psychiatric Ward. A chill runs up my spine.

He seems to sense my nervousness. "I can go first and get the lay of the land and tell you about it when I get back. It won't be like the movies, I'm sure."

I haven't seen any movies about such places, but I nod my head quickly.

Jake heads down the hall toward the elevator, and I sit in the large waiting room. A TV is on in the corner, and I watch it but nothing registers.

Jake returns, flushed, and doesn't look me in the eye. "She seems good, and the place is pretty nice," he reports. "She has her own room. No crazies hanging around that I can see."

I shush him. "Don't say that. That isn't nice."

Looking sheepish, he says, "She wants to see you."

Vee is in room 525, sitting on her bed with a smile on her pale face. She starts in a rush, "Come in, come in. I'm so sorry I left you at the party."

"What?" I can't believe *she's* apologizing to *me*. "No, that was fine. I'm so sorry you had to go home by yourself. I should have been there. I totally messed up."

Vee clasps my hands in hers, looking much wiser than her twenty-one years. "There was nothing you could have done, Emma. If you were there, I would have just done it when we went to bed. It's been building for a while, and I knew there was no stopping it. It's like watching a movie I already know the ending to. I can only pause the movie to delay the inevitable for so long. I can't keep pushing pause forever; the ending is eventually going to come. The ending came last night."

I sit down on the edge of the bed. "You seemed okay to me. I mean, some days you couldn't do your sun salutations but other than that—"

Vee smiles thinly. "It's all a bit of a show. I can put up a good front—until I can't."

I sniffle. *This is all my fault. I should have been able to see the pain Vee was in. Why couldn't I see it? That was my one job. I got caught up in living my life and forgot I wasn't the only player in this little story, and, in fact, I was a nobody in this story. How could I have failed so miserably? Probably this is why Jake was so sickened after having sex with me. He remembered this was all my fault. God, he probably thinks I deceived him into sex when he was distraught and not thinking clearly. Maybe I did. It is what I've wanted. When did I become so self-centered? I don't blame Jake for being unable to look at me this morning. I make myself sick, too.* The weight of the Jablonski's sacrifices suffocates me, pinning me to the mattress, constricting my breath. What an embarrassment to the family name.

Vee is silently watching me, letting me run through my internal gyrations.

A tear escapes from my eye, and I brush it away. "I'm so sorry." I'm not sure if I'm talking to Vee or all my dead ancestors.

Vee is the only one that answers. "I told you; this is not your fault. Don't blame yourself for a minute. Our time together is what has made life bearable lately and that is why I lasted as long as I did. I just can't seem to find meaning in life without drinking or doing drugs, and I really need to figure out why or else this is going to keep happening. I need to get off this merry-go-round once and for all. So, I decided this morning, I'm going home for a while. Jackson has a great rehab place, close to home. I need to fix things with my mom and get my issues out on the table. I'm tired of hiding everything."

"Wow," I say, trying to take in all this new information. "Okay. What can I do to help?"

Vee laughs. "Well, first you need to tell me what the heck happened last night. Jake is very cagey about, well, *everything.* And now that I really look at you, you look guilty and weird, too. Or, as my momma would say, 'You look as nervous as a cat in a room full of rockers.'"

Shaking my head in confusion at the expression, my cheeks burn, and I look down at my hands in my lap, clenched into tight fists. Vee takes my chin in her hand and raises my face to look at her. I meet her eyes and try valiantly to keep my features calm, but my blush deepens, and I drop my eyes. I know I'm wearing my emotions on my sleeve again, but I can't mask the hurt and embarrassment of this morning.

Holding her gaze steady, she let out a loud, "No way."

I cover my face with my hands, even more embarrassed, if that's possible. Vee gently takes my hands away and says softly, "Come on, Emma. It can't be that awful. If it's what I'm guessing, it's good news."

Shaking my head, I don't look up.

"Emma, come on," she whispers. "I'm piecing together that something happened between y'all. Tell me what happened, and I can let you know if it is really anything you need to repent to your God." Vee pleads.

Looking up at Vee in surprise, more guilt washes over me. *How did I forget about the huge sin I committed?* I make the sign of the cross, wondering why I haven't been struck by lightning yet. I must go to church this Sunday and make reparations.

"Okay, did you have sex?" Vee smiles tentatively, "That's really okay."

"He didn't like it and got mad because I was a virgin," I whisper. "It was awful—I mean it wasn't awful, at least *I* didn't think it was. I thought it was great, but this morning was awful."

Taking my hands in hers, Vee rubs them absentmindedly. "This is cool. So cool. I can't believe Jake is angry at you. He didn't seem angry when we just talked. He did seem weird and off, but not angry." She squeezes my hands. "Listen. He can't be too mad. Wait until you hear my idea and don't worry, he thinks it's a great one. Well, he may not have called it great. But give him time. You both will come to love it."

Glancing up, I ask, "Your idea?"

"Well, you know Jake is really miserable, right? Living with Oliver and Carol. They're really pressuring him to settle down with someone like that dead fish, Jessica. Ugh!—and start working in the firm—double Ugh! He just wants some peace and quiet to finish his thesis in the next three months. Then he's either running off to some safari or he'll join the firm. When you and I talked about how you were a perfect marriage candidate, it got me thinking. I told Jake our idea the other day and—"

"What?" I spring off the bed and start pacing back and forth. My arms tightly clamped round my chest. "You didn't! That isn't—"

"Okay, calm down. That isn't what I told him. I'm just messing with you." She hits my arm playfully and gives me a smirk. "But I did tell him he *should* get engaged to you."

"You didn't," I hiss.

"Calm down and come back and sit down." Vee gestures toward the spot I had vacated. I sit down as tense as an over-wound toy. "This way, he can get the peace and quiet he needs for the next couple of months. He can move into my place with you and his parents will stop pushing that awful Jessica on him. He can finish his thesis and decide his fate in March. Jake loves the idea."

I gape at Vee. "I don't believe it. What are you saying?"

"What part didn't you understand?" she retorts. "This is really your idea. Remember, after the dinner party, you asked, *Why can't Jake get engaged to me?*"

I blush ferociously and sputter, "That is not what I said. I said it *couldn't* be me."

Vee laughs—this time it is a full snort—and wraps her arm around my shoulders. "I'm just teasing ya. I know you didn't say that. It's just that you always talk about trying to live a little or a lot until March. I have no idea why March, but it fits perfectly with Jake's plans. In four months, he is either throwing off the shackles of his family or he'll join and die a slow death at Henderson Investment. Either way, he needs the next four months of no pressure from his parents and no fix-ups with Jessica or any other Jessica sort. So, a pretend engagement will work perfectly for both of you. I did say it would be a pretend engagement, right? This way he finishes his thesis, and you don't have to move back home yet. It is like it was meant to be."

I stand and start pacing. I'm speechless. It sounds almost reasonable when Vee describes it, but it's the craziest, stupidest thing I've ever heard. I open my mouth and then close it again. I can't believe after last night and this morning, Jake would agree to any such thing. A fake engagement. That only happens in my romance books I read sometimes. I chew my lip. He hated me this morning. Nothing makes sense.

Vee rushes on, "And I know you are religious and all that—an engagement these days makes it okay with the church, right? They've moved into the twenty-first century, right?"

I shake my head.

"Really!" Vee insists. "Come on, an engagement does the trick."

"Not a *fake* engagement," I shoot back.

"Put that right out of your mind. No one knows if it's real or not." She nods vigorously. "Yes, go with that. It *is* real, because who knows what can happen?"

I respond indignantly, "God knows. But even if he is okay with it, I can't believe Jake would go along with this. Not after . . ." I trail off, unable to speak the words.

Vee pats my hand. "Let me talk to him and see what I can figure out. Guys can be really weird about the whole virgin thing. He seemed fine with the plan when we talked, but I'll make sure it isn't going to be a problem. When I came up with my plan, I figured you guys would just continue to be good friends. Of course, I had my hopes . . . but this new wrinkle needs to be figured out. It adds a little complexity, for sure. Give me a day or two to make sure this is as brilliant a plan as I think it is."

I shake my head, incredulous that I'm considering agreeing to Vee's harebrained plan.

Chapter 17:

The Engagement

After leaving Vee's bright sunny room, I approach Jake in the waiting area, unable to meet his gaze. My cheeks are burning.

"I'm going to visit my parents," I mumble. "Vee wants to see you again if you have a minute."

Without waiting for a response, I dart into the elevator bank, eager to escape. Stumbling out into the fall sunshine, I head toward Central Park. Gulping in the crisp air, trying to breathe. I watch a leaf seesawing gently down to the ground, and my shoulders soften and my mind quiets. Suddenly, I'm certain I'll join Jake in this crazy plan if he agrees.

I questioned the existence of my guardian angel just this morning, but I realize they must still be watching over me as they handed me my next four months on a silver platter.

This is not the time to shrink back into my shell. At least not yet. Excitement races down my spine, I feel taller than my five foot two.

After a friendly visit with my mom and babcia, I make one stop on the way back to Vee's: purchasing a cell phone. Vee may not blame me, but it's certainly my fault we couldn't find each other at the party. If I had a phone, Vee could have reached me last night when she needed me the most. That will never happen again.

The next morning, I unplug my new shiny phone from the charger and turn it on. I feel invincible when I figure out how to google the hospital to get their phone number.

"Hello, room 525 please." I say.

"Hello."

"Hi Vee. It's me . . . Em. Guess what?"

"Uh-huh, let's see. Did you have sex again?"

"Oh, my god. No! Now you've ruined my surprise!" I harrumph. "I'm calling on my new cell phone. Let me give you the number so you can call me anytime."

"Oh, that is cool. Very nice Em. I just was thinking about how I'll miss our late-night conversations when I head to Jackson. But now I can call you whenever I want to hear your sweet voice." Vee lowers her voice to a whisper. "Just to let you know, Jake is totally still into the plan."

"The plan?" I ask hesitantly.

"Yes, the plan, silly goose. The engagement and moving in and stuff."

Staring at the phone, I struggle to register what Vee just said, but my mind has completely seized up. My calm and rational decision to agree to the plan yesterday has completely vanished, replaced by a tangled mess of nerves that's on the verge of unleashing tears at the mere thought of Vee's ridiculous plan.

"Are you still there? Did you hear me?"

"Yes. I'm here." My voice catches. "I'm not sure what to say or do. Why would he want to do a fake engagement? It all seems crazy, doesn't it?"

"It isn't crazy at all. It's brilliant. You know kill two birds with one stone and all—"

I cut her off, "You know I can't stand that expression."

"Oh right, I forgot." I hear a smile through the phone. "You and Jake are perfect for each other."

Perfect for each other echoes in my ears.

Vee remains in the hospital for one more day. Jake picks her up and brings her to the apartment.

The second she walks through the door, I hug and hold her tight, whispering, "I'm so, so sorry."

She grips me back and whispers fiercely, "Emma, listen to me. You actually may have saved me. This experience made me realize I needed to get clean for good. Stop being a goose and help me figure out what one packs for a stint in rehab."

We all laugh, and the somber mood in the room lightens.

"Come along," she says lightly and leads us to her room.

I watch her as she slowly packs; she looks tired and scared, but the hollowness behind her eyes is gone and in its place is a hint of a spark of determination. She almost seems relaxed.

When her single large bag is full to the brim, Jake carries it downstairs for her and we hail a cab for the airport. She'll fly straight to Jackson, Mississippi, and her parents will meet her there to drive her to the Jackson Rehabilitation Center.

The three of us squeeze into the back of the cab with Vee in the middle. She smiles at each of us. She has brokered our *deal*, and we will be starting *the plan* once she leaves.

Glancing at Jake and with a whine in her voice, Vee begs, "You need to promise to call me with details when you drop the bomb on Carol and Oliver."

Jake coughs uncomfortably.

"Come on. Do it just like I laid out. At dinner at your parents', get down on one knee and pop the question. Oh, I just wish I could be there."

Shaking his head, Jake fires back, "Absolutely not. We will go over there with the story already concocted and Emma will have the ring on her finger. God, in front of my parents? You are truly nuts."

Watching Vee and Jake argue back and forth, I can't remember what made me agree to this insanity. Perspiration drips down my side, and I cross my arms, wedging my hands under each armpit.

Vee turns to me and notes my posture, as I'm trying to disappear into the seat. She tugs at one of my arms, looking way too happy for someone heading to rehab. "I have a gift for you that you must promise you will use," she says.

I reply, mystified, "I'm sure I will use it; I never waste a thing. What is it?"

"I got you a four-month pass to Asana. Promise me you'll go."

I clap my hand over my mouth. "You didn't."

"I did."

"Oh, that's so nice . . . but I can't go without you."

Vee tuts, "You are getting pretty good, and you know you really love it."

I incline my head sheepishly, "I do think I kinda like it sometimes."

Vee smirks. "I knew all your complaining was just a big show. Now try to go at least three times a week, and you'll be a pro in no time."

Jake snorts and we both turn to him. He mutters something about yoga instructors and then he shifts in his seat, looking chagrined, and stares out the window.

The taxi pulls up to JFK, and we hustle out, taking turns giving Vee hugs. She tears up as we say our goodbyes. As soon as I see her tears, the waterworks start flowing from me, and soon I'm a mess, blowing my nose and wiping my eyes.

Jake and I jump back into the taxi, and we watch Vee strut into the airport. She looks tall and strong. She turns at the automatic doors and gives us a jaunty wave.

On the drive back, I silently chew my lip, making sure our shoulders don't touch when we take a turn. We haven't been alone or talked since *that* morning and the tension between us makes my stomach cramp. A picture flashes before my eyes of me in the stiff dining room with a fake ring on my finger, and Jake's parents' cold eyes staring at the ring in horror. I shudder.

Jake takes my hand and gives it a squeeze. It's the first time we have touched each other since . . .

A shiver shoots right through me, and I pull my hand away.

Jake asks quietly, "How do you want to be proposed to?"

I shake my head, "I have no idea. I've never thought about it."

"Aww come on, all girls dream of this and have their perfect proposal all planned out in their head."

"Nope, not me," I say firmly. "Maybe if it was remotely possible, I may have started spinning scenarios—but with no prospects, I never saw the point."

Jake nudges me. "No prospects, that can't be true. There must have been some boys at the bakery that wanted to butter that roll . . ."

My cheeks heat up as I picture the red smear on the sheet.

"Sorry, that was kind of crass. I don't know why I even said that. Dammit, I'm a little nervous."

I look up sharply to see if he is making fun of my bundle of nerves. His cheeks are a little flushed. I manage to reply evenly, "No problem."

He regains his composure. "Leave it to me. I will plan the perfect surprise, fake proposal."

I try to smile. "It just can't be Vee's idea. Please make it just the two of us. I'm an awful actress, so no audience, please."

Jake's lips twitch, and he leans back appearing to be pondering possible proposals.

Two days later, my new cell phone rings and breathless I pick it up.

"Hello."

"Hi, guess what?" Without waiting for an answer, Jake continues, "I heard there's a Cooper's hawk in the Ramble. I thought we could go and see if we can spot it. It's a recent arrival that will likely spend the winter."

I clap my free hand to my mouth. "Oh, how exciting, I've never seen one before." I pause and continue. "I can meet you there in fifteen minutes. I was going to visit my mother and my babcia this afternoon, so this will be on the way."

Grabbing my coat, I fly out the door, only to come to a screeching halt and rush back into the apartment. I sit at Vee's little vanity with a mirror and cute mini-chair, trying to apply a little makeup artfully and quickly without Vee's supervision.

When I finish, I inspect myself in the mirror; I think I've done a pretty good job, although my cheeks barely need any added blush as they already are pink with excitement.

Time to go! I remind myself, and I fly out the door.

Spotting Jake with binoculars in hand, I think, *I'm such an idiot. I forgot to bring along my binoculars.*

I get closer and stamp my foot in exasperation. "I forgot your special gift. I just flew out the door." I turn bright red, recalling how I had enough time to put on makeup but didn't have enough wherewithal to bring the one thing I needed.

Jake smiles pleasantly and takes the strap from over his head and places his binoculars in my hands, putting the strap securely over my head. "Well then it's a good thing I brought these, isn't it?"

I quickly recover my excitement and put the bins to my eyes and breathe, "Okay, have you spotted it?"

There is silence. I take the binoculars down and look to my left—Jake is gone.

I hear a sound and look down; he's on one knee and holding something in his hand up towards me. I tilt my head and peer down at him. Then I pull back in confusion and shock. It's a delicate ring that looks like a diamond.

"Emma," he says, "will you get engaged to me for the next four months?"

I blush a red-hot crimson and tears threaten to spill down my cheeks. I can't believe it; I can't believe any of it. This is so special and awful all at the same time.

I choke out, "You idiot! What are you doing?"

Jake calmly gets up and replies, "We need to do this properly, and I thought what better place than your favorite spot in New York."

I look around; we are right near my favorite bench in the middle of the Ramble. I ask with a pout, "So, no Cooper's hawk? No lifer?"

Jake explodes with a laugh, "Sorry. No Cooper's hawk. I tried, but he wouldn't cooperate."

I look around again and remember watching couples holding hands and cuddling and being so envious. It's right here that I used to watch the world go by. I admit to myself that this is exactly how I would have wanted my real proposal to be.

Sighing, I ask, "How did you know this is my favorite spot?"

Jake suddenly looks a little sheepish. "I've seen you here over the years, so I figured you liked it."

"You have? I've never seen you."

Jake shrugs. "Try it on. It's the ring my dad gave my mom when they were still pretty poor, so it isn't much, but I always liked it. It's certainly better than the huge bauble my mom has now from Oliver. We can get it adjusted."

I slide it on my finger; it fits perfectly. I flash it at Jake, and he smiles.

"Does your mom know what you are doing with it?"

Jake kicks the ground with his foot and admits, "Not really. She gave me the ring years ago—I think in case I might need to sell it someday, if she and Oliver fell apart or he kicked me out."

Holding my hand out, I stare at the delicate band with the perfect, oval-shaped, sparkling diamond. It is perfect. I clutch my hand to my chest and ask hesitantly, "Do we have to tell your parents now?"

Jake shakes his head. "We don't have to yet. We just needed a story of where and when I popped the question. So, we can tell them it when we are ready."

I nod relieved.

Jake responds lightly, "But pretty soon, I've got to get out of the pressure cooker, or I may explode all over their lovely rug and walls."

I'm still reeling from what's just transpired, but I can't shake my anxiety over the next step in our ruse. *Why did I ever agree to this?*

I clench my fists and swallow the lump in my throat. "I'm going to visit my mom and grandmother right now, like I said. Do you want to practice on them—tell them and see how it goes? I feel bad about the—the whole thing, but I've got to tell them something about losing my personal assistant job and see if they need me back at the bakery. We could tell them everything all at once."

This way, we will be able to tell my mother without my father there. This will give my father some time to adjust to the idea of a pending marriage—especially to the dreaded Jake. My stomach clenches. I'm not sure if I'm more jittery about my dad's reaction or about being engaged to Jake.

Jake frowns. "You aren't going back to the bakery, are you? They don't pay you, remember? Maybe you could get a different job. You know, one that pays."

I shrug. I have almost $5,000 saved from my month of working for Vee so I'm rich beyond belief.

Jake tugs at my arm and leads me over to my bench. I go willingly, as I've always wanted to sit there with someone. We're both silent for a few minutes—a nice, comfortable silence. I lean back and relax. Then I hear the familiar song of a robin, and I relax even more.

Finally, Jake turns to me. "Maybe you could apply for a job at Columbia. They always have openings for some low-paid assistant to a professor or something like that."

I straighten up, frowning. "No, I'm not qualified for anything like that."

"You are much more qualified than some student who's doing it for the money or for the resume-building," Jake says. "You're a hard worker, and I may know a professor who is looking for an assistant. Not a teaching assistant, but for a study that needs someone to help with the organizing and tracking. I'll ask him about it and see if it's still open. If it is, I'll recommend you. Honestly, you would be perfect."

"Jake, I couldn't," I protest. "You couldn't. I won't know what to do."

Jake leans back with a satisfied smile on his face. "You will be perfect. More than perfect. Remember how worried you were about figuring out how to be a personal assistant? And you were fantastic."

Until I wasn't and then look what happened.

Jake jumps up. "Let's do it!" he exclaims. "Let's tell your parents."

He puts out his hand and pulls me to stand. "Come on, this will be the easy one."

His enthusiasm is infectious. As we walk to 933 Fifth Avenue, I practically bounce down the street. My earlier nerves are almost completely gone.

Chapter 18:

Testing the Waters

Softly knocking, I use my key to enter the apartment, followed by Jake. I cringe as the smell of onions and garlic that has seeped into the curtains and furniture from fifty years of Polish cooking hits us. I only noticed the smell once I moved out, and now when I drop by to visit, I realize how pervasive it is.

Walking ahead of Jake, I head down the hallway and into the kitchen. My mother is sitting at the old Formica table with her walker nearby. She is sipping a mug of tea.

I say tentatively, "Hi, Mama. How are you doing?"

My mom looks up and smiles, then her eyes slide past me and register surprise at seeing someone else. I try to say something, but all the words turn to dust in my mouth. Jake steps forward with his hand outstretched and reaches for my mother's hand.

"Mrs. Jablonski, I'm Jake. We've been neighbors for years. I'm so glad to meet you finally."

My mother recovers and straightens up. "Yes, nice to meet you, too."

I usher Jake to a seat across from my mother and pull up the chair next to her.

"Mama, we just got engaged, and we ran right over here to tell you first. Jake surprised me completely, hmm, in the park." I slip my hand out of my pocket and hold it out to her. "Isn't it lovely?"

She takes hold of my hand, and I feel a slight tremor. She peers at the ring and then at me. "Emma, what a surprise," she whispers.

"I know. It all happened so fast. Jake is Veronica's cousin and when I started working for her, we saw a lot of each other," I blurt. "We started dating a while ago and it just happened so fast, but I'm really happy."

I'm not sure what is true and what isn't, and it all flows out as naturally as rain. Jake takes over the conversation, telling my mother about his teaching position at Columbia and how he is working on his PhD dissertation. I'm not sure my mother understands much of what he shares, but she listens intently and nods at all the right times.

She pats his hand when he finishes. "Ahh, you take good care of my Emma, won't you?"

I look sharply at my mother. Calling me *my Emma* is the most endearing thing she has ever said. Amazing. All it took was a fake engagement.

Standing, I announce, "I'm going to go show Babcia."

Jake starts to get up, but I shake my head. "No, please. You stay."

He settles back into the hard chair obediently.

I walk to Babcia's room and fumble through the story of my engagement again. When I'm done, she says, "Well, good for you. About time you did something for yourself."

While her comment is not as sweet as my mother's, it's even more surprising.

Stepping back into the kitchen, I glance at our wall clock. It's almost 4:00 p.m. and my father could be home anytime.

"We have to run," I say in a rush.

Jake pops up out of his chair.

My mother looks disappointed, but states evenly, "I will tell your papa. Congratulations to both of you."

Out on Fifth Avenue, I'm giddy with my audacity and my ring. But I slow and my shoulders slump. I shouldn't be gloating about lying to my parents and the world. Sending a quick prayer of forgiveness up toward the heavens, I glance furtively down the street for my father. Relieved that I don't see him, I hurry Jake toward the park anyway, knowing my father never uses my shortcut.

"And you said you couldn't act." He laughs. "You were marvelous."

A surge of pride swells in my chest despite my best efforts to contain it. Lying is nothing one should be proud of, but I practically skip back to Vee's. As we approach her apartment door, Jake is still next to me and suddenly the ring feels like a weight on my finger and my palms get clammy.

Jake, as always, senses my nervousness. "I'm just walking my fiancée safely home," he says lightly. "I have class in a few minutes, so I'll see you tomorrow, okay?"

Equal measures of relief and disappointment course through me.

Turning quickly, I impulsively say, "If you need to do work or stuff, you can come here after class . . ." I rush on, "I can make you pierogies or naleski or even pasta."

Jake pauses for a minute. "Make it pierogies and you have yourself a deal."

I laugh and he turns, striding quickly away.

The pierogies are sizzling in the pan when Jake knocks, even though I know he has a key, and I rush to let him in.

He inhales dramatically, "Oh, I've been waiting all class for this. I almost dismissed them early today."

Serving up the pierogies with sour cream onto a plate, I pull a beer from the fridge—I ran to get some after he agreed to come for dinner—and open it for him. He smiles appreciatively, lets out a satisfied sigh, and quickly works his way through six pierogies, then spreads some papers on the breakfast nook and starts working with another beer nearby.

After I clean up, I wander through the apartment, unsure of what to do. Jake has his computer out and I hear the whirl of the printer hidden in Vee's bookcase kick in.

Jake gets up and collects the handful of papers that were just spit out from the printer and hands them to me. He beams. "Your application for the job at Columbia. Fill it out, and I'll hand deliver it to Professor Montgomery tomorrow. I already talked to him. Turns out he just let go another assistant in a long line of assistants, and he is willing to hire anyone at this point." He slaps a hand over his mouth. "Oh, that didn't come out right. He is willing to hire *you*. He's tough but fair. It really is the assistants who have been awful."

I hesitate, then take the papers and head off to find a pen. If I've learned anything these past months, it's that living is scary, and I need to face those fears because time is marching on. In just over four months, there won't be any more fears to face, only boredom. Oh, except for MS. So, maybe there will be a *few* scary things to face.

As I work through the application, I pepper Jake with questions, mainly regarding what address I should use—Vee's or my old one—and what I should say about college, as all I have are a bunch of community college courses taken over the years.

Jake is thrilled when I tell him I've taken a basic Excel course, as he says that will be really helpful.

Staring at the completed application, I'm not sure what I'm feeling. My stomach is unsettled, and a knot of anxiety settles in the pit of it.

"Remember how nervous you were for Vee's job?" Jake nudges me. "How many times did you ask us, *what does a personal assistant do?*" He chuckles and continues, "You survived and even thrived."

I stretch out my tense neck muscles, twisting my head and shoulders to loosen them, trying to smile confidently. I did figure out how to be a personal assistant. And if I were to believe Vee, I didn't mess it all up at the end; according to her, I may have even helped. Just the other day on the phone she said, "I'm where I should be, and I have you to thank for that. Not because you are to blame for my issues, but because having you as a friend showed me life is not that complex if you approach it honestly and openly."

Handing Jake the papers, my fingers graze his open palm. I glance up and catch a look of surprise in Jake's eyes, like he forgot all about our recent indiscretion and my touch suddenly raised it from his subconscious. A rush of blush stains my cheeks as I remember the morning after and how repulsed he was. I yank my hand back quickly, and he has to make a mad grab for the last of the papers when I do.

Jake continues to work for another hour on the papers he has spread out. I glance at them; they are complex spreadsheets and maps, and I can't decipher anything. I settle down on the couch with my trusty guidebook and read about the birds and their secret world. I lose track of time until Jake gets up, yawns and piles up the scattered papers. Our eyes meet.

"Why don't we plan to tell my parents about our engagement this weekend? We can stop over there this Saturday. They'll be busy getting ready for a dinner party, so it will be quick and painless." Jake's casual tone belies the crease of worry on his forehead.

"Can't you just tell them, and I'll come over some other time?"

Laughing, he retorts, "I'm not going into the lion's den alone. You need to be there, or they will never believe me. We can run through some scenarios on Friday night after my class, and maybe by then you'll have Professor Montgomery's job. They know you were working for Vee, and I don't want them to find any more issues with this than they have to."

The words, *any more issues*, echo in my head and my heart sinks. I know Jake is completely out of my league, but it is still painful to hear him state it so bluntly.

Chapter 19:

Sharing the News

Jake's "any more issues" is stuck in my head on repeat. On Friday, as I'm finishing up the bolognese in Vee's kitchen, he walks in with a huge smile, and despite my worries, I can't help but grin back.

"It smells delicious." He grabs my arms and swings me around the kitchen. "Oh, wait a minute, the smell almost made me forget my good news. Professor Montgomery wants you to start on Monday!"

I cover my mouth in surprise. "Really? Wow, that's great. I think."

"It's for a special project he's working on; researching declining populations of some sort of bird in the area, as well as something about rare or extinct birds, so you should be in seventh heaven."

I clasp my hands together at my chest and squeak, "No way! It's a bird project. Why didn't you tell me?"

"I wanted to make sure you had the job before I told you, just in case. Professor Montgomery isn't easy, and I didn't want to disappoint you if he didn't go for it."

"This just keeps getting better and better." I shake my head in wonder. "Do you know what I'll be doing?"

Jake tousles my hair. "You'll be organizing and filing reports. Your Excel skills will definitely come in handy. Maybe doing some research, I would guess. You won't be out in the field looking for birds, if that's what you're asking."

I narrow my eyes at him with mock-anger. "Hmph! You never know."

He sniffs the air. "Is something burning?"

I yelp and rush back to the stove, quickly stirring the simmering sauce, chagrined that I may have ruined the whole dinner. But when I serve it up a few minutes later, I think it tastes pretty good—and Jake assures me it's delicious.

Hating to change the mood, I shift in my chair uncomfortably until I can't bite back the words. "What did you mean when you said we should *run through scenarios*?" I ask as I spear a bite of pasta.

"We need to be prepared for Oliver and Carol to question us a bit," Jake says seriously. "They'll think it's sudden, so we need to tell them our story and make it believable."

I suck in a breath at his words, "our story." It sounds so romantic.

Jake continues, "It's best to stick to the truth as much as possible, so here's what I'm thinking. We went on a few casual dates and were getting to know each other. Let's say neither of us was interested in anything too serious."

I nod in agreement. "Will you tell them I live next door?"

"Umm, oh, I don't think that would be smart. Let's stick with what we told them, that Vee met you at a bakery. We don't want to get into that whole, er . . . mess." Jake replies.

"Oh." I mumble.

"Then the night Vee overdosed, we were both so upset and ended up talking all night long, sharing our innermost thoughts." Jake continues in a rush. "It made us realize that life is too short to waste a moment of it, and we both admitted to each other that we were in love."

I blush and look at him, dismayed. "Do we have to tell them everything about that night?"

Jake vehemently shakes his head. "No, of course not. They won't ask about anything like that. It will just be easier to keep track of things if we follow a real timeline of sorts. I'll just say what I just did to you about life being short, yada yada, yada and then we can share my romantic proposal in Central Park and how you said yes and how we're both thrilled. How's that?"

I bite my lip. I'm doubtful I can pull it off. Jake sidles close to me as I'm standing holding the half empty pasta bowl. Gently taking it from my hand, he sets it down. Taking my arm, he pulls me close and my body sways toward him automatically.

He looks down at me. "We need to act like we are in love, so we need to show it."

I feel his body against mine as I lean on him. I tilt my head back so I can continue to look at him, and he smiles lazily. With his other hand, he pulls me closer; I fit into his body like a snug puzzle piece. He leans down and gently touches his lips to mine. My lips part in surprise, and then I reach up for more. I'm drowning and the only thing that can save me are his beautiful lips. Pressing my lips harder against his, he slides his tongue slightly into my mouth. Reaching around his neck, I feel his hair against my palm, and something ignites deep in my soul. I pull him down closer so I can explore his mouth, longing for his touch—and suddenly I feel his hands on my hips, pushing me away.

He straightens back up, and I lose purchase. I'm lost.

Closing my eyes, I slowly get my bearings. When I open them, Jake is gazing at me strangely. I clutch my arms around my chest and turn away in humiliation, as I've again thrown myself at him.

Jake takes my shoulders in his hands and turns me to face him. "We may need to dial it down a bit for my parents," he says mildly. "We can't go jumping each other's bones on their living room floor."

I redden, Jake's lips quirk in a grin.

"But it certainly was believable, right?"

Feeling cold, I suddenly shiver. Is he saying we were acting just now? Was I *supposed* to be acting? I'm very confused. Confused by my actions and by Jake's reaction.

"I can't wait for tomorrow to be over," I say peevishly.

Jake looks solemn. "Right. Oh, one more thing. We need to make sure we are ready to discuss our wedding plans."

"Our *wedding plans*?" I'm completely flummoxed.

"Just a few ideas, but mainly we need to give them an idea of when," he says, as he paces the room. "We need to control the narrative. Umm, let's tell 'em we're going to move in together immediately, but we're planning to get married in . . . maybe two years and that we want just a small family affair." Jake nods to himself. "Yes, I think that's the ticket. We can't have my mother start planning anything yet. We'll explain that we know it was a quick proposal, so we want a longer engagement. That sets things up nicely to explain when things don't work out."

Watching Jake muttering to himself, I struggle to follow what he's saying. I'm still confused by the kiss—I'm trying to figure out exactly what happened and whether it was real. I examine it from every direction, and no answers are forthcoming.

Saturday dawns cold and rainy, which fits my mood perfectly, dismal. I'm sitting stonily on Vee's couch when Jake calls.

"Hey, I'm downstairs in a taxi," he says. "Want me to run up?"

"No, no, I'll be right down." I plod down the three flights like a condemned man, heading to the guillotine. I give myself a squeeze on the last step to shake off the melancholy. Jake gallantly comes around and opens my door. My cheeks pinken despite my anxiety. He is in a good mood—or maybe he's already acting.

As we near the apartment building, he pats my leg.

"Just follow my lead. This will be easy. They're all excited about this dinner party with some potential big investor, so they won't linger over our announcement." Jake continues in a voice sounding a little pinched. "Who knows, they may even be happy as this is what they've been pushing for."

We head up to the third floor and I glance nervously at apartment 325 as we pass, praying my father doesn't step out the door.

Jake gives a soft rap on his door before opening it and announcing loudly, "Mom, Dad, I've got news."

I rarely hear him refer to his stepdad as *Dad,* and it dawns on me he's doing it on purpose, to get everyone in a good mood. Carol and Oliver step out of their bedroom. Carol, in a cream-colored dress with lace sleeves and a pair of black pumps, is putting on a pair of drop pearl earrings and she looks up distractedly. Oliver is wearing an expensive-looking black suit, and his red power tie is already tight around his thick neck.

As they approach, Jake pulls me forward by my hand, continuing with even more enthusiasm, "You remember Emma? Well, we wanted to tell you both our big news. We just got engaged."

Shock and dismay replace the look of distraction on Carol's face. Staring at Jake, she opens her mouth, then snaps it closed. She glances helplessly at Oliver, who steps up and shakes Jake's hand, then turns to me, giving me a perfunctory hug. This breaks Carol out of her mute phase.

"What did you just say?" she gasps.

Jake wraps his arm around my shoulders. "Let's all sit down, and we can tell you our story. We're just thrilled beyond belief."

Oliver promptly announces, "Well, this calls for a drink."

Jake's arm tightens around me, and I feel the tension in it.

"No, Oliver!" Carol shoots him a look. "I need to hear this first before we go off celebrating anything." She pointedly stares at my stomach.

I cross my arms in front of me as if that may shield me from the daggers she is aiming at me, then peek at Jake, who looks down and gives me a wink and a squeeze. Immediately, I feel better. I can do this. This whole thing could be true. We could be in love.

I extract an arm from my stomach and wrap it around Jake's waist. We sit down on the love seat. Carol perches on the chair closest to us and turns her steely eyes onto Jake. Oliver stands behind her with a hand on her shoulder. I hope it is firm enough to keep her from leaping across the coffee table and scratching my eyes out.

Jake says sheepishly, "I know it is quite a surprise. It really surprised us, too." He pulls me tighter. "Emma, do you want to tell our story, or should I?"

Tilting my head just a touch, I say sweetly, "Why don't you? You tell it so nicely. I just love hearing it."

Jake drops a light kiss on my mouth and my eyes widen. I smile and then turn toward his parents, trying to confidently meet their eyes as Jake launches into his story, somberly talking about Vee's tragic night.

Jake ends with a flourish, "And right there in Central Park, next to our favorite bench, I got down on one knee while Emma was scanning the sky for the hawk and asked, 'Emma, darling! Will you marry me?' And bless her heart, she said yes."

His parents don't look amused, but I laugh and give him a smack on the leg. "I fell for it hook, line, and sinker. Jake knows my weakness."

Carol's eyes turn even colder; I decide to stay quiet.

Jake takes my hand and, staring into my eyes, turns it over in his hand and kisses my palm. The room fades to just his bright brown eyes that are filled with such tenderness. I'm lost momentarily but am brought back to reality when I hear Carol clear her throat and ask stiffly, "May I see the ring?"

Jake pulls me up by my hand and draws me over to Carol and Oliver. He holds out my hand for inspection.

Carol reaches out and her finger lightly touches the delicate ring; a caress. Looking at Jake, she pauses. Her eyes mist over, and for a second, she looks as if she is going to pull Jake, or maybe even both of us, into a hug. But then her eyes shift toward Oliver, and when she looks back toward us, all the softness is gone.

She stands. "Well, now we are going to be late to dinner. Really, Jake, you know how important this dinner party is to Oliver."

Jake replies comfortably, "Of course, I'm so sorry. I forgot all about the Andersons. You both look smashing. That is really all we wanted to share. Oh, and that we are planning to move in together." Jake drapes an arm around my shoulder loosely.

Carol gives him one more stern look that seems to say, *I'm not fooled by any of this*, and then marches back to her room with Oliver in tow.

Jake sits back down on the loveseat and pats the spot next to him, and I obediently sit.

"The worst is over," he whispers. "They'll be gone momentarily." A smile splits his face and the relief is pouring off him. I try to breathe but I'm still on edge waiting for some explosion. Carol and Oliver rush through the room with a curt *bye*, and sail out the door, clearly focused on the dinner party and not the little drama that just occurred. As soon as the door clicks shut, I let my breath out in a *whoosh*; Jake springs up pulling me with him. Twirling me around, he does a little waltz, humming something catchy in my ear. His enthusiasm is contagious, and I laugh for no reason other than the stress is gone. He pulls me closer; we stop circling the living room, and he nuzzles my neck.

My knees go weak.

I place my arms around his shoulders and feel his muscles through his sweater. Warmth spreads through me. Jake shifts his head, and his lips graze mine just like he did in front of Carol and Oliver, but as he is pulling back, I stand on my tiptoes and press my mouth against his.

He sighs into me, and his hand slips lower to cup my bottom, pressing me firmly against him. Our lips and our tongues dance with each other and our bodies still. He steps back half a pace and takes my hand and pulls me to his bedroom.

My stomach is in knots, but right below my stomach, I'm pulsating with heat and need. Jake tugs me down on the bed next to him. We sit side by side, and I try to figure out how to kiss him again from this angle.

Leaning forward with his head in his hands, he states simply, "Look, I need to apologize about the last time—hmm, the first time, our first time. I really messed the whole thing up."

He rakes his hands through his tousled hair. I watch, mesmerized, as a strand falls across his cheek. I want to reach out and push it back into place and then pull him to me to make him stop talking. I can't concentrate on anything but his lock of hair reflecting in the celestial light, a thousand shades of brown.

Turning to me suddenly, he catches me staring and I flush.

Looking uncomfortable, he blurts out, "I shouldn't have been so rough. I didn't know—you know about—but there really isn't an excuse. I was lost that night and then that morning, I made a mess out of that too. I shouldn't have said what I said. I'm sorry if it seemed like I blamed you for anything. I didn't mean to; it was all my fault."

Staring at him, some of what he is saying sinks in. He doesn't blame me, and he isn't saying I was awful either. He's apologizing for something. What exactly, I'm not sure, but I feel light and happy inside. I spontaneously throw my arms around him and kiss him, as now the angle is perfect. Our lips touch and I slide my lips against his, pressing and angling. I can't formulate any words to accept his apology, so instead I shift to press my body into him, and he lies back willingly. He moves, pulling me further on top of him, and I slide between his legs. He loosens my shirt from my pants and his hands trace my curves. I concentrate on kissing his mouth and then rain kisses along his neck. Reaching my hand up slowly, I tentatively push the hair from his face, and my insides melt, and wetness gathers.

Jake is slow and gentle.

The pressure builds slowly and overtakes my brain as I push and writhe against him. "Please, please hurry." I beg.

Lying under his expert fingers, I'm taut with a need I don't have words to express. He rubs and teases and I'm left panting, gazing up at his fancy light, bathed in its little stars. Suddenly they explode into a flash of light and I'm floating far away on a different plane, in a different world.

As I slowly come back to reality, Jake comes into focus. He's watching me.

He murmurs in my ear, "Lie still. Just relax, this time won't be as bad, I promise."

And that is what I do. He is slow and careful, and I understand now what he meant by his *rough* comment. While he wasn't rough by any means, he wasn't like this. I experience the same fullness where I think I can't take any more. I see how beautiful Jake is in his power and something ignites in me when he gets lost in his own urgency, he too has left this realm for a moment. I feel all woman and all powerful. I'm both softness and strength. I'm as old as the ancient trees and also as new as the fawn I saw last spring.

Suddenly, we are moving as one, in and out, pushing and pulling, my hips moving wildly. I can't get enough of the fullness. Jake explodes and freezes, and his muscles clench and release. I'm back floating, staring at the pinpoints of light above my head.

Kissing me gently, he rolls off me but pulls me into the crook of his elbow. After a few deep breaths, Jake props himself onto his elbow and gazes down at me. I don't even have the decency to blush. I'm naked and don't try to cover myself as he scans my body. He smiles at me and again, I've lost the ability to move or show any modesty.

Tracing circles on my stomach, Jake begins softly. "Have I told you why I don't want to work for Oliver's hedge fund?"

I shake my head, as my tongue doesn't seem able to form words.

"My dad, my real dad, worked on Wall Street. Carol and he met at Ole Miss. After graduating, they came to New York to make their mark. It was the eighties and was a crazy time. My dad had a finance degree and started working at some brokerage firm on Wall Street. He started slowly, but it being the eighties, he couldn't help but make money. It just started rolling in. My mom had Sandy and then me a few years later, and she quit working. She started hanging out with all the other rich, bored Wall Street wives. They had it all: cars, fancy apartment, the place in the Hamptons, kids and my dad seemed to have the Midas touch."

Jake pauses and takes a deep breath. I sit up and touch his tense arm encouragingly.

"After a few more years, my dad started doing coke and other drugs, it was all part of the game. You needed uppers to stay awake and then downers to come down. Have you ever read *Wolf of Wall Street*?"

I shake my head. "Is it good? I love to read."

"Well, they are making it into a movie now, but probably not your cup of tea." Jake quirks his lips, "I read it because I wanted to get an idea of what it was like for my dad; you know investing, drugs, cheating, and all that shit. I think there were a lot of parallels except my dad died and Gordon just went to jail. For my dad, the money started to ebb and flow and suddenly what was so easy, wasn't so easy anymore. The stress skyrocketed. I was five when the market took a bad downturn. Because they were mortgaged to the hilt, they were about to lose everything. My mom was crazy with fear and anger. The fights and the tension were awful, while I didn't understand any of it, I felt it. My father was too coked up to figure a way out of the mess, so instead hatched some shady deals that failed miserably. All my dad had left was a life insurance policy." Jake wipes at his eyes. "So, he OD'd on May 12, 1982, and Carol got the million-dollar payout." I suck in my breath and Jake lets out a sad hollow noise. "The money allowed her to pay off the apartment and the house in the Hamptons, but we didn't have any money to live on. She was desperate. Then, in walked Oliver to save the day, and she did what she had to do—for me and Sandy and our future."

I give a pitiful sigh. "That is so sad. For everyone."

Jake continues, "Auntie Beth, Vee's mom, told me this story when I was ten, and I vowed I'd never work in such a crazy world where making money is all you're doing. I wanted to be a police officer or a builder or maybe save the world. Something real, something you can see and feel, not just pushing around make-believe money. I'm not sure why Auntie Beth told me the story when I was so young. I don't think I asked her, but maybe I did. I don't really remember my dad. I remember some stuff from that time, mainly the fights and the screaming, but Auntie Beth filled in the stuff I didn't know or understand."

Jake lays his head back down on the bed, facing me, and I shift so I'm on my side too.

Taking his face in my hands, I respond fervently, "That's a sad story, but it doesn't mean you have to do something you don't want to do. You can be a builder or a police officer, or a doctor. That's something you can feel and touch." I pause and when Jake doesn't respond, I continue, "You don't have to work at a hedge fund. It's your life and your choice. Your mother made her choice."

Jake smiles wistfully, "But she did something she didn't want to. Sometimes you gotta do stuff no matter what vows you made when you were ten. Family is family."

Knowing all too well the weight of family obligations, I shake my head. Then try another tack. "But you don't have to. You aren't a single mother in desperate straits. You don't have to save anyone. You need to do what's right for you." I like the sound of that. That is what I'm doing on a tiny scale.

"I find doing the right thing rarely means doing the right thing for *you*." Jake gives me a soft kiss. "Who knows what will happen? All I want to do now is move out of here and finish my thesis. I can barely breathe, never mind think, with them on my back all the time pushing this girl or that girl at me."

Jumping up, Jake starts pulling on his clothes. His contemplative mood evaporates.

"Come on!" he says. "Let's pack up my stuff. Now that we are legit, we can move in together, right? I know it isn't quite the same as being married, but your church has loosened up a little on those puritan beliefs, right?" He continues without letting me answer, "I may actually finish my dissertation by March. Come on, my little minx, before I lose my focus again."

He playfully slaps my thigh, and that gets me up and scrambling for my clothes. I'm thrilled to feel the heat and sting of embarrassment, as I was worried I may be lost forever in the dreamy world Jake seems to catapult me into with just a touch or a look.

"What can I do to help?" I ask.

Jake hands me a small suitcase. "How about if you pack up everything in the bathroom?"

I head to the bathroom and carefully begin to clear out the drawers. As I do, I get a clearer picture of Jake. He keeps everything neat and uncluttered. His toothpaste cap is screwed on tight, and neatly squeezed from the bottom. I'm relieved, as Vee was a complete mess. Vee never put the caps back on, or if she did, she never tightened them.

I investigate his razor drawer and the cord to the electric razor is wound up neatly. I'm going to like living with him—a thought causes another blush to stain my cheeks.

Looking into his bathroom mirror, a disheveled, feverish stranger stares back at me.

I whisper, "Please, Father, forgive me for my sins. I know it doesn't make it right, but it is only for a short while. Please understand why I must do this and forgive me. I promise to try to make up for it for the rest of my days. Amen."

Shooting a quick glance out the bathroom door, I spot Jake still in his closet, taking items off hangers and folding them into a large suitcase. I look heavenward and make the sign of the cross. Boy, I hope God is the understanding and all-knowing God Vee thinks he is and not the fire and brimstone God of St. Augustine.

I return to the job at hand: I lug the suitcase out of the bathroom, swing it up on the bed with the other suitcase Jake has quickly filled, and help him finish emptying his closet.

Chapter 20:

The Apartment

We hail a taxi back to Vee's, four overstuffed suitcases in tow. Once inside Vee's, I hang back to watch where Jake puts his belongings. A surge of happiness fills my chest when he walks straight to my light blue room and not Vee's. I grab a suitcase and follow him, almost at a run. "There is plenty of room in the closet and the bureau. Let me just move a few of my things. I don't have much."

Jake tosses his bags onto my bed. "I promised Vee I would leave her bedroom, so it is ready any time Vee can come back. I think it's important for her mental health to know she is coming back sooner rather than later, right?"

Nodding, I can't keep the smile from my face. Vee's presence is powerful as I snap open the suitcase.

We leave Vee a message that night and when she calls back an hour later, she sounds like her old self. She talks to Jake first, peppering him with questions about how Carol and Oliver took the news. She loves the Central Park proposal but is a bit disappointed there weren't more fireworks at 933 Fifth Avenue.

Jake says quietly without looking at me, "Oh, there will be fireworks. They are just tamping the powder down, so it will be a really big show."

When it's my turn to talk to her, I ask, "So, how are you doing? Everyone at yoga misses you terribly, especially Jasmine. Are you doing your sun salutations down there?"

Vee laughs and I hear a little hollowness in the sound, "Slow down, too many questions. I'm going to ask you one, and all you have to say is yes or no, okay?"

"Sure," I say.

"Are you guys sleeping together? Say yes, please, please, please."

Mortified and keeping my eyes averted from Jake, I breathe out and whisper, "Yes, oh yes."

Vee squeals. "Oh, I knew if I didn't let Jake sleep in my room, that would force things. I don't mean force. Eh, not force, but expedite. You made my day. My week. Clearly not much of that stuff is happening down here. Although Kim and Stan, who are in my same therapy group, may be sneaking around."

I giggle, forgetting my embarrassment. I'm glad I made Vee happy even if just for this moment. When I hand the phone back to Jake, I'm still smiling.

On Sunday, Jake is pouring over papers that are spread over the table. I take a quick peek and silently try to sound out the words on the top of the worksheet; *campephilus principalis*. My Lord, it must be Latin or something. I can't imagine what a premed biology class would involve. I barely passed my high school biology test about the circulatory system, and that was just a small part of what doctors need to know.

Turning toward the door, I quickly state, "Hey, I'm going to church with my parents." I've been going every Sunday as they requested.

He looks up and contemplates me for a minute, taking in my black pants and bulky cream sweater. Then he chuckles. "Enjoy. Say a prayer for me too, will you?"

I hesitate, wondering if he has caught me reciting my Hail Marys or other prayers of forgiveness. I thought I was being careful, but maybe I've been doing them without even being aware. Ducking my head sheepishly, I can't come up with any response, so instead head out into the brisk but sunny day.

I spot my parents in their normal pew, and they don't look up when I slide in next to them. Only when I reach out and give my mother's hand a squeeze does she look at me, smiling tiredly. I give my father a quick glance and I can't tell if he is sitting more stonily than normal as church is serious business for him. I'm sure he has been told the news, and I wish I could decipher his mood.

During the sermon, I wonder what Jake is doing back in the apartment, then think about what to cook for dinner. Suddenly, the service is over, and I help my mother get positioned in front of her walker. My father, with a grunt, heads out to hail the taxi they now take back and forth to church.

As we make our way up the aisle, she says quietly, "He is still in shock, give him time. He's worried about you."

I shrug and spot my father up ahead in the taxi, sitting ramrod straight as if he is still on the hard, unforgiving pew.

I sigh as we approach him. My mother grabs my hand and gives it a squeeze, and I smile at her. She murmurs, "We want you to be happy. That is all Emma."

I look down at her hand clasped in mine and I feel an unexpected warmth swell in my chest. *Could that be true?* Leaning into the taxi I say, "Bye Mama. Bye Papa."

Turning, I rush back to Vee's as the day has gotten colder in the last couple of hours. I rub my hands together after shutting the door behind me; the warmth of the apartment eases my muscles that are shivering with the cold and the bleakness of November. I am happy. At least right at this moment.

Jake is still working, but he stretches his arms over his head and twists back and forth. I hear the bones in his back crack as he does.

"I'm thinking of making some beef stew," I say. "It will warm us up. Do you like beef stew?"

"Gosh, sounds perfect." He flashes me a wide smile. "How long will it take? I'm starving."

"I'll get cracking, so maybe forty-five minutes."

"Perfect. That will force me to correct a few more papers before I call it quits. How was church? Are we both going to Hell?" He grins.

Frowning, I pull the vegetables out of the refrigerator.

"Aww sorry. I shouldn't joke. As Vee says, you're an angel. So, you don't need saving, it's just me and I'm a lost cause."

Smiling, I hum a tuneless tune as I chop the carrots. Normally, all this talk about *saving* would riddle me with guilt and remorse, but I can't seem to muster up either of those typical feelings. Instead, I'm filled with a lightness and ease that has me flying through the meal prep.

Chapter 21:

The Wood Thrush

I lay awake Sunday night, listening to Jake's quiet snores beside me. Worry is gnawing at my gut. Rolling onto my side, I lose myself in my new favorite pastime: staring at Jake.

I can't believe he is sleeping next to me, close enough to touch if I dared. I scan the vague outline of his body under the quilt. He sleeps in a pair of silky-looking shorts. So, he isn't naked right now, but I have vivid pictures of him naked that parade through my head. I swing between my two current realities: one minute butterflies are drumming against my chest at the worry of starting my new job tomorrow, the next a pulsating heat takes over, making me squirm from Jake's nearness, making coherent thoughts impossible.

Fortunately, sleep finally comes to save me from the seesaw that is my life.

The moment I drift off, the forest grows and deepens to a dark olive, with sunlight filtering through the layers of leaves and limbs, painting the air mossy gold. I'm dwarfed by the pillar of trees but feel at home among the giants. Smiling, I hear whistling just ahead. I pick my way along a barely discernible path, feeling safe and cared for. There is a shout up in front of me, and a jab of excitement. Suddenly I'm awake and blinking my eyes open groggily, I then close them softly. I lie still, wrapped in the cocoon of my dream, until it slowly dawns on me: it's Monday.

Snuggling a little deeper into the comfort of the quilt, I stretch, thankful again for the comfort of my dream, but it feels different from before. More like it was trying to show me something rather than just taking me away for a moment, a night.

Sitting up, I notice Jake's empty spot next to me, and I hear sounds coming from the kitchen. Then he pokes his head in the bedroom.

"Oh good. I thought I was going to wake you. Tea is ready, and I have oatmeal, too."

Forcing a brave smile, I exclaim, "Thanks, but I'm too nervous to eat."

"Oatmeal will settle your stomach. You need something like that. Now come on, get moving. You will be great. I promise."

A real smile breaks out on my face, and I glide into the bathroom, feeling pampered and special.

Jake walks me right to Professor Montgomery's office door. Thank goodness, because Columbia is a maze of buildings, paths and signs. I never would have made it without Jake leading the way.

"It will get easier," he reassures me, "don't worry."

He's going to work on his thesis in his office today while I'm at my new job and will come back to escort me when my four hours are over. The sensation of being cared for and protected settles more firmly around my shoulders as we stand outside the door. The feeling is just as delicious as in my dream, perhaps even more so as my dream has been recurring for years, but in my real life, I've never experienced this warmth. Certainly not from my parents. I think they care for me, but they don't demonstrate it—that kind of affection is not necessary or appropriate, but boy, it feels nice.

Jake leans down and drops a kiss on my lips. "Good luck. You'll be fine."

Walking into the office clutching my pen and notebook, I channel my best Vee, shoulders back, head high.

Clearing my throat, I squeak out, "Hello, Professor, I'm Emma." Horrified at the tremor in my voice, I fight to keep my eyes raised, trying to smile.

A large man wearing an old plaid suit jacket regards me from behind his desk. He has penetrating, dark eyes. He inclines his head toward a chair in front of his desk and says gruffly, "Sit, sit. Let's talk."

He is a hulking presence, but I'm used to my father, uncle, and grandfather, who are of a similar size and seriousness. I sit obediently.

Professor Montgomery is slow and precise in his words and movements. He looks at me with sharp intelligence. His hair is a tousle of gray points sticking out in all directions. He absentmindedly yanks on one of his hair tufts and I realize this is the reason for his unique hairdo.

"I started at Columbia as a young man doing my thesis, just like Jake is doing now. It was a much smaller department back then. And once I completed my thesis, I stayed on. I've been teaching ornithology for many years here and always spent the summers and some sabbaticals doing fieldwork. Those were the best times. But now, my knees and my back, traitors that they are, require that I stay behind, sifting through the nidification research, letting the young ones do the fieldwork. The dirt, the bugs, and the late nights are for the young, not old men like me."

I smile slightly. He looks like he is a sturdy sixty, and I can easily picture him tramping through woods.

I'm thankful I have my trusty notebook. I jot notes down, including the words I don't understand. *Ornithology* and *nidification* both go on the list under "ask Jake."

Professor Montgomery continues, "One of the long-running research projects is on the IBWO and that is the Hail Mary of all Hail Marys."

Looking up in confusion, I glance at my purse to make sure my rosary beads aren't showing. I add *IBWO* and *Hail Mary* to the list. I thought I knew a lot of bird terminology but clearly my bird guide didn't teach me as much as I thought.

He begins to run out of steam and peers over his glasses at me. "So, who is Emma Jablonski?"

Blushing, I begin haltingly, "I've worked in my parents' bakery my whole life, until recently. I've taken some community college courses and most recently was a personal assistant to a model, but now want to help with . . ." I pause. "Whatever you need." I take a deep breath and continue in a rush, "I'm a hard worker and a fast learner—at least that is what others have said. I may not be as smart as some of your students, but I will try my hardest."

Professor Montgomery leans back, smiling encouragingly. "You are already well ahead of those snot-nosed kids. They show up here thinking they can get by on their brains or their parents' money. They don't know the first thing about hard work and diligence. Not one of them has ever shown up with a notebook and pen. They aren't interested in working, not really."

A little crack opens in my chest and a bit of warmth from a gentle sun spread through my body.

Professor Montgomery comes from around his desk, and I notice for the first time his rumpled khakis and an untucked shirt. "The first thing we need to do is input all these field reports into the spreadsheet on the computer. I was doing a few earlier. It's kind of mindless work, but it must be done. Here is where I left off. The wood thrush nest observation #23 is the one I just input. Look at the paper report and you will see how I transferred the information into the spreadsheet. Make sure the sections match up to what you are inputting and start typing."

"Did you say wood thrush?" I ask timidly.

He turns; eyebrows raised. "Yes, wood thrush. Jake said you liked birds. Is there an issue with wood thrushes?"

"No, not at all. I just can't believe it. I love birds, and the only thing better than a wood thrush would be a kingfisher study."

Professor Montgomery barks out a laugh. "How refreshing. But tell me why the kingfisher?"

"Oh, kingfishers are my favorite, ever since seventh grade. My teacher let us pick a Greek myth to do a report on, and I picked the myth of Halcyon and Ceyx. It was so lovely. Not many people have heard of it, but it is both tragic and romantic."

"Oh, we are going to get along marvelously." Professor Montgomery gives me a warm smile. "Halcyon and Ceyx are way better than silly Hercules. Your myth is required reading in my Ornithology 101 course. A lot of my students don't remember much of the class, but they all remember that story."

Staring at Professor Montgomery, a smile stretches across my face. Life is so amazing. I don't need to ask Jake what ornithologist means, as now I realize it must be someone who studies birds. Now, I remember that from my guidebook. *I'm the luckiest girl alive!* Sitting down, I get to work deciphering the field reports.

I'm deep into double-checking my entries when suddenly there is a soft knock at the door, and Jake's head pokes through the door.

He whispers, "Hi there, how are you doing? It's one p.m., so I'm checking to see if you're ready to head back."

Peering at my watch, I can't believe it's been four hours. I glance over at Professor Montgomery; he's engrossed in reading something and didn't hear the knock.

Standing, I announce, "Professor, I've completed all the reports from April. I'll be back tomorrow and can start on May."

Looking up, he smiles distractedly. "Yes, great. A genuine pleasure."

Jake steps into the room. "Professor, how are you doing?"

A smile breaks out on his face. "Jake, I didn't see you there. So nice to see you. Marvelous recommendation. She didn't look at her phone once and didn't chatter incessantly like my last assistant. A real keeper, this one is."

Jake smiles, "Yep, she sure is."

I grab my coat, and we head out the door. Once we are in the elevator, I start jotting down the directions to get in and out of the building.

"I can't believe this project," I blurt out. "It's so cool. I feel I'm helping those poor birds trying to nest and raise their babies out in the middle of Pennsylvania."

Jake grins. "Fate, isn't it?"

"Oh, I have a bunch of words I need help with." I pull out my notebook. "First, do you have any idea what IBWO means?"

He replies softly, reverently, "Oh, I sure do. It's an ivory-billed woodpecker, one of those really rare, possibly extinct birds."

"Oh, I've heard of them. John Foster's book has something about them."

I dig into my bag and take out my constant companion. Flipping to the first page I read aloud, "When it was discovered the ivory-billed woodpecker may have been spotted in Arkansas after years of thinking them extinct, my first response was not to jump into my car and start driving all night as I've done for countless other rare-bird sightings. Instead, it was to sit with the idea of an ivory-bill still living in this world. And that is just what I did for several days, savoring the idea that I may be living in a world that such a wonderful creature still inhabits. That is all I needed. To know the bird lives in the same world as I." I pause and continue, "That's from the foreword by David Marshall. He must be a fellow birder like John Foster, right?"

Jake chuckles and throws his arm around me companionably. I'm thankful he doesn't react as he normally does when I go off spouting John Foster, as I don't want anything to mar the wondrous mood I'm in.

I'm up and out of the apartment every morning to walk to Columbia, where I spend a fascinating four hours logging in data about the breeding and nesting habits of the wood thrush, a lovely little brown spotted bird I've heard and seen in the woods of Central Park.

Professor Montgomery shares the details and the focus of the project, and I learn that the wood thrush population has been declining since 1970, and this study is trying to determine at what age and in which type of forest the birds have the highest success rate for reproducing. It's tracking over one hundred nests during this past nesting season. Professor Montgomery thinks the issue may not be so much the nesting and breeding habitat, although climate change is messing up every habitat for so many species. He thinks the issue may lie in their wintering habitat down in South America. Those countries are struggling with deforestation and overdevelopment that is eliminating the woodlands these birds count on to survive.

Soaking it all in, I imagine I'm the one trudging through the woods of Pennsylvania, counting eggs and reporting nest destruction or successes. I feel the pain as I complete the spreadsheet for a particular nest with zero successful fledglings. So many things can go wrong and seem to go wrong. I now hate the brown-headed cowbird. These birds have the audacity to lay their extra-large egg in a thrush's nest, and the mother thrush sits on all the eggs, but when the cowbird baby hatches, it is so much bigger than the thrush babies, it ends up taking all the food and the thrush babies wither and die. Each time this happens, my heart breaks for those poor, starving little babies that end up weak and trampled. And that is only one of the possible problems. Snakes, raccoons, wind, rain, heat, or cold all wreak havoc on the delicate nesting process.

Today, around noon, Professor Montgomery sighs heavily. "I can't look at another spreadsheet today." Leaning back in his chair, he says amicably, "I don't imagine your bird guide includes anything about the Gunnison sage-grouse?"

I shake my head.

"Well now, that bird has the fanciest mating dance I've ever witnessed. Of course, it's in an impossible place to get to. One must tramp through the mud and cold of Colorado before dawn to see it. But I tell you, it's truly amazing. You must stay until the last grouse leaves the dance floor, so as not to disturb the birds from their all-important mating ritual."

I give a soft hoot. "Really? That sounds crazy."

"The grouse have these special areas called a lek they use year after year, every spring, to strut their stuff," he says, growing more animated. "The males will inflate their yellowish air sacs, making a special popping sound to attract a female."

I shake my head in disbelief. "Amazing."

After a pause, Professor Montgomery queries, "What made you interested in birds? Was it just the myth of Halcyon?"

Smiling at the memory that jumps into my head, I shake my head. "It was even before that. I was in fourth grade in Bridgeport, Connecticut. My teacher was Mrs. King. She loved birds and had real nests and ceramic birds sprinkled throughout her classroom. I loved Mrs. King. The spring of the school year, she took the entire class out to a bird box attached to a metal pole at the edge of the playground. I had never noticed it before, as it was near the woods that surrounded the back of our school. Each of us got to climb up a little stepladder and peek through the plastic side of the box. Inside were four of the tiniest bluebird babies, they were little pink wrinkled sacs with bug eyes that weren't even open yet. Their little beaks covered their whole heads, and their necks were so weak and wobbly, I couldn't believe they could hold that huge beak up for more than a second. Staring at them, I felt something open in my chest. I thought, *What a miracle that these things will one day fly.*"

I hesitate, I've never shared this with anyone before. The professor gives me an encouraging nod, so I take a deep breath and keep going.

"When we got back to class, Mrs. King had us all draw a picture of the nest and the babies. She explained that there are three species of bluebirds in the USA, and these were eastern bluebirds. She gave us all the most beautiful blue crayons to draw the parents. We only once in a while got so see the brilliant flash of blue."

The professor smiles. "There are birders everywhere. Sounds like your Mrs. King knew her stuff."

"We got to do this every other day for two weeks, and I watched those birds grow and grow, morphing from pink sacs into beautiful birds with sleek feathers and heads that matched their bodies. Then one day when we went out, they were gone. All that was left was some matted grass that had been their little nest. I looked for those birds everywhere, hoping to see my little bluebird family, but I never did. I saw other birds, but no bluebirds." I feel a small lump in my throat, remembering how desperately I missed those little birds when they were gone. "Ever since then, I've felt a kinship to birds and quite simply fell in love with them. I was part of something bigger and better than I had ever thought possible. That year was special and unforgettable. Toward the end of the year, because I continued to draw pictures of birds and write stories, Mrs. King suggested that when I get to seventh grade English to make sure I select the story of Halcyon and Ceyx for my myth and that is exactly what I did."

Professor Montgomery chuckles. "We all have our spark story that led us to birding. Someday I will tell you mine . . . but enough chitchat for now, back to work."

My world is slowly becoming what I always dreamed of—normal. And that it is a true miracle. I go to work each day and catalog birds, I come home to a lovely, bright apartment. Sometimes I squeeze in a hot yoga class. I say hi to a few of the regulars and often, we stop and chat. On my way home, I grab a few things to make dinner. Jake comes back from his class at 6:00 p.m., and we eat together, sharing news from our day. He tells me the progress he is making on his thesis. And then the best part of the day happens: I curl up to sleep with Jake every night. Sometimes we have the most wonderful sex, sometimes we just chat and fall asleep. He's more relaxed than I've ever seen him and I'm happier than I ever have been, just a typical girl doing typical things.

On weekends, Jake indulges me, and we walk through Central Park with our *bins*—Jake taught me to call our binoculars that—searching for birds. For someone with little or no interest in birds, Jake is really good at spotting and identifying them. Because of him, I've added some great finds to my life list, including the ring-necked duck and golden-crowned kinglet.

Chapter 22:

Family Dinner

We are in our own special happy bubble. But all that evaporates, when Jake's parents invite us over to dinner the weekend before Thanksgiving, ostensibly to meet his sister and her husband.

When Jake tells me the news, I ask flatly, "Do I have to go? I hate fireworks."

Smiling sheepishly, he says, "There won't be any fireworks. Showy and extravagant isn't really their style. Chinese water torture is more their style. If my mother takes out toothpicks, hide your finger, okay?"

I force a laugh. Jake swings his arm around me, stating, "It's only for a couple of hours. You'll get to meet my big sister, Sandy. She isn't too bad. We can bear it."

Can we? I wonder darkly.

On Saturday, we make our way over. It's already dark at five, so we don't get to look for birds as we cross the park. The air smells cold and brittle, leaves crunch underfoot.

Sandy has Jake's coloring; russet, wavy hair, and she is wearing it up in a high ponytail. Smiling, she rushes over to shake my hand. My palm is sweaty, and I try to wipe it against my pants furtively. Sandy doesn't seem to notice. She tugs at her dress. It is tight in some areas and loose in others, and she appears a little disheveled.

Carol gives me a quick hug, barely touching me as she does it. It must be something they teach in rich-people's class, how to hug without really hugging.

Oliver claps me on my back in a fatherly way, loudly exclaiming, "Hello again and welcome to the family er, ah, Emma."

I'm relieved he got my name right.

Jake lightly kisses his sister on the cheek and shakes hands with a distracted, balding man who must be Sandy's husband, Glen. He is sitting at the kitchen nook talking on his phone and gesturing wildly.

He waves to me and mouths, "Nice to meet you."

He is heavyset, with bushy eyebrows and a meaty face.

Sandy rolls her eyes and says, "Emergency consult. Just ignore him for now. Doctors; they make the most awful dinner guests."

Catching Jake's eye, I raise a confused eyebrow; he told me both Sandy and Glen were doctors. He winks and gives me a shrug that seems to say ignore her.

Turning to Carol, I remark brightly, "Well, something smells delicious." I'm glad that I can speak tonight, unlike the dinner with Jessica, where I kept losing my ability to string words together.

"Nothing special, just something Maria put together," Carol replies curtly. "Keeping it simple, as it's just family, right?"

I try to ignore the edge she has to her voice, but I think I hear the *drip*, *drip*, *drip* of water and I clench my hands into fists.

At least I get to sit next to Jake in the dreadful dining room tonight. He immediately takes my hand under the table and gives it a squeeze. Then, leaning over, he presses a kiss lightly on my open lips.

Looking into his eyes, all my nerves melt away and all I can think about is wanting more of his lips. My eyes glaze over and time freezes.

With some irritation, Sandy grumbles, "Really! At the dinner table."

I tear my attention away from Jake's lips and see Sandy has her face screwed up in a look of disgust and something else, maybe envy. She takes a bite of her steak with unnecessary viciousness. I focus on the food and am delighted to find that it's delicious. The meat melts in my mouth; one barely needs to chew it.

Glen finally sits down next to Sandy, and she gives him an exasperated look.

"So, what did I miss?" he asks congenially. "Have we grilled Emma yet on her intentions?" He barks out a laugh while the rest of the people at the table ignore him.

Oliver clears his throat. "Emma, what do you do now that you have lost your job as a secretary for Vee?"

I glance at Jake, and he smiles encouragingly.

Taking a deep breath, I respond, "Well, I got the most wonderful job working at Columbia with a professor on a bird project. Jake got me the job, and it couldn't be more perfect."

"Birds," Oliver sputters, "you have got to be kidding me."

Jake straightens up in his seat. "Yes, she is working on the wood thrush study. It's been going on for several years. You may remember Professor Montgomery. He's just wrapping it up."

I add bravely, "I don't get to do any fieldwork, but maybe one day. Right now, I'm cataloguing and organizing the final work. It really is very exciting."

Carol looks over at me and in a voice dripping with condescension says, "Oh yes, sounds so rewarding. What would the world do without wood thrushes?"

Glen, who's been quietly stuffing the dinner down as if he was starving, looks up. "Speaking of birds, is everyone set to come to our place for Thanksgiving? We both have it off this year and we want to do it up right with all the bells and whistles."

"Absolutely," Carol gushes.

Jake looks tense and angry. "Oh hey, thanks for the invite. Unfortunately, Emma and I are going to visit Vee for Thanksgiving. I guess we will see Aunt Beth and Uncle Joe, but mainly it's hanging with Vee over the holiday weekend."

This is the first time I've heard of a visit. I honestly don't know what is going on here, but there is again this undercurrent that makes me feel like I am walking on quicksand, and one wrong step will be the end of me.

The table is silent, and Jake seems unaffected by the stony stares that are being leveled at him. He gives me a quick tilt of his head. "It's no big deal; you guys won't even miss us. Have a wonderful time." The silence is deafening.

"I'll make sure I tell Aunt Beth hi from you and Oliver," he says sweetly, meeting his mother's icy stare.

Carol keeps herself ramrod straight, saying nothing. The tension is thick, and I'm losing my appetite, even though the steak and green beans are to die for.

"How is the thesis coming?" Oliver bites off. "March still the target for it to be done, so you can get serious about joining the firm?"

"Well, I'm not sure how March is looking now," Jake shoots back. "I have such a distraction at home these days, I can't seem to do much of any actual schoolwork. Can I, dear?"

He locks eyes with me, pulling me close for a searing kiss. It is hard and demanding. And then he pulls away.

I put my fingers to my lips, staring at Jake. This kiss felt dirty.

We suffer through a dessert of lemon meringue pie that leaves a sour taste in my mouth, and then, finally, we say our goodbyes.

Jake sets a brisk pace as we walk back to Vee's; I must hurry to keep up.

I reach out and tug on his arm, and he doesn't break his stride. I give another yank, making him stop.

"What was that kiss for? I didn't like it."

Jake's expression softens, and he looks at me deeply, with total sincerity.

"I'm sorry about that. Sometimes I get so angry at all the innuendos and veiled threats, I do stupid things. I knew it would annoy them, so I did it. I wasn't thinking, I mean I wasn't thinking about you. That was thoughtless." He hangs his head and quirks an eyebrow at me. "I promise never to use our kisses as a weapon to get back at my stupid parents, okay?"

He has a lazy smile on his face and leans toward me capturing my lips in his. We stand in the middle of Central

Park and neck, completely oblivious to people passing by or the birds flitting nearby. I've become one of those magical couples I used to watch from my bench. I'd forgive him for anything if it meant I can keep kissing him. Kissing him now in front of strangers is so much better than in front of his family, with all its undercurrents and tension.

Electricity shoots between us as we stride quickly back to the apartment.

Jake is quick and a little rough, but afterwards, he is back to himself. I'm mesmerized as he twirls a strand of my hair between his fingers. Then I remember and sit up and hit him playfully on his shoulder. "I almost forgot, what is this about a visit to Vee? That was a complete surprise."

"Oh yeah. I've been thinking about a visit to Vee's but didn't have any proper plans. Then in the middle of the miserable dinner, the idea of going to Sandy and Glen's next week was so unappetizing the idea just popped out." He chuckles, "This way we can kill two birds with one stone."

"That is a truly despicable expression." I frown at him. "But with that said, I agree wholeheartedly with your scheme."

I wonder what would ever happen if Jake's parents found out I'm the girl next door. *Could they disapprove of our arrangement even more?*

Chapter 23:

Thanksgiving

Today is the day. I'm going to fly. It's the Tuesday before Thanksgiving and I give myself a squeeze as I lie under my blankets and then spring out of bed. I'm two months into my six-month plan to live and I never imagined it would include flying off to Mississippi. *I definitely didn't dream big enough*. Living is crazy. Ever since Jake knocked on my door two months ago, I've been a bundle of nerves, anxiety and excitement; wondrous things have happened and awful, awful things have happened. The picture of Vee face down on her bed flashes through my mind.

I slide into a pair of leggings and an oversized gray sweater, feeling oh so trendy in a comfortable pair of chunky sneakers I bought just for the trip. Vee gave me advice on flying that I should wear layers, as planes are notoriously cold or hot but never just right.

Jake and I have seats next to each other and he graciously offers me the window seat. The takeoff is indescribable. One minute I'm chatting excitedly with Jake and the next minute there is a deafening roar that goes on and on and I'm pressed flat against my seat, unable to move or breathe. Jake smiles at me as panic rises in my eyes. I couldn't scream because the roar forced all the air out of my lungs.

He pats my hand. "It will be over in a few minutes."

I don't know how he can lift his hand when I can't even blink. Then, just like that, the noise level drops to just a buzz, and I can move and breathe again.

"Wow." I gasp.

Twisting in my seat, I stare out the window as we pass the Statue of Liberty—and my eyes tear up. I've never seen anything so beautiful. Of course, I've seen Lady Liberty hundreds of times in my life, but this bird's-eye view is majestic. An unbidden picture jumps into my head: my grandfather all alone on the bridge of a ship and seeing her for the first time, with his shirt and the jewels pressing against his sides. My family's story suddenly seems so real and tears prick my eyes. How strange that a change in perspective makes a common experience completely new and different.

I nudge Jake without taking my eyes off the statue. Jake leans over to see what I'm looking at then he gently wipes my tears away. He starts to say something but then smiles at me with such tenderness in his eyes, I must look away.

Together, we watch her fade from view.

The landing is the exact reverse of the takeoff. Thank God my seatbelt held; otherwise, I would have been thrown into the seat in front of me. This time, I can't breathe because my seatbelt is cutting through my midsection as it strains to keep me in seat 14A.

When we get off the plane with our bags, I'm a new person—a world traveler. I'm someone who has seen Lady Liberty from above and understands the world a bit more in all its complexities and perspectives. My smile keeps getting bigger and bigger as we work through renting a car and checking into our hotel.

We eat dinner at an Applebee's, and then it's time for me to spend my first night in a hotel. I flop on the crisp white sheets, thinking, *I'm really living, and living is beyond my wildest dreams.*

The next day on the short drive to Aunt Beth and Uncle Joe's, Jake explains, "We are doing this to keep the peace. Auntie Beth is pissed we aren't coming to her place for Thanksgiving. I explained we are down to visit Vee, but sometimes she can be awfully pigheaded. We'll have lunch with them today and then spend Thanksgiving with Vee tomorrow."

"It's strange they aren't going to the clinic's Thanksgiving. Vee would have been all alone if we weren't visiting, right?"

Jake shakes his head. "I know. Auntie Beth I guess still hasn't forgiven Vee for sending her packing a year ago. I'm so glad this plan *popped* into my head. Vee tried to tell me it isn't a big deal, but it is. And the icing on the cake is we miss dinner at Sandy's." He chuckles softly.

Five minutes later, right at 1:00 p.m., we pull up to a white clapboard house. The house is modest but nice. Jake rings the bell, and we stand outside in the warm sunshine. A large buxom woman in a housecoat opens the door and swallows Jake up in a hug. She turns to me and engulfs me as well. Ushering us in, she yells, "Joe, Jake and Emma are here! Get up here and greet our guests."

A lanky man comes up from the basement, wiping his hands on his work pants, smiling. He has a kind face.

Aunt Beth *tssks* and exclaims, "Joe! Jesus, wash your hands. Jake and Emma are from New York City; they aren't used to dust and dirt from your hobbies." She holds her fingers up in air quotes when she says hobbies.

Joe gives us a sheepish look and scurries off to the kitchen in the back. Jake whispers, "She clearly hasn't seen the subway, huh?"

Beth ushers us into the living room, and we sink into an uncomfortable, bright floral couch. She hurries off and returns quickly with a tray of iced tea and some little rolled sandwiches. As she places everything on the low table in front of the couch, Joe comes in and shakes Jake's hand, then reaches for mine.

Holding my hand, he states sincerely, "Girl, I can tell just by looking at ya', I like ya'. We've been wondering who the lucky lady is that snared our Johnny."

Beth cuts in, "You know he likes to be called Jake now. Jesus, Joe, hush up."

She pours the tea and hands around little China plates for the sandwiches. Smiling, I take the plate and glass, but each time I try to shift them from hand to hand, my butt sinks deeper into the overstuffed cushions. Any deeper and I may never get off this couch. I spot Jake setting his glass down on the low table in front of the couch, so I hoist myself out of the couch pillows and scoot a bit forward to do the same. I'm going to be exhausted by the time I finish my tea with all the scooting and sinking I'm doing. We chew quietly on the dainty sandwiches.

Beth breaks the silence and asks, "How is your mother and Oliver?"

Jake replies evenly, "They're doing fine. They seem reasonably content, but would be more so if I buckled down and went to work at the firm."

"Yep, I'm sure that sticks in Oliver's craw," Beth says. "But you're a grown man, you can do what you want, honey. But clearly you know that, as you got engaged to Emma. Boy, that must have blown your mother's top."

Jake gives my hand a squeeze. "Aww, they're fine with it. I was just telling Emma the story of *my* parents and what happened. I wanted to ask you about how they met and what they were like in college. You were at Ole Miss when they were there, weren't you?" Jake asks these questions rapid fire, clearly trying to change the subject.

Beth pauses, looking reflective. Glancing at Joe, she says, "Joe, go get us some beers. If I'm going to tell this one, I need something stronger than sweet tea."

Joe hops up and comes back in short order with four beers. As soon as he hands Beth hers, she takes a long swig. Then she pulls herself up and goes over to a cabinet along the wall, taking out a bottle of bourbon and splashing some of the brown liquid in the bottom of a stout glass.

Bringing the glass back to her chair, she raises it in a solo toast and states, "Turns out I need something even stronger than beer."

Joe frowns but doesn't say anything. I'm relieved she doesn't offer us any.

Leaning back in her chair, Beth says, "Carol and John were two years ahead of me at Ole Miss. Both of 'em beautiful, smart, and nice. They met when they were juniors and took the same finance class. They fell hard for each other. They let me hang out with them, and we would go on double dates whenever I had a boyfriend. Their connection was beautiful. Honestly, I was jealous of them, but you couldn't not like them because they were swell to everyone and so great together."

Taking a sip from her glass, Beth continues quietly, "Ever since we were little, Carol and I had dreams of moving to New York City. The plan was, once I graduated, we were going to go. Acting was our first plan and that morphed into stewardesses, but by college we were dead set on advertising. Carol was a really good artist, and I loved words. We were going to work at an ad agency, that was our plan, and I was okay with John coming along too. As I said, everyone loved John."

Pausing, she downs the rest of the bourbon with a quick swallow.

Her voice hardens, "Well, that isn't quite how it went down. Carol and John went to New York as soon as they graduated. I figured this way they'd work things out, so by the time I show up two years later, they'd have everything set. But on the day of my graduation, Carol came down from New York for it. She was pregnant with your sister and told me I couldn't come. It hit me like a ton of bricks, and it hurt." Beth's face flushes an angry red. "Oh, I know she couldn't ban me from going to New York if I wanted to, but what she was telling me was I was on my own. She wasn't going to be my advertising partner or any other sort of partner. She never told me why or explained anything to me. Boy, was I pissed." Beth sits quietly for a moment and her shoulders droop.

Joe injects congenially, "Well, if you had gone to New York, we never would have met and remember things didn't work out so well for either one of them, did it?"

Looking over at Joe, a little fondness creeps into her voice, "You are right. And we never would have created a supermodel, would we?"

Goose bumps rise on my arms. Looking at Jake, I raise my eyebrow. It's strange to hear Beth refer to her daughter as a supermodel. Especially when she's sitting in rehab, probably needing her mother right now.

Jake adroitly shifts the conversation. "So, did Vee tell you Emma was her personal assistant for a while, and that's how the two of us met?"

Beth regards me with a smile, "Oh, I did hear that. Do tell us some stories of Vee's modeling? I just loved going to shoots with her. I felt like I was part of them."

We spent the next hour talking about photoshoots, and Beth and Joe share some funny stories of Vee when she was a gangly kid. Beth has two more refills from the bourbon bottle, and just as she is getting a little sloppy, Joe stands. "Hey, Jake, let's show Emma the basement, for old time's sake."

"Yes, go and enjoy." Beth nods her head agreeably.

As I start down the basement steps, I watch Beth pull herself up and walk a little unsteadily over to the liquor cabinet.

A brightly lit woodworking shop that smells of fresh sawdust occupies most of the basement. There are half-finished chairs and tables and lots of large tools and tables with saws embedded in them. Framed pictures of old jets and airplanes adorn the walls. I look around, intrigued; this must be Uncle Joe's little hideaway, where he comes when he needs to be alone for some peace and quiet. It feels miles away from the stuffy room upstairs infused with bourbon and broken dreams.

Touching a few of the tools and pieces of wood, Jake says warmly, "This was always my favorite place when we came to visit. I loved coming down here with you." He turns to me and adds, "Uncle Joe taught me how to plane and cut wood. He can build pretty much anything."

Uncle Joe whispers conspiratorially, "It was my favorite place to come during those visits too. Beth and Carol one upping each other the whole time, and Oliver pontificating about this or that. Lord, I was glad you were there to have an excuse to take you down here to teach you a few things. I knew we were safe because Oliver would never dirty his hands.

Jake cracks a smile and nods in agreement.

Joe picks up a small rectangular box about a foot in length. When he turns it around, I spot a little hole in the front panel.

"Oh, a bluebird box!" I exclaim clapping my hands.

"Yup," Joe says proudly, "been makin 'em for the Mississippi Audubon Society's annual Christmas bazaar since 1995 or so. Right, Jake? So, just about fifteen years now."

"Sounds about right," Jake says.

Glancing at the wall behind Uncle Joe, there is a wall of boxes stacked one on top of another. "Wow, there must be a hundred."

Joe asks, "How about it, Jake? Let's put one together. Your girl here can do some sanding. She looks as if she can handle getting her hands dirty. Even Vee never minded helping me down here occasionally."

The two of them start working as a team, and I find a stool to sit on and watch them. They are relaxed and focused, and in no time, they produce a finished box.

"I didn't get to do anything," I protest.

Joe hands me some sandpaper and plops the box in my lap. "Okay, just start rubbing out any rough spots. Mainly focus on the edges."

Joe leans against the table. "Have you seen Vee yet?"

"No," Jake says. "Tomorrow we'll go for a visit and a turkey dinner."

Joe states matter-of-factly, "I'm just glad she won't be alone for Thanksgiving. I'm not sure why Beth dug her heels in, but she did and just refuses to be inconvenienced. If you have an addicted son or daughter, far worse things could happen to you than being inconvenienced." Joe shakes his head. "Beth just wants it all to go away and go back to having a model for a daughter, but that ain't going to happen. She is slowly coming around, though. The sessions we attend pretty much make you face facts. Of course, it's tough as some of Vee's issues are because of Beth, and Beth is going to have to come to terms with that. She pushed Vee way too fast, and Vee was clearly too young to be left alone in the city. The pressure that little girl was under would have been too much for most people. Modeling can really do a number on someone whose self-confidence was low to begin with. I've picked up these things in the sessions, and I see we did a lot of things wrong with Vee. It's tough when she's your only child."

Pensively picking up a box, Joe absentmindedly begins to rhythmically sand it. *Scrape, scrape, scrape.*

"Beth felt cheated out of a life and blamed your mother unfairly. But I think that's what made Beth put a lot of unfair expectations on Vee. The focus on Vee's looks did a lot of damage. I should've stepped in more to stop what was happening, I now see that. But it was easier to come down here and escape. But I'm dealing with things now, and I don't want to escape it anymore. I just want to help my little girl. Those stories at the therapy sessions are scary. Kids die if they can't get their heads on straight."

Jake seems at a loss for words; all he does after this lengthy speech from Joe is nod soberly. Joe looks unhappy but resolved. I'm glad Vee has her dad in her corner.

We head back upstairs and find Beth sitting serenely on the couch in the family room with a snifter of something nearby. She's watching TV and waves to us to come in. "My legs are plumb tuckered out from all the preparations and shopping I've done for tomorrow's dinner."

We each give her a quick hug, and I smell the alcohol oozing from her pores. Joe walks us to the front door and gives us a hearty wave as we drive away.

The next day, we drive to Jackson Clinic. Dinner is at 2:00 p.m., and we arrive early so we can visit Vee first.

We knock lightly on her door, and peek into a bright and sunny small room. Vee shrieks, leaps off the bed, and throws herself at Jake, giving him a big hug. She then spins to me, lifts me off my feet, doing her classic laugh snort, which leaves us all giggling like kids.

Jake sits on the one chair in the room; Vee and I sit on her bed. She appears healthy and almost happy.

I ask, "So how is it?"

"I'm learning a lot in therapy about myself and why I use or misuse alcohol and drugs. I'm now on antidepressants and antianxiety medication, and it's starting to help. I realize that when I used to get anxious or feel bad about myself, I would turn to alcohol or drugs, which only worked in the moment—in the long run everything became much worse." Vee says in a rush. "So, I would do it again and again, causing a spiral that was very hard to climb out of. It's called self-medicating, and it isn't good."

Vee pauses, and I picture Beth over at the liquor cabinet. Jake gets up and gives Vee another hug and sits on the other side of her.

He murmurs quietly, "You can do this. You are really strong, and you have people who care about you as a person and not just a pretty face. You'll figure it out."

Shrugging, Vee says, "I'm getting there. I really am." Then she turns to me. "Tell me all about it. What's it like living with this jerk?"

I smile shyly, "It's alright. He at least puts the cap back on the toothpaste, unlike someone I know."

Vee scoffs, "Oh! A match made in heaven." She continues, "Okay, Jake, how are Carol and Oliver taking it? Wait, wait, what about Jessica? Did someone tell her the news?"

Jake visibly cringes. "I imagine my mom broke the news to her. I have no idea."

Vee leans back. "Okay, I imagine she pursed her little prissy lips and didn't say a word. What an uptight bitch."

I love how Vee says things I never even dare to think. I give her arm a squeeze and say sincerely, "I miss you."

Vee replies, "Miss you more."

We spend another hour updating each other and sharing stories. I gush on about my wood thrush project with Professor Montgomery.

Vee says to no one in particular, "Jesus, birds! I can't imagine what is so interesting about birds. I remember you in our basement years ago, Jake, building those boxes with my dad."

Jake responds playfully, "Guilty as charged. We built one with him yesterday for old times' sake. It was great."

Vee glances at her phone and announces, "Chow time. Come on, I'm starving."

Each family has their own table, so the three of us sit together after serving ourselves from the buffet. There is a large table of *clients,* as Vee tells us they are called, who are sitting together because they don't have any family visiting. The table looks fun, and the clients appear happy, but I'm so glad we are here to be Vee's family, and she doesn't have to sit over there. The turkey dinner and all the fixings are delicious.

Vee shares, "My dad visits me almost every day, but my mom only comes for family therapy sessions, and she isn't happy about that."

"If anyone can use a little therapy, it's your mom," Jake says. "She told some stories about my mom and dad yesterday. Boy, she's still holding on to some actual anger from way back in college . . . and still drowning that anger with bourbon. She definitely was living vicariously through you to prove something to my mom or to get back at my mom for ditching her. My guess is she wasn't looking out for you so much as trying to rub my mom's nose in your success. I guess she forgot my dad died from it all and she should be thanking her lucky stars she wasn't any part of the New York City scene that ruined my family."

Vee gazes at Jake, raising an eyebrow. "Jake, you should be a therapist. You clearly have real potential. That's exactly what my therapist says to me in my sessions. Not exactly, but pretty darn close. She thinks my mom used me and didn't do enough to protect me and should never have left me at eighteen like she did, even though I told her to go. My therapist is trying to work on my mom, baby steps, she says."

Her voice trails off with a bitter little laugh. We sit quietly for a moment.

How hard life is sometimes, I think. *For everyone, even the beautiful. I never realized that when I was watching from the sidelines.*

Our melancholy is broken when they announce the pies are now served and the three of us make a dash for the dessert table. Jake is an apple guy. Vee and I pick the pumpkin.

After dinner, we're back in Vee's room, and when Jake goes to find a bathroom, Vee clutches my arm and giggles, "Okay, quickly tell me everything. How is the sex? Is it like you imagined it would be? Come on, out with it."

Turning a bright pink, I stare at Vee in utter embarrassment.

"I'm teasing!" she exclaims, laughing. "I don't want to hear about my cousin, yuck. Don't say a thing. I'm just making sure my plan is working. Oh, you guys make the cutest couple."

Shushing her as I glance at the door, I reply, "Vee, you of all people should know, this is all fake. You haven't forgotten that part, have you?"

"Oh, that." She swishes her hand in the air. "Well, it can become real anytime you guys want it to. Or keep calling it pretend, as long as you're having fun. That's all right too. For another six months, is it?"

I shake my head and mutter, "Closer to four now, but who's counting?" I picture my calendar up on Vee's wall and I know the exact days remaining in my deal with the devil or God or whomever.

Walking back into the room, Jake narrows his eyes at us suspiciously and we jump apart.

He says casually, "Vee, what have you been saying to Emma? She's as pink as your hair was when you were fifteen. Remember that phase?"

Vee and Jake laugh.

After visiting Vee several more times over the weekend, we fly home on Sunday night. I fall asleep against Jake on the plane ride, though I wake long enough at one point to hear the flight attendant ask Jake if his fiancée wants a snack. He whispers, "No, she's fine."

My body fills with a warmth like someone has wrapped me in the softest blanket. I take a mental picture of this moment. This will be one of those memories I store away to take out and examine once I'm back in my real world that will help sustain me.

Chapter 24:

Professor Montgomery

Back in New York, I dive right back into the wood thrush project. I'm thrilled to use my very basic Excel skills to make improvements to the tracking spreadsheet. I introduce color coding that applies red, yellow or green automatically based on the final outcome of the nest. Professor Montgomery didn't think it was necessary, but even he starts referring to the *green* nests when we review the findings. I find organizing and analyzing data is a lot like getting ready to make a recipe at the bakery. You need to organize all the ingredients before you mix things together. Then you put all the things together and create something new and different. Professor Montgomery says I have a knack for this type of work.

Today he drops a sheet of paper on my desk while I'm transferring data into the spreadsheet.

"These are the classes I would recommend you try out next semester," he says.

Without looking up, I shake my head and state simply, "I can't."

I don't want to tell him I need to save all my money for my bleak future that is bearing down on me; that is my secret. Never mind I have no idea if I'll even be able to make it to classes in the coming months.

"Emma, you know the expression 'A mind is a terrible thing to waste'?" He pauses. "You can do great things. And you should take advantage of all the perks Columbia provides, as I know they aren't paying you very well."

"Perks? What do you mean perks?"

"The courses are free to anyone who works at the university. Didn't I tell you this when I hired you? Uhh, maybe I didn't. I guess I didn't expect a model's assistant to last the semester. My bad. Well, you better sign up before I find your tragic flaw and decide I must fire you." Professor Montgomery grins.

In disbelief I ask, "So, I can take classes for free because I work for you?"

He nods.

Scooping up the paper, I scan the list of classes, asking him several questions about each of them. They all sound very intimidating, but Professor Montgomery distills them down to simple explanations, and I put notes next to each one on the list. I circle Introduction to Natural Resource Conservation; Ornithology Studies; The Early Days of Bird Studies; and Conservation of Populations and Ecosystems. They sound fascinating and scary. But as I now know, that is life—and I don't want to stop living until I have to.

Sighing, I go back to working, keying in the latest reports, but keep the list on my desk where I steal a glance at it periodically. A possible future lies in those classes.

"These classes sound amazing," I muse aloud after a few

minutes of working. "I wonder what the early days of birding were like. I never thought about that."

Professor Montgomery looks over his computer. "Oh yes, that one may be a tough course for you. The early days were barbaric. Those first birders had no other tools except for a gun; no bins, no cameras, no nothing. So, if they wanted to study a bird, they shot it, stuffed it, and then studied it. Can't blame 'em but sometimes I scratch my head. Did they have to kill so many to study them? Most were collectors too, and if they could collect one, they wanted a hundred. They didn't realize the impact, but it really is shameful. These so-called early birders more than likely caused the demise of the ivory-billed or at least contributed to their downfall."

I sit quietly digesting this and quickly cross out the Early Day's class from the list.

A few hours later, one report includes a picture of a nest in a bird box that has a plexiglass side, just like the one we had in fourth grade. Remembering his promise to tell me how he got into birding and since I'm too keyed up to fill in one more tracker, I peek over at Professor Montgomery. He is getting up to get another cup of coffee.

"Professor, you never told me your, er did you call it a spark story? You know what got you interested in birds. Is now a good time?"

He turns and smiles, "Oh, I wondered if you remembered that." He shakes his head. "Well, this is no sweet baby bluebird story like yours."

He refills his mug and sits back down at his desk.

"Here goes." He waves his hand dramatically, "I was eleven and with my family at the beach on Cape Cod for our annual summer vacation. Growing up, we would spend a week each year enjoying the beaches, exploring the marshes, and walking the tidal flats. It was getting toward four or five o'clock, and the beach was emptying out. My parents loved the beach in the evening. We'd been there all day, and I was kind of bored, so I started goofing around and hunting the seagulls. The seagulls were getting bolder and bolder as the beach emptied." He gives me a stern look. "To be clear, at the time, I referred to them as seagulls like everyone else, but you know there is no such thing."

"Of course." I nod eagerly. "They are gulls and have different names like herring gull or great black-backed gull, but not a one is called seagull."

"Exactly!" Professor Montgomery grins. "So, I start by hiding in a little dip in the sand and jumping out and running after them. That proved not overly effective, so I dug a bit of a deeper hole with a wall of sand and stayed in it with a rock in my hand. Now, mind you, I didn't think this would be any more successful than me chasing after them, but I had nothing better to do so I lay in wait and then popped up and hurled my stone as hard as I could. It was a million-to-one shot. That rock sailed like it was shot out of a cannon and hit a gull right in its head. The bird flapped its wings once, took a few wobbly steps, and just tipped over in the sand, right at the edge of the water. I was horrified."

"Did you kill it?" I ask, covering my mouth with my hand.

"I thought so," Professor Montgomery says grimly. "So, I did what any full-blooded American boy would do. I ran and got my mommy. She rushed over to the bird, and I stood behind her staring at that poor gull. Waves were starting to slap at the big bird, so she wrapped it in a towel and brought it up to dry sand, laying it down carefully. I couldn't believe how big it was up close. It was huge. I now know it was an adult great black-backed gull. We retreated and sat down to see what would happen. You know your little prayers you send up to the big guy throughout the day?"

I glance up in surprise. I didn't realize he noticed my crossing and whispered amens. I nod sheepishly.

"Well, I sent up some major ones that day. I told the big guy I would never harm another bird or animal as long as I lived, if he let this one live. Well, wouldn't you know it, after about five minutes, the gull lifted its head, shook it, then stumbled to his feet, shook his head again, walked a couple of feet, flapped his big black wings and took off. It was truly a miracle. In my infinite wisdom, I figured I needed to do more than just not hurt a bird ever again; I needed to help them. So, there you have it. That's why I do what I do. A pact with God I made when I was eleven. You can't mess with that."

I'm not sure if he's being serious about the God references, but he certainly seems sincere. I picture him as a young boy hiding behind his mother and smile. Professor Montgomery grins back.

Just then a soft knock sounds and Jake pokes his head in.

Professor Montgomery exclaims, "There's our boy, right on time. Do tell, how is the work coming? Will you ever be done with that thesis?"

Beaming, Jake replies, "Thanks to my fiancée here, I can actually say I'm making good progress. I can think and breathe and turns out that helps a lot with getting those critical thinking juices flowing."

Professor Montgomery barks out a laugh. "Yes, this one is a real wonder. The wood thrushes will have her to thank if we can turn around their decline. Between your thesis and this project, she will have helped . . ."

"Oh, come on, we've got to run." Jake interjects. He grabs my coat off the hook and hustles me out. I'm glowing at Professor Montgomery's praise that I'm helping thrushes, and I guess Jake's future patients. I'm on cloud nine.

After dropping my things and changing at the apartment, I leave Jake to his work and head to yoga.

In class today, I stay up in crow pose for several breaths. Which seems fitting because of my bird infatuation. Yoga doesn't measure things in counts or minutes. It uses breath as its timer, and I appreciate this.

A girl I see quite often, Robin, is in class today. When Vee introduced us last month, I remember Vee rolling her eyes when I told Robin how I loved her name.

After class when we are both dripping sweat, Robin asks, "How are you?"

I respond energetically, "Doing just great."

Robin replies, "What do you do for work? Just curious how you get to come to class at two."

I gush, "Oh, I'm working with a professor at Columbia University on a bird study. It is so cool. I love it." Robin beams, "Gee, that's nice to hear. Someone who loves their job. So many people around my office just grouse and complain about their job, but they never do anything about it. I like my job too. I work in human resources and love trying to get people into the right spot and showing them how loving your job makes such a difference."

"Wow! That sounds cool, too."

We walk out together and chat companionably for a few blocks until she turns off and I continue to Vee's. It's so nice to have a simple exchange with a person, I take a mental picture of us sweaty and me having a friendly conversation with someone that is genuinely interested in my story.

After settling into bed tonight, Jake and I chat a bit, which is our normal routine. Soon, he drops off to sleep and I prop myself up on my elbow and work to memorize every angle and plane of his aristocratic face. His eyebrows are perfect arches above his eyes. His eyes have long lashes that frame the speckled brown eyes now hidden under his closed lids. I continue my perusal; I never want to forget what he looks like sleeping next to me.

I'm scrutinizing his bare chest—the sheet is pulled up only to his midsection—when suddenly I hear, "Why don't you reach out and touch it, instead of just ogling."

My eyes flash up to Jake's face and I gasp, "Oh my gosh! Oh, my . . ." I blush furiously.

Jake smirks. "While I do like being ogled by you, I've dreamed of you reaching out and touching me one of these times. Come on, you can't just look."

I sputter, unable to come up with a retort. He's known all along that I've been staring at him when I thought he was asleep. I'm horrified. My eyes start to tear, which only makes me more mortified.

Jake catches my hand in his. "I'm just teasing you. Don't be upset. I shouldn't have said anything. Come here and let's forget the whole thing."

He wraps his other arm around me and pulls me alongside him. Ducking my head into the slight hollow on his chest, I take a deep breath. I press against the muscles along his side with my knees bent upward, pressing against his thighs. Melting into him, feeling safe and warm. His skin feels delicious against my burning cheek.

The now-familiar warmth gathers, and I squirm a little to try to make the discomfort go away.

Jake's voice near my ear whispers fiercely, "Emma, one more wiggle like that and I'll make you touch me."

Gasping, I shift again, moving my hips without thinking.

He chuckles. "This is your fault. I was *way* too tired to even think about sex until you started with your eyes and now your hips. I'm still very tired, though, so why don't you climb on and get those hips over here?"

Unsure of what he wants, I freeze. Jake opens a lazy eye and swings me on top of him with one muscled arm. He quickly dispenses with my night shirt and then my panties.

I'm holding my breath; my mind is racing. *Oh God, what is happening?* But my body takes over, sliding down over him, which feels completely different. How weird. I'm now controlling things; I pull back a little and then work back down a bit further only to pull back again.

Jake groans and I gaze down at him. Groaning again, he says, "Don't tease, Emma."

A surge of power fills me, and I lower myself again. Jake has a look of pure ecstasy on his face. I move to a primal rhythm. I can't stop or tease or control anything. I start to spiral and lift away for a moment; Jake moans my name; the release is heaven. Collapsing down on Jake's chest, my breath labored. I hear Jake's heart beneath my ear, and I listen to its steady beat.

He stirs, nuzzles and kisses my neck. "Ah, baby, you are killing me."

With my face against his chest, I recalled seeing Lady Liberty from the plane; it made me realize the world transforms based on one's viewpoint. At this moment, I feel like I'm on cloud nine and even though I have much more to discover about the world and life, I believe I have the courage to face it.

Chapter 25:

Christmas

Skipping into our little office at Columbia, I make a beeline to the calendar on the wall, joyfully flipping over the page to December. Stepping back, I stare at the bright red cardinal on a branch in a snowy pine tree. *Perfect!* While the day looks like the prior November days, cold and dreary, I feel the difference. December means magic where everything is possible. I've always loved December. It is the one month of the year that hope spills out of me despite myself.

Professor Montgomery breaks my reverie by barking, "Emma, what the hell happened to Nest Observation #12? Did it just disappear into thin air?"

I turn, smiling at him. *Hmm, I guess he doesn't feel the Christmas magic in the air.*

"Seriously, are you smiling at me?" His brow furrows. "I'm used to tears or anger or both, but not a smile. You're the most confounding assistant I've ever had." Shaking his head, he tries to hide his smile.

I whisper, "Magic." And then more loudly state, "Let me check on Nest #12, I remember inputting something about a knockdown of the nest a week ago. Maybe I entered something wrong," I pause for effect. "Highly unlikely, but it's possible." I'm surprised at my audacity, but boy, it feels good being *almost* positive I didn't enter something wrong.

Professor Montgomery replies calmly, "Okay, no problem. Just check it out."

Shuffling through the field notes, I find the knockdown and my chest swells with pride. *I knew it! That explains why it isn't showing up on the report.*

What is even better than being good at my job is being good at Jake. A picture of Jake in bed flashes through my head suddenly. I understand him more and more every day and can decipher his moods. When stressed, he fidgets distractedly, running his hand through his hair with a furrow in his brow. The stress is normally from an altercation with a student or, more likely, a discussion with his mother. Typically, a good meal or a funny story distracts him from such worries. If that doesn't work, I've learned that a few touches of his arm and tosses of my hair, or a simple worried biting of my lip can get his focus on something else altogether. While I haven't had the nerve to initiate something overtly, I've learned it doesn't have to be anything obvious to do the trick. I can't believe it, but I think he enjoys this side of our relationship almost as much as I do. The awful memory of the morning after our first time has faded little by little, and the look of disgust on Jake's face and the stained sheet rears its ugly head less and less, in these past weeks. Even though those images are permanently etched in my memory, I can cope with them.

The only thing marring the perfectness of the approaching Christmas is that we are attending the Christmas Eve service with my parents and then spending Christmas day with Jake's parents and Sandy and Glen. Ugh! I've tried everything I can think of to get out of either or both. I suggested another Vee visit, but she is going home for a few days over Christmas, so that didn't pan out. I told Jake that I may come down with the flu, but he is standing firm, that everything will be fine. He just doesn't understand all the landmines that are out there waiting for me to step on. My stomach cramps in protest every time I picture us back in his family's cold dining room.

Jake and I finish work for the semester in mid-December and even though I love my job, I'm thrilled to have a month off for winter break. Jake immerses himself even further into his thesis work; I go to yoga, watch the winter birds in the park, and visit my parents.

My father is home today when I drop by for a visit, and I'm happy as he is talking to me again. When I'm getting ready to leave, he gruffly says, "You look happy, Emma."

I stand still, letting the warmth of his words spread through my body.

I guess I was pretty sad in the past. I didn't think anyone really noticed.

"I can work at the bakery during my winter break to help during the Christmas rush," I offer.

A rare smile breaks out on Papa's face, "Oh, Emma."

I explain quickly, "I can't do four a.m. but I can get there at nine or ten and work until two or three."

"Of course, of course you can't do four a.m.," he says quickly. "Ten will be fine. We need you, the new girl can't add two plus two."

My cheeks pinken with pleasure. That is as close to a compliment I've ever received from my father. Maybe Christmas Eve won't be a complete nightmare after all.

Jake isn't happy about me going back to the bakery, but he doesn't get it, family obligations are family obligations. When I come home from my first shift, I hand him a bag of powdered paczki. "A peace offering."

He begrudgingly takes the bag and sticks his nose into it, taking a deep sniff, "Mmmm, smells like heaven." He lifts out one of the heavy donuts and takes a bite.

"Oh, my god! This is so good. What are they?"

"They're a Polish donut called paczki. I grabbed the leftover paczki, which doesn't happen often."

Taking another bite, he murmurs, "You must bring these home every day."

I tease, "Wait a minute, what about this being slave labor and that I shouldn't do it?"

Jake replies with his mouth full of a donut, "Completely changed my mind on that front. You need to work there for the rest of your days so you can supply me with Polish delights forever."

Smiling wistfully, I think, *Forever, that would be nice . . . but the days, weeks and months are ticking away.* I keep marking them off on the calendar.

Watching Jake devour the rest of the donut, an idea of a Christmas gift for Jake's family materializes. I've been worried about what to get on my limited budget, but now I have the answer. I'll make them kołaczki, a favorite Polish Christmas cookie. Everyone loves homemade treats, and these are special.

On Christmas Eve, we close the bakery at 2:00 p.m., and I take the dough I made earlier today out of the refrigerator. I'm ready to put together the kolaczki.

Rolling out the dough into an even sheet, I then cut pieces with a pastry cutter, scalloping the edges. I have two fillings, a tangy apricot preserve, and a sweet nut filling. Humming jingle bells, I place a dot of the apricot filling in the center of the first cookie and carefully roll the corners using a drop of water to help seal the edges. Nothing is worse than when your sweet little rolls unseal and bloom in the oven. The cookies don't take long to bake. When they're done, I remove the pans from the oven, dusting the cookies with powdered sugar. The sweet dust settles on my arms and hands as I pass the sifter back and forth over the pans.

I place ten cookies in each of the four boxes I lined with fancy red tissue paper. The cookies nestle into the boxes looking delicate, fancy and oh so perfect. Placing the boxes carefully in a large bag I brought, I head out to get ready for Christmas Eve with my parents.

Jake and I walk to my parents and, as planned, we stay outside to hail a taxi, so my mother and father don't need to wait outside in the cold. This also ensures we won't run into Jake's family.

The wind is biting, and after a few quick hellos and Merry Christmases, we pile into the taxi. Jake is in the front seat, and my parents and I settle in the back.

The church is crowded as it always is on Christmas Eve for the 5:00 p.m. mass. We settle into a pew a few rows behind our normal one, my father stares stonily at the backs of the heads of the family that took our spot.

He leans toward me and Jake, stating gruffly, "Chreasters, should be relegated to the balcony or at the very least the back, eh?"

Jake leans toward my father and asks solemnly, "What is a Chreaster, sir?"

My father almost smirks as he stage-whispers, "It's pretty much all these folks. You know, the ones who only show up on Christmas and Easter . . . . Chreasters."

Jake laughs, "Oh, I get it. That's funny."

My father replies, "Careful there, I'm pretty sure you're a Chreaster."

"Guilty as charged. But who knows, this one"—he glances at me—"has been changing me in more ways than I ever imagined. Anything's possible."

My father harrumphs but not in a bad way, and we all turn to face the front as the priest makes his way down the aisle to the altar.

We get right to the business of singing and genuflecting and I almost relax, with Jake's baritone ringing in my ear.

I never imagined I would have someone to come to Christmas Eve mass with my family. It's not that I didn't have dreams. I did. I dreamed of holding hands on my bench and walking through Central Park with my Ceyx. But the idea that I would sit on this hard pew with my parents and someone special—I never dared to dream something like this could ever happen. Some things are impossible to imagine.

I'm not worrying about tomorrow or the next day or the next, I'm just in the moment, singing hymns, being told of the miracle of miracles. It is all beautiful and something resonates deep within me. The next hour and a half went by quickly.

After church, we hail another taxi and ride back to my

parents. When we get to their apartment, I rush into my old bedroom and grab the bag I hid there last week.

While my parents and Jake get ready for a light dinner of pierogis, I head into Babcia's room. Leaning over her bed, I hand her the Metropolitan Museum's Masterpiece Paintings book I bought for her. "Merry Christmas, Babcia."

She takes the enormous book and slowly starts flipping through the pages, touching some pictures with her hands gnarled with arthritis.

"Remember when I first came to live here, you pushed me to explore the city, especially the museums? I know I never was good at describing what I saw. I didn't have the words or the soul of an artist like you do, and I know I was not a good stand-in. So, I thought for Christmas I would bring the paintings to you, and you could feel them again like you wanted me to."

She looks up at me, tears in her eyes, and whispers, "Thank you." She closes the book reverently and reaches out, clutching my hand. "You know the family legacy was never meant to bend and bow you. I'm glad you are standing tall these days as the Jablonski weight sits much better on shoulders that are strong and straight. That is perhaps the most important trait of us Jablonski's, eh?" She smiles and then opens the book and continues flipping the pages slowly.

I straighten my shoulders, looking down at her, now so small and frail in her bed. She did once stand tall, cherishing her museums, art, painting, and her beloved family. She was always the most ardent advocate of *the legacy*, yet it did not constrain her life; rather, it was enriched by it. Remembering her before my grandfather died, I realize she didn't shy away from her hopes and dreams. Instead, she embraced her happiness, appreciating it even more because of the legacy. *Wow! I've forgotten what she was like before age robbed her of her zest. I wish I paid more attention back then instead of being so miserable and sad about my life.*

Quietly, I leave her. She is enfolded in a world she thought she had left behind. Her present was the most expensive of the three, and I hesitated to buy it, but I'm so happy I splurged as the gift she just gave me with her words are of much greater value than she will ever know.

Stepping back into the kitchen, I see my mother taking the pierogis out of the boiling pot of water and Jake, with an old, faded apron on, is ready to start flipping them in the sizzling pan in front of him. My father is sitting at the table, so I sit down next to him. Reaching into my bag, I bring out a large package of smoked salmon and slide it toward him.

"Merry Christmas, Papa. Enjoy."

Picking it up, my father bounces it in his hand as if estimating its weight.

He declares, "Ahh, Emma, my favorite. My Christmas bagel tomorrow is going to be extra special."

My mother turns away from her pot and eyes the salmon. "That is enough to feed us for a month. You spoil us, Emma."

Standing, I take a pretty box out of my bag and say, "This is for you, Mama. You deserve something pretty and this will match your eyes."

Mama slides the top off the box and takes out a dark-blue scarf. My mother wears scarves on her head when she goes out, and all her scarves are old and as faded as the apron Jake is wearing. This one has gold thread running through it. My mother drapes it over her shoulder and rubs it against her face. She smiles and her eyes sparkle, she sits down and holds the scarf out for my papa to feel.

He smiles into her shining eyes, "Very pretty."

Jake and I serve the pierogis bursting with potato and cheese paired with sauerkraut that is crisp and tangy. The table is silent except for the scraping of forks on our simple white plates. Remembering the tense quiet I experienced across the hall during the last dinner, I am glad I don't have perspiration dripping down my armpit tonight—but I know soon enough, I will.

When Jake and I step out onto Fifth Avenue, the cold whips through our bulky coats. The air has that expectant heaviness that feels as if it will snow at any moment. We hurry home and make hot chocolate. My boxes of cookies are hidden away, ready for tomorrow.

"I have something for you," I say shyly as we sit in the living room, sipping our hot chocolate. "I don't want to give it to you at your parents'. Do you want it now or tomorrow morning?"

Jake looks up from his mug; he has a chocolate mustache. "Now, please," he blurts.

I go into Vee's room, where I hid Jake's present, and pull it out from under her bed. I carry it back to the couch and hand him the wrapped gift, and he grins, "I love surprises."

He tears open the wrapping, revealing the framed collage inside. There is a Snowy Owl in the center and then in seven smaller pictures around the edge: there is a yellow-rumped warbler, a palm warbler, a northern cardinal, a white-throated sparrow, a black-capped chickadee and a dark-eyed junco. The last one is a lovely wood thrush to commemorate the job he got me.

"These are the birds we've seen when we were together in the park, not the actual picture as I don't have a camera, but pictures of the birds plus, of course, the wood thrush," I babble. "I know you hate John Foster, but you seem to like birds, and I thought this could be something for you to remember me by—you know, for when this whole thing is over." I wave my hands nervously then clasp them at my chest, waiting.

Jake tilts his head and replies, "I love it. You are right. I do like seeing birds with you. This is great, but let's not talk about this whole thing being over. That will just make me sad."

He actually looks stricken. My heart swells, "Deal."

We sit sipping our cocoa and talk about each of the birds. I made myself the exact same collage so I will have it to brighten my dreary room at my parents' and will remember each bird sighting once I'm back there, all alone. I'll remember this exact moment too. I'm squirreling away each of these memories, to be taken out and examined when my days drag on and my body begins its halting slide to infirmity.

The next morning dawns bright and clear, I catch the rich scent of pancakes, Jake must be making breakfast. *Oh, how delightful.*

I snuggle under the quilt for a bit. Everything feels . . . the only word to describe it is *happiness*. Lying perfectly still, I work to capture this in my memory bank. If only I could take a picture of my happiness, like the bird pictures, so it could stay with me forever, reminding me of this Christmas morning when my fiancé was making me breakfast after going to church with my family on Christmas Eve.

I grab my robe and run to the window to peek out. Frowning, disappointed when I don't see any magic snow to transform the city. Quickly washing up, I head down the hallway. Standing just behind Jake, I say, "Merry Christmas," and kiss him shyly on his neck. This is the first time I've done something so bold, but it was the feeling I had lying in bed that gave me this newfound surge of courage.

Jake turns and gives me a quick squeeze. "Pancakes are ready, I'll grab your tea and then we can eat."

We munch quietly, passing the syrup back and forth. I get up to refill Jake's coffee, pouring a touch of creamer in it just as he likes. It feels as though we have been doing this for years.

Suddenly, Jake reaches over and pulls out a little blue box hidden behind the napkin holder on the island.

"Emma, here's your Christmas gift. I want to give it to you now instead of at my mom's."

Gazing at the box, I see the name etched on the edge. I clap my hand over my mouth and breathe, "Tiffany's. Oh, my."

Jake beams. "Vee told me you've never gotten a blue box from Tiffany's before, and every girl needs to get at least one box once in her life."

Staring into Jake's speckled brown eyes, I throw my arms around him. "Thank you, thank you so much."

Jake peels me off, chuckling, "But you haven't even opened it. You do know there's something in the box?"

I swat at his arm and slowly lift the top off the box. Nestled inside are the most delicate pair of diamond earring studs, with a little blue stone on either side of the diamond.

"They are lovely. So beautiful. Oh, I can wear them today. Jake, how can I ever thank you?"

Looking pleased, Jake says, "I thought the blue stones match your pretty blue eyes."

Carefully, I take them out of the box and try to figure out how to put them on. They have back screws, I guess to make sure they are extra secure. I finally figure them out and do a twirl in the kitchen and then dash off to the mirror in the hallway to admire them.

Yelling over my shoulder, I'm ecstatic, "They are just perfect. I can't believe I have diamond earrings. I never dreamed of owning such a thing."

We head over to Jake's parents at 3:00 p.m. for an early Christmas dinner. Jake and I are each carrying our bags with gifts in them. We walk through the park and we both slow to a crawl, dragging our feet the closer we get to the apartment building.

Suddenly, the first snowflakes start softly falling, and I think my heart is going to split at the seam. Grabbing Jake, I pull him over to my bench, and we silently watch the snow fall.

Every snowfall in my life seemed to send me a message. A message that transformation and magic are possible, and for me to never stop believing in magic. I remember when I'd step outside at 4:00 a.m. and discover a city blanketed with fresh snow. The world transformed in a heartbeat, and one day that same magic will paint my life with its magical brush just as it does the trees and the sidewalks, changing the city from drab to dreamy.

Finally, Jake pulls me up and gives me a kiss on the tip of my nose, stating, "Listen, Emma, we must go, or we both may freeze."

We run the rest of the way and burst through his parents' door all red-faced and giggling. The apartment smells delicious. Sandy and Glen are already there, and both are holding glasses with some thick-looking yellow mixture in them.

Jake loudly announces, "We're here, let the party begin."

Carol gives Jake a quick look of reproach, but then smiles indulgently, "Merry Christmas, son."

Jake gives her a long hug and I hang back, feeling uncomfortable. Jake nods his head in Sandy and Glen's direction and says, "Merry Christmas, guys. What have you got there? Oliver's famous eggnog?"

They both grimace and nod. Jake calls into the kitchen,

"Oliver! Merry Christmas. Emma and I are dying for your eggnog. Is there any left?"

Poking his head out of the kitchen, Oliver replies jovially, "Coming right up. No need to worry, we have plenty."

Jake whispers in my ear, "Just pretend to drink it. It's pretty awful and watch out, it's strong."

When Oliver brings over two glasses with a thick yellow liquid and I take a small sip. *Hmm, maybe this will help me make it through the evening.*

We sit down for dinner and I'm glad I can identify everything on my plate, and it tastes as good as it smells—except for the little legs of lamb. They are too raw and too strong for my taste. After trying a few bites, I leave them alone and decide I'll just eat everything else.

Jake reaches his fork over and takes a few morsels of lamb off my plate when he notices I'm avoiding it. I, meanwhile, sink my fork in his twice-baked potato when I finish mine. We are like an old married couple, eating off each other's plates. Next thing you know, we'll be finishing each other's sentences.

Maria clears the plates, and I stay firmly rooted to my chair to avoid any repeat of the Jessica dinner fiasco.

Carol announces dramatically, "Before dessert, let's retire to the sitting room for presents."

We shuffle into the living room and there are a few gifts under the huge, sparkly, fake tree. I rush to tuck my cookie boxes underneath the tree with the other gifts.

Carol clears her throat, making sure all eyes are on her, before handing Sandy and Glen a large, heavy box. They open a huge juicer or blender thingy they call a *Vitamix*.

Sandy gushes, "Thanks so much. This is great. I hear it can make juice out of anything."

Hopping up, she gives Carol and Oliver a quick hug and turns to regard Glen pointedly. "Glen and I have been trying to eat healthier, and the Vitamix is just what we need to help."

Rolling his eyes, Glen responds sarcastically, "Great. Juice."

Reaching under the tree, Carol pulls out a long rectangular box. She reads the tag, "To Jake, From Oliver and Carol." When Jake doesn't get up, she places it in his lap, and Jake slowly, hesitantly unwraps it. Inside the elegant Brooks Brother's box is a lovely pinstripe suit with a shirt and tie.

Jake grimaces. "Gee, thanks. This is really too much."

Carol comes over and hugs Jake. "Jake, really. You need to start thinking about when." Her voice drops. "Oliver is losing patience."

Jake gives her a stony look. "Really?" he asks flatly. "On Christmas, Ma?"

Looking annoyed, Carol retorts, "You know I hate when you call me that."

Jake turns to me. "Emma, do you want to give out your pretty little boxes you've brought?"

My cookies aren't an expensive suit or a Vitamix, but they are lovely and certainly won't evoke any of the ill will that seems connected to the more expensive gifts. I quickly retrieve my boxes and hand one to Oliver, Carol, Sandy, and Glen.

Glen opens his first and exclaims, "Now we're talking. These look delicious." He grabs a cookie out of his box and pops it in his mouth, "Aah, heavenly."

Carol lifts out a cookie, takes a sniff, and then sets it back into the box, "Yes, they do smell and look lovely. But we have dessert coming."

Sandy and Oliver don't bother to open their boxes.

Smiling reassuringly, Jake says loudly, "Emma, they look lovely. Did you make these?"

"Yes, I did," I say gratefully. "They're called kolaczki, a traditional Polish Christmas cookie."

"Okay," Carol says as if I haven't even spoken, "now here is something for Emma." She pulls an envelope from the tree that was hidden in the branch and hands it to me.

I'm not sure if I should open it.

She nods encouragingly, "Open it, dear. It's something everyone can use."

Opening the envelope, I find a pretty card inside. As I flip open the card, an Amazon gift card drops onto my lap. Jake reaches over, picks it up, and hands it back to me with a frown.

"Thank you so much," I say sincerely. "That is so generous. And you are right, I can certainly use it."

Sandy gets up and pulls an envelope from her purse and quips, "Like mother, like daughter. Here open mine—uh—mine and Glen's gift."

I slide open the card and this time manage to keep the Amazon gift card from dropping. It is another $50 gift card. I smile at Sandy. "Oh, that is a funny coincidence. Thank you both so much. I have a hundred things I can buy with this."

Jake levels a sharp gaze at both Sandy and Carol and says, his voice dripping with insincerity, "Yes, what a wonderful *personal* gift from both of you. Is this what you gave the doorman too?"

I peer at him, confused by his tone. "Jake, it's very nice and, as they said, very useful."

Jake cuts me off with a glare. "No, really. This is so welcoming and filled with such thoughtfulness. I really must go on—"

"Enough! Let's go have dessert," Carol warns, waving her hand dismissively. She marches back into the dining room.

On his way out, Glen sneaks one more cookie into his mouth and nudges me whispering, "Thanks for the cookies.

They are the best I've ever tasted. And I'm not just saying that because I may be drinking only juice for the new year."

He winks. He is a nice guy when he's allowed to talk.

As we are packing up the gifts, getting ready to leave, I run to the bathroom. When I walk by the front door, I see the maid has placed her bag next to the front door before returning to the dining room to do some last-minute cleanup. I spot one of my boxes of cookies peeking out of the side of her bag.

Only now do I remember hearing Carol say something to Maria earlier about taking something because "they will only go to waste." I thought they were talking about leftover lamb, but now I realize she was talking about my cookies. My heart stings with the hurt. I'll never fit into Jake's family, but they didn't even give me a chance. I'd been holding on to a little hope that I would be accepted and even welcomed, but now it is as clear as the red box shoved into the maid's bag that I'll never fit in.

Making my way into the dining room, I woodenly say, "Merry Christmas and thank you for the meal."

I can't bring myself to say anything about the Amazon gift cards, as I now understand Jake's anger: they are a pathetic gift that, unlike my cookies, didn't take an ounce of time or effort.

Jake and I step out onto Fifth Avenue, and I take a sharp inhale, the world is now blanketed with snow, turning it into a winter wonderland. We stand perfectly still, taking in the magical sight. The city has completely changed in the four hours since we arrived at Jake's parents.

Jake breathes, "I don't even care if my family gave you the lamest gifts anymore. That isn't what Christmas is about, is it?"

I shake my head in agreement. "I don't even care your mom gave my cookies to Maria. That isn't what Christmas is about either."

"What?" Jake barks. "She gave your lovely cookies to the maid?"

I nod, feeling the sting of tears despite the magic in the air.

Jake shakes his head. "If I knew that was an option, I would have given Maria my stupid suit, too." He smiles ruefully.

"Well, at least Glen won't give his box of cookies away, am I right?" I quip.

Jake hoots. "Oh! Aren't you something? I better watch out. You have some claws hidden under all that innocence and sweetness."

I giggle and our anger and hurt melt away with our laughter. The soft covering of snow turns the hurt and disappointment into something enchanting and mystical. Our little drama isn't important in the larger scheme of things. The world and nature contain secrets, and the power of Christmas snow heals and fixes everything. Its magic lets a pretend couple walk with the fairies and elves on this one special night.

As darkness descends on us, we hear the distinctive *who cooks for you* call of a nearby barred owl. Magic!

Chapter 26:

New Year's Eve

I'm more than halfway through my *living* time allotment and I can't believe how quickly it is going. The magical Christmas snow has melted, leaving only brown, slushy patches in the sidewalk's shadows. A hundred stomping feet have leached all the sorcery out of it.

It's New Year's Eve, and my old calendar is in the trash. I've hung up the new one Jake gave me. It's the 2014 Audubon bird calendar, making my monthly countdown almost fun because the Ruby-crowned Kinglet, the Great Spotted Woodpecker, and the Juniper Titmouse marks each of the next three months.

Jake and I are going to a New Year's Eve party Jake's parents insisted we attend. We're not thrilled, but to keep the peace, as Jake says, we're going. Jake uses so many war terms when dealing with his family. All the references make me worry that something bigger is gathering just over the horizon, and we need to be prepared for some sort of flank attack.

"You promise this won't be another *Vogue* party?" I ask. "I really don't want to go if it is."

"Definitely, it won't be anything like that. There will be no random Danny running around accosting you," he states emphatically. Jake had insisted on knowing the whole story, so a few weeks ago, I finally told him. He winced his way through every sordid detail.

"What you need to worry about is being bored to death. These people are miserable. Nothing's worse than a bunch of Wall Street fat cats trying to make merry and ring in the New Year so they can continue to fleece America," he snorts with a laugh.

Jake shrugs on his suit jacket and eyes the frosted window, looking miserable. My heart aches for him. He really hates everything about what his parents are forcing him into.

Glancing down, I smooth my new party dress. Since I will never wear my maroon dress again, I bought this one at Barneys—on the discount rack; the cost wasn't absurd—and my mother and I made the few adjustments needed, as there is no fancy fitting service for the discount rack. The dress is black with silver piping around the edges with a little silver belt. My silver shoes go perfectly with it.

I consulted Vee for makeup help earlier, and she worked her magic from far away through FaceTime. She had me reblend my eyeshadow twice, but overall, she gave me a big thumbs up by the end of the session. Jake was very accommodating, holding the phone through the whole consultation, all the while peppering Vee with questions about what was going on with her. She's home now for good (fingers crossed) and attending AA meetings every day. She sounded strong and upbeat. When we hang up, Jake peruses my face and nods his head approvingly, whispering, "Stunning," almost to himself. I feel my cheeks flush, and I glance in the mirror again, tilting my head at my reflection. *Stunning* echoes in my head.

We head down to our waiting taxi and jump into the backseat. As we drive to the party, I get a rush of excitement despite Jake's description of the party.

A fancy New Year's Eve party with my fiancé, who just said I was stunning. What could be better?

The party is in a large hotel ballroom, and champagne is flowing when we arrive. I see immediately, this party is very different from the *Vogue* party. You can hear yourself talk over the band that is playing off to one side. They're playing a swaying waltz and not the electronic pulsating beat that made my heart pound erratically and assaulted my eardrums. People are dressed up, but there are no angels walking around in the crowd.

We spot Carol and Oliver sitting at a table with two other couples on the far side of the ballroom. We introduce ourselves to the table and take the two available chairs. Oliver is all business and barely acknowledges us.

He waves over a server, "Bottle of Pappy's bourbon for the table. Make it quick, I'm thirsty."

George, the man at the table with a southern accent, claps Oliver on the back announcing loudly, "Now we're talking! The best deals always happen with good bourbon."

The server brings eight glasses, and all the women demur when offered a glass. Jake does the same, but when Oliver shoots him a look, he sighs and signals to the server that he will take a glass.

"And a side of water, too, please," Jake says.

"I'd like water too, thank you!" I pipe up.

George does a little eye roll to Oliver who shrugs and mouths, "Amateurs."

Once the bottle is set in the center of the table, Oliver grabs for it and pours generously.

Servers with food trays come by periodically, and Carol and the other two women keep declining while Jake and I are trying many delectable items.

Turning to the ladies, I gush, "This one is really good. You should try it. It's shrimp and something else."

Winnie replies drily, "Oh yes, I'm sure it is, but do you know how many calories are in one of those bites?"

Scrutinizing the little tidbit, I shake my head. Winnie doesn't respond and I realize it was a rhetorical question. Winnie is pencil-thin, like Carol, and her face looks tight and drawn.

Jake leans toward me and whispers, "Eat it. Don't listen to them. They haven't been able to enjoy food for years."

Studying the women, I see a weird similarity despite the obvious difference in height, coloring and facial features. What is similar is how they all hold themselves rigidly, as if they aren't breathing. It's like they are trying to hold themselves together, seemingly worried they may shatter into a million pieces at any moment, revealing their true selves to the harsh world.

Studying them, something dawns on me: I'm not looking to swap one box for another—especially not one so confining it tells you what to eat, what to wear, even how to think. My box may be small, but now I realize there is room for joy within it. We savor good and hearty Polish food without guilt, relishing every bite. And as for work, I'll gladly stick with my humble job helping feathered friends rather than spending my days feathering my nest. I giggle at my cleverness.

Jake elbows me and whispers, "What's so funny?"

"A bird pun," I say cheekily. "I'll tell you later."

Jake shoots back, "A bird pun? Now that I must hear."

I shush him, reddening. The other man, whose name I forgot, glances over, shakes his head, and remarks snidely, "You and those birds."

My face falls at his tone and I raise my eyebrows in surprise, as I didn't think anyone even knew about my job. Carol or Oliver must have said something about it before we arrived. Although that seems unlikely, as this crowd presumes women don't have jobs worth talking about.

Easing out of his chair, Jake takes my hand and says, "Be back shortly," to the table.

Over the clink of glasses, no one pays us any attention.

We stroll around the ballroom together. Jake says hi to a few people and introduces me as his fiancée, which is met with appraising looks, and I try to meet their questioning stares with confidence and warmth. It's draining for both of us. We stumble upon a sumptuous buffet tucked in a corner and we dig in, loading up our plates with a selection of extravagant meat carvings and fancy side dishes. We find ourselves a secluded tall table where we eat standing up. I enjoy every bite; glad the women's disapproving eyes are no longer drilling into me.

After we've eaten our fill, we wander over to a bar area and Jake orders us sparkling water that comes in fancy fluted glasses. We meander back to the table, knowing we must, as it would be rude to stay away too long.

George and Oliver are now talking loudly, both intent on one upping the other in telling stories of their less than scrupulous business dealings. They are both red-faced, and the bourbon bottle is almost empty. Carol has a pained look on her normally placid face.

When we sit down at the table, Oliver focuses his glassy

eyes on Jake, exclaiming loudly, "There's my boy. Jake, where have you been? I've been telling George here how you are going to start working at the firm soon. Can't wait to have you on board. We need new thinking and fresh eyes. I'm thinking, George, he may be your account manager if we seal our deal. Jake is great. He just needs to get his head out of the clouds and start pulling his weight."

Jake smiles tightly and inclines his head in George's direction.

Glancing at Jake's watch, I see it's 11:30 p.pm. I figure we have another hour before we can make our escape. As I'm making my calculations, Carol leans over to Jake and whispers something I can't hear. Jake flashes his eyes towards Oliver and then back at Carol, who looks agitated.

Jake puts his arm around me and pulls me close to him. "We are going to try to get Oliver out of here without making a scene," he whispers. "Oliver drunk can be pretty ugly. Okay?"

I nod quickly, glad we don't need to hang out for another hour.

Suddenly, George shoves the table a bit and warns angrily, "Watch it, Oliver. Let's not get nasty here. We're all enjoying ourselves."

Oliver's face flushes red and spittle forms in the corners of his mouth as he struggles to come up with a retort. He violently pushes up from the table and his chair bangs over behind him.

Jake jumps up, grabs the chair, and says smoothly, "Oliver, let's go make the rounds. You wanted to introduce me to some other folks here tonight, right?"

Oliver squints at Jake, looking a little confused, but Jake links arms with him and he allows himself to be led away.

Carol watches them go, then just as smoothly as her son says, "Well, it was a lovely evening. Such wonderful company. Happy New Year to you all. Emma, dear, come along."

I get up obediently and mumble something about how nice it was to meet them all and rush to catch up with Carol. Her eyes are darting around the ballroom. She breathes a sigh of relief when she spots Oliver and Jake heading to the hallway where the bathrooms are. Oliver is staggering a bit, but Jake is propping him up.

We follow and wait in an uncomfortable silence in the hallway outside the men's room.

I spy the ladies' room down the hall. "I think I'll go the ladies' room," I say, wanting to escape Carol for a moment.

"Don't you dare," Carol hisses. "We need to get him out of here and I need Jake's help." Her face softens. "Unless it is an emergency. Then of course you can go."

I shake my head. "No emergency. I'm good."

Jake and Oliver come out of the bathroom and Oliver looks better. He has water around his hairline and his face isn't as flushed as it was.

Carol rushes over to him. "Darling, there you are. I have a splitting headache, and Emma isn't feeling so well either. All those hors d'oeuvres aren't sitting well with her." She tosses a disapproving look in my direction. "We have a taxi waiting."

Oliver gazes at Carol, then at me, hesitating. "Sure," he finally mutters. "Just need to say our goodbyes."

"All taken care of." Carol pats his arm. "George and Winnie are heading out too, so no one is left at the table."

Oliver pauses, then lets Jake take his limp arm and we all walk out onto the street. There is, in fact, a taxi sitting there, as promised, as it is not yet midnight and no one else leaves this early. I sit in the front seat, and Jake, Carol and Oliver settle in the back.

Oliver turns to Jake. "Jake, a deal's a deal, right? You

are coming to work for me. That's the plan since . . . well, since forever, right?"

Jake starts to shake his head but Carol cuts in, "Yes, Oliver. Of course, that's the plan. Jake will start in March as soon as he completes his PhD. He will be the only investment fund broker with a PhD in—"

"Yes," Jake interrupts. "March it is. This is the new year, so time to start new things for all of us."

I turn to gaze at Jake, and he doesn't meet my eyes.

We pull up to the apartment building and stumble out into the cold air. Oliver has shifted into a mellow, almost sleepy state and Jake and I help him up the stairs, into the elevator and lead him down the hallway. A shiver of déjà vu runs down my spine as I remember carrying Vee down this same hallway three months ago. I smile softly to myself, as only I know how much I've changed since that day.

As we pass my parents' door, Carol grumbles in a voice dripping with disgust, "Jesus, those dirty, smelly Polacks are at it again. Do they ever cook anything other than onions and cabbage?"

I freeze.

I look at my parent's apartment door and want to reach out and touch the worn wood.

Jake reaches out with his hand and tugs me along, mouthing, "Just ignore it." He looks pained. "Please."

My heart stutters and seizes. Ignore it! His mother just called my family dirty, smelly Polacks. I look up ahead at Carol, who hasn't missed a step. This isn't something new for Jake. She probably says it every time she walks by our apartment. He's probably heard it his whole life. But this is the first time I've heard such a thing, and my stomach sours and I feel sick.

I continue walking but my legs aren't working right. It's like I'm walking through mud. My feet are dragging. I trail a hand along the wall both to help guide me, but I also want to press through those walls and pass on a modicum of comfort to my hardworking parents. They are sleeping on the other side after a long day of surviving. I don't want to see Carol or Jake, so instead I focus up at the ceiling. The painted ceiling is peeling and cracked. My eyes trace a crack that is circular, the exact size of a head of cabbage. Fall is when cabbage is cheap and fresh, retaining a lot of juice. Last month, I watched my mother cut the cabbage into thin slices and put it into the crock pot with salt to start the process. I remember saying gently, "Mama, let me cut the cabbage." And my mother replying, "No Emma, I can do it. I've been doing it forever. This disease can't take everything from me." My eyes burn with unshed tears that I try desperately not to let fall. To distract myself from the group moving to the next apartment, I calculate how many heads of cabbage we've carried into our apartment. My grandparents moved in in 1950; therefore, they have been making sauerkraut for sixty years. Roughly five cabbages a year means I need to multiply five times sixty. I'm trying to remember basic multiplication when my foot snags on nothing and I stumble. Jake grabs hold of me again and I continue in a daze through their apartment door, seeing the plush apartment once more with fresh eyes. I shiver with a chill. Jake continues ahead, bringing Oliver into his bedroom and deposits him on the bed. I'm careful not to make eye contact with Carol, who is now in the kitchen. Jake leaves Oliver sitting on the bed taking off his shoes slowly. Jake takes my hand and pulls me along.

Carol asks sweetly, "Do either of you want any coffee, er, or I guess tea for you, Emma?"

Any other time I would be elated, but this time, I slowly shake my head and search Jake's face for any response. He looks resigned and deflated, leaning against the counter. My stomach roils and I glance toward the bathroom door as a sour taste forms in my mouth. The coffee maker hisses and gurgles. Suddenly, a roar emanates from the bedroom and Carol's face blanches. She gives Jake a push, and he gets up robotically, walking down the hall like a man condemned.

I'm not sure what is going on, but I can't summon up any genuine interest. I'm watching things from inside my bubble; I'm not part of this little drama. Carol called my family something terrible, and Jake isn't going to do anything about it. I grab my coat and head in the other direction—yank open the apartment door and step out. I smell the aroma from my parents' apartment, knowing my mother finally cooked the cabbage to make sauerkraut, which has been fermenting for the past month.

The burning in the pit of my stomach intensifies when I think of Carol calling my mother dirty and smelly. She's just trying to cook and provide for her family, all the while fighting MS. The nerve of that shell of a woman, with her lily-white hands and her upright posture, to judge my parents and me.

Walking blindly past my door, my eyes are burning. Down on Fifth Avenue, I blindly march towards Vee's. I'm tempted to cut through the park, but that seems foolhardy on New Year's Eve, so close to midnight. I stick to the sidewalk. I will grab a cab once my anger dissipates a bit.

Then suddenly I'm sprawled face down on the hard cement. I remember the weakness I felt in my legs in the hallway earlier. *My god, MS has a cruel sense of humor.*

I hear a voice ask, "Are you okay? That was a nasty fall. Can you get up?"

I roll over, sit up, and survey my dress. Ruined. My ankle throbs, and I may have broken my wrist. I cradle it in my other hand.

Looking up, I try to smile at the concerned faces above me. I respond, "I think I'm okay. My ankle hurts."

The man gingerly takes my good arm, and I stand with most of my weight on my left foot. We make our way to the bus enclosure nearby and I sink down thankfully onto the hard bench. They hover over me, clearly worried. I try to smile, but it feels as if my face may break in two.

Taking a deep breath, I steady myself and say firmly, "I'm fine. I'm just going to sit and rest for a minute. My apartment is right over there."

I tilt my head. Although they don't appear convinced, they step out of the bus area and continue walking down the sidewalk, glancing back in my direction as they go.

I breathe deeply and fight back tears. Everything is too much. My MS, Jake's mom's spitefulness, Oliver's drunkenness and Jake's unwillingness to . . . to do anything. I need to end this whole charade now. It feels too real for me, and I must stop before I become more deluded. A single tear spills over and falls onto the arm of my coat. I'm just the dirty, smelly Polack girl from next door. God, it hurts just thinking those words.

My ankle is beginning to swell and I'm glad it's freezing cold; it's like having an ice pack on both my wrist and my ankle. Suddenly, my cell phone rings. Taking it out of my purse with my good hand, I eye it warily. It's Jake. As it continues ringing, my gaze remains fixed upon it. I'm torn. I would love to ignore it, but I doubt I can make it back to Vee's or my parents by myself.

I pick up and resignedly say, "Hello."

Jake shouts, "Where are you, Emma? I came back to Vee's

expecting you to be here. Are you with your parents?" His voice drops when he says *your parents*.

"Uh, I fell, and I'm sitting on Fifth Avenue between Ninety-Seventh and Ninety-Sixth."

"Dammit, I cut through the park to get home quicker when I realized you left. What a shit show. Okay, stay right there. I'm coming."

I punch the red button on my phone and wait. My toes and fingers are slowly going numb, along with my heart. I've made my decision. I need to go back to my old life. I have enough memories stored away, and I've learned enough, so I'll no longer pine for the life I think others have. There is no need to be jealous, no one's life is perfect or easy. That's just a fantasy. As my grandmother told me, I can stand tall on my own and try to figure out what I want that fits into my world.

I'm in a semi-dream state when Jake rushes up to me and takes my ice-cold cheeks in his hands and kisses me. "Listen, I'm so sorry," he pleads. "I should have said something. I don't know why I didn't. Well, I know why I didn't, and it was cowardly. I just wanted the night to be over and get Oliver into bed before something really bad happened. I didn't mean what my mother said wasn't really bad. It was. It's just Oliver can be volatile, and I didn't want you to see that. Listen, tell me what happened. Oh God, you look awful."

I hear words tumbling out of Jake's mouth, but I can't grasp them. I'm off in my own world and I know now he is not part of it.

I speak softly, "My wrist may be broken, and my ankle hurts too."

Jake examines both carefully. Standing quickly, he hails a taxi driving by. I'm surprised we found one so quickly, until I look down at his watch and see that it's only a little past midnight. We're still in the sweet spot of time, just after midnight, even though it feels like a lifetime has passed since we left the party.

Jake settles me into the taxi and kisses me again, "Happy New Year, Emma."

Normally I would melt into him, but both the pain and my recent realizations keep me in my place.

He scrutinizes me, a perplexed look on his face, as he tells the cabbie, "Mount Sinai hospital."

We drive the few blocks in silence.

The emergency room is busy but not crazy; that will come later. We sit and wait; finally, my name is called, and we go back to a small exam room. The medical assistant asks me several questions as she takes my vitals. Sitting on the crinkly tissue paper, I'm swept back to the last time I sat on such a bed. I'm lost in my musings.

Jake gets up from the chair, his forehead creased with concern. "Emma, are you okay? You look kind of out of it. Do you think you hit your head?"

He takes his hands and starts feeling my head, moving my hair off my forehead.

Taking hold of his hands, I push them back down and say flatly, "I didn't hit my head, Jake."

He sits back down only to jump back up when the doctor enters the room. The doctor is young and has a chart in hand. He asks me the same questions the medical assistant just asked.

Examining my wrist and ankle, he states, "We need to order X-rays, but I'd say you're right. Broken wrist and a sprained ankle."

I ask quietly, "Jake, can you step out of the room for a moment, please?"

Jake glances up in surprise and I keep my gaze steady. He gets up and closes the door behind him.

Turning to the doctor, I state matter-of-factly, "So, I have MS, I was diagnosed with it a few months ago. I'm not on any medication yet, but that is what caused my fall. Dr. Liam is my MS doctor. I'm not sure if that makes any difference at all, but I wanted to tell you just in case."

I stop talking and try to meet the doctor's eyes but can't. I don't want to see the pity that comes with such a revelation. I've seen it from too many doctors over the years for my mother. I'm not ready to see it directed at me—not yet. Doctor Tremont sits down and starts punching information into the computer, intently reading the information that comes up.

He finally twirls around. "I'm just reviewing your records. Dr. Liam's office is part of the Mt. Sinai healthcare system. This says they suspected MS back in September, but your Lyme disease test came back positive, and they treated you for Lyme; that should have resolved your problems. Did it?"

I stare dumbfounded. "What did you say?" I stammer.

He regards me steadily, and this time I meet his eyes. "Your chart says it was Lyme disease, and you were treated for it. Are you still having muscle weakness and swollen joints? You may need another dose of antibiotics—sometimes Lyme can be persistent."

"Dr. Liam doesn't think it's MS?"

Dr. Tremont replies, "You definitely had Lyme, but only you know if you still have symptoms but if you do, I would treat you for Lyme again before I jumped to MS, despite your family history."

Thinking back, I realize I have had no symptoms since that first month after my visit to Dr. Liam. I've been just fine right until this fall. *Could the horrible sidewalks explain my fall coupled with my distraction because of the wretched evening and not MS?*

I don't know what to think about that. My diagnosis has been a part of me for almost four months. It is why I agreed to this ruse with Jake and what made me break out of my shell to live a little. Without MS, suddenly I have no idea what I'm doing. My shoulders hunch, curling into myself. I lost my security blanket.

There is a knock on the door and two orderlies poke their heads in.

"X-Ray," one of them says.

Right behind them is Jake, looking more worried than I've ever seen him. I glance away. I've played an awful trick on him. I was planning to disappear into my little cocoon come March, fading away into my illness. Now, I'm not going to do that, and suddenly my entire plan is much messier and more problematic than I expected. Now, apparently, I am going to be alive and well, which means I have a lifetime to wonder what Jake is doing and who he's marrying. *Oh, no!* My stomach clenches. I'll bump into Jake going and coming from his parents' place at 4:00 a.m. once I'm back at my bakery job soon enough. *Ugh!* I want to scream.

The orderlies shift me to a gurney, and I'm wheeled down the hall to X-ray. After we get the results, I get a boot for my sprained ankle and a cast for my broken wrist. As soon as both are on, the throbbing lessens and then the two prescription-strength Tylenol kicks in, and I almost feel normal, at least physically. Jake continues to survey me quizzically. Dr. Tremont tells me to make an appointment with Dr. Liam and wishes me luck, and it's over—we are heading *home*.

We crawl into bed and as we lie side by side, Jake rambles, "You scared me tonight. When I didn't find you here, I panicked. I was really scared something happened to you, and I never want anything bad to happen to you. And then at the hospital, it seemed like something weird was going on . . . it just got me worried, that's all." He continues in a rush, "Do you want to tell me anything? Who is Dr. Liam?"

Turning toward him, I study the gorgeous angles and planes of his face. Suddenly, tears well in my eyes. "Not tonight, please," I beg. "Not tonight."

Chapter 27:

Good News

First thing Monday morning, I call Dr. Liam's office. When I tell the receptionist who I am, she exclaims, "Emma, I'm so happy you finally called us back. We've been trying to get a hold of you for months. Why didn't you call us back?"

"Uhm, I recently moved out of my house and I . . . I need to see Dr. Liam," I say. "Can you squeeze me in as soon as possible?"

"Of course," she chirps. "Just hold on one moment.

When she gets back on the line, she tells me they've penciled me in for that Wednesday at 7:30 a.m., before Dr. Liam normally sees patients.

I guess they don't get to share good news with patients very often.

The office is empty when I get there, but Dr. Liam bursts in and leads me to an examination room.

She hugs me and then scolds, "Why didn't you ever call us back? We've left messages at the number you provided but couldn't leave any other information on the test results. We expected you would call us back." Glancing at my boot and cast, she says, "And what in the world happened to you?"

I shrug and sheepishly say, "I fell on New Year's Eve. I want to know if that was me just being clumsy or if it was MS acting up."

"And the no call backs?" Dr. Liam presses.

"My mom mentioned the messages, but I ignored them. I moved out of my parents' house and didn't want to deal with reality yet." I look directly into Dr. Liam's eyes. "Are you sure it's Lyme and not MS?"

"Well, let's have a look."

She goes through the normal checks of balance, reflexes, keeping up a steady stream of questions.

At the end, she remarks, "I don't see any indication of physical issues. The ones we noted in September have cleared up. Your responses to my questions tell the same story. No indication of MS symptoms. We both know that doesn't guarantee they won't emerge at some point, but for now, no MS is my diagnosis. I think we can safely assume the antibiotics I gave you for the Lyme worked."

Dr. Liam regards me with raised eyebrows. I am sure she is expecting me to be jumping for joy, but all I can muster is a wan smile as I feel the crush of my crazy decisions coming home to roost. What am I going to do? I no longer have just the next few months to figure out and deal with . . . suddenly I have my whole life, and that is overwhelming. Being brave is much easier when you don't have a future ahead of you. I hug myself as fear and worry consume me, making breathing difficult. Life is too scary; I just want to run back to my safe cocoon. I realize without MS, I'm not sure I can stand tall. A single tear makes its way down my cheek. *Goddamn it.*

I step out of Dr. Liam's building. People are rushing around, heading to work, and on errands; the feeling of being disconnected from the world pervades my mind. I wander through Central Park, sit on my favorite bench, but all the birds are quiet. I try to think about my future, but it makes my head hurt. Jake, my parents, everything keeps tumbling around and around.

Getting up slowly, I limp behind the bench and melt into the woods. Ten feet in, my mind quiets, my body seems to reconnect with the world—this world. Blindly, I reach with my one good hand and press it into the sturdy trunk of my tree. My breath eases, my senses sharpen, and my mind clears. The life I've been living is untenable, but that doesn't mean I have to crawl back into my cocoon. Maybe, just maybe, I can figure things out on my own.

The rough bark against my hand brings a sense of certainty. I'm no longer lost. *I can do this. I can make a life for myself.* My shoulders lift and I retrace my steps and reemerge behind my bench, no longer disconnected from the hustle and bustle of the people and the city. With my head up high and a lopsided bounce in my step, I walk back to Vee's.

Sitting on the couch after I get home, I contemplate what my new world could look like. I'll move home, keep working with Professor Montgomery, I'll take some real college classes, I'll work at the bakery on weekends, I'll sign up for another three months of yoga . . .

I don't realize Jake's come into the room until he comes over and sits down next to me. He picks up my good hand in his larger one, and we both stare at our entwined hands. He places his other hand over mine and rubs it gently.

"Emma, what is going on? Please let's talk. This seems like it's about more than just what my bigoted mother said."

I lock my eyes with him. The brown speckles glow with an intensity as well as a lovely sweetness. A smile starts to break out on my face, despite my inner turmoil. His eyes make me smile, even when my world is shifting beneath my feet.

But then I glance away. I'm not ready to tell him everything. He's been very patient since the emergency room, but my future is starting to take shape, and I don't yet have words to explain things. The bubble closes around me a little tighter. I'm hoping with time the words will come.

"Emma?"

"It's okay, really, nothing is wrong," I state, trying to keep my tone light. "I'm just trying to figure out some stuff."

He shakes his head. "I'm worried about you. I've never seen you like this. Maybe we should talk to Vee?"

Now I shake my head. "No. Really, I'm fine."

Extracting my hand from the warmth of Jake's grip, I go through the motions of getting dinner ready. It's a simple cacio e pepe, which Pinterest describes as simple but elegant. I try to make small talk, but all I can think about is how my future won't include this anymore. I stir the white sauce staring at the black flakes of pepper. I drift back into my head, losing the connection I found in my secret grove—I'm disconnecting again.

After we finish dinner, sleep pulls at me. Even though it is only 8:30 p.m., I head to bed and immediately fall into a deep, dreamless sleep. I don't even wake when Jake comes to bed.

My zombie state continues. Jake shares that he's making good progress on his thesis and I smile, but the smile doesn't reach my eyes or my heart. I try, but I can't feel the emotions I did before.

On Friday morning, my cell rings. Vee. Picking it up, I feel more grounded as soon as I hear her voice. She sounds relaxed and happy.

"How are things going down there?" I ask.

"I'm going to meetings every day, and I feel free," she says. "It's so liberating to attend these meetings. All these people are so wrapped up in staying sober and trying to fix themselves, they don't have time to care or even notice that I'm a model or even beautiful. They see the broken person inside me, and don't notice the outside person. We are all the same on the inside. Remember my yoga religion? Well, I found a place to worship it, and it's AA. No masks allowed."

"Seriously," I warn her, "you *will* be struck by lightning." But I don't really mean it.

Vee snorts a laugh, replying, "Someday you will find your nature church you described that day, and you'll see the wonder in it too. But really, I've never felt like this before: not special because I'm beautiful or tall or thin. God, I love it. They see the real me and the real me is fucked up. I'm not the face with airbrushed cheekbones, you know what I mean?"

"No, I'm not sure I do," I admit. "But you sound happy, and that's what matters."

"So, what's going on up there?" she probes. "Just to be straight with you, Jake called me and asked me to talk to you. He's worried about you. He told me about stupid Aunt Carol and her comments. So, what's up? If I've learned anything through rehab, it's that talking really does help. It helps with everything."

"I know you're right." I pause and take a deep breath, "First, I don't really care about Carol and what she said. She's miserable and so self-centered. What hurt was that Jake didn't say anything or stand up for me." I sniff loudly and fight back tears. "I know I'm just a fake fiancée, but still. But that isn't the real issue."

"Not the real issue?" Vee questions.

"The real issue is . . ." I inhale. "I thought I had Multiple Sclerosis. I told you my mom has MS, and back in September I was sure I had it too. Even my mother's specialist thought so. MS can be genetic. Well, after that doctor's appointment, I decided I would give myself six months to live a little before I start the treatment."

I feel a weight lift from my shoulders. Saying it out loud does help, and it actually doesn't sound as crazy as I thought it would.

"Oh, *that's* why," Vee interrupts. "Now I finally get your fixation on six months! But MS . . ." Her voice goes somber. "That's really bad, isn't it?"

"Yes," I say simply. "There's no cure, and the medications you take for the symptoms are dreadful, so I decided I would be okay with my sucky destiny if I could live a little first. And that was right when you and Jake came along and handed me a life. It was the answer to my prayers, and I can never express what you guys did for me." I gather myself, taking a deep breath. "But I just found out I *don't* have MS. It was Lyme disease, and it's all cleared up now. So now my plan is ruined."

"Emma, wow!" Vee says slowly. "That's heavy. But I'm thrilled you don't have MS. Aren't you?"

"I know I should be really happy, but I'm just confused and very lost. I know it's crazy, but now I have to live my whole life instead of just six months—and I'm not sure how to. MS meant my parents had to take me back after my little rebellion and the church would too. Now I'm not sure either will take me back, and . . . What will I do?" Tears spring into my eyes.

"Okay, slow down. You don't need to figure out everything right now," Vee says firmly. "This is what I've learned down here. Take it little by little. Start with the positive. First, you have a job; you have a place to live that isn't with your parents. You don't have to squeeze yourself back into that shell of an old life. The small box you were living in isn't fair or right. You deserve so much more."

Shaking my head, knowing she can't see it, I whisper, "I don't deserve anything."

I'm not sure if Vee hears me. She states emphatically, "Emma, what about Jake? He really likes you; I know it."

"It's all fake, Vee, remember? All so he could get away from his parents for a little while. I'm not even good enough to be a fake fiancée. Jake needs someone real like Jessica, not me."

"That is bullshit." Vee says emphatically. "Jake needs you more than you know."

I reply quickly, "I'm just a smelly, dirty Pollack and no one needs that."

"Well, we're back where we started. Carol is a snob and a bigot, but Jake isn't."

A flash of energy surges through me. "Jake needs to stand up to Carol and Oliver—not about me or my family, but for *himself*," I blurt. "He needs to stand up to them and tell them he won't work at the firm. He should do what *he* wants. Gosh, he's almost thirty, and he's going to cave and end up being just as miserable as they are."

I'm shocked at my bold words, but Vee is right. It feels good to get them out into the open instead of holding them inside letting them twist and turn in my head.

Vee responds eventually, "Yes, Jake does need to do that, but we can't control others. We only control ourselves, our actions, and reactions. So, let's focus on you and what you want."

"But I don't know," I implore.

"Think about it. Really think about it and we can talk again."

I feel lighter after we hang up. Not back to normal, but a little more part of the world.

Chapter 28:

Field Study

In mid-January, the semester starts again and I'm relieved to be back at work, finding solace in my job. Professor Montgomery keeps looking at me askance, but he doesn't press, and I'm glad of that.

Taking a deep breath, I ask, "Professor, you told me about a field study back in November. I know I said I wasn't interested, but I wonder if they are still looking for people? I'm thinking I may want to do it now."

Professor Montgomery chuckles. "Ah, the magnificent *Campephilus principalis*. Yes, yes, they're always looking for someone who is willing to work for practically nothing and get eaten alive by mosquitoes, slogging through woods and swamps. Hold on a moment." He prints off a page and hands it to me. "Here is the information on the IBWO study. It started a year after Gene Sparling spotted or thinks he spotted an ivory-bill deep in the Cache River National

Wildlife Refuge, in February 2004, which set off a cascade of crazy events. Most call it the *ivory-bill* but its tag code is IBWO. Jim Tanner tagged the only ivory-bill ever tagged. Good old Sonny Boy. Well, a group of the top birders, searchers, and conservationists set up a secret mission to confirm there were ivory-bills still living down there. They had numerous documented sightings where these experts were almost one hundred percent sure they spotted an ivory-bill. And then it happened."

I breathe, "What? What happened?"

"Well, this guy, David Luneau, went down there and actually got a picture and video of it. Nothing really clear, but it was something. That was April 25, 2004, and that's when the birding world blew up. Every birder worth their salt remembers where they were when they first heard the news." He takes a deep breath and continues in a calmer tone, "We are now nine years in and still nothing is resolved. Many people believe that the experts in April 2004 were so eager to find the ivory-bill alive that they mistook it for a common pileated woodpecker. Others are sure they spotted one or more. The video is so grainy, it doesn't settle anything either. So, you'll be going down there to figure out who is right."

"Wow. That is amazing." My brow crinkles. "But how am I going to spot this bird if even the experts aren't sure?"

"Well, I, for one, believe those experts really did see the ivory-bill. Those folks can't mix up an ivory-bill and a pileated. Christ! They can distinguish a cattle egret from a snowy egret at thirty paces. They wouldn't mix up a goddamn ivory-bill with a pileated." He thumps his fist on his desk. "Let me find a book that will help. It tells the whole sordid story of this magical bird and its awful demise. It's around here somewhere." He ambles over to his overflowing bookcase and sorts through the books resting on the shelves in a jumbled mess. "Ah! Here it is. *The Race to Save the Lord God Bird* by Phillip Hoose. This will tell you what you need to know. Pictures and everything."

On the cover is a huge, wild, amber-eyed, black-and-white bird with a scarlet crest and a white bill. He looks like he thundered down straight out of Zeus's bow. I flip through some pages, examining the drawings and pictures of the ivory-bill, and something cracks open in my chest. This is a creature from another world, or at least another time, it feels like magic.

Professor Montgomery interrupts my thoughts. "This book will fill in the facts and the history, but ask Jake—"

"No, Professor, I don't want to ask Jake, and I don't want you to mention this to him. I want to do this on my own."

Frowning, he presses, "But Jake—"

"Nothing about Jake on this," I cut him off again. "This is me on my own."

Professor Montgomery looks wounded. "Emma, if something is wrong, you need to talk to Jake and not run away. Running away never solved anything. You aren't the sort."

I turn away with a jerk. *I'm not running away. I'm just hoping time and distance will help heal a broken heart.* I can't bear to tell Professor that talking is futile, as it was all a charade.

Instead, to change the subject back to safer ground, I say, "I found this wonderful quote by someone, I forget his name, but he said just knowing ivory-bills may still inhabit our world is enough for him at this moment."

Smiling, I remember sharing that quote with Jake. Maybe this will be my life from now on. Remembering memories from this special time. *God, I hope that will be enough.*

"Oh, that was David Marshall. One of the premier west coast ornithologists. We have a healthy rivalry. I'm the king of the east coast and he is king of the west. We both have life lists of over eight hundred. I think he might be one or two birds ahead of me now. I agree with his sentiment, but we do want to know for sure."

Professor Montgomery jabs his finger at the book in my hand.

"You'll find the crazy story about Sonny Boy in this book. Look at that picture. They are the most majestic of all avian creatures. They stand over two feet tall and have an iridescent black body, with a jagged white eye stripe, and show a large amount of white in the wings. Truly a magnificent bird. The males have a red cap, and they fly like soaring eagles, according to John Muir. I would give my eye tooth to see one in flight." He pauses reverently. "You'll be trying to solve the most hotly debated topic among ornithologists. Are they still living and somehow have found a way to survive far from us humans who have fragmented and cut down so much of their habitat, which is the old-growth forests? Ivory-bills need at least seven acres of old-wood growth forest, and we clear cut those long ago. Researchers rediscovered a nesting pair in Florida in 1924, complete with photographs. You'll see the pictures of the lovely pair in the book. Ivory-bills mate for life, you know. Can you guess what some idiot did after finding them?"

I shake my head having no clue. I've never seen Professor Montgomery quite so incensed.

"They shot them both, stuffed and mounted them. Idiots, we are all idiots."

I can't let myself dwell too long on the image of those two beautiful birds stuffed and hanging on a wall or I'll start blubbering right here. *Why is life so cruel?*

Squaring my shoulders, I ask, "How do I go about applying? I would love to be even a small part of trying to find such a bird." I pause and add playfully, "Although, what will you do without me for a few months?"

Professor Montgomery gazes at me, smiling. "Ah, to be young and able to get back into the field. I'm jealous, for sure. When you return, you must tell me all about it, promise? Let's go on the website and apply together."

Laughing, I feel a part of my heart thaw just a touch. On the home page is a beautiful picture of the ivory-bill. I'm humbled at the thought of it. I quickly complete the required information and hit *submit*. Professor Montgomery said he would send a personal email to the project team in Arkansas and assured me there won't be any issue with me joining.

While Professor Montgomery is confident, I'm less so. They would need to be desperate to accept me with my paltry months of organizing and cataloguing thrush data in a cozy office. I try not to get my hopes up.

Professor Montgomery was right! They are desperate.

With this new adventure awaiting me, my life, which felt so unhinged since my un-diagnosis, feels a little bit more under control. I decide I won't tell Jake anything until I have everything all figured out for my new job. I need to do this myself, or at least without Jake.

We are coexisting. I'm using Vee's bedroom to sleep, and while she isn't happy about that, she's not meddling too much. I make dinner for us, as it seems petty not to when I'm making something for myself, but I draw the line at making pasta Bolognese. Jake is busy emailing someone back and forth, spending a lot of time on his phone or computer. It appears he's not working on his thesis; his papers aren't spread out on the table as they normally are when he's working. I try not to keep tabs on his comings and goings, but habits are hard to break. I'm always aware of where he is in the apartment. And when he is gone from the apartment to teach his class, the emptiness sometimes makes me collapse in a heap on the couch.

I hope my change in venue will stop this. If I didn't know better, I'd think it was MS again.

I'm sitting, staring blankly at the pages of one of Vee's *Vogue* magazines, when Jake comes into the apartment and comes directly over to me. I received acceptance into the IBWO project a week ago, and I still haven't told him. The cushions shift as he sits on the edge of the couch.

He takes my hand and says earnestly, "Emma, I want to talk."

Looking up at him, I give a barely perceptible shrug.

"I know I should have said something to my mother when she said those awful things. But I want to explain the reason I didn't do anything then. I'm not making excuses, just explaining things. I didn't want you to see Oliver like that. He gets mean when he drinks and that is nothing you need to deal with. My mom and I have been dealing with it since . . . umm . . . forever. It goes way back. So, my sole focus that night was to keep things smooth and calm and get him into bed."

Jake stands and starts pacing.

"This has been playing out my whole life; it's what we learned to do. I'm not sure I even registered what my mom said, I was so focused on Oliver. Well, that isn't true—I knew what she said. But I knew not to say anything then. God, if I had ever said anything to her, with Oliver in that state, he would have reacted and reacted badly."

Jake takes a deep breath and runs his hands through his hair. I'm digesting what he's sharing, trying to understand it.

"Well, I've thought and thought about this and all the messed-up crap that got me to the place where I wouldn't open my mouth when my mom said something despicable. I finally confronted my mom. I told her who you are and how wrong it is for her to call her neighbors' horrible names. She feels really bad. Well, once she got over the shock, she did."

I imagine Carol's shock and disdain at the news of her son's engagement to the Polack next door; a painful lump rose in my throat. I try to formulate my thoughts at this revelation. I almost say thank you but bite the words back. "I'm sure she's not happy with you or me."

He shrugs. "She'll come around."

"Well, she won't need to come around for too much longer, will she? Our time is almost up," I remark dully, although something flickers in my chest at the thought that Jake told his mother.

"Look, we need to talk about that. This whole thing needs to be figured out." He waves his arms in a circle. "But I've got to go away for a week or so. I have a mini-crisis I need to take care of. I'm working on a special project but not scheduled to start working on it again until March, but I need to make a quick check now. I'll be back soon, and then we can talk. This will give us both time to think about what we really want."

Looking into those deep brown eyes, I ache to run my hands through his hair one last time. If only I had known the last time I'd done it was going to be my last, I would have committed it to memory. Now all I have is the hazy memory of running my hand through his unruly hair the afternoon of the party, but I don't have all the sharp details I need so I can hold on to them long after our time is over.

"Emma, okay?" he pleads. "We can talk when I get back. We need to talk about our future."

I vacillate on whether I should just tell him the whole sordid MS story and be done with it. But I'm still not sure how to explain it all to him. And does it even matter? All I know is I don't want to come up with our breakup story and tell the few people who need to hear it, especially Carol. Just disappearing will be best because I'm done. I squash the little flicker and something akin to relief loosens the muscles deep in my chest. I will survive this, and one day, breathing will not hurt so much.

I watch as Jake packs a small bag. Within an hour, he is gone. I ask myself, *Should I have told him my secret?*

The apartment is quieter than ever.

Chapter 29:

Surprises

Three days later, there's a knock on the apartment door. Believing Jake has returned, my heart races, and I dash to the door, boot notwithstanding. Flinging open the door, I find Carol in the hallway, looking like she has bitten into a lemon.

"Carol?" I squeak.

Brushing past me, she murmurs, "Hello, Emma."

I perch awkwardly on one of the kitchen chairs and watch her apprehensively. "Would you like coffee or something?" God, what am I thinking? I shouldn't be offering her anything.

She shakes her head, her eyes sliding past mine, and exhales. "Look," she begins softly, "I shouldn't have said what I said. If I had known who you were, I would never have said such a thing."

She wouldn't have said it out loud, at least.

"But Jake should have told us who you were. I'm not sure if it was you or Jake who was hiding . . . everything." She waves her arm dramatically.

I start to respond but stop myself before any words come out.

She slips an envelope out of her purse and slides it across the table, still not looking me in the eye. "This is for you, if you agree to disappear and forget this whole thing. I mean you can move back to your parents and all. Just no more engagement or anything like that. This is for your future so you can move on and live the life meant for you.

My good hand slowly reaches for the envelope and picks it up. I'm repulsed by my actions, but I can't seem to stop myself. I need to know the Henderson's assessment of what my future is worth. Jake wanted to talk about my future when he got back, but his mother clearly couldn't wait for him to return to share this plan. The envelope is unsealed, and I pull out a check. I count the zeros. $10,000. One part of me is relieved, as I feared my value would be a lot less. But then a wave of nausea hits me. This is so messed up—Carol with her perfectly coiffed hair, rigid posture, and manicured nails and hatefulness.

Regarding her, in a voice that isn't mine, I say, "Please leave."

Gaping at me, Carol gets up clutching her purse. "So, we have an understanding. The money is yours; you just need to forget all about this." She waves her hand around again.

Sitting perfectly still, I repeat coldly, "I understand. Now please leave."

Carol bolts up and practically runs to the door. When she reaches the safety of the open door, she regains her composure and, with a good bit of irritation, says, "This is for the best, really."

I nod and she yanks the door closed behind her.

Clasping the check to my chest, I turn my eyes heavenward and beseech, "Jake, how could you? My God, please no."

The memory of Jake saying, *We need to keep the peace,* flashes through my mind. A knife slides into my heart and twists. The pain is searing but slowly lessens as I breathe in and out. The voice in my head starts gaining traction. *There is no future with Jake. This is actually good. A clean break.*

I put my head in my hands. *I won't take their money. I can't take their money.* Unseeing, a tear falls onto the check. The check's pain is too deep for a thousand tears to erase. But as tears stream down my face, I realize I've got to try. I deserve that.

The next morning, I wake and think, *Yoga.* That's what I need. I'm able to do only the most basic moves because of my boot and cast, but it is something. I have two more weeks until I'm out of both, the doctor says. Pulling on my leggings, I'm glad I haven't let Carol's visit completely unhinge me. I smile thinking like Vee, if I get to yoga, it means today will be okay, and that is all I need right now.

As I'm heading for the door, the phone rings. It's the landline in the kitchen, which hasn't rung for the three months I've been living here.

I walk over and pick up the phone gingerly. "Hello?"

A man's voice snaps, "Hello, is Jake there?"

"No, I'm sorry, he's traveling right now." I fumble with the handset. "Can I ask who's calling?"

"Yes, yes of course. This is Arnie, his poor overworked agent. Any chance he's in the middle of Central Park updating his guidebook?" He laughs.

"Guidebook?"

"Yes, The Birds of Central Park. Please tell me he's working on it."

I move the phone away from my ear and stare at it. *Is this some sort of joke or am I dreaming?* I put the phone back to my ear. "The guidebook by John Foster?"

"Yes, John Foster."

"The—the author?" I stammer.

"Yes, the author. Really, I must find him. It's really getting urgent."

Trying to calm my racing heart, I ask, "Why would you think he is here?"

"Well, I know it's a long shot, but Jake listed this phone number as an emergency contact years ago, and I've given up trying his cell. It just goes straight to voicemail."

"Did you say Jake or John Foster?" I ask, getting more flustered by the minute.

The man laughs. "Well, both or either. Jake Henderson or John Foster. One and the same."

I inhale sharply. "What do you mean one and the same?"

"Well, Jake is John and John is Jake. Now, is he there or not?"

"They are the same person?"

The man sighs but responds patiently, "Why, yes. Jake Henderson uses the pseudonym John Foster for his books. Now, who am I speaking to? I assumed this was the number of a close friend. I shouldn't be spouting out such information to just anyone."

I reply automatically, "I'm his fiancée. Well, Jake's fiancée. Oh, and I guess John's too. I didn't know he was John Foster, so maybe I'm not John's fiancée."

Ugh! Stop saying fiancée. I sound completely deranged.

"Oh, the mysterious fiancée. Well, nice to finally meet you and hey congratulations! Jake is a wonderful guy. So glad he's settling down. He deserves to be happy. But what matters now is whether he's there or not. He needs to sign his latest contract, or the publisher is going to kill him or me. So, is he there?"

"Well, no. He left on an emergency trip. Something to do with a special project. It was unexpected. He will be back in, let's see . . . six days."

"Okay, that could be okay. He must be out in the middle of nowhere, as usual, with no cell service. I just don't get it, but I guess that's why I'm an agent and not a famous author. Can I stop over and drop the contract off, so he'll have it as soon as he gets back? He needs to sign it and then needs to call me and I will come pick it up—or the little bastard can drop it off in my office. Tell him no snail mail."

Laughing, I give him Vee's address.

"I'll bring it over tomorrow afternoon, since there's no rush now that I know Jake won't be signing it for a while."

"Okay," I agree dazedly, and hang up the phone.

Forgetting about yoga, I sit on the couch, mulling over this unbelievable turn of events. *Jake is John Foster.* Playing things back in my head, I remember all the times, he told me to stop spouting John Foster quotes. All that time, they were *his* quotes. And then I clap my hand over my mouth and gasp out loud. "Jake is a *birding expert!*"

How did I miss that? He spotted the palm warbler walking to Vee's that first time. And there was the birdfeeder in his bedroom window. My God, it is so obvious now. He knew about the snowy owls and even taught me the fancy word *irruptive.* I thought everyone must know the word because regular old Jake knew it. Probably only John Foster knows that term and how to use it. Suddenly, I picture Jake showing me how to focus and spot a bird with my new binoculars. A famous birder taught me to use binoculars. Wow! That is very cool.

Cool but really annoying.

Cringing, I remember going through my little life list with Jake. He probably laughed at my pathetic list compared to his. But he didn't seem to be laughing at me back when I was sharing it.

Then there was the time I told him my magpie story.

I was maybe eighteen and had just gotten my book—*his* book—when I saw a woman with binoculars looking up in a tree. I approached her and asked what she was looking at.

She responded with barely a glance at me, "A group of magpies are up in the tree."

When I got to this part of my story, Jake laughed and then immediately responded that the woman was being a jerk. He knew immediately the women was being mean. Back when it happened, it wasn't until I went home and looked up magpies and discovered they weren't anywhere around here that I figured out she was being rude. But Jake knew right away. Of course, John Foster knew that magpies aren't found in Central Park.

How did I miss all those clear signs that Jake was John Foster? Well maybe not that he was John Foster, but at least that he was a real birder. He knew too much about birds not to be.

Sitting quietly for the rest of the day, I consider this revelation from every angle. Even after hours of this, I can't figure out if I'm angry or really impressed.

Marching into work the next day, I demand, "Professor, why didn't you tell me Jake was John Foster?"

Squinting up at me through his bushy eyebrows in surprise, Professor Montgomery leans back in his chair.

"Well, Jake keeps the John Foster thing tight under his wing, as we birders like to say. Never really understood it; what I gathered is it has a lot to do with his parents. Or his stepparents. Glad he finally told you. I thought it was strange when he swore me to secrecy. I mean, you're his fiancée, for goodness' sake."

I don't correct him, and he continues.

"John Foster is his birth name, and when his mom remarried, his stepfather adopted him, so he changed his last name from Foster to Henderson. His legal first name is John, but everyone calls him Jake. I never could quite follow it. I think he liked the idea of publishing under his real name, and it served the most important purpose of avoiding his parents' wrath. As the book became popular, he became a little paranoid and wanted to ensure his parents didn't find out about it. I think because his parents hate the idea of Jake's chosen profession and also, he knew using his real name would not sit well with them—or, rather, one of them. The whole thing is a little asinine."

"His chosen profession?" I squeak.

"Yes, well, he's a pretty good bird guy. As soon as he finishes his thesis, he'll officially be an ornithologist. One day, he'll give me a run for my money. He's good, and his students love him."

I squeak, "Jake teaches classes on birds?"

"Why, yes, of course. What did you think he taught?"

Shaking my head, I say dumbly, "I thought he was a doctor . . . He's not a doctor?"

"Well not a medical one, but he'll have his PhD, so he is a bird doctor, as we like to call ourselves." He laughs quietly.

"Oh dear." I pause disconcerted. "Wow! This is so weird. It's as if I don't know him at all."

"Of course, you know Jake," Professor Montgomery says firmly. "He's your fiancé. He certainly dotes on you. I've never seen him happier."

Feeling even more confused, I take my seat at my little desk and fail miserably at filling in this week's progress reports.

In the apartment in the afternoon, the doorbell rings. When I open the door, a massive giant stands in the doorway.

Everything about him is big: his hands, his head. A custom-made, light brown suit fits his massive waist.

He delicately shakes my hand and asks, "Emma?"

"Yes, I'm Emma."

He enters, ducking his head as he comes through the doorway. "I'm Arnie, Jake's agent. We talked on the phone yesterday."

"Yes, of course, nice to meet you."

Arnie smiles and taps a folder of papers, "So, you must promise as soon as Jake returns, he must sign this and call me. I will pick them up immediately."

I nod obediently.

Arnie continues, "So, you are the one who's captured Jake's heart. I wasn't sure if he was so distracted due to his darn dissertation or due to you. But now that I've met you, I believe I have my answer. I've been hounding him to work on his update to the bird guide for months and he's been ignoring me which isn't like him at all."

I turn a bright red.

"Oh my, a blushing bride. How quaint." Arnie pats my arm gently and says, "Dear, I didn't mean to embarrass you."

Collecting myself, I ask, "Can I get you a coffee or tea perhaps?" and I direct him toward the couch.

Arnie sits down with a loud exhale and waves a hand in my direction. "Maybe I will sit for a quick minute. Coffee would be great—light milk, with two sugars, if you would be so kind."

I hurry off to the kitchen, and in short order bring back a cup of coffee for Arnie and tea for me.

As soon as I sit down across from Arnie, I can't stop myself, "How long have you known Jake?"

"Well, it was back eight or nine years ago. Jake came wandering in off the street into my agency with his idea of a guidebook for Central Park birds. I have a soft spot for birders, as my mother loved to feed the birds back on Long Island. He pitched me the book idea and I called my mother on the spot and asked her if she would buy such a book. She said absolutely, so I signed Jake right then and there." He takes a large gulp of coffee and nods appreciatively. "He was still wet behind the ears, but my mother knew. Now, the book isn't a bestseller, mind you, but every spring and fall migration, it has steady sales and that's been true for years. Have you seen the book?"

"Oh yes, I've seen it," I say eagerly. "It was the first book I bought and that was before I even knew Jake. It's my bible—oops, I don't mean that." I hurriedly cross myself and do a quick "I'm sorry" under my breath.

Arnie watches me with interest, causing my blush to start anew. Then he finishes his coffee in one long slurp, sets his cup down on the table, and heaves himself up.

Leaning over and tapping the paperwork he left on the coffee table, he demands with a smile, "Promise, as soon as Jake gets back!"

I nod my head solemnly. "Promise."

Chapter 30:

Taking Flight

My upcoming IBWO study's logistical details arrive in an email. I'm both thrilled at the prospect and achingly sad, as this will be the end. My bones are slowly healing and I'm hoping time and distance will do the same to my shattered heart.

I print off the long list of items provided in the email and hand it to Professor Montgomery, who skims it over and rubbing his hands together murmurs, "Oh, to be young." He rummages through his desk drawers until he pulls out a compass. Moving over to a chest of drawers, he extracts a small pack of matches in a sealed pouch, water disinfectant pills, some sort of pumping filtering device, and a beautiful pocketknife.

Staring at the growing pile, "Am I going into the jungle?"

Professor Montgomery laughs. "No, not really. But you spend days in the woods, and you always need your survival pack just in case you can't make it back to base camp by nightfall."

He holds up a small pouch with a silver blanket inside.

"Voila! Emergency blanket. You probably won't use half this stuff, but you need it just in case. Let me find my backpack and we can put everything in there. Oh, I'm getting excited just thinking about you down there searching for the most magnificent bird known to man."

Professor Montgomery crosses off quite a few items from my list. For the rest, he tells me, I'll need to head to Kaufman's Army Navy. He calls ahead so they'll be waiting for me when I arrive.

On the way home, my stomach keeps flipping and flopping and I feel dizzy. I was surprised I held it together at Kaufman's, but I somehow managed by deep breathing as I retrieved the remaining items from the shelves. *This is living and this is what I want. This is what I need.*

When I get upstairs in the apartment, I call Vee to ask her to help me book my flight to Little Rock.

"So why do you need to go to Arkansas?" she asks for the fourth time. "As far as I know, there is absolutely nothing in Arkansas."

"Please Vee," I beg her. "Can you just do this for me and keep it a secret? I must do it. I'll call you when I'm down there and give you all the details."

"I don't like this, not one bit," she grumbles. But she books me my flight.

Before hanging up, she asks, "What about Jake?"

"I can't do the fake fiancée thing anymore," I say. "I'm trying to carve out a life for me on my terms—a real life. I'm absolutely scared to death, but I've learned that is what life is all about, so I need to just grit my teeth and do it."

"I'm so happy to hear you aren't crawling back into your

little cocoon and shutting out the world," she says. "But the two of you had something real. You must know that."

"It was just a crazy dream." I sigh. "When Jake's mother called me a dirty, smelly Polack, that was when I finally understood there was no hope for anything real, and there never will be. I was deluding myself—maybe Jake was too, for a while—but now it's clear."

I can't bring myself to tell her that Carol tried to get rid of me with a $10,000 payoff. The pain and humiliation of that is too fresh. And the thought that this is what Jake meant when he said he wanted to talk about our future when he returns, cuts deep into my psyche. Maybe someday I will figure out how to put those words out into the world, but not now.

After hanging up, I reread the field study instructions. I email a girl named Kate my flight details as requested so they can have someone at the airport to pick me up. I'm set on my next step in my plan to live a life on my terms.

I try on my cargo pants that have zippers around the knee, so I can change them into shorts at a moment's notice. I check out the instructions for the water pumping device and the water tablets and hope that I won't ever have to use the contraption. I repack everything into the backpack Professor Montgomery gave me and the duffel bag I bought at Kaufman's. I fold up the vest with so many pockets I can't count them all. I add some socks and underwear and toiletries and my trusty winter parka. I can't believe it's going to be that cold in Arkansas, but the list says warm gear, so I include my wool hat and mittens. I flex my fingers, glad my wrist is now in a removable splint. In two more weeks, I will have completely healed. My ankle is a little weak and stiff, but it is out of the boot now and I've been walking daily to strengthen it.

Leaning back on my heels, I inspect the room. I will be leaving this lovely sunny place in two days. I check my list. *My* list, not Kate's. The one remaining item on it is, *Tell mama and papa.*

I'm glad it's too late to do it tonight—but tomorrow after work, I must.

The next day, I bid a fond farewell to Professor Montgomery, hugging awkwardly.

"People either love the deep forest or hate it. Remember Emma, when you are sick of being eaten alive by insects and the sweltering heat or getting rained on, I have a spot for you back here in my cozy office."

I smile bravely. "I'll be back before you know it."

I practically run down the hallway to my parents' door, petrified I'll bump into Carol. Remembering Jake's advice to keep our story as close to the truth as possible, I sit with my mother and explain, "We've decided to call off the engagement. Jake and I realized it just wouldn't work—we come from two different worlds." I rush on, "I'm going to Arkansas for a bird project, and then I'm going to figure things out from there."

My mother reaches for my hand and tears slip down my cheeks, I rub them away with my hand. Even though it was a fake engagement, something about telling my mother starts my tears flowing and I can't stop them. As they run silently down my cheeks, my mother just holds my hand.

"I'll tell Babcia and Papa," she finally says, gently. Then she gives me a squeeze and gets up to make tea.

"I hope you find happiness, Emma," Mama says after we take our first sip of the tea. "You are a good girl and deserve that. Everyone has to break free to fully understand their destiny."

I squint at her, I wonder if she is talking about my father or the church. "Really, did you ever do that?"

"Of course." She says with a soft chuckle. "You don't have to live by anyone else's expectations—not your parents', not anyone's. I remember what it was like to be young. Go—find yourself."

I smile at her in wonder. No argument at the insanity of going to Arkansas to work on a bird project, no recrimination for failing to be a good fiancée, nothing about my family obligations. Could my parents have been waiting all along for me to break out of my shell? Waiting for me to grow up and start making my own decisions.

Back at Vee's, I leave Arnie's contract with a note that reads, "Please sign it and call Arnie." On top of that, I place the envelope with the $10,000 check in it, and on top of that, I carefully place my *Birds of Central Park* guide.

My heart cracks wide open when I slip Jake's diamond ring off my finger. I clutch my chest as if trying to hold my heart together. My finger feels strangely empty without the weight of the ring. *How did I get so caught up in the lie?*

Eyes stinging, I lay the delicate ring on top of my little pile. My chest aches. I've read so many books that described heartbreak as actual pain, and I always thought it was hyperbole, but it's not, it hurts. The rest of my body feels normal, but the space in my chest is heavy and painfully so. *How can your heart, an organ that just pumps blood, feel? This is a part of living I wish I never learned.*

I look around Vee's apartment. There is no trace I was ever there. I took the rest of my stuff back to my parent's apartment yesterday. When I shut Vee's apartment door, it feels like I'm shutting the door on this whole crazy couple of months. I'm hoping one day it won't seem so real but will feel like a dream and I will only remember the happy times.

Chapter 31:

The Field

Standing awkwardly in the baggage-claim area in Little Rock, I glance around, and panic rises in my chest. *I've made a terrible mistake. What was I thinking?*

Then my eyes alight on a rugged-looking young man and spot my name on the sign he is holding.

Get a grip, there is no turning back. Channeling Vee's confident stride, I head in his direction and reach out a hand—but my huge duffel bag swings off my shoulder when I do this, and I stumble as it hits the floor with a thump.

The young man lets out a contagious howl and I suddenly feel lighter than I have in weeks. I let out a little giggle.

The young man clasps my hand, "Hey, Emma. I'm Evan. Are you all set there?"

Nodding, I struggle to get my duffel bag settled back in place. Evan slips it off my shoulder without a word, flips it over his shoulder, and heads toward the large exit door.

We get into a dirty F-150 pickup and start driving. Evan is pleasant, but taciturn. I watch out the window as the highway narrows into a two-lane road and the signs indicate we are on I 40. I don't see many houses and only occasionally, we pass through a town. One is called Fargo, and another is Cotton Plant.

I'm not in Kansas anymore, I think wryly.

On the outskirts of a town called McCrory, Evan pulls into a long winding driveway with a peeling, weatherworn sign for the Pine Knot Motel.

"This is our good old base camp. We're right on the edge of Cache River National Wildlife Refuge," he says.

Evan shows me to my room and introduces me to my roommate, Jenny, a fresh-faced girl a few years younger than me, with dark hair plaited into two braids. I test the small bed with a few gentle bounces. There is a small fridge, a desk, and a small table in the room.

"Most of the volunteers are kids right out of high school who are trying to make a little money or just get out of their parents' house, or both," Jenny explains. "Today's my break day. Normally, ten to twelve people go out into the field each day."

Hearing the roar of a truck, I quickly finish putting my clothes away into my two assigned drawers. Poking my head out our open door; I see two pickups returning from the field. Out tumble ten people who look dirty and hungry. Most of them hurry off to their rooms, but a tall, thin man with curly blonde hair who appears a little older than the rest pauses in front of me.

"Emma?"

I nod.

"Glad you're here. I'm Trevor." He sticks out a hand, then looks down at the grime covering it and snatches it back.

He wipes both his hands on his pants. "Sorry about that; I'm still dirty from the field. Handshakes can wait for later. You want to come and help with dinner?"

"Sure."

I follow him to his room, where two people—Sally and Nick, they introduce themselves—are already in his room and working in a little kitchenette.

"Is this your first field study?" Sally asks.

"Yes," I admit. "I've only ever done the organizing of the bird information back in the office. I'm kinda nervous. What's it like?"

Nick responds with a chuckle, "Oh, it's great if you enjoy wandering around a forest from dawn 'til dusk and then cooking dinner for fourteen."

Trevor sticks his head out of his bedroom and retorts, "Don't listen to him. We rotate the cooking. Teams do it once a week, even less if I decide to spring for pizza."

"Yeah, Nick's my partner and he can't boil eggs, so he hates his rotation because he gets a lot of grief." Sally laughs. "I'm glad you agreed to lend a hand. Can you cook?"

Remembering Vee describing her cooking skills in relation to boiling eggs, smiling I respond, "I can make a few things. Can we make anything we want?"

"Pretty much," Nick says. "I mean, you can't say you're going to cook filet mignon each time as we have a weekly budget, but it's not bad. Because of my handicap in the kitchen, we pretty much stick to spaghetti and meatballs, right, Sally?"

"Affirmative. I can't be too creative." Sally grins.

"Umm, I could probably turn it into a nice pasta Bolognese if you want," I suggest. "It's pretty easy, and we should have all the ingredients, or most of them."

Sally perks up, sounding impressed. "Super. Sounds great."

I immediately feel comfortable, as the kitchen reminds me of my parents' kitchen in its functional austerity. I give Nick the job of getting the pot filled with water for the pasta, and Sally nods approvingly. Sally and I dice onions, and I find a few carrots to include, as well as plenty of garlic and spices. We throw in the hamburger meat and let everything simmer. Trevor walks into the kitchen with his hair still wet, wearing clean clothes.

He pauses, inhaling. "What smells so good?"

Sally pipes up, "Looks like you may have gotten more than you bargained for. Emma is a gourmet chef."

My cheeks flush, "Definitely not. I can make a few dishes, most of them are Polish. Nothing special, just simple stuff."

Trevor straddles a chair and says, "Shopping day is in two days. Put together a list. My grandmother is Polish, and I loved her pierogis. If you can make something even close to hers, you won't need to go into the field at all."

I laugh. "But that is what I came down to do. I really want to go out."

"You may change your mind once you've experienced it!" Trevor winks at me. "Just keep it as an option."

A warmth spreads through my body; I feel part of this group already. *Have I ever felt a part of a group before? Certainly not at school.* Sally watches the sauce, and I put the spaghetti in to cook. Trevor tells Nick to get the plates ready and then calls in the troops.

We are putting the finishing touches on the sauce by sprinkling it with parmesan cheese out of a can—I smile remembering the freshly grated fanfare of Vee's presentation; that must not be within the budget here—as the group of newly washed and dressed folks make their way into the room. We have rolls, pasta, and sauce. Everyone is pushing in the line and exclaiming how good everything smells. They introduce themselves to me as they funnel past. All of them are smiling and friendly.

Once they've filled their plates, most of the folks go outside and sit in chairs and eat on a tiny patch of lawn. Trevor, Sally, Jenny and I stay inside around the little kitchen table.

"Six pairs of field teams go out each day," Trevor says through a mouthful of pasta. "The other two people stay back to do laundry and other chores, but there's time to do whatever they want. The entire team has Sunday off, and that is when we do the shopping. So, everyone does fieldwork five days a week and cooks one day."

"So, what will I do tomorrow?" I ask.

"Tomorrow, I'll give you a crash course on the ivory-bill so you know what you're looking for," Trevor says. "We will assign you to one of the senior teams for the first couple of days. When you're comfortable, you'll get your own tract to search, and you're on your own. We all head in the same exact direction following our compass for a couple of miles. One leader marks the spot where we turn around. You'll have a walkie talkie that is for if you spot *the* bird." He pauses dramatically, "Or, more often when it's time to mark and turn around. You'll get the hang of it. You're just listening and searching for signs of the ivory-bill. Of course, if you find a good bird, you can call it through the walkie talkie and see who wants to come take a look at it, we all want to add a few good birds to our life lists while we're here. Are you good with birds?"

I shrug. "I'm pretty good with birds in Central Park but not anywhere else. I don't think I'll be calling in any rare birds."

Trevor laughs, "Okay, great, another Central Park expert."

I wonder what he means by that, but he's already getting up to start cleaning. I decide to save my questions for later.

The next morning, Trevor stays back with me while most of the group pile into two pickup trucks and head out into the woods.

When the last rumble of the pickup trucks' motors fade, he announces enthusiastically, "Okay, let's get started. Here are the best pictures we have of the bird. Study them. You see the splash of white along the back when they have their wings closed; that is the best way to make sure you don't sound the alarm over a pileated woodpecker. But don't worry, even the best birders can mix up those two from afar."

I drink in the pictures. Those yellow eyes touch something deep within me.

Trevor points to the red cap, pointing backwards from the bird's head, "The male. The female has a black crest that points forward. Weird right?"

He passes more pictures, showing the majestic bird clinging comfortably to an old, dead tree. I squint at one grainy picture that looks like a black arrow flying through a dense forest.

"It is supposed to be amazing to see one fly." His eyes gleam with excitement. "Straight and true like an arrow. This is a picture taken by the Cornell team in 1934 in Florida of a nesting pair. Isn't it gorgeous? They call them Lord God Birds in some places. I think that's the right name for them."

"I read that book called *The Race to Save the Lord God Bird*."

"Cool. That is a good one."

We both sit quietly, passing the pictures back and forth until Trevor jumps up.

"Okay, those are the visuals, but most of the time, you hear it and only after that may spot its roosting hole or nesting cavity. Of course, this is how James Tanner explained it happened back in the 1930s. Who really knows today? But let's listen to what the bird sounds like."

He takes out a small recorder from his bag and presses a button. Static fills the room, then a clear *toot toot*, like a toy horn, is audible. There is more static and then the loud reverberations of a *da-BAM*.

I whisper, "Is that really the bird? The Lord God Bird?"

"Yep. The same bunch of crazy ornithologists from Cornell who took that picture recorded it. They invented a sound machine, built it into a truck and drove down to Louisiana to try to record the ivory-bill and every other rare bird in the USA back in 1934. They dragged their equipment through the swamps and bayous and ended up getting this recording. It's a goddamn miracle. Whenever I think I have it tough, traipsing in and out of these woods, I think of Jim Tanner and his crew taking a wagon and mules into the swamp and sleeping on the ground every night. They didn't have a warm bed to come back to or a kitchen. Can you imagine?"

I shake my head reverently. "I can't."

Trevor takes out his compass and says, "Okay, let's see if we can get you in and out of these woods now. Grab your compass and I'll walk you through that part of the process."

Over the next couple of hours, I learn how to make sure I don't get lost in the woods, and how to shoot an azimuth—which, I learn, means "compass direction."

By that afternoon, I almost feel ready.

The next morning, we pile into the pickups and drive over the bumpiest dirt road I ever imagined for what seems like an eternity. When my butt is protesting, I remember those birders from Cornell, stuck sitting on a hard wagon bench, and suppress a smile.

Trevor gives the group our intended azimuth and we line up the mirror that is part of the compass and then get the red arrow into the shed.

He calls out in my direction, "Remember: Red Fred goes into the shed."

I move around, staring at my arrow until it points north, and then I find a distant object and start hiking to that spot. And then do the entire process again. This way, we are all spread out over an extensive area and searching in the same direction, keeping the right amount of separation between the teams. I'm paired with Claire and Dan, but they let me figure it out on my own.

Once I reach each spot, I tie a yellow string to it so we can find our way back when we turn around. Claire and Dan explain they don't need the strings anymore, but it is important for new searchers to use them for quite a while.

Nodding my head, I think; *I won't ever be comfortable without my bright security string leading me back to the rendezvous spot.*

Staring at my compass, I keep tripping over the roots and stones, but I eventually get the hang of trusting my direction, so I only consult my compass periodically. As I work deeper into the square, I look up at the trees.

"These trees are so big," I muse aloud. "I can't believe it."

Ten or fifteen feet separate us, but Dan yells back, "Cypress! Some of them have been here for a hundred years. Silently growing and doing their thing."

A sense of peace washes over me.

As the days go on, I find comfort in this forest; it feels a lot like my little hidden patch of woods behind my bench in Central Park, except the size is something I never dreamed of.

In the forest, the weight of life lifts off my shoulders and the wall of separation that has been there as long as I remember things, and I'm able to breathe easier. The pain of the last few weeks lessens, and I'm not as hemmed in by fear or worry over others' perceptions of me. I can't hear the whisperings of my ancestral ghosts or the demanding God from church; instead, nature whispers sweet nothings in my ear all day long. All those yoga teachings become real out here. Remembering them as I walk through the trees soothes me. I'm beginning to put the pieces of my heart back together.

In the middle of the deep woods, the forest seems to watch, ancient eyes hidden in the underbrush, I'm wandering the earth before man, before time, when there was just earth, leaves, roots and magic. The Garden of Eden before the fall—all nurturing and all goodness. Cleansing. When I return to the motel, I'm dirty and bug bitten like everyone else, but inside I'm purified. I have cleansed myself of my sins. A place like this does not care that I lived in sin with Jake and lied to my parents and to myself. The forest forgives all. I'm at peace, no longer feeling alone. This is where God dwells. This is his church, and I'm home and comforted like I've never been at St. Augustine's. I can't believe that Vee was right. Church can be anywhere, and I shake my head in wonder when I don't have the urge to send up a prayer of forgiveness for my blasphemous thoughts. *Wow, who am I?*

On Friday I'm on my own, working my block and I've reached the farthest distance when Trevor calls over the walkie talkie for the group to turn and head back. I spot my yellow string in the distance and I start walking.

For the first time, I let myself think about Jake, remembering one morning, lying in bed with him, watching him sleep. The sun was just starting to chase away the darkness, and I watched him breathe. My breathing slowed to match his slower breath, and we were one.

Suddenly, I'm knocked out of my musings and find myself flat on my face on the soft ground. Rolling over gingerly, I move my shoulders and neck. Sitting up, I see the offending root I tripped over. I roll my ankles, and I feel a twinge in my right ankle; the same one I sprained. It doesn't feel as bad as it did on New Year's Eve, though.

I hobble over to a tree that has fallen down and sit. I start to take my boot off and then think better of it. Instead, I tie my laces as tight as I can, figuring my hiking boot will act like my walking boot I wore after my last spill. Sitting on the wide tree trunk, I raise my leg to elevate my foot. Sinking deeper into my seat, I lean back against the part of the tree that remains standing. Last time I tripped, my mind immediately jumped to MS, but this time, it doesn't. I'm just clumsy, not doomed.

Peering upwards, I say out loud, "Thank you. I'm truly happy I don't have MS. Sorry it took me this long to realize that. I've been pretty stupid."

Pausing, a wave of serenity wells up inside me. I'm not sure who I'm speaking to. *God, maybe . . . mother nature, perhaps*. Whoever it is, they are taking care of me and will take care of me, as they believe I deserve to be happy.

I close my eyes for a minute; warmth envelops me as if I've been covered with a blanket, replacing the usual coldness of the glass. *Boy, this feels nice.*

After a moment of rest, I pull myself up and am caught in the threads of a giant cobweb. Looking down, I see the silver chains clinging to my vest, connecting me back to the tree, the woods, the world. Laughing, I wipe the clinging threads from my face. I marvel at how I didn't disturb it when I first sat down and head off toward the trucks with a warm flame flickering in my belly.

My ankle hurts a little, but it is bearable. I smile at the dirty faces of my fellow field team members and slide into the closest truck. They haven't been waiting for me too long and don't notice my limp. Back at base camp, after ice and ibuprofen, my ankle feels almost normal.

Lying awake that night, I give myself permission to think about Jake. Closing my eyes, I remember his fresh citrusy smell and tears prick my eyes. I picture the dreamy smile he gives when he is downing one of the bakery treats. Then I picture his head against the white of the pillow as the morning sun hits his hair. Oh, his lovely hair. By now, he will be back and have found the pile of items I left for him. For the hundredth time, I wonder if I should have written a note. But the pile says it all. I release him and am gone from his life. I'm now shooting my azimuth. Maybe I will move back with my parents, but as Vee coached, I don't need to fit myself back into that tight box. I can continue to work for Professor Montgomery, keep doing yoga, and maybe take a class or two at Columbia. I will find a life of my own. I've figured out that it was me that was walling myself off from wanting and from dreaming to protect myself from the pain of wanting and not getting. But it turns out that barricade—my bubble— was even worse. It was a life unlived. The picture of my lovely, little cobweb in the corner of my drab bedroom flashes through my head. Of course! I need to spin webs to connect myself to the world instead of shielding myself from it. I was the one keeping myself locked away, not my parents or the church or anyone else.

The following Tuesday is my first day off. Jenny and I hang around the motel and she shows me the laundry room and we do a little cleaning in our room. The project team gets a special low rate at the motel, but we must do our own towels, sheets, and cleaning. We spend the afternoon making pierogis and Jenny loves it.

The day flies by, but I miss the woods and the trees. Just before the pickup trucks should be returning, I decide to give Vee a call. The cell service is iffy in the room, but Jenny has shown me the best spot to stand, which is in the middle of the driveway of the motel.

Vee picks up and exclaims, "Well, hello there. Boy oh boy, you have someone pretty worked up. Jake is fit to be tied. Where are you? He's been to your parents' place, and he's ready to call the police."

Taken aback, I stutter, "W-what? What do you mean?"

"Well, he wants to talk. He said he told you he wanted to talk to you when he returned, and you just up and disappeared."

"I thought about leaving a note, but wasn't sure it mattered," I whisper. "He went to my parents' apartment?"

"Yep, he sure did. They wouldn't speak to him, so he got nowhere, and now they won't open their door to him."

"I didn't want him to worry. You know I'm in Arkansas. I'm on a bird study project. He could have asked Professor Montgomery. He would have told him. I wasn't running away or anything. Well, er, maybe I was."

Vee laughs. "I knew you flew to Arkansas, but nothing else. Remember? You were all secretive when I helped you book your flights. Where the hell are you? In some swamp or backwoods?"

"Pretty much. I'm in the panhandle, looking for the ivory-billed woodpecker. We're in the forest and it's really cool. I'm just trying to figure out my life, and this seemed like a good idea. What should I do? I can call him, but I really need to start dinner, and this is the only spot for cell service."

Vee laughs louder. "Christ, Emma, you and Jake are perfect for each other, really. That sounds awful by the way. I'll call him to let him know aliens have not abducted you and you are safe and just need time to think about things. How about that? Is that okay?"

I started to say why that's *not* okay, but change my mind. The exact explanation doesn't matter. I'm gone, and it's over.

"Just tell him goodbye, okay?"

Vee lets out an exasperated harrumph. "I will not tell him goodbye. You need to call him and tell him that if that's what you want."

The call ends and I stare at the phone in my hand. *Call Jake and say goodbye.* I can't imagine doing that. Is that why I couldn't leave a note saying the same thing? Victoria from *The Language of Flowers* flashes through my head. Victoria and all her running away. Could I be doing that too? I sigh in frustration. The one thing I do know for sure is I was running away from that damn check.

The pierogis are a huge hit. Trevor's first bite almost brings him to tears, and he spends the entire dinner reminiscing about his babcia. It's so sweet. Remembering those kids in fourth grade turning up their noses at my special dish, that old hurt lifts off me and floats away. *What do fourth graders know? They are a bunch of idiots.*

Chapter 32:

Lost

On Saturday night, Trevor treats everyone to pizza. Afterwards, Susan enters Trevor's kitchen area while I'm washing the remaining plates.

"Hey, make Trevor do those dishes," she says indignantly. "He'll do anything to get more of those things you made the other night. Come on, we're going on an owl hunt!"

My ankle is back to one hundred percent, and I remember the wonder of seeing the snowy owl in Central Park fly on its silent wings. Tossing my dishrag down, I follow Susan out.

Susan, Skip, Matt, and I head off in the pickup, but in a different direction than the quadrants we've been working. A few miles from camp, we stop and begin hiking along a trail until we reach a beautiful meadow.

"Look at this place," Skip exclaims. "It's the perfect hunting area for the eastern screech owl. And it is the perfect time for their flyout. Keep your eyes peeled." He continues,

"We've spotted the great horned owl, but not recently. Now that owl is impressive."

Standing at the edge of the meadow, we have our bins at the ready. After a bit, we begin slowly trekking along the edge, making a half circle around to the other side of the meadow.

Suddenly Susan whispers urgently, "There it is. It just flew into the tallest tree directly across from us. It looks bigger than a screech. Could be a barred. That would be great. We haven't seen one on this trip. Let's work our way back toward the tree."

Suddenly, a flash of wings catch my attention. Pointing, I exclaim in a hushed tone, "It just flew away!"

While the group tracks the owl, I step into the meadow to see if I can find where it went.

I'm searching with my bins, but the light is tricky as the moon is out, but it gets really dark every time a cloud passes in front of it. I keep scanning. When I finally drop my bins, I glance around and don't see the group. I hear voices to the left, so head in that direction, toward the tree I thought the owl landed in. But as I get closer to the tree, I realize this doesn't look like the right tree. I'm disoriented and it is dark now, as the clouds have completely blocked the moonlight.

I strain to hear voices, but all is silent—just a rustling of leaves or branches. I wait for ten minutes. Maybe they didn't realize I wasn't with them, and they already started back. Walking around the perimeter of the meadow, I reach the spot where I thought we entered. I mark it with a yellow string and start walking back through the woods. It was only a mile, and no one used their compass because they knew where they were going, so I paid little attention to the trail as I followed them. I won't make that mistake again.

I tie another string to a branch. Seeing the yellow marker makes me feel better. This way, I can always come back to the meadow and hunker down if I need to. I have my pack, so I have the emergency blanket, and the meadow is quite lovely. Marching with more confidence than I feel, I tie a string every hundred feet or so. The magic of the forest keeps me calm and focused. It will do me no harm. Checking my watch, I realize I've been walking and tying ropes for thirty minutes. If this was the right direction, I should have hit the road and the truck by now.

Pausing, I sit and take a sip of water from my canteen, thankful it's full. This is why Trevor drilled into all of us to never go anywhere in the woods without our basic survival gear.

My only option is to head back to the meadow. I easily retrace my steps, picking up the markers as I go. Stepping back into the peaceful field, I try to reorient myself again to the trail. Deciding to try the opposite side, figuring I may have gotten completely turned around when the owl flew out. Walking halfway around the perimeter, I spot what appears to be a trail and I start the process again of marking my trail.

My legs are aching, and my feet are dragging. It's now 10:30 p.m., and it was a long day in the field. Sitting down again. I take stock and decide to turn back and sleep in the meadow. Walking quickly, I find my string but can't locate the next one.

"I'm okay. I'm going to be okay." I announce firmly to the trees and any nighttime creatures that are roaming about.

I say it louder, "I'm going to be okay."

Yes, I truly love Jake, but I deserve to be loved in return. I want that. I need that. I deserve that. Stopping in my tracks, I repeat to myself, *I deserve to be loved*. I never imagined that was possible. As I stare up into the tree branches, I recall the warmth and love of the forest surrounding me when I sat on the dead tree after I twisted my ankle. The cobweb reaching out to connect me back to this place. That didn't come from God or Mother Nature, that came from within me. I love myself and who I am, and no one can take that away from me. Not the mean kids from my past, not Father Kowalski, not Jake or his parents. The gentlest of breezes caress my face and with a soft whoosh the bubble that has kept me from living and loving in this world finally thins to the barest of film and then the last vestige of it disintegrates into a thousand specks and they fall softly down into the bed of decaying leaves.

I see the moon between the clouds and the emerald canopy above. The smell of the solid earth is comforting. I'm safe, even though I'm lost and alone. The forest will shelter me and show me the way. Life is the combination of both bright yellow happiness and sad, heartbreaking blue that combines to make the loveliest vibrant green.

Getting up, I continue walking when I hear a noise, a rustling, and then someone calls, "Emma!"

I turn toward it and suddenly I'm transported into my dream . . . . *I'm working my way through a green forest, and I'm lost but not afraid . . . feelings of safety and security wash over me.*

Pulling myself out of my revery, I choke out, "I'm over here."

Suddenly, up ahead, I see—Jake?

I stop in my tracks. It *is* my dream.

Standing rooted to the spot, my brow furrows in consternation. This is too weird. I'm conscious as never before in my dream. I reach out to touch a branch and use it to steady myself. I can touch and feel things. *Am I dreaming or is this real?* Jake charges down the path. As he gets close, he waves his arm and brushes furiously at his face. "Eww! A spider web," he exclaims.

Smiling dreamily, I muse, *The web's magic threads are intertwining all things, even reaching into my dream world.*

Closing the last few feet between us, he wraps his arms around me. I can feel his touch; it's as real as the branch in my hand. Dropping the branch, I gingerly reach up and touch his face, feeling some threads of web still clinging to the side of his face. A laugh gurgles up from deep within me. He grabs my hand, kisses it, and wraps me again in a bear hug.

Am I in my dream?

Staring at me, Jake asks hurriedly, "Are you okay? You're white as a sheet."

He holds my arms in his hands; I sway, and my legs go weak. I feel such a strong connection to this man, this place, and this world. Dreams are such magic.

He takes a firmer hold of me, and with a corded arm around my shoulder, says, "Let's get you back to base camp. Oh, wait a minute."

He slides a walkie-talkie out of his hip pocket and over the crackle announces, "I found her. Everyone head back to the trucks. We'll meet you there in twenty minutes. The first group of six who get to the truck, head back to camp, and the rest of you wait for me and Emma."

I hear cheers through the device. Shaking my head, I ask, "This isn't a dream?"

Jake peers at me sharply. "What? A dream? Seriously, Emma, what happened to you out here? You really sound like you're losing it."

"No, I'm fine. It's just that there's this dream I've been having my whole life, and suddenly it's . . . real."

Jake's lips quirk into a smile. "You've been dreaming about me saving you your whole life? And I thought you couldn't stand me for the first ten years."

Hitting his arm with my one free arm, I shoot back, "That

isn't exactly what I meant or what I dreamed about. It's this forest and being lost with someone who is . . . well it's hard to explain." I turn a bright red. "Forget it. My Ceyx may resemble you a little, alright?"

Jake leans in and touches his lips to mine. I melt.

Straightening, he says, "We've got to get going, the others are waiting."

My déjà vu continues as we trek out of the woods. I try to get my brain to work, but it is stuck halfway between my dream and the real world and won't cooperate at all. I stop trying and instead just exist in the bubble of happiness that my dream always creates. No questions, no worries or concerns about the future or the past.

We make it back to the pickup, and my dream state dissipates a bit more. The group waiting isn't just the owl hunters, it's the entire camp. I begin to apologize for making everyone search for me.

Trevor is one of the people waiting, and he states emphatically, "Not your fault at all. Those idiots went off following the owl and were deep in the woods before they realized they lost you. By the time they got back to the meadow, you were gone, so they came back to camp to get more recruits to help search, and that was when our captain surprised us by showing up rather unexpectedly."

Jake shakes his head and grins. "Very funny."

Trevor continues, "Well, Emma, we couldn't very well let you spend the night in the woods, and Evan learned quickly that such a suggestion wasn't advisable. Boy, Jake, you ripped him a new one." He says with a smirk. "I'm still trying to figure out why you're back here. You were just down here, and there hasn't even been a report of a dead tree with its bark stripped or a hole large enough for an ivory-billed. What's up?"

Trevor stares at Jake pointedly, and then his gaze slowly travels along his arm, which is wrapped tightly around my shoulders. As his eyes move back and forth between the two of us, he scratches his head. "Ah, I'm putting two and two together . . . sweet. And she can cook, too. Jake, you're one lucky guy."

Jake knocks his fist lightly into Trevor's arm. "Cut it out, Trevor. But you are right about Evan. I probably do need to apologize to him. I seem to remember we left him out in the woods on one expedition last year when we lost him, right?"

Trevor nods, "Sure did. The kid was scared shitless. Emma, were you scared out there? The woods at night can be freaking intimidating."

Grinning, I state proudly, "Nope, not really. I kind of liked it. I was trying to find my way back to the meadow because I thought that would be a great place to spend the night."

Shaking his head, Trevor remarks, "A match made in heaven. How many times have you spent the night out there, Jake? The big dark woods don't mess with your head either."

My thoughts are getting clearer. Turning to Jake, I ask, "What are you doing here?"

Appearing a little uncomfortable, he says quietly, "Looking for you. I've been looking for you for a week. Thank God you called Vee. I was really going to call the police or make your parents answer their damn door."

Trevor turns around again. "Now, this is interesting. Jake, how could you not know your girlfriend joined your team?"

"*Your* team? *Captain*? What the hell!" I shock myself with my swear and squeeze my eyes shut for a quick second, asking for forgiveness.

Trevor pipes up, "This is Jake's project. He got the grant from Columbia and oversees the whole thing. You're writing your dissertation on it, right?"

Jake nods his head affirmatively.

I gaze at him in amazement. "This is *your* project? I signed up for this to get away from you!" I shake my head. "Hey, wait a minute. Professor Montgomery knew I wanted to get away, and instead, he led me right back to you, kind of. Boy, oh boy, he is a sneak."

Jake shakes his head. "God, I'm such an idiot. I should've asked him first. That would have saved me a lot of heartache. I only went to him after Vee told me it was some bird study in Arkansas. Of course, the old coot is meddling in my business. He's been doing that for years."

He said heartache, I think. *What does that mean?*

We arrive at camp and the rest of the team is still up and the owl hunters continue to apologize for running off. I assure them it was all my fault for getting separated. Jake pulls Evan aside and they chat for a bit and then Jake slaps him on his back, and they smile when they rejoin the group.

I'm dead tired; I get up from my chair to head to my room.

Jake intercepts me. "I have a room around the corner. I'll wait if you need to grab some of your stuff. We need to talk."

The word *talk* sends a shiver down my spine. I obediently walk into my room and look around, but I quickly realize I'm too tired to make any sound decisions or listen to any of Jake's explanations or thoughts.

When I turn around, I see Jake standing at the doorway.

"Jake, I can't," I murmur. "We can talk tomorrow, but tonight it won't be talk, and we need to talk first. I really said goodbye to you back in New York, even though you weren't there. Sorry about that, but I know what will happen if I go back to your room."

Jake dips his head in defeat. "I'm just glad I found you. So, anything you want. Okay. See you tomorrow."

Chapter 33:

Found

Sunlight angles through my window as I wake. Stretching, I check my body from last night's adventure. Aside from a few aches and pains, I'm feeling normal. Even my head feels fine. The only part of me I'm not sure about is my heart. But it slowly dawns on me, *I'll be all right, no matter what.*

I step out of my room and spot Jake dressed and standing next to Trevor. The sun is shining, making his hair look like burnished gold. As I stare, he turns as if he senses me. He slowly walks over, and I ache to reach for him. His body looks warm and welcoming. Taking my hand, he leads me over to chairs set off to the side. I sit in one as Jake jogs quickly over to Trevor's room and comes back with a cup of coffee in one hand and tea in the other. Smiling wistfully, I remember the dreadful dinner when he served me tea in front of his parents. That seems like so long ago and isn't as painful as it once was.

"Look, Emma, I've been an idiot," he says as soon as he sits down. "Ever since I met you, really met you, I've sensed you were just dipping your toe into my world, and you were going to disappear at any moment back into hiding. When I came home from my trip and you were gone, I knew that was what happened. It was awful."

A smile is plastered on my face, but I can't seem to find the right words. Finally I say, "I wasn't running back into hiding, I was running forward, I think trying to find myself or save myself. I assumed the check was from you and your mother."

He smiles ruefully and his shoulders relax, "Oh my god. Absolutely not. When I found the check my mother gave you and realized what she had done, I couldn't believe it. I'm truly sorry. That was so wrong. I was so pissed. I confronted her and told her everything. I told her the whole engagement was fake, and I did it just to avoid World War III, but I'm not avoiding it any longer. I explained to her I can't work at Oliver's firm, and while the first engagement may have been a fake, I told her I'm going to try for a second engagement and this one is real."

Staring into Jake's chestnut eyes, I see genuine pain. My hand goes to my mouth and my eyes well up.

"Emma, my blue-eyed princess," he says, going down on one knee. "This isn't your favorite bench in Central Park, but we've done that already. Somehow, this feels right. Will you marry me?"

He slips his mother's ring out of his pocket and holds it out to me. I'm momentarily frozen. *Is this real or am I still in a dream?* Ernest's hand slips into mine and lifts it up towards the ring, gently guiding me. Clasping the ring, I turn it over in my hand. I missed this lovely little ring on my finger. Slipping it back into place feels perfect. I feel Ernest's reassuring presence slip away, and I wonder if I will ever see him again.

Suddenly, I'm in Jake's arms with my arms and legs wrapped around him. I hear clapping from the group, and I unwind myself from Jake, blushing. Jake sweeps me up and, despite my embarrassed protests, carries me off around the corner.

We're in his room before I knew it.

Laying me on the bed, he touches the ring on my finger. "Did you say yes for real?"

I nod enthusiastically, and he swoops down and kisses me. I press my lips against his and weave my hand through his copper hair.

We kiss until I think I've bruised my lips. We've been apart for only two weeks, but it felt like a lifetime. I was sure I wouldn't ever kiss him again, and I'm like someone dying of thirst who has found a cool spring. I can't get enough.

Jake sits up a bit and begins to unbutton his shirt and I'm mesmerized. I want to memorize every tiny detail. You never know when the best things in life might disappear into a poof of smoke. I watch him through heavily lidded eyes. When he tosses his shirt onto the floor, I reach my hand out to touch him and my hand skims over his chest and the long muscles that play beneath his skin. Jake's eyes fly up to mine and I smile tentatively.

After these weeks of connecting with nature and the forest, I've connected to who I am as a woman. The rhythms of the forest and the birth and rebirth of life through the plants and trees that grow flowers to produce seeds and then die, only to be reborn again and again flow through me. It's natural and good. It's how God made the earth, and nothing is bad when done from a place of love. Tracing my hand around his chest, I trail it down his flat abdomen. I'm powerless to stop my hand from exploring. Jake remains perfectly still, and my hand completes a circle and then reaches up for his head and I play with his beautiful hair. I pull him back down to me. He quickly kicks off his shoes and slides out of his pants.

He says playfully, "You look good in field gear. Different, but good."

Grinning up at him, I respond, "I really like it in the woods. It's so peaceful, yet alive. I don't think I was meant to live in a city. I should have grown up here or somewhere like it. That must be why I like Central Park so much. It's closer to where I belong."

Jake chuckles, "Yup. I can only take so much city living, and then I need to get back to this to recharge. This is where you feel what the earth is meant to be like. I remember reading a poem by Gary Snyder. He said, 'Nature is not a place to visit. It is home.' I believe that. Civilization has ruined so many things. So many species are extinct now or are going extinct. It will break my heart if the ivory-bill is extinct. But if it's lost forever, we need to know. Because if we killed off such a magnificent bird, I'm not sure I can forgive us or the human race." He shakes his head. "What am I doing, yammering on like that, when I was just about to get you naked? Emma, stop distracting me with poetry and philosophy. I have a much more primal need. God, when I got back to the apartment and saw the pile of stuff, I went crazy, thinking I had lost you."

Kissing me passionately, Jake slides his hands down to work on the buttons on my shirt and then my pants. We separate a fraction and lay on our sides, staring at each other in amazement. Our eyes reflect wonder. He slowly reaches out and wraps a hand around my back. I reach around his broad shoulders and press my hands, feeling his muscles, hard and taut. His hand slips lower, and he caresses and rubs, and the heat rises, and need fills my head and wetness pools down low.

I hear myself beg, "Jake, please."

He hesitates for a second and I reach for him urging him on. It feels as if it has been forever. He plunges into me without hesitation. I gasp. My body reorients itself to him, and I'm home. There is no yesterday, no tomorrow, only this. The two of us together. I press into him as close as possible while the need builds. Jake murmurs, "You feel so good." His words and the friction drive me to thrash and clutch at him until finally I tip over the edge with an explosion of white behind my eyelids. I relax into the shudders until my muscles quiet. Jake had stopped and is watching me with a look of wonder and he then resumes his rhythm until he drives deep and releases and gasps, "Emma."

He lowers himself down, so he is partially on top of me, and we stay connected at our cores. When he finally withdraws, the loss of that connection causes my eyes to start to fill. I move closer to him, pressing our bodies together. I wedge myself into the crook of his arm, a perfect fit.

I nuzzle into him and say, "So, tell me everything. What did Oliver say about the news that you aren't going to work at the firm? And do you really think your mom is alright with this?"

"Well—"

"Oh, wait a minute. Forget about your parents. Start with John Foster. I cannot believe that. What the hell? You lied to me for all this time . . . why?"

Jake raises his eyebrows. "Wow. You really have changed out here. You *never* swear." Then he hangs his head. "I am so sorry. That one was just stupid and it just kind of happened." He traces a finger down my cheek. "I don't tell anyone about my book—well, I mean a few people know, like Vee, not that I think she even remembers. Professor Montgomery, and Arnie, of course. But I never say anything to other people, especially strangers. So, when I met you and you started spouting off quotes from my book, I did what I always do. I clammed up. And I figured it would be a good idea to act as if I didn't even like the guy.

"I figured you'd look after Vee a couple times and that would be it. Then things started snowballing, and after that I couldn't figure out how to tell you that I was John Foster. Stupid, I know. I kept hoping you would figure it out. Remember when Uncle Joe called me John? I waited for you to connect the dots while we were making bluebird boxes. But you didn't."

I sputter, "Seriously, you thought I would somehow come up with the idea that you were a famous birder who wrote my favorite bird book? You put way too much faith in my detective skills. Of course, after the whole Arnie thing, I could see all the signs, but no way would I have ever put two and two together. Arnie practically had to hit me over the head with it before I believed any of it. Honestly, that may be the most maddening thing about"—I wave my hands in a wide circle—"this crazy situation. My favorite birder. That is just nuts."

I catch sight of the sunlight reflecting off my ring and twist my hand around so I can stare at the diamond.

"Do you think this can really work?" I ask solemnly. Jake grabs my hand and presses it to his chest.

"Look, when I came home and you were gone, I suddenly realized that all this time that I've been searching for the ivory-bill, I was really looking for you. You make me a better person, a stronger person. So yes, I think it can work." Jake takes a deep breath and, with a quirk of his lips, says, "Didn't you say you've been dreaming about me for years?" he pauses and I punch his arm blushing. "But seriously, it feels like fate or destiny to me. I'm your Ceyx and you're my Halcyon."

"Fate or destiny, my Ceyx," I murmur. *Could it be?* Then, taking a deep breath, I share my story and the MS diagnosis, wanting nothing hidden between us.

Chapter 34:

New Beginnings

We searched Arkansas for five months but found no sign of the elusive ivory-billed woodpecker. Scientists and birders have pored over the 2004 grainy pictures from David Luneau's camera and video recorder, trying to decipher if the pictures are of the pileated woodpecker or the ivory-bill. Some strongly support Professor Montgomery's contention that the ivory-bill sighting was accurate. These weren't naive dreamers; they were expert scientists who knew the differences between the ivory-bill and any other bird. Others are of the opinion that all the recordings and supposed sightings are exactly that: a misidentified pileated woodpecker. They firmly believe that the experts out in those woods conjured up an ivory-bill, because they so desperately wanted it to be one. *I can relate*. My dream world collided with the real world out in the forest five months ago and delivered me my most fervent wish; to be loved and to love.

When we left the research team, I hugged each one and gave a silent prayer that their dream will come true one day and they will find some evidence of this majestic bird. Some team members remain hopeful that the Lord God bird, pursued for over a century, has evaded humans entirely and is secretly thriving in isolation. The rest of the team suspects the ivory-bill's last confirmed sighting was in the 1930s, by Jim Tanner and the Cornell team.

As soon as we return from the woods, we visit my parents and show them the ring *again*. I called them from Arkansas; therefore, they knew about our re-engagement, but they said that they needed to see me to ensure my happiness.

Jake and I share an abbreviated version of our story with them. The memory I will always cherish is my father stating loudly, "I understand happiness, and Emma, I can see you are happy. If Jake has given you that, that is all we have ever wanted for you."

This from the man who ranted about Jake my whole life. Miracles do happen. Then my mother squeezed my hand, her eyes warm. Now, without the shell I built around myself, I can clearly see their love. A love that was there all along.

Jake submitted his thesis before he ran off to find me, and he had to defend it when we returned. He was thrilled that only minor revisions were needed in order to pass. I was incredibly proud and excited as I finally could fully grasp his presentation—thesis, charts, graphs, and all—but also was so grateful that I played a small part in the research work. Watching Jake present, I could feel a delicate thread connecting me to the graph displayed on the big screen that reached all the way down to a swamp in Arkansas.

Shortly after that, the University of Connecticut offered Jake a teaching position in rural Storrs, Connecticut. Professor Montgomery provided me with an excellent recommendation, and I landed a full-time position as an assistant to a professor in the university's ecology department.

Vee decided to stay in Mississippi. She's working for a large department store as a buyer and sounds strong and content, working every day to maintain her sobriety. Her parents are happy to have her. While her mom holds out hope of her rekindling her modeling career, she's considering going to college to get a degree in fashion merchandizing. Jake and I continue to live in her condo, and Vee says she will sell it once we move to Connecticut.

Amid the July summer heat, Carol invites us over for lunch.

Picturing her icy hand sliding the envelope across the table, I plead, "Jake, I don't want to go. I can't. You understand?"

"Mom really has changed," he begs. "She seems truly contrite and is working on herself and her own happiness. Please, give her another chance."

Gazing into his warm brown eyes, I vacillate. I can't imagine she has changed, but Jake's eyes plead with me. Finally, I nod. Jake yanks me into a bearhug, pulling a laugh from deep within me.

Walking through the park to see Carol later that week, I squeeze Jake's hand and say, "I'm really nervous."

"I know, sweetheart. It will be okay, I promise. She really has changed."

Shrugging my shoulders, I continue to walk toward Fifth Avenue, despite wanting to run in the other direction.

We gather around the kitchen island with Carol; Maria is nowhere in sight. Carol appears relaxed and actually hugs me like she means it. But it is her apology that finally wins me over.

"Emma, I can only say that I was wrong and I'm deeply ashamed. I want to meet your parents and really get to know you," she says, looking directly into my eyes. "I was in a dark place, and from that place, I could not recognize the love you had for my son and he for you—a love like I had with Jake's father. That memory was too much to remember—what real love looked like and felt like. But enough of this maudlin stuff—believe me when I say welcome to the family. I'm truly happy for you both." She reaches for our hands and grips them tightly.

I reply simply, "Thank you."

Carol *tssks* and waves us over to sit down at the kitchen island. "Just some sandwiches and salad. I didn't want anything stuffy or overdone. Is that okay?"

I glance at Jake. He looks as surprised as I do. I didn't think Carol ever did anything that wasn't overdone. As we crowd around the island, it reminds me of Vee and the cooking lessons we held in this very kitchen. I meet Jake's eyes. He smiles, I'm sure he's remembering the same. That was the start of our crazy adventure.

He grabs three plates, and we make our sandwiches. Carol even makes me a cup of tea when she gets herself coffee.

Once we're seated and eating, Carol clears her throat and announces, "So, I'm divorcing Oliver."

We halt mid bite and forget all about our food.

Jake charges around the island and wraps her in a hug. "Mom, really? Are you sure?"

Carol pushes him away and retorts, "Yes, I've made up my mind. I already visited with an attorney, and it turns out because your father and I owned this apartment and the beach house before I married Oliver, I will get them both as the prenup doesn't just protect Oliver, it protects me as well. Also if everything works out, I'll receive a considerable amount of alimony for the past twenty years of suffering. I'm just sorry I didn't investigate this sooner, to see if I could find some genuine happiness for myself." She pauses, and with a slight catch in her throat continues, "I'll never find the happiness I had with your dad. He was one in a million. But I may find something more than the miserable excuse of a life I have with Oliver. God, that man is impossible. I could never admit that until now."

Jake gives her another quick hug and responds, "You deserve all the happiness in the world, Mom, and I know you'll find it."

Carol smiles wistfully. "I'm planning to spend the rest of the summer at the beach house while the lawyers work on the details, just in case they're wrong, and I lose everything." She laughs—a tinkling, lighthearted laugh I've never heard before. "I'd love it if you both could come for the summer. It's so lovely there, with tons of birds." She laughs again. "I'm planning to invite Beth and Joe and Vee. It's about time I righted that wrong, too. I've ignored it for too long, and Beth deserved better from me."

Sitting back, I look back and forth from mother to son. I suddenly see more of a resemblance. Carol seems softer and certainly happier.

"We'll see," Jake says, darting an uncertain glance in my direction.

"That sounds just lovely," I jump in. "I've always wanted to stay in the Hamptons for the summer. I've watched that bus leave every day, all summer long, for years. I'm itching to get on it and see what all the fuss is about."

Carol's face brightens, and she smiles at me with a tenderness that takes my breath away. For the first time, I see the person she was before life happened to her.

Later that summer, Jake and I marry in a small backyard wedding at Carol's beach house. My parents make the trip to the Hamptons on the bus and no one notices when they are an hour early for the ceremony, but that is only because they stayed overnight in the carriage house. We chose the weekend Aunt Beth, Uncle Joe, and Vee were visiting. Everything is perfect until Vee lightly touches my cheek with her makeup brush, which starts my tears. They only stop when Vee sternly tells me I'm ruining everything and that she won't be blamed for a bad makeup job.

I look out at the small group of people gathered for the ceremony and think, *These are my people.* When the Justice of the Peace is going through our commitment to each other, I glance behind Jake and spot a blue-and-black kingfisher awkwardly perched on the scrubby bush up on the bluff. The bird looks at me with his opaque black eyes and it's as if he can see all the colors of the rainbow that fill me. I stretch my hand towards him, and he dips his head and takes flight, swooping into a denser corpse of trees. The wind kicks up, and I know the gods are pulling their magic strings high above us.

Epilogue

Jake and I are sitting at our comfortable breakfast nook, the morning sun is angling through the window, and the kids are still sleeping. Jake is reviewing some students' tests on his laptop. Chewing my lip, I'm working on my morning crossword puzzle, when Jake's phone beeps. He idly looks at the message, then, with more intensity, picks up his phone and starts scrolling. I watch curiously.

He finally sets his phone down and states flatly, "Well, it's official. The U.S. Fish and Wildlife Service announced it plans to list the ivory-billed woodpecker as extinct."

It's been seven years since our field study in Arkansas, but Jake's passion for the ivory-bill has continued to burn as brightly as it did all that time ago. When I look at him now, his eyes carry a pain that makes me reach over and clutch his arm.

I stand and slide onto his lap, holding him tight. "What does that mean, exactly?"

"Well, in a few more years, if nothing turns up, they'll consider it truly gone. A casualty of human stupidity and greed that makes me want to scream and break heads. All those so-called birders that shot, killed and stuffed thousands of these creatures and those logging companies that didn't give a rat's ass that they were clear-cutting old growth forest that will never stand again." He wipes his eyes. "It just kills me."

I hold him tighter and murmur, "Have faith. Maybe a hundred years from now, we'll clone ivory-bills from all the dead specimens that those idiots collected. Or maybe they are still living and thriving in the deep mountains of Ojito de Agua in Cuba. Just because it's too late here doesn't mean it's too late everywhere."

"I know." He pauses and leans back to gaze into my eyes. "I'm truly grateful to the ivory bill no matter what. I have the search to thank for bringing us together. We just need to keep trying and maybe one day the gods will have mercy as they did with Ceyx and Halcyon and the forest's dreams will come true and make the world a perfect place, not just for a nesting pair of kingfishers but for a pair of ivory-bills to live in. That's what your story tells us, right?"

I nod and touch my lips softly to his. Remembering my life from long ago, I think, *Dreams are what keeps you going day after day, even when the world is bleak and dull. Dreams live within all of us including the forests and we must hold and cherish them.*

I say, "I believe the ivory-bill is biding its time. They'll only reveal themselves when things are right with the world, when they know it's safe and people won't shoot and stuff them." Laying my hand on Jake's shoulder, I feel him relax under my touch. I continue, "Until we prove that to them, they'll remain hidden, elusive, waiting for us to get our shit together. But they are out there, patiently waiting and watching until we learn to share the world with them. I'm hoping it happens within our lifetime, but if not, maybe our children's."

Ivory-billed Woodpecker, Dr. James T. Tanner,
Public Domain

Author's Note

My story is a modern retelling of L. M. Montgomery's *The Blue Castle*. A hundred years ago, *The Blue Castle* was a contemporary romance. I liken it to Emily Henry's books of today. If you aren't familiar with it, it's a charming story of dreams, empowerment and what you can do when you think you have nothing to lose. You should check it out.

I made every effort to ensure the bird facts in this story were accurate, though I did take a few creative liberties. Snowy owls didn't quite make it as far south as Central Park during the 2013/2014 irruption. I found a dead snowy on a walk with my dog back during the irruption and I so wanted to see one alive. Because of that, I decided to let Emma experience the wonder of seeing such a magical creature with Jake.

Another liberty is that I chose to place the renowned ornithology program at Columbia University, when it's located at Cornell Lab of Ornithology, world renowned for its study of birds and the wonderful Merlin Bird ID and eBird app. This allowed Emma and Jake to live in New York

City, near the wild and wonderful Central Park, allowing for the contrast between one of the world's most urban environments and the natural oasis the park provides—for people, plants, and wildlife alike.

As for the ivory-billed woodpecker, well . . . that's an entirely different can of worms. Since the 1930s, the existence of the ivory-bill has been the most divisive topic among birders and ornithologists. Only recently eclipsed by Flaco, the escaped Eurasian eagle-owl of Central Park. Me, I'm a firm believer that the ivory-bill still exists in the United States and after reading *Woody's Last Laugh* by J. Christopher Haney (thank you for the gift, Edgar), I'm even more resolute in that belief.

Acknowledgements

I never imagined I'd be writing another acknowledgements section—but here I am, thanks in no small part to Tricia Scully. After my first book, she challenged me by stating, "Everyone has one book in them. It's whether you have a second that's the real test." Her challenge inspired me to return to my desk and begin writing before my first book was even published. So it's only fitting that I thank her first. She also strongly recommended that I add more sex which I did for this one.

Of course, I want to thank L. M. Montgomery for her lovely book, *The Blue Castle,* that was the inspiration for this one. Her contribution to literature is unparalleled, and she continues to find new fans through her books and the many adaptations of her most famous book, *Anne of Green Gables*. I'm thrilled to be doing my part in helping to continue to spread the word.

I'm also deeply grateful to my brother Dave Bradford, who not only helped ensure the bird facts were accurate but also nurtured my growing passion for all things avian in recent years. Heartfelt thanks go to Mark MacGougan, Dan Aramini and John Ciurylo, my steadfast beta readers, whose thoughtful insights, feedback and creative ideas made this story stronger and more layered. Many thanks to Brenda Geiling, my number one fan, for her invaluable advice and support.

To the She Writes Press community: you lifted me through the journey of my first book and have continued to carry me through this second one. I raise a glass to you—a truly remarkable group of collaborators and friends.

Finally, thank you to Brooke Warner, a tireless champion of books and women, and to Addison Gallegos, whose support I felt in every step of this process.

And of course, endless thanks to my children and my husband, Edgar. I couldn't have done it without you.

About the Author

Andrea Ezerins grew up in the small town of Columbia, Connecticut, and earned a bachelor's degree in business administration from the University of Connecticut. After spending three decades in the insurance industry, she traded risk assessments for plot twists, publishing her debut novel, *Again and Again Back to You*, in 2024 which placed third in Fiction-Literary-Love Story & Romance category of the BookFest awards in 2025. She followed it up with her second novel, *When the Forest Dreams* proving that an empty nest (and a spoiled German shepherd) is the perfect recipe for creativity. Andrea lives in Hebron, Connecticut, with her husband and is the proud mom of two daughters and identical twin sons. When she's not writing, she's raising bluebirds and monarch butterflies, running, or flowing through yoga—probably while plotting her next book.

Looking for your next great read?

We can help!

Visit www.shewritespress.com/next-read
or scan the QR code below for a list
of our recommended titles.

She Writes Press is an award-winning
independent publishing company founded to
serve women writers everywhere.